Pursuit

By W. J. Prior

For everyone I love, and all who inspired me. This is for you.

Prologue

The cat was pinned firmly by the back of the neck. Mewls of distress desperately vibrated out of its throat as it struggled to escape. Thrashing about, its legs slapped at the puddles that punctuated the floor of the narrow alleyway. The smell of wet fur clung to the air. A musky aroma, the scent was thick and stifling.

A sound, like the snapping of a dry twig, split the atmosphere with a dull crack. Curdled cries of pain sprang up from the cat, warbling and distorted in agony.

The gruesome sound of bone breaking repeated. Over and over again. Always brief, and always followed by more cries of pain.

In the dark of the night, the blood swallowed all of the light, appearing quite black. Bone was visible; the splintered ends peeking out of the fur as if to say hello. The stifling smell of damp was replaced by the coppery scent of blood.

A firm grip pressed into the top of the cat's head, as the pressure on the neck intensified. One single practiced movement later, and the neck was broken. The grinding crunch of the spine breaking lingered in the air for a moment.

No more than a second later and the body was in the sack.

A playful voice, softly humming a tune, echoed down the alley.

Chapter 1

Scott Willard awoke to the steady rhythmic beeping of the alarm clock sat beside his bed.

Roused from his slumber by the harsh synthetic sound, Scott opened one eye and checked the time. Half-heartedly sighing to himself, he removed one hand from beneath his bedsheets and struck the top of the plastic device, silencing the wailing.

Rising, he moved about his room slowly before opening the door and traversing the landing. Snatching up a towel, he made his way to the bathroom and showered quickly.

Once he was clean and dressed, he made his way downstairs, checking his watch as he went.

Satisfied that he had sufficient time, he clicked on the radio and made his way to the kitchen. Rooting through the cupboards, one of his hands drummed out the rhythm to the song currently playing as his other searched for food.

Settling on a jar of marmite, Scott made up his mind and began to prepare his toast; all the while keeping one ear on the rhythmic thrum of the radio.

As he ate, he felt a shape move past his leg.

"Never too early to bother me, is it Louis?"

Reaching down absent-mindedly, Scott scratched the top of the cat's head. Pushing its head up into his fingers, the small feline began to purr. His digits slipped through the silky fur, momentarily distorting the brown tortoise shell pattern that decorated the cat.

Finishing his breakfast, Scott scooped up his plate and set it down in the sink, before fixing the cat his own bowl of food.

"See you later," Scott said, waving at the cat as he made his way to the door. "Try not to get up to too much trouble while I'm gone."

The street outside his house was relatively empty. Every so often a car would pass him by on his left hand side but, aside from that and the occasional pedestrian, Scott had no company on his walk.

Above his head the sky was a clear and crisp blue, white clouds crawling sparsely across it like lone swimmers in an empty sea. Darting through the air, a chaffinch settled down in the branches of an overlooking tree and peered at the young man through the pale pink blossoms.

Readjusting the bag slung over his shoulder, Scott again checked his watch. He was running almost perfectly on time.

"I could almost set my watch to you, you know that?"

Prudence Harding was stood just past the bend of an intersecting road, leaning against a low garden wall. Dangling from one of her ears was the wire from a pair of headphones.

"I like being on time. There's nothing wrong with that."

"How you holding up on your own?"

Scott's family were away on holiday, having left the previous morning. Not wanting to miss any of his classes, he had elected to stay behind and look after the house.

"Better than I thought. I actually like the peace and quiet."

"Surviving? If you want, I can come round and make you dinner some time."

Scott laughed. "Thanks, but I'm gonna have to pass on that. I've seen you cook. I'm not about to go down that road again."

"You're such a bastard." While her words were harsh, her tone was light-hearted.

"I try."

Scott and Pru had been friends for so many years that casual insults like those had become commonplace. It had gotten to the point where he hardly noticed them anymore.

"How's the boyfriend?"

Pru grinned and interlocked her fingers behind her head as she walked. "He's doing okay. I still haven't put him through the ringer yet, though."

"I feel sorry for him. He still doesn't know how much of a nightmare you can be."

"Well aren't you nice today."

"Sarcasm is unbecoming of you."

"I can think of plenty of thing about me that are unbecoming, and you're picking sarcasm?"

"Honestly, I take what I can get."

Pru grinned, seizing the opportunity to play off of the unintentional innuendo. "Speaking of: You going to Tom's party on Thursday?"

"Ugh, mind out of the gutter." Scott peered out of the corner of his eye at the dark haired girl to his right. "That was one time, alright. Why do you bring it up every chance you get?"

"Because you torture me. It's only fair."

Scott allowed himself a silent smirk.

"You still haven't said if you're going or not. Come on, it's not like you have to give your parents an excuse. And you don't have a curfew to stick to."

"Yeah but it's the night before a school day."

"I swear to god, you don't even need parents. You do a damn good job of policing yourself as it is." Pru began to walk backwards so that she could look at Scott while she talked to him. "Tell you what... I'll drive you there and take you home. Then all you have to do is play designated drinker."

"Why are you so up for getting me to go out?"

"Because you need to live a little."

The pair reached the gates to the school building. Passing through the wrought iron structures, they entered a gaggle of students. Fragments of conversations could be heard as they maneuvered their way through the herd.

"-I watch a lot of it but, like, I'd never actually do it."

"-It's obviously coming back for another season. Plus-"

"-and who the hell does he think he is, saying that to-"

"-is their best single. Give it a listen, man."

Scott dipped between the swarm of bodies, all the while replying to his friend; raising his voice to be heard over the crowd. "I live plenty, thank you very much. You seem to be forgetting that time when-" His speech pattern was broken momentarily as he bumped into the arm of a younger girl. "Oh, sorry about that- That time when I jumped out of Lizzie's window."

"That was like a year ago," Pru replied. "I haven't forgotten. It's just nobody cares anymore."

"So what you're saying is I need to do something crazy to spice up my rep?"

"Pretty much."

"Why do I get the feeling that this is going to somehow end very badly for me?"

"You don't know that. This could be exactly what you need."

Finally settling into a steady pace, and falling in line with the other students, Scott half groaned under his breath. "If I say I'll go, will you get off my back?"

Pru's face brightened. "Almost definitely."

"I'm not liking the sound of that 'almost' you put there."

"Well I always have to be on your back about something. Them's the rules if you want me as a best friend."

"I don't recall ever saying that I wanted you as a best friend in the first place."

"Oh shut up. You love me and you know it."

Scott said nothing. He merely smirked and shook his head.

*

Constable St. Claire was sat at his desk, spinning a pen around his thumb. The tendons of his wrist rose up as he finally stopped and gripped it tightly.

Scattered across the surface in front of him were numerous different files and folders of paperwork, all in varying stages of completion. A mug of tea, long since turned tepid and cold, sat on the corner of one such file. A dull ring of moisture was left clinging to the brown paper as he lifted the cup to his lips and attempted to force down the liquid.

His eyes were bloodshot, from where he had been rubbing them. Snatching up a packet of antihistamine, set down next to where his mug had been placed, St. Claire unwrapped the foil and swallowed two of the pills.

"Damn hay fever..." he muttered under his breath, grunting from the back of his throat.

"Mornin' Officer."

Leaning back in his chair, St. Claire's dark brown eyes fell on the upside-down form of David Stafford. "Morning Dave."

"Pulling another all-nighter again?"

"Got it in one." He swivelled his chair around so that he could talk to his co-worker face to face. "Tryin' to pack in as much overtime as possible."

"I'd hold back on it if I were you. Don't want you making the rest of us look bad." David smirked. "Gotta say though, the overtime pay is pretty cushy."

"Not doing it for the pay. I'm takin' the hours in lieu. Looking to get a bit of time off at the end of the month; take Jess somewhere nice."

"I was gonna say," David half-laughed. "It did seem strange to see you actually getting some paperwork done. All things said, I thought you enjoyed running the beat."

"Name me a single Constable in this station that likes paperwork and I'll eat my fuckin' hat," St. Claire replied.

"Point taken. So anything interesting happen in the early hours?"

"Not really. We got a drunk and disorderly in Three, but that's about as exciting as it gets. Julie brought him in. Apparently he mistook a park bench for his ex-wife."

"I take it that didn't end well?"

"Kicked the absolute shit out of it. Got a fine for the damages."

"Good thing I wasn't there."

"Whys that?"

"I'd have probably laughed at him," David said, grinning and leaning back against the desk behind him.

"That's why we keep you locked up in here most of the time," St. Claire chuckled in reply. "Can't be trusted out there, you'll stop people takin' us seriously."

"So where you thinking of taking Jess?"

"Old friend of my Dad's has a place out in Majorca. Said I could have it for a couple of weeks, if no-ones renting it."

"Oh nice."

"Yeah, I thought so. Love a nice bit of hot weather."

"It's out by Spain, isn't it?" Scratching the side of his scalp, David tilted his head to the side.

"Maybe," St. Claire shrugged. "They speak Spanish out there, but I dunno if it's near there. They speak Spanish in Tenerife and that's all the way down by Africa."

"Fair enough. The DCI's Spanish, isn't he?"

"Who, Franko? Yeah. He doesn't speak the lingo very much, but it tends to come out when he's had a few."

"I still find it weird that you go out drinking with him."

"Hey, he's nice enough. Plus it helps to be in close with the boss."

"Yeah but has it even once worked in getting you a favour?"

"Well not yet." St. Claire laughed. "But hey, you wait. Sooner or later all those whiskeys are gonna add up."

"Yeah, you keep telling yourself that."

"Don't you have anything productive to be getting on with? Or are you just makin' it your mission to pester me?"

"I actually wanted your help with something."

St. Claire took note of this. Very rare was it that Dave would admit he needed help with anything.

"What is it?"

"Cats."

"Come again?"

"Over the last few weeks, a load of cats have been going missing from Lindum. It's not isolated to one spot either, and it's too high a number to be coincidence."

"You know this isn't usually police business, right? There are dozens of lost pet agencies that should be able to find them. Not to mention nowadays almost every animal is microchipped."

"Yeah, you'd think that but all of them are turning up zip. It's weird. Usually with a high number of pet disappearances like this, most of them would have ended up in shelters. But the report I got yesterday says that the number of cats picked up by these places has actually been going down."

St. Claire had already lost interest with the conversation, however decided to humour his co-worker. At least that way he would be able to say he tried to help. "Maybe they were just hit by cars or something?"

Almost two hundred and thirty thousand cats had been killed in motor collisions in the UK, the previous year. It was a fair assumption to believe that the happenings had something to do with adding to that figure.

"See at first I thought that too, but no. I went and asked around the council, to see if the street cleaners reported higher levels of roadkill, but no dice."

"Is this actually a case you've been assigned?" St. Claire didn't want Dave to be getting into something off the books. It wasn't that they were busy, and his time could be devoted elsewhere; far from it in fact. Franko, the DCI in charge of their station, didn't approve of officers spending excessive amount of time on things that didn't concern them.

"Well no, but I just thought it was strange."

St. Claire reached down absent-mindedly and picked up his mug of tea, only remembering too late that it was almost ice cold. "Look, you want to work this on your own time, fine. I'm not going to be the one to stop you. Just make sure it's actually on your own time. You know how the DCI gets when it comes to stuff he doesn't think is important. Not to mention, Lindum is outside our jurisdiction."

"We use the Lindum crime labs for almost all of our cases. Not to mention, we always work with their Police Department."

It was at that point that St. Claire realised he wouldn't be able to argue with David any more about the matter. He was going to continue to look into it, no matter what he said to him. "So what exactly did you need my help with?"

"Jess's sister still works as a receptionist in Parks Veterinary, doesn't she?"

"Mhmm?"

"Give her my number. Tell her to call me if they get any injured cats. Anything that seems suspicious."

He knew where Dave was going with his train of thought. "You think someone's killing all of them."

"It's just a theory. Honestly, I hope I'm wrong about it, but it doesn't hurt to cover all of my bases."

Chapter 2

Constable David Stafford pulled into the parking bay of the petrol station just off of Lyefield high street. The dark rubber wheels of his neon green and white police cruiser rolled over the Tarmac, grinding down on the gravel embedded in the treads.

Walking from his car, he snatched up a copy of the Times from the newsstand; readily avoiding the neighbouring issue of the Mayfair Star. Walking inside the store, his shoes squeaked against the dull linoleum floor as he traversed the aisles. Paper still clasped underneath his arm, David picked out a tub of fruit and a sandwich from the refrigerated shelves, before making his way to the register.

Meeting him with a bright smile, the cashier greeted him cheerfully. At around forty years old, her neatly groomed blonde hair held a few flecks of grey that caught the light. Crow's feet extended from the corners of her eyes, betraying her friendly attitude. In her younger years, she may have been considered quite pretty.

"Morning Dave," she said, slowly reaching out to scan his items.

"Morning Paula. Not very busy in here is it?"

"It never is at this time of day. Eleven in the morning isn't exactly rush hour."

"I guess not."

David's eyes creased slightly as he smiled. A kindly man of thirty eight, the signs of middle age were slowly beginning to creep onto his face. Mousey brown hair clung to the top of his head in a thin crop, offsetting his deep brown eyes. His shoulders were broad, highlighting an athletic frame. Jutting from the sides of his head, David's ears belied his younger years in the scrum of Lyefield's local rugby club.

"You seem distracted?"

"I was just thinking... Things have been too quiet recently. Not that I'm complaining, it's just I get a bad feeling from it." David placed his large hands on the counter in front of him and sighed. "I don't know. Maybe I'm just being paranoid."

"I think you need to take a break, get your mind off work."

"Is that right?"

"I'm free Friday at seven."

"Well, aren't you a bit forward today?" He broke into a grin.

Paula met David's sarcasm by leaning forward against the counter and smiling back. "Helps me get what I want."

"Well I can't exactly say no now, can I?"

"I should hope not."

David laughed and lifted up the food items in his hands in a half wave. "I better be getting back to work now."

"Uh-uh." She pointed to her lips. "Aren't you forgetting something?"

"Oh how could I forget?"

Leaning over the till, David planted a quick peck on her lips before making his way out of the shop and waving at her through the window.

Paula Stafford stifled a blush and laughed under her breath. After ten years of marriage, he was still as charming as when they first met. Granted his hair was thinning and he had packed on a bit more weight around his mid-section, but she still found him every bit as attractive as she did in her youth. He was still tall, dark and handsome. The thing she loved most about him were his broad shoulders; the way he held himself.

Beginning to busy herself behind the counter, Paula rearranged the packets of cigarettes displayed on the wall behind her. In front of her eyes, the multitude of colours threw flashes of rainbow images over her dark pupils.

She started to think of ways that she could help take her husband's mind off of work. The train of thought soon elicited a slight giggle, in response to some of her naughtier ideas.

David had always been that way. When work was particularly quiet was when his mind worked the hardest. Paula guessed that it was his way of staving off boredom. He couldn't stand having nothing to do.

There was a dull hiss as the automatic doors to the shop swung open.

Sighing to herself, Paula returned her attention to the till.

*

Scott sat in his class staring across the room at the door. The sounds of pens scratching against paper scraped through his head, numbing him and drowning out the subtle sound of the clock at the front of the room ticking away. Every so often a mutter would rise out of the silence as two students quietly spoke. The sound of a chair slowly scraping against the floor suddenly pierced through the atmosphere as someone readjusted their sitting position.

As he broke into a soft sigh, he allowed his mind to wander across Tom's soon-to-be party. Despite his earlier reluctance, Scott was actually beginning to look forward to it. While he wasn't old enough to legally drink in a bar, at seventeen years old, he really enjoyed the drinking and party atmosphere. He'd been to enough house parties to know that much. The only reason for his earlier hesitation at saying yes to attending was due to a particular occurrence at a previous similar event.

He was suddenly snapped from his daze by the feeling of something tapping against his shoulder.

Glancing to his right, Scott was met with the smiling face of Alice Goodacre. She was a short girl stood at around five foot three, with honey blonde hair. Her fringe was parted at a seven-to-three ratio, framing her neatly plucked eyebrows and clear grey eyes.

"Hm?"

"Are you going to Tom's on Thursday?" As she spoke, her voice was plucked by a restrained and hopeful expectation.

"I should be, yeah." He kept his voice low, so as not to disturb the other students working around him.

"That's great. I haven't seen you out in so long."

"I've been hiding," he replied, slightly laughing.

"How are you getting there? I live down the road from him, so if you want you can come around mine after school Thursday. Then we could go together."

"Usually I'd love to, but I can't. My family's away right now, so I need be at home to feed the cat. Plus Pru already said she would take me."

"I can't believe you just blew me off because of your cat." Alice began to laugh.

"Hey, it's not my fault. If my family were home, we wouldn't be having this problem."

"Well at least I get to see you there."

"Do you know who else is going? Besides Tom and Pru, obviously."

"You know what he's like. Tom's probably invited half the school. Odds are, anyone you want to be there is probably going to be."

The bell signalling the end of the lesson began to ring, the piercing sound rattling through the air. Roused from their semi-silent study, Scott's fellows began to pack their belongings into their bags.

"Hey! Hey! The bell doesn't dismiss you, I do!"

The History teacher, Mr Smyth, placed himself between the students and the door. A tall, yet surprisingly frail man, his hair shimmered silver, drawing even more attention towards his pale face. Two small and round blue eyes peered from beneath his stout brows. White saliva clung to the edge of his lip; a side-effect of his diabetes medication.

A number of the students began to groan and protest the situation.

"Looks like we're going to be here for a while..." Scott sighed, leaning back in his chair.

"Don't sound too disappointed about having to spend more time with me." Alice chuckled, however Scott sensed something serious behind her words.

"You mean to tell me you'd prefer to sit in this class, instead of going to lunch with your friends?"

She pulled a comical face. "Maybe."

"You're weird."

Alice smiled and glanced out of the corner of her eye at him. Peering through her dark lashes, she studied Scott's profile. His skin was clear, lacking any form of bump or blemish. The faint signs of stubble clung to his cheeks and chin, having grown since his shave the previous morning. Muddled hazel eyes, flecked with tinges of brown, were set into his attractive face, beneath a light brown pair of eyebrows.

Scott interrupted her brooding with a question. "So do you think Naomi is finally going to try it on with Leon? On Thursday, I mean."

"Are you saying she needs to be drunk to try anything with him?" Scott's reference to her friend earned a slight laugh from Alice.

Scott merely raised an eyebrow, suggestively.

"Okay, you may be right about that. Well, she better do is all I have to say. She's been crushing on him for so long, if she doesn't do anything about it, I'm going to kill her."

"Wow. That was a bit extreme."

Laughing off the remark, Alice pushed her hair behind her ear.

At the head of the class, Mr Smyth had finally relented and allowed the other students to leave. Rising to his feet and joining Alice in laughing, Scott slung his bag up onto his shoulder.

"So where are you going to be spending your lunch period?"

Without even hesitating, Scott responded. "The same place I always do."

"The grass bank by the Science rooms?"

"Got it in one."

"Well, I guess I'll see you next time we have a History class."

"So it would seem." Scott broke into a smile and waved Alice off as they both exited the room and ventured down different directions in the hallway.

Stuffing his hands into his pockets, Scott tilted his head back as he walked. Above him, the ceiling lights passed by one-by-one. Cracks in the plaster held his attention, spiderwebbing out from the plastic fixtures that held the bulbs.

Having been delayed in his departure from the classroom, the hallway was relatively empty, allowing him to settle into a casual pace. As he settled into the slow tempo of walking, his mind drifted back to Alice.

While not entirely oblivious to her advances, Scott still found himself unable to tell if she was being serious or not, whenever she expressed a particular interest in him. He found himself constantly second-guessing whether her advances towards him were earnest or in jest.

Pushing his thumb down onto the back of his middle finger, he cracked his knuckle. Lifting his left hand, Scott pushed one hand back through his messy light brown hair.

He considered running the Alice situation past his friends, to see if they had any thoughts on the matter. While not usually one to ask for advice, Scott had been curious of the girl's intentions since she had first sat next to him in their history class, six months earlier.

A positive of discussing it with his friends was that Pru would be present. She was never one to mince words and would undoubtedly tell him straight. Add into the equation that she herself was a girl, Scott felt confident that she would be able to help him.

Exiting the main school building, he made his way across the green stretch of field immediately opposite the exit until he came to a sloping grass bank. Purposely ignoring the stairs and path to his right, Scott scaled the incline and made his way towards the group of students sat on the lip.

"Smyth pitch a fit again?"

"It was pretty mild today. All he did was block the door for a few minutes."

Kyle Ballard leaned back against the turf, crossing his arms behind his short cropped black hair. His dark eyes twisted in amusement. "You remember the time when he locked us in the class and Adam jumped out the window?"

"And when he went out to go and chase him, we all just walked out." Scott began to laugh as he sat down amidst the group.

"How about last year when the bell was broken and we wound the clock forwards forty five minutes, when he left the room?"

Jack Gibson groaned and rolled onto his side, so that he could look at the others without constantly tilting his head. "Is that why you all got split up into different classes?"

"That's why Tom and Kyle got put into other classes. I had no part in any of it. All I did was watch." As Scott spoke, he splayed his fingers against the ground and leant back.

"You make it sound like I'm a bad influence." Kyle attempted an innocent expression but soon devolved into laughing, unable to keep a straight face.

"You *are* a bad influence," Pru said, leaning her head on the shoulder of Daniel, who was sat in front of her.

"What can I say; it helps me get the ladies."

Pru scoffed and abandoned her boyfriend's shoulder, so that she could lay back on the green. Her dark hair spread out on the ground around her head, stark against the bright emerald grass, like tendrils of seaweed.

As the rest of the gathered students began to talk amongst themselves, Scott shuffled over towards Daniel and Pru.

"Hey there, Scotty boy," Pru said, looking up at him. "How's life been in these four hours we've been apart?"

"Not bad. Hey… I've got a few things I wanna run by you. Get your opinion on."

"Having girl trouble?" She began to snicker slightly.

"You could say that."

"Aww, look at you growing up."

"Shut up."

"So, this girl got a name?"

*

Sat beneath the undergrowth that bordered the school field, a small domestic cat licked its paws and basked in the midday sunlight. Its tortoiseshell pattern glimmered in the green-tinged light, throwing a bright glare upwards.

All of a sudden, it's lounging was disturbed. Rolling back onto its stomach, the cat addressed the noise of something wading through the trees that lay just past the ferns. Thrown into shadow by the overhead leaves, the fence that marked the perimeter of the school grounds was barely visible.

Cautiously edging towards the trees, the cat kept its centre of gravity low, in case it felt the need to either pounce or flee.

A figure approached, stepping out into the sun.

Reaching down, as if to pet the feline, it scooped it up and retreated back into the shadows.

Chapter 3

Scott Willard lay back on his sofa, thumbing through a dog-eared paperback. He held it carefully, resting it on his fingers and turning the pages lightly. The book was so worn down that there wasn't much spine to speak of, and the print had faded considerably.

As he finished the chapter, he shifted his position to something more comfortable. Creasing out around his body, the black leather of the couch caught the light in a bright shimmer.

He felt listless. Distracted.

Scott had originally picked up the novel as a way to distract himself and escape into fantasy. This attempt, however, had proved futile. His mind ticked over, seemingly trapped in an unending loop. His conversation with Pru replayed over and over inside his head.

"What, are you some kind of idiot? How long has this been going on?"
"I don't know, since she sat next to me?"
"And you haven't figured out that she likes you?"
"I just thought that's what she was like. Y'know, like she was joking with me?"
"For six months...? Damn. Well one thing I have to give that girl is she's persistent."

Placing his book down onto the low coffee table, Scott folded his arms behind his head and stared up at the ceiling. A warmth spread through his limbs as blood rushed into his muscles and dispelled the beginning traces of pins and needles.

Reaching down over the edge of the furniture, he felt around for the downy fur of his cat; attempting to find distraction in the feline. As his fingers brushed against the pelt, the sensation elicited an aggressive hiss from Louis. Glancing down at his pet, Scott took note of the cat's temperament. He could practically hear it telling him to fuck off.

Cats confused Scott. One minute they could be your best friend in the world, however at the drop of a hat they could turn on you, leaving you a broken husk, complete with matching claw marks. He never was quite able to wrap his head around why. He remembered

Pru telling him once that she thought it just meant that they were honest with their emotions. That, unlike humans, if they didn't feel in the mood for anything, they wouldn't smile past the discomfort and pay lip service; they would quickly and readily make it known. Scott, however, had pointed out that there was no need for them to be such little bastards about it.

"You know, if they were any bigger, they would probably eat you. Fuck, you hear about it all the time: Some crazy old bitch tops it alone in her house, and the cats make a meal out of her. Literally."

Remembering Kyle's words elicited a small chuckle from between Scott's lips.

In spite of being, for the most part, confused by them, Scott liked cats. They were low maintenance and required nowhere near as much attention as something like a dog. Dogs were practically small children, what with their constant need for attention and companionship. He also enjoyed that, all things considered, cats were jerks. Cats could always tell when someone either didn't like them, or was allergic, and made a point of climbing all over them. Scott respected that. If someone doesn't like you, then fuck with them, just to spite them.

His problem, unfortunately, had to do with the fact that someone did like him; a concept that, while not altogether alien, confused him immensely.

No matter what he did, his mind kept coming back to it, like he was continuously walking in circles. Over and over he would depart the issue and focus on something else, yet eventually, he would always find himself back where he had started. Alice.

He remembered a song that the old drunks who drank in The Bear Tavern used to sing. ("Alice! Alice! Who the fuck is Alice?") Scott used to frequent the pub, in his younger teenage years. Seeing as he was still not yet old enough to legally consume alcohol, his reasons for visiting the establishment were not as unsavoury as one would assume (even considering the fact that he had, for all intents and purposes, been drinking since the age of fourteen). Situated in the small companion town of Lyefield, just outside of Scott's home city of Lindum, The Bear was an urban pub that still somehow managed to maintain an air of the countryside to it. The majority of the locals who called the pub home were crusty old drunks who had long ago claimed their pensions, and decided that the best way to end their lives was to drink them. Scott's Grandfather being one of them.

He wondered what his Grandfather would have said about the Alice situation, had he still been with them.

And like that, Scott was back to where he started again.

The repeated backing-and-forthing was starting to annoy him, grating on his nerves and turning them red raw. Frustration boiled up inside him, and Scott found himself seriously needing some form of release. Emotional or physical, he didn't care which. As things stood, he had three possible options: One, raid his Father's liquor cabinet and deal with the earful when his family got home; Two, make full use of his empty house and search online for porn, to help with a quick fumble; or Three, text Pru for advice.

Scott settled on the final option.

Reaching into the pocket of his black trousers, Scott pulled out his phone and pushed the menu button. As the touch screen came to life, white rectangles of light were reflected in Scott's eyes. Quickly opening his messenger app, he tapped out a short text, to check to see if Pru was busy, and hit 'send'.

He got a reply almost instantly.

"Not busy. Pretty bored... What's up?"

Scott's thumbs blurred in front of his half-focussed eyes as he typed a reply.

"Sounds like you need a friend. And nm, just all this Alice shit..."

"I got you, don't I? What do you mean by Alice shit? Has something happened since I told you to nut up?"

"More like nothing's happened. I'm stressing big time :/"

"Aw, are you getting cold feet? ;)"

"Shut up. I don't even know if I'm gonna go anywhere with it! That's what I meant when I said I was stressing"

"You want some advice on what to say to her?"

Scott began to chew on the corner of his lip.

"I'm not even sure if I want to say anything to her... That's the problem"

*

Constable Stafford could feel the onset of drowsiness start to set in. The warm embrace of sleep wound itself around his body, clinging to him like the arms of a beautiful woman, clouding his thoughts.

The sharp twinge of his heartburn shocked him back into his right mind. Popping a pair of antacids out of their foil wrapping, David slipped them into his mouth and knocked the pills back with a slug of water. As he felt them drop into his stomach, the small capsules neutralised the acid burning through his system, providing several moments of psychosomatic relief. It would still take another few minutes until the medication actually resolved the problem.

He had been sat in his cruiser in the back parking lot of the Station for close to twenty minutes. Try as he might, David couldn't bring himself to walk inside and clock out just yet. Clocking out meant facing St. Claire and finding out if there was any news from the Vet (or worse, finding out that there was none). It also meant potentially having to deal with the DCI, and explaining why there were rumours floating around about him working a case off the books. He wasn't CID, and Franko was an unforgiving bastard towards anyone who worked on anything they hadn't been assigned.

Flipping down the sun visor, he swept aside the plastic cover of the mirror and examined his eyes. It had been a long day, addled with stress, and the signs were clear on his face. He looked like shit, and he knew it. Despite his cheerful attitude that morning, David's mood had quickly gone downhill after his patrol had passed the noon mark. Bags hung beneath his eyes, drooping like carrier bags weighed down with the contents of a weekly shop, indicative of his need for sleep.

He found himself wondering if DCI Franko ever slept, or if he had simply evolved past the need to.

Sighing heavily, David rubbed his face with the palms of his hands and snapped the visor back up into place. He was glad that his usual partner was off sick. The last thing that he wanted was someone sat next to him in the car all day, pointing out how tired and run down he was. As if he wasn't aware of it himself.

That isn't to say that he disliked his partner. Constable Klajdi Alikaj was a strange if not amusing man, with an equally strange and amusing name. He claimed that his first name was pronounced "Clyde", and that his last name was of Italian origin; both of which were statements that David believed sparingly, if at all. Klajdi had a talent for bullshit unlike anything David had ever seen before. On a good day, it was nothing if not amusing, however given the situation, he was glad that he didn't have to deal with it.

Exiting the vehicle, David made his was across the steadily filling lot and towards the door that lead into the station. As he stepped inside, the door swung back on heavy hinges and ground against the dark concrete of the floor.

He was met with a bright glare from the overhead lights, catching the pale green of the Linoleum floor. Some of the other officers might have referred to it as the colour of faded limes, however David had always thought of it as closer in hue to snot. A milky off-green, typically reserved for nasty colds and the flu.

Signing in his cruiser on the wall-mounted check-in sheet, David walked past the two interview rooms and made a beeline for the open-plan office. Looking out over the numerous desktops and accompanying Constables, the Detective Chief Inspector's office was to his left, framed by the enormous window that seemed to cover the entire front wall, so that Franko could keep an eye on the officers. David could see him sitting at his desk, head bent and reading something laid flat on his desk.

Hoping that his superior wouldn't notice him, he made his way over to St. Claire's desk and tapped him on the shoulder.

"Christ, did you even go home?"

Cocking his head to the side as he worked, St. Claire muttered out a vaguely interested response to David's question. "I went home for about four hours, between ten and two. Wanted to get all of this done before I called it a day, but turns out I underestimated just how deep this hole I'd dug myself was. Franko wants to have a word with you."

"Figured he would," David replied. "You heard back from Jess's sister, yet?"

St. Claire barely even looked up from the severely diminished paperwork set down in front of him. Grasping a single sheet of A4 paper, he held it up beside his head, for his colleague to snatch. "Called me around three thirty; said that there had been a few unusual pet injuries these past two weeks. I asked her to email me the details. You know I think you might actually be onto something here."

"Don't say it too loud, people might hear you."

"Just make sure you're workin' it on your own free time. I don't want to have the DCI breathing down my neck about you, I get enough stick from him as it is. I might drink with him, but that just means he notices me more."

"You've never been the type to care before," David replied, coyly. He was right. St. Claire was always the first man on the Force to mouth off and share some of his more unsavoury opinions; however, over the past few months, this attitude had been waning.

"Yeah well before, I wasn't being considered for a promotion."

"You're aiming for Sergeant?" David asked, visibly impressed by his colleague's aspirations.

"*Detective* Sergeant," St. Claire corrected, still scribbling away at the sheet in front of him. Beneath the tip of his ballpoint, trails of ink looped into words. His handwriting was surprisingly neat. "Give it a few more weeks and I'll probably be a part of CID, but at the moment that's not enough for me. I want to lead a team."

"And all this time, you told me that you enjoyed running the beat?"

"I do enjoy it, but it's not something that I want to still be doing twenty years from now. Plus the pay is better as a Detective Sergeant. Not by much, mind you, but it's still better. I'd much rather have something that's going to set me up well for the future."

"So when do you take the Detective's exam?"

"No plans on that, yet. This promotion comes first. Take each hurdle as it comes is a pretty good philosophy to live by. Hopefully this means I won't get distracted by much."

"Here's hoping." David broke into a slight chuckle and started to move away from the desk, paper in hand.

"You know Franko wanted a word with you," St. Claire said, still not looking up from his paperwork.

"He can talk to me if he catches me. Otherwise, I didn't know."

Turning halfway to his left, David made a beeline for the men's locker room, to change out of his uniform. The sooner he was out, the lower the chances were of him receiving a grilling from Franko, at least for the moment. It would have to wait until at least the next day, and that would give him more than enough time to think through all of his potential answers to the questions his superior would undoubtedly ask him.

"Stafford!"

The voice slammed into David like the closing of a coffin lid. His body jolted to a stop and he felt his breath sigh out from between his lips. He briefly shut his eyes. He should have known that he wouldn't be lucky enough to escape his superior's attention.

Especially with that damn window of his, he thought, bitterly.

"Yes sir?" he asked, turning towards the opposite side of the room, and calling over the heads of the other officers.

"I want a quick word with you. I won't be long. And shut the door."

David entered the office and closed the door behind him, the dull click of the catch sliding home echoing inside his head. "Is there anything I can help you with, sir?" His best course of action would be to play dumb; though he wasn't sure how well, if at all, it would work to his advantage.

Detective Chief Inspector James Franko was a man that many of the officers working under him would have described as being akin to a rusty nail. A man of fifty nine years old, he had iron grey hair and blunt features; his leathery skin holding a slight tan to it and sagging around the corners of his eyes and mouth. Despite his appearance, dealing with Franko was best done with care and at your own peril. Extraordinarily sharp (and in most cases likely to cause tetanus, if the rumours proved true), he had a particular way of digging at your skin and reaching the deepest part of your being. This was best observed in his eyes. Small and discerning, they held a dark sheen to them, like lacquered rosewood, that reflected a peculiar hardness. In spite of never having seen it in the eyes of anyone other than Franko (and maybe even *because* of that same fact), David recognised this hardness. James Franko had seen some serious shit.

The eyes narrowed behind Franko's glasses. "I've heard some of the other Officers talking. You're working on something you haven't been assigned." He spoke in a blunt and direct fashion that many would often mistake as rudeness, however it was never intended as such. It was efficiency, pure and simple.

"I am, yes." There wasn't any use in lying about it. The most David could hope for was the opportunity to explain himself.

"You know how I feel about my Officers working cases that aren't theirs."

"I do. But this is only in my free time, sir. It's something that's been bothering me for a while, and I really think I'm onto something with it."

"The cats, right?" Franko placed his elbows down onto his desk and steepled his fingers, resting the digits on his lips.

"Yes sir. I think someone is killing them."

Franko closed his eyes and broke into a laboured sigh. He knew the signs; he'd seen them before, back when he worked at the MET. He was about to explain when he stopped himself short. This wasn't the time to talk about The Butcher.

"Listen," he said. "You're not a part of the Criminal Investigation Department. You shouldn't even be working this sort of job. Not to mention, you're going almost entirely off of a hunch. A suspicion. That's not how we do things around here."

David had prepared himself for this. He was all but ready to receive a right royal grilling from Franko. However, in a strange twist of events, it never came.

"But I'm going to let it slide just this once. Only if you promise – and it damn well better be sincere – that if anything more comes out of this, you bring it straight to me."

Blinking twice, David stared across the table and into his superior's eyes. He caught a glimpse of something different in them; something that he never expected he would ever see. Vulnerability. It was faint and distant, but it was undeniably there.

Distracted by what he had seen, David just about managed a nod.

"I'm going to need that verbally," Franko said, the flicker of emotion disappearing from his dark eyes.

"I promise."

"Good. You can go now. And make sure you shut the door behind you."

Chapter 4

David drove home from the Station, feeling a strange mixture of numbness and confusion. He was stunned that the DCI had allowed him to continue to look into the matter. It was the last thing he had expected would happen, and even twenty minutes later, he was having trouble processing it. Franko was never this accommodating, never as understanding as he had been when they talked about the cats.

The cats.

He had skimmed the notes from Jess's sister while he walked from the front desk to his car. Multiple legs broken in at least three places; all injuries similar or the same across four of the animals. So far his suspicions were proving correct. Nothing about this felt like it was natural.

Franko had obviously felt the same, when he had given him permission to pursue the case. Franko with his vicious, penetrating intelligence that, given the misfortune of a bad mood, could do damage that you couldn't walk away from. It pierced and drove deep into enigmas, and if it was telling Franko, even in vague intuition, that there was something there, then it was worth David listening to as well.

That being said, the strange expression David had noted on the DCI's face may have been an indication of a temporary lapse in judgement. Anything was possible. Common opinion amongst the other officers was that he was growing listless and distracted as of late; though the reason why was anybody's guess.

David preferred not to think about it. Speculations about Franko would take up far too much of his time; fill his brain with a myriad of nugatory thoughts. Not to mention, said speculations would involve spending far too much time thinking about his boss. And such was a practice that he hoped to avoid, for the most part. It was true that he admired Franko to a certain degree, but past that the older man unnerved David. Talking to him held a peculiar detachment to it; like you were being observed through a two way mirror.

He took a deep breath and blinked hard twice, in an attempt to clear his mind and focus on more pleasant thoughts.

He thought of Paula waiting for him when he arrived back home, having just finished her own shift in the petrol station's accompanying shop. Feeling his lips brush against hers, coming back slightly slick and smelling of aloe, from the balm that she used. Catching the scent of her makeup removal wipes as he held her, the smell of cucumbers clearing his head and making him feel fresh and calm.

David's mind wandered from the sensations and feelings to the experiences. To what his evening would be filled with after he walked through the threshold of his home. The playful back-and-forths he and Paula shared, discussing each other's days, sitting in each other's presence on the settee. He would read the papers from the Vets while she would watch something on the television; more than likely the baking show that she loved so much, the name of which constantly escaped David. They would sit just within arm's reach, him occasionally reaching over to touch her with his fingertips, the sensation comforting and familiar. In their youth, back when they had first met, they had hungered for each other's touch, enamouring themselves in the feeling of their bodies, worried that such would be their last moments together. They used to sit tangled in a tightly wound knot of limbs, taking turns to nuzzle their faces into the crooks of each other's neck. Such intimacy had long ago evaporated into the ether, replaced by mutual comfort, appreciation, content and the occasional night of passionate fucking.

As David flicked on his indicator, the green blinking light on his dash flickered in his eye; a single bright spark in the blackness of his pupil. Pulling into his driveway, he shut off his headlights and killed the engine.

The gravel beneath his feet was damp from rain, and shifted wetly as he traversed the path leading up to his front door and slipped the key into the lock. Removing his shoes, David turned back on himself and sealed the entrance behind him; the snap of the bolt as it slid into place providing him with a dull comfort.

He could smell garlic and tomatoes, wafting through the air and coming from the kitchen. Paula was cooking. Pasta most likely.

Heading towards the kitchen, David slowed his pace and dropped his centre of gravity low. His socks padded softly against the floor, making little to no sound. He steadied his breathing, eliminating the sound.

From his slightly crouched position, he could see his wife's back. She was turned away from him, busying herself searching for something in one of the cupboards over the kitchen worktop.

Lifting his arms, David prepared himself to grab her.

"You jump me, and I swear to god I'm going to lamp you one." Paula laughed slightly and turned around to face David.

"How'd you know I was there?"

"Because you're predictable," she said. "And childish." Looping her arms over his head, Paula lifted herself up onto her toes and tilted her head to the side, smiling. "But mostly because I heard the door."

David planted a kiss on her and came away tasting aloe vera on his lips, exactly as he had expected. "I guess I'm going to have to be a bit more sneaky next time then."

Paula grinned. A sly and astute smile, indicative of how well she knew her husband. David knew the look all too well. He could almost imagine her calling him out, telling him that she was well aware of the fact that he let himself get caught by her on purpose. But she didn't say that. The smile was a conversation without words, punctuated by glances.

"So, you going to tell me what's wrong?" Paula asked, brushing a stray hair off of David's shoulder. "Or do I have to dig it out of you?"

David smirked slightly and let out a sigh, the air escaping his lips bearing a heavy sound. He knew that she would pick upon how tired he looked; how out of place the bags under his eyes were. "Just a long day," he answered, scratching the side of his head and revelling in the soothing sensation of the nails dragging over his scalp. "Domestic down in Parkside. You know how those can sometimes get."

"*And?*" she asked, as astute as ever.

"And I've finally started getting somewhere with this feeling I've been getting," he muttered, leaning back against the countertop behind him. His arms folded over his chest. "Though I'm not exactly sure if that's a good thing. Thought that the DCI was gonna rip me a new one..."

"Well did he?"

"No... God knows why."

"Maybe he thought that you were on to something? That or he's finally at that age where he's stopped caring."

"Franko doesn't stop caring," David grinned. "He's more machine than he is human. You know what he's lived through. Shit, you were the one that told me, when I found out he was gonna be my new boss."

"Blame all those garbage True Crime shows that I watch."

"I'd do no such thing," he smiled. "But still... It's unsettling: Him giving me his approval to continue on this."

"Why?" Paula asked, gripping the sides of his face and laughing as she hooked her thumbs on the corners of his mouth, in an attempt to force David's lips into a smile. "Not everything has to be doom and gloom. He could just be being nice."

Finally giving in to his wife's prodding, David let his mouth curl into a smile. Warmth flooded his face and laughter started to escape his lips. As he waved off Paula's hands, he found himself wondering if Franko had been programmed for niceness.

*

James Franko felt his eyes grow weary behind his glasses. His lids flickered and dared to close, weights seemingly hanging from his lashes and trying to drag them down. Closing his book, he placed the paperback on the table beside him and removed his glasses. Pinching the bridge of his nose, Franko blinked hard, to rid himself of the lingering effects of tiredness.

Past the haze of sleep, he watched Sarah. She had fallen asleep in her armchair, the pale light from the television licking over her milky skin. The shawl wrapped around her head had slipped ever so slightly, exposing the smooth skin of her scalp.

The cancer had been in remission for the past two weeks.

Thank God... he thought, before he stopped himself. This was a time where relief was a concept barely spoken of. It came sparingly and fled quickly. Franko knew the dangers and pitfalls of giving in to relief. He knew that as soon as it settled you were dragged back into despair by the hair.

It was the second in four months that Sarah had supposedly been in remission. Franko couldn't allow himself to fall back into the trap of feeling relief; he couldn't stand another heartbreak.

Sarah stirred slightly and Franko felt his breath catch in his throat. He didn't want to wake her.

As he watched her sleep, Franko caught himself thinking that this wasn't how it was meant to be. He had transferred out of the MET to take command of a station in the countryside, spend time in quiet comfort, accumulating funds for retirement. They were supposed to leave it all behind, move to sunny Spain to be with his family. A tranquil life as expats. Franko pictured a stout wooden beach hut, a stone's throw away from the sea. Stephanie would have brought the grandchildren to visit in the summer, while they were out of school, and Arthur would come to see them in the sparse time that he had off of work.

Their dreams of the future had been crushed when Sarah had received her diagnosis. Stage 2 breast cancer. The doctor had told them they had been lucky to catch it when they did. At the time, Franko had to hold himself back from punching him in the face. There wasn't anything lucky about it at all. He didn't trust doctors. Even less so after they had claimed the mastectomy had been a success. It wasn't more than a week later that they discovered the cancer had spread to her chest wall. At that point, it had developed into Stage 3. They started her on chemotherapy almost immediately.

Reaching out, through the dull fog of sleep, Franko fumbled for his book and placed his glasses back onto his face. After several seconds he realised, with bitter disappointment, that he had lost his place. He hated bookmarks (and despised with a fiery passion anyone uncultured enough to *fold over* the pages of a book). He hated the way they left even a slight crease in the page when you looked down at the top of a book, but now he was regretting his practice of simply remembering page numbers. With all of the stress brought on by Sarah's illness his brain had been rattled and slow. He was nowhere near as sharp as he used to be.

His mind crawled back towards David Stafford. Franko was surprised at how astute the Constable was. Not since he had been part of the Murder Squad in the London Metropolitan Police had Franko seen anyone pick up on signs like that, and very rarely was it noticed *before* anybody had been killed. Signs like those were often caught in hindsight. (Early indications of psychopathy included marked cruelty towards, and even the killing of, animals. Typically it began with smaller domestic pets such as cats and dogs.) They were often things quoted by reporters and newscasters as something seemingly obvious that the local police should have picked up on. Franko found himself recalling a journalist who once felt the need to question him on why the harming of animals wasn't caught much earlier. The reply that he gave him was the same as the thought currently settling in the forefront of his mind: *"The patterns of animal cruelty are almost impossible to pick up on. And when they are recognised it's usually by a family member, and the child responsible is put into therapy. The level of animal abuse that is indicative of a psychopath of this degree is massive and, more often than not, extremely difficult to connect and track, unless you already know where to look."*

And yet David had managed to recognise a pattern.

The prospect of finding such an individual early in their life both thrilled and daunted Franko. It left him with a cordial of confused feelings mixing inside him, swirling together yet still remaining separate and distinct, like an imperfect emulsion. On one hand, it allowed for early apprehension and identification. It meant that the person responsible could be entered into treatment to curb the impulses that could potentially lead to murder. On the other, should they be too far gone, Franko would be confronted with a particular breed of monster that he hadn't encountered since the Butcher. And, given Sarah's current condition, he didn't know if his emotions would be able to hold strong.

Rubbing his face, Franko tried to clear his head. Flipping open his paperback, he managed to find a sentence that he recognised. It may not have been exactly where he had been, but it was good enough.

He needed to dismiss the thoughts of David and the cats. Dwelling on them was doing nothing for Sarah.

More importantly, he had no concrete proof that the disappearances of the cats were a result of a blooming psychopath. It was in his best interests to leave it to David. He would only become involved when, and more importantly *if*, it came about that his suspicions were one hundred percent correct.

For a second time Sarah moved in her sleep, teetering on the edge of waking. Franko rose to his feet and fetched her a glass of water. He set it down on the high table next to her armchair before sinking back down into his space, in the corner of the sofa closest to her.

Flipping the novel open he realised, once again, that he had lost his place.

Chapter 5

Scott was on his morning walk to school when he finally decided how he was going to progress with the predicament he had landed himself in. The solution he came to, however, was the decision that he wasn't going to decide. As opposed to acting on the signals himself and talking to Alice, he would wait for her to make a move on him. Granted it was the coward's way out, but it was also the easiest. He would attend the party on Thursday night, make it known that he was available and if Alice gravitated towards him, then he would know that it was acceptable to proceed. And if, during that moment, he didn't feel the connection he was looking for, he would know exactly where to end it.

Scott was thankful for finally reaching some kind of conclusion. It filled him with a sense of ease and allowed him to focus more readily on other aspects of his life, like the millstone hanging around his neck had finally been cut loose. His mind slipped back into the ease of the mundane, holding focus in small distractions: The sound of leaves, dangling from overlooking trees, rustling as they were caught in the breeze; the occasional flash of colour as a car passed him on his left; the rough feeling of red brick beneath his fingertips as he trailed his hand over the top of the wall beside him; the sight of a younger girl walking parallel to him, across the street.

The damp veil of rain descending on him left his clear skin damp and the gentle lick of the wind chilled him into delicious sense of alertness; like he had just woken up from a refreshing nap. Scott had a brief flash of a memory, long since passed. (Waking up early in the morning after a gathering at Kyle's house, Pru suggesting that, to clear their hangovers, they should go for a walk in the pouring rain.) The edge of his mouth slipped up into a partial grin.

A dull buzz coursed across the skin of Scott's right thigh. Pulling out his vibrating phone, he peered down at the screen before hitting the green icon and lifting the device to his ear.

"Who the hell calls people these days?"

"I do," Pru's voice replied. "You got a problem with that?"

"I've got a few problems with it," he chuckled. "So, what do you want?"

"I'm running kind of more than a bit late," she rattled out, her numerous double negatives drilling into Scott's brain. "Could you be an absolute doll and run to the IT labs for me. I was supposed to print out this essay for Lincoln's class, but my printer ran out of ink, and I can't get in early enough to do it myself."

"What, do I look like a gofer to you? And why can't you get Dan to do it? I'm pretty sure this falls into the spectrum of 'boyfriend duties'."

"You know he always skips first period on a Wednesday," she said. Her voice took on a whining, pleading tone. Like a small child vying for its parents' attention. "Come on, Scott. I'll love you forever!"

"You damn well better," he replied, grunting and scratching the side of his head, with his free hand.

"So that means you'll do it?"

"What can I say, it seems you convinced me."

After a rushed round of 'thank you's from Pru, Scott hung up and wiped the phone against his shirt, to remove the rain clinging to the back of the device.

Up ahead of him, the school started to come into view. He remembered a time when he enjoyed going to school. The memory was distant and detached, almost as if it wasn't his own. School was a place filled with rules and restrictions, both of which were concepts that Scott held in a small amount of contempt. He didn't like being regulated; didn't like being told what he needed to learn. All things considered, he would have enjoyed school a lot more if he had a choice in the specifics of his studying. He preferred the people to the place. His friends were the only thing that made it tolerable.

Entering the crowd of crushed bodies as they streamed through the gates, Scott pushed through the swarm and picked up his pace. He didn't like to be late, and if he was going to print the papers for Pru before first period, he would need to move quickly.

He arrived at the Computer Lab with time to spare, collapsing into one of the chairs and dragging the keyboard of the closest desktop towards him. The tips of his fingers clacked across the keys, filling his head with a rapid and rhythmic click. Blue flared across his hazel eyes, as the screen came to life and he logged onto Pru's user.

It was then that he felt a strange sensation.

A slight tingle raced across his skin, traversing the bridge between his shoulder blades before shooting down his spine. Goosebumps rose up on the skin of his arms. It was a sensation that his mother had often referred to as happening when "someone walked over your grave". The phrase had never sat right with Scott, leaving him with a sickening feeling of disrespect, deep in the pit of his stomach. It implied that, eventually, everybody stopped caring. That one day all that would be left of him was a neglected patch of ground in the middle of an overgrown church yard; only disturbed when someone casually stepped on his sacred piece of earth.

Turning his head slowly Scott eyed the room. It wasn't that he expected to see anything, however the tingle had granted him an unfounded sense of paranoia. His eyes dragged across the surroundings, reassuring him that nothing was amiss.

In his mind, he counted off everything that his gaze fell upon. Three other students sat at desktops dotted around the room, no doubt busying themselves completing some urgent piece of homework. In the corner a large portable fan, typically reserved for the summer heat, stood dejected, pointed into the corner like a punished child. A pile of broken monitors took up residence on the top of a desk in the corner opposite the fan, ignored by the staff and crying out for repair. Past that were several more computers, leading up to Scott's own.

And through the glass window, set into the door to his right, someone was watching him.

*

David stared down at the monochrome sheets in front of him and cursed himself for deciding to enter into Law Enforcement. Set down onto his desk was the bane of his life: Paperwork.

He didn't know a single Officer that didn't complain about it. Without a doubt the worst part of the entire career, everybody (with the current exception of St. Claire) avoided it like the plague. Nothing compared to it. Traffic duty, while monotonous, had brief moments of exciting reprise. Battery and assault often ended ugly, but the satisfaction of putting away those responsible trumped all negative connotations. Domestic abuse was soul crushing, however you left it feeling as if you'd actually made some kind of a difference, no matter how small. Paperwork, unfortunately, offered no sense of excitement or satisfaction; no feeling that you were making a difference. All it provided was the dull pleasure of relief once it was all finished. Despite the fact that it never, really, finished.

It was why David hated Cop Shows and action movies with an Officer as the main character. He knew for a fact that nobody would be able to perpetuate such an astounding level of carnage without being struck by the unforgiving mistress that was paperwork.

Sipping from the mug of tea that Julie had made him, David closed one eye and shook his head. It was too sweet. No matter how many times he said to her that he didn't take sugar, she always made the tea how she liked to drink it. Next time he would brew the tea how he wanted and see how she liked it.

Actually... he thought. *Better not.*

Julie Chambers was the Station's resident badass and crossing her in any way shape or form was best done at one's own peril. At sixty four years old and standing at just under five foot four, her appearance led to many people mistakenly assuming that Julie was frail. Several minutes of talking to the woman, however, would indicate otherwise. Intimidating was an understatement. In a good mood she was one of the most loving and kind women anyone had ever met, but once her switch was flipped she was utterly ruthless. She bowled through everything in her way with all the force of an air compressor. David recalled an incident a few years earlier when they had gone out for drinks with a number of the other Officers. Julie offered to buy him a drink and he had politely declined. Within seconds David's answer did an about face. She was so forceful and insistent, he thought she was going to slug him if he refused for a second time.

David could just about see the flat top of her silver-white bob over the top of his computer monitor.

"I can see you looking at me." Her blunt voice struck him like a mallet.

"Sorry about that Ju," he apologised, half standing so that he could look at her while he spoke. "I was just thinking... We've been working together a long time, right?"

"Indeed we have, my love," she replied, leaning back in her chair and training her pale grey eyes onto David's face.

"So that means that we know each other pretty well."

"Well enough for me to know that you're dancing around the issue right now, you big div. You going to actually ask me what's on your mind, or do I have to dig it out of you?"

David emitted a single faint laugh, hidden in the undercurrent of his breath. "What I'm trying to ask is: Do you think I think too much?"

"What kind of question is that?"

"I dunno, it's just something that's been on my mind for a little while." The irony of his statement wasn't lost on him.

"Has this got something to do with them bloody cats?" Julie asked, lifting one of her stout white eyebrows. Noting David's stunned expression, she pursed her lips together. "St. Claire told me."

"I can't trust him with anything."

"Don't blame him, love. He's proud of you; thinks you're actually on to something with this. Said that Franko thought the same." She nodded her head towards the enormous window that framed the DCI's office. "Hell of a thing, that. Never thought I'd see the day when that old bastard actually cared about someone like you."

"Thanks... I think. But what do you mean 'old bastard'? He's younger than you."

Julie's face creased up as she started to laugh. "It's rude to ask a woman about her age!"

"I didn't ask," David teased. "All I did was make a statement."

"Yeah, well next time you keep it to yourself."

"So what exactly did St. Claire say about the cats?"

"That you noticed a lot of them are going missing. And that you're trying to figure out why."

"You think that it's all a bit pointless, don't you?" Julie's nature kept very little about what she was thinking a secret. David could see her judgement as clear as day, almost as if it had been written in block capitals across the flat skin of her Botoxed forehead. It said: 'You're wasting your time.'

Julie was unashamed of her straightforward, and often brash, nature. She wore it like a badge of honour and, in fitting with her personality, was not one to wear it in silence. "I think that you're going to do what you want, regardless of what I say. But if it's all the same, I wouldn't be doing all of this extra work on a hunch."

The older woman's response didn't surprise him. Rather, David had expected the reply. The corners of his eyes creased as he broke into a smile. "I knew you'd say something like that."

"I'm just saying don't stress yourself out about it. Life is too fucking short, just do what makes you happy."

Strangely enough her words gave David a second wind, clearing his head and helping to focus his thoughts. Talking to the female Officer always gave him a strange amount of encouragement, even (and sometimes especially) when she was telling him to give up. It helped to reaffirm his thoughts and gain clarity of mind. She had told him to do what made him happy. And right then, in that moment, the thing that would make him happier than anything else was potentially discovering the cause of the feline disappearances.

Reaching into the top drawer of her desk, Julie pulled out a packet of cigarettes and a cheap disposable lighter. As she shook the device, the fluid inside the translucent neon body rippled and flashed in the light. "I'm going out for a fag. By the time I get back you better be feeling better, or so help me."

David laughed at the threat, only half sure that she was joking.

Waving Julie off, he collapsed back into his chair and sank down into the fabric-covered foam. His head newly refreshed, he allowed a smile to pluck at his mouth. Picking up a nearly worn out ballpoint from his desk, he began to tap out a simple rhythm on his desk.

The memory of the notes lapped through his brain, like waves at high tide. They advanced from the recesses of his mind, encroaching more and more into the forefront of his consciousness.

There were a lot of things that had bothered him about the injuries the cats had sustained. The similar injuries between the animals he had taken to mean that something (or rather some*one*) was behind it; but he wasn't a doctor. The damage may have been caused by other incidents: Cars or even falls. He would need to visit the Vets himself, after he finished work, to talk through what could cause the wounds. He hoped that there was a reasonable explanation behind it all. That the Vet would tell him that the sustained trauma was normal.

The hope vanished as the latest wave of thoughts washed through him. It wasn't the wounded cats that had drawn him in. It was the missing. The numbers were vast. Too vast for it to merely be coincidence.

And he needed to figure out where they were. Who was responsible, and why.

David needed to know.

Such was the curse of the police. The overwhelming desire to figure out; to discern the nature of things. It wouldn't let him give up. It scratched at the inside of his head like a toothpick against mortar. Slow, yet persistent and purposeful. And over time the effects grew more and more pronounced.

Righting the pen in his hand, he scribbled out a post-it note and stuck it to the corner of his computer monitor, reminding him to call the Vet after he finished work to arrange an appointment.

Chapter 6

He blinked several times, to make sure that he wasn't seeing things.

The face disappeared from the window, leaving behind the grey condensation of warm breath against the glass. An afterimage of blonde hair remained in Scott's vision. If he didn't know any better, he would have said that the girl staring at him looked like-

"Alice?" he muttered, knitting his brows together and pulling a confused expression.

Standing up and making his way across the room, Scott tentatively opened the door and stuck his head out into the busy hallway. The swarm of uniforms that usually occupied the school met him in a canvas of black jackets, punctuated by the occasional flash of white shirts and red striped ties. A multitude of hair colours floated over the top of the scene; seaweed in a black ocean.

He recognised a few of the faces, and just as many of the bags, from students whose backs had been turned on him. But no Alice. If it had, in fact, been her that he had caught spying on him, then she was long gone.

Making his way back to the desktop and clicking the printer icon, the image of the face remained fixed in his mind. Already it had started to blur and distort, to the point where he wasn't even sure if it belonged to a boy or girl.

Perhaps he was just seeing things.

Alice had been on his mind so much lately that he wouldn't be surprised if he had mistaken another student for the girl. He convinced himself that it was just some random student, checking to see if their friend was one of the room's occupants. That must have been it. There wasn't a chance that Alice had been staring at him.

Logging off, Scott walked over to the printer and snatched up the assignment. He took a second to appreciate the warm feeling of the paper. The comforting heat spread up his hands and eased his mind. Scott had always enjoyed the sensations of newly printed sheets. A subtle scent caught his nose, from the fresh ink, and he broke into a gentle smile.

Checking the time on the wall-mounted clock, he reassured himself that he wasn't running late before carefully slipping the homework into his bag and exiting the room. His plan for the day cycled methodically through his head, ensuring that he accurately kept time. First period was free study, meaning that he would have the opportunity to give Pru the work he had printed for her.

Her first lesson was Geography with Mr Lincoln, the class that the assignment was due to be handed in to. As long as Scott headed directly to the room, and met Pru in the hallway, he would have enough time to hand her the homework before her class started. After that, he would find himself an empty classroom and relax. More than likely listen to music. He was all caught up with any assignments due, so it wasn't as if the opportunity would be wasted. And as long as he made it look like he was doing work, Scott knew that he wouldn't be bothered by anybody.

*

When David Stafford arrived at the Parks Veterinary Practice, there were a number of problems.

First of which was the Border Collie that emptied its bowels over the floor (and, by association of proximity, David's shoes). From what he could gather from the hurried apologies of the too-friendly nurse, the dog had consumed almost an entire box of chocolates and was feeling appropriately worse-for-wear.

Well now, so are my shoes... he thought, bitterly.

The second problem was that, due to the staff being preoccupied with the poisoned canine, no-one was available to point him in the right direction. He stood lingering in the waiting room, checking his phone for any messages that he may have received during the day.

Awkwardly shifting from one foot to the other, he quickly scanned the room and immediately noticed the third problem: There wasn't a single cat.

He had started work early, so that he could take the afternoon off and look into the details he was having trouble with. Set onto the wall, above the unmanned reception window, the clock read the time as 1:00PM.

"Mr Stafford?"

Stood in the hallway, leading off from the waiting room, the Vet noted David and waved him over.

Dr Copeck was a young man of twenty six, standing at six foot one and weighing around one hundred and eighty pounds. Hanging across his forehead was a thin fringe of light brown hair, framing a pair of striking green eyes. His face was fresh and bright, indicating a love for his job, however the stress of his workload was evident in the thin lines extending from the corners of his eyes.

"Sorry for taking up your time, I'll try and make this quick," David said, following the Vet into his office.

"It's okay. I've already attended to all of the serious cases today, and I'm sure the nurses can cover anything that comes up while we're talking. Just be prepared that if there is an emergency, then I will have to rush off."

"That's fine, Dr Copeck. You're doing me a big favour, so any time you're willing to give me is perfect."

"Ollie," the Vet said, offering his first name at the same time as his hand.

Wrapping his fingers around Ollie's hand, David shook. "David."

"So what can I help you with? Maria told me yesterday that you needed information about cat injuries. I'm guessing this has something to do with that?"

"I just had a few questions about what could cause the type of wounds you described in the email Maria forwarded to my colleague."

"I'll admit I was curious about why you needed the information. Now I think I know what you're getting at. You think someone did this to them on purpose."

"Didn't you come to that conclusion?"

"I did, but I didn't think the different instances were connected."

"So what do you think now?"

"Now... I'm still hesitant to agree with you. I don't like thinking that someone would intentionally harm this many animals." Ollie's face was gripped by a dry sympathy. He was used to seeing animal abuse, but that didn't mean that he was immune to the effects.

David decided not to tell him about the number of missings. If his theory was correct, someone was responsible for hurting far more than four.

"So... How can you tell that these injuries weren't the result of accidents?" David asked. "Like traffic collisions?"

"Bones break differently depending on the direction and degree of force involved," Ollie replied. "If these cats had been hit by cars, the bones would be completely shattered, and the damage would be distributed across the entire body. The fractures here are focussed entirely on the legs. Not to mention, a car would cause haemorrhaging of the internal organs, and here there is none."

"Well then, what about falls? Wouldn't that only cause damage to the legs."

"It'd have to be from a pretty massive height to result in damage like this. Cats are damn good at falling: they distribute their weight evenly and land feet first to reduce impact. I've seen cats go off of multi-story buildings and come out without a scratch." He reached into the drawer of his desk and pulled out a series of X-Rays. "These are compound fractures. Not to mention... All of the legs are broken in different directions. In multiple places. It's almost like..."

"Almost like what?"

"Like someone systematically snapped the bones one by one."

David unintentionally flinched. "That's sick."

"You're telling me."

"Is there any evidence of abuse before?" He was holding out on the hope that, even if the damage was caused by a person, the incidents weren't connected. There was no such luck.

"None. Prior abuse would have left scars; evidence of old healed breaks. And if this level of abuse were long term, there would be signs other than injuries. The cat would have a poor coat, and maybe even fleas or mange. Besides the broken legs, these four cats were all perfectly healthy."

"Damn..."

"This isn't the answer you were hoping for?"

David sighed and shook his head. "Not exactly. It's complicated. At least now I don't feel like I'm going completely mad."

Ollie folded his arms across his chest and sat back against the edge of his desk. His face was difficult to read. It didn't move much. Behind his eyes, there was a faint air of what appeared to be sadness. "And is that a good thing, or a bad thing?"

"Honestly? A little bit of both."

David thanked the Vet and shook his hand again. Exiting the office, he shut the door behind him and rubbed his hands over his face. A dull tingle clung to his skin in the wake of his palms.

Walking down the hallway, he came out into the waiting room and stopped for a second at the window set into the wall, shielding the receptionist's desk. Maria Brown, Jess's sister, sat on the other side of the transparent shield, filling in details of appointments, on the desktop.

"Thanks for the help, yesterday," he said. His voice was flat and level.

Looking up from the computer screen, Maria broke into a half smile. "Don't mention it. Are you any closer to figuring out whatever it is you're working on?"

"Right now I don't know," David admitted. It felt like he was running on a treadmill. He knew that there was an end goal to reach, a point to aim for, but for the most part he felt static.

He watched the remaining occupants of the waiting room. A woman was sat across the room, cradling a guinea pig in her hands and cooing down at it. The terracotta fur caught the light and glimmered, throwing an orange glow up across its owners face. Several seats down from her, a greyhound had managed to weave its body through the legs of the young lady holding its leash. The dog's eyes were sad, staring at a fixed spot on the wall across from it.

"Do you have any?" Maria asked, looking up at the Constable through tea-coloured eyes.

"Pets? Me and Paula both work, so no. I had a turtle when I was a kid, though. His name was Sheldon."

"What happened to him?"

"He ran away."

Maria pulled a face. Unsure over whether David was telling the truth, or if the entire conversation had been based on an elaborate lie, she looked up at the older man from her position behind her desk.

Catching the look that the girl was directing at him, David broke into a sly grin.

"You know you almost had me fooled," she said, half exasperated, but not without a smile.

David found some form of solace in that. She appreciated his coy attempt at humour. It was something that Maria had in common with Paula. That and her earlobes. Connected to the sides of her jaw, they would stay exactly where they were, even after the sag of old age inevitably started to set in. Quite the opposite to himself. He figured that by the time he was fifty, his earlobes would be hanging by his ankles.

The curious association reminded him of a song he used to sing to his niece, when she was little. ("Do your ears hang low, can you swing them to and fro? Can you tie them in a knot, can you tie them in a bow?")

David was brought back to the world by the dull hum of his mobile phone, buzzing inside his pocket. Fumbling slightly with the older model device, he slid up the screen and peered at the display.

"Out of milk can you grab some on way home? Xxx love you xxx"

"That your wife?" Maria asked, leaning forward and looking up at David, through the spiderwebs of her mascara.

"Yeah," he replied, quickly typing out a reply before slipping the phone back into his pocket. "Listen, I've got to head off now, but if anything else comes up, anything at all, send it my way."

"Do you want to give me your email? I can get it to you quicker that way."

"Could you? That would be perfect. Do you have a pen?"

As Maria took down the email address, David watched her slender fingers, gripping the transparent plastic of the pen. Again, a strange detail to focus on. He figured that as a young girl she must have played the piano; could still, as far as he knew.

"Thank you."

"That's okay," Maria said, smiling warmly as he moved to leave. "Have a good night." And then she added: "Treat your wife to something nice."

Walking out of the Vets, and making his way to his car, David considered her words. It wasn't such a bad idea to do something special for Paula. A spontaneous gesture of love.

He was already in Lindum, and his route back home to Lyefield would take him past a number of shops. There was a florist halfway along West Avenue, just down the road from St Matthew's School.

Paula loved lilies.

Chapter 7

The Technical Support office of St Matthew's Comprehensive School was a rectangular room measuring roughly ten foot by twelve foot. The three separate workstations all bore at least two monitors, as well as a large free-standing console, tucked into place beneath the lip of each respective desk. The off cream walls were tacked with a number of different charts, timetables and images, and the high ceiling housed several circular light fixtures. Through the door that provided entrance to the office the sounds of students, midway through a class, were often heard.

Derrick Harshen (Junior IT Technician) sat at his desk working at the underside of a laptop, with a bright red screwdriver. He had been attempting to fix it for the past hour and was so far having very little luck.

After changing the wireless card and trying to boot up the device, he discovered that the laptop refused to turn on. Initially assuming that the battery had run out of charge, he plugged it in figuring that would solve the problem. It didn't.

Thus he found himself removing the case, in an attempt to access the motherboard and circuits. So far, he hadn't found anything abnormal. His face scrunched up as he pulled his thick-lensed glasses down from on top of his head.

Troubleshooting was always the worst part of his job. His Line Manager hated the phrase 'I think'. It meant that he needed to be absolutely sure of what the problem was, before trying to solve it. Overall it minimised mistakes, however Derrick found it tedious and draining.

"It's probably a problem with the battery," Kent Haolin said, leaning over from his own station and peering down at the seemingly dead piece of hardware.

Kent's face was broad and his nose slightly crooked, as if he had been struck square between the eyes with a hockey stick (and, given his penchant for sports in his free time, it was highly likely that this was in fact the cause). His hair was black and flecked with sparse strands of solid white, despite him not being much older than thirty. He had a pen tucked behind his ear.

"Yeah, but I've already plugged in the charging cable. It-it should have turned on. I don't know why it's not working." Derrick fumbled his words slightly at the stress of the situation.

Having recently come back from three months sick leave, this was the last thing he needed. His doctor had told him to avoid unnecessary stress and confrontation. Even with his pills, the mood swings still hit him. One minute he could be on cloud nine, only for something to suddenly snip the wires and send him plummeting back down to earth. He sometimes wondered if the pills even worked at all.

The heat he was feeling dismissed the curiosity. A side effect of his medication was increased body temperature, and at that moment he felt like there was a furnace inside him. Set onto his desk, the miniature fan whirled away, blasting cold air into his face.

"But if one of the cells inside the battery is burnt out, it ruins the circuit," Kent said, reaching over and taking the laptop. Unhooking the battery from its port, he checked the power cable before flipping the device back over and hitting the 'on' button. The screen immediately lit up. "See. Without the battery the power goes in a circular route instead of a figure of eight."

"So does that mean we only need to order a new battery?"

"Yeah. Yeah. I mean we may not even have to do that." Kent placed the laptop down on the floor and fell back into his chair. "Johnny's got a couple of spares laying around; you could probably get away with just using one of them."

Derrick nodded. He was glad that the problem was a simple one. Easy to resolve. All he would need to do was wait until his other colleague returned from the job he was on. Then Derrick could have him unlock his desk drawer, to get at the spare parts.

A chime filled the room, cutting through the hum of the computers and the whoosh of Derrick's fan, as they both received the same email.

"Got another one," Kent muttered, spinning his chair around to face his monitors.

"What is it this time?"

"Kevin's having problems with the desktop in the security room. For some reason, when he came back from his lunch, it was turned off and wouldn't come back online."

Derrick's simian face crumpled. The freckles set onto the tanned skin around his eyes disappeared beneath the scrunched folds, the motion magnified by his glasses. "That ain't right. That computer never should have been turned off."

"I know. Look, I'm really busy clearing out the directory here, so could you head upstairs and sort it out?"

Grumbling under his breath, Derrick pushed his glasses back on top of his shaved head and folded his arms across the flat of his chest. "Can't we just leave him to it? He probably just knocked the socket or something." Grasping a handful of mints from the tub next to his keyboard, he shovelled them into his mouth.

"Don't you start getting complacent," Kent said, wagging his finger at the larger man. "You're a lot better than you used to be, but that doesn't mean you can start cutting corners. That's how you fall back into old habits. Even if Kev did accidentally turn it off, that security room is important. Without the computer they can't view the video feed, or store the recordings."

"Okay, okay." Giving in, Derrick threw his hands up and heaved himself out of his seat. "I'll be back in a minute. Did you want me to check the printers on my way back?"

Kent checked his watch. "Nah, best leave that for now. It's nearly time for the period six change over. I don't want you getting caught up in the rush of kids."

Derrick exited the office, through the conjoined IT classroom, and started making his way upstairs. As he walked his eyes trained on a number of black domed security cameras, positioned along the ceiling. They were located all over the school and fed live video to the computer in the security room. The recordings were stored digitally on the mainframe. However, if the desktop controlling them went down, the cameras were little more than expensive pieces of glass and plastic.

In the security room Kevin Hendrickson, the school's caretaker, was sat uncomfortably at the sole desk. A tall man of fifty two, his powerful build was crammed into a set of black khakis and a matching fleece. He rubbed one large hand backwards through his thinning white hair, and glanced over at Derrick through his half-frame glasses. In front of him, the three separate monitor screens were a solid and unmoving black.

"I don't know what it is," Kevin said, indicating the hardware with a wave of his right hand. "I came back from my lunch break, and it was just dead."

"Alright," Derrick said. "Let's have a look at it."

He checked the socket first, just to make sure that the power was in fact turned on. After finding no problems, he grunted and sank down to his knees, to check the back of the console. There was always the possibility that the cable connecting the monitor had come loose.

What he found was far more than just a loose wire.

Every single cable had been yanked out of its port. There was no way that this had been done by accident. Someone had purposely unplugged them.

Derrick's job, however, did not revolve around the why or even the how. His job was to fix what was broken. Plugging everything back in, he hefted himself onto his feet and tried to power on the computer.

The screens came to life, flashing blue light across his and Kevin's glasses.

"That should do it," Derrick said, watching the display and moving the mouse to test that the cursor was working.

"Cheers mate," Kevin replied. "Would you mind just staying until the system comes back online? I don't want to have to call you down again in five minutes, if anything goes wrong."

"Yeah, sure thing."

They waited in silence for the software to resurrect itself. Derrick wasn't known for his conversational skills, much preferring to distance himself from the rest of the faculty. As such, he was often at a loss of exactly what to say during such encounters where he had to hang around for an extended amount of time.

"Okay, just give me a second." Kevin leaned forwards and began to type on the keyboard, moving the mouse in several sharp motions. "I'm just going to bring up the display of all the video feeds, just to make sure that they're all working, and-"

"What's that?"

"What's what?" Kevin looked up over his shoulder at the Technician.

Derrick reached out and pointed at the screen on the left. "That there, third row down."

Confused, the caretaker turned back around and double clicked on the small moving thumbnail. As the image filled the screen, he felt his stomach lurch up into his throat.

"What the fuck is that?"

Chapter 8

Mr Spencer Hemming taught his class in a manner vaguely reminiscent of his sex life: Boring and monotonous, yet with an ever so slight amount of humour. His voice droned and dragged, leaving the air thick and heavy. Most of the students dotted around the room struggled to fight off the drowsiness induced by the sound. Just as they were about to completely nod off, however, he would drop a pun so terrible that the students would have to wake up, just to cringe.

A relatively squat man, Mr Hemming's most striking feature was his nose. Long on knobbly, the slope jutted out of his face and into the open air. This, coupled with his drooping eyes and small teeth, reminded Scott of The Child Catcher, from Chitty Chitty Bang Bang (though he would have never said this to his face).

Chewing on the corner of his lip, Scott allowed his eyes to lose focus. During these sections of the lesson, he could afford to slip into a daze. Period six on a Wednesday was typically reserved for watching videos of psychology case studies, interspaced with sections of class discussion. The video, currently streaming from the front-facing projector at the back of the class, allowed him the chance to daydream unnoticed.

The blinds had been drawn for the entire lesson, throwing the room into shadow. The beam of light from the projector sliced through darkness; particles of dust rendering it visible.

As the final video clip of the class finished, Mr Hemming flicked the light back on and took his position at the front of the room. "Well, that was educational wasn't it?"

When he received no response, the teacher glanced around the room at the group of blank, disinterested faces staring back at him.

Just as he was about to open his mouth to pose a question, however, a piercing sound filled the air. The bell, signalling the end of the lesson, cut him off.

Not even waiting to be dismissed, the students all rose to their feet and stuffed their things into their bags. Making their way towards the door, the chatter of conversation filled the room.

While his fellow students were preoccupied with fleeing the class, Scott lingered behind. He always made a point of helping the teacher, whenever he was able. More often than not, he found himself moving textbooks, rearranging tables or, as was currently the case, helping with the blinds. Having a free slot on period seven of a Wednesday, he usually made a point of staying behind to help pack things away.

Walking towards the window on the far left, and grasping hold of the knobbly white cord, Scott tugged hard.

What he saw, as the blackout blind rolled out of view, caused his stomach to churn.

Piled in clear view of the window was an undefinable bloody mass. Patches of sticky and mottled hair stuck out in various directions, crimson beads rolling down them and glinting in the light. Flashes of pink flesh and white bone could be seen, through bright red lacerations, like stained teeth and tongues through red lips. Every so often a grey jelly-like substance, that Scott could only assume was brain matter, had globed together. The thing that most gripped his attention, however, was the eye. Set down at least three feet away from the pile, the eggy yellow orb stared towards him, through a single slit pupil.

"Jesus fucking Christ..."

*

The sound of sirens carried up the road and entered David's car, through the open sliver of his window. The flashing blue lights followed closely behind, flickering over his windshield and reflecting across his mahogany eyes.

He knew he was off duty; that he wasn't obligated to stop, but something convinced him otherwise. The fact that the origin of the light show was the school may have had a hand in it, but all in all it was something more than that. It was a feeling; an ominous sense that told David that he needed to stop.

Slowly, with every inch he edged down the road, his mind began to unspool. Like the strands of his thoughts were connected to the hubcaps of his car, unwinding while he drove.

As he drew closer, he could see two patrol cars in the visitor section of the school car park. Neon green and muggy white clashed against one-another, the difference in colour becoming more and more pronounced as David's car drew closer to the scene. Turning left, he drove through the wrought iron gates and pulled into a vacant space.

Exiting the car and approaching the closer of the two cruisers, he noticed a strange scent in the air. Mildly pungent and sour, he recognised the smell as that of nervous sweat. And it was coming from him.

There was no logical reason for him to feel nervous. It was almost as if his body knew something that his mind had not been privy too. Like all of his organs had organised a meeting amongst themselves and purposely not invited the man upstairs.

David knew that, as soon as he opened his mouth, his voice was going to waver. Rapping against the window, to gain the attention of the Officer in the car, he attempted to cover his anxiety with humour. "Ello ello ello, what's all this then?"

The other Officer didn't respond well. "Are you takin' the fuckin' piss?"

"Oh! No! Sorry, mate, just having a bit of fun." He fumbled out an apology and pulled his warrant card from the back pocket of his trousers. "I'm with the Lyefield Station. Was driving past and wondered what happened."

"Nothing like anything I'd ever seen before..." the man muttered and stared out of the windshield, towards the entrance to the main school building.

"What is it?"

"Fucked up is what it is."

A cocktail of thoughts stirred through David's mind. Within a split second numerous hopeful theories poured through him, filling his head to the brim and daring to spill over. A curious mixture of intrigue and fear gripped him.

He lifted an eyebrow, prompting his associate to elaborate.

"Got a call from the caretaker about thirty minutes ago, said he'd seen something on the security cameras," he answered. "Said it looked like a load of dead bodies. One of the guys from tech support was with him too; he was the one that first noticed it. Poor bastard. Sensitive soul. Don't think he ever thought he'd see anything like that in his life. Threw up everywhere. Fuckin' mess. He's on his way down the station now, along with the kid."

"Kid?"

"Yeah. Around the same time, a student opened the blinds for his class. Got a real good look, up close."

"How had no one else noticed it before that? And why so few now?"

"Whoever dumped it picked a good spot," the Officer said, lowering his brows and staring vacantly into the distance. "It's outside an annex on the south-facing side of the building. Only one room has windows facing that direction, and according to the teacher, the blinds are always closed on a Wednesday, from 1:05 to 1:50."

"That was pre-meditated," David confirmed, joining the man in staring at the building.

"Yeah. We think whoever's responsible came in through a gap in the fence, and made the dump." He started to pick at his fingernails. "Must have carried it in a bin bag or something."

"Sorry for all the questions," David said, before coming to his main point of interest. "But... You said the caretaker thought it was a load of dead bodies."

"Yeah?"

"Well... Was he right?"

The man sighed and leaned back in his car seat. His head rolled backwards and he started to rub the thin stubble that gripped his throat.

While he waited for a response, David's thoughts whirled out of control. They thrashed inside his skull, like centipedes scurrying about.

Dead bodies. Dead *bodies*. It meant that there was more than one. And, based on the way his comrade was talking, they were assuming that one person was responsible. Coupled with the lack of CID personnel and a proper restriction of the site, it meant that the deceased clearly wasn't human.

Behind his ribcage, David's heart skipped in an avian flutter.

"Officially we don't know yet. They're mangled beyond recognition. Personally? I'd say they look a hell of a lot like-"

"Cats?" David interrupted, unable to contain his thoughts any longer.

"How'd you guess that?"

The curious mixture of conflicting emotions that he had felt earlier in the Vets slammed into him with all the force of a truck. His stomach wound itself into a tight knot, while a strange sense of elation floated up past his ears. He had to stop himself from both smiling and grimacing.

Luck and chance was a curious thing.

Most police work operated through a mental state that most of David's fellows referred to as 'the machine'. A state of mind that embodied efficiency, it was how most investigations and inquiries were resolved. The machine reached conclusions through sheer persistence and mechanical tenacity.

However even the most well-oiled machine was nothing compared to luck. To spontaneous instances of divine grace; where all of the pieces just magically fit together.

If he hadn't gone out of his way to buy his wife flowers, he would never have stumbled across this. It was exactly the break that he needed, and given how serious the situation had become, David was sure that he'd be allowed to pursue it during his work hours.

Thank you, Paula, he thought. *I swear to God I'm going to buy you so many flowers. Shit, I'll buy you the whole fucking florist!*

"It's something I've been looking into. If you wouldn't mind, could I get the number of the Chief Superintendent of the Lindum Station?"

Fishing around in his glove compartment, for a card with his boss's line extension, the Officer squinted his eyes. "What d'you need it for?"

"There's been a lot of cats going missing recently... Dozens of them." Inside his pocket, David's hand started to tremble. "And I think you've just found some of them."

Chapter 9

The Sergeant about to interview Scott bore a number of conflicting aspects to his appearance; the most striking being his stature. Tall and broad, Joshua Akinfe's body was trim and extraordinarily muscular, much like that of a rugby player. His raised shoulders and straining biceps sprouted out of his tree trunk of a body and were so large that he found himself incapable of holding them at his sides. The enormous limbs ended in a matching set of massive hands; so large in fact that Scott figured the Officer would be able to wrap the fingers of one hand completely around his head. His physique, however, failed to match his face; and similarly, his sense of style clashed with both. Framed by a wide pair of wire-frame glasses, his eyes were coal black, yet bore a comforting reassurance to them. His expression was sympathetic and caring, emphasised by the way he subtly moved the thick lips of his mouth. As they parted to speak, Scott recognised the distant twinkle of a gold tooth.

"Now son, I don't want to pressure you into anything." He spoke with a slight twang of a Nigerian accent. "If you want to tell me what you saw, then that would be great. But if you don't feel up to it, then we can take as much time as you want, until you're okay. How does that sound?"

Joshua was a calming and considerate man. The sound of his voice rolled gently, like swaying wheat in a field. It soothed and settled anyone he talked to into comfort, whereby he would simply need to wait for them to ultimately reveal what was stirring away inside their head.

His penchant for waiting and patience had been forged through numerous years working for the Police Service. In his earlier days, before he had grounded himself as an established member of the Lindum community, he had often been targeted by a number of unsavoury individuals who "*[wouldn't] let no fuckin' coon tell [them] what to do.*" Needless to say, they had eventually come around. Not through physical force, or intimidation of stature, but through a calm and personable tone.

When he received no reply from Scott, Joshua clasped his hands together on the table and gave his head an understanding tilt. "Would you prefer if we waited for your parents?"

At the mention of his family, Scott became more respondent. "No, it's okay. They're... They're on holiday at the moment. I stayed behind to look after the house."

"That's awfully responsible of you," Joshua said, his tone friendly. "You like helping out your parents?"

Scott shrugged. A half-hearted admission that he was a good son, just too self-conscious to admit it.

"Hey," he suddenly said, looking up at the strangely comforting face of the hulking Sergeant. "I... I was wondering."

Joshua raised an eyebrow and pushed his glasses up his nose. "What were you wondering?"

"What kind of person would do something like that?"

The question surprised the Officer. The kid was tougher than he looked. If he was at all shaken by what he had seen, he wasn't letting it come across in his voice. If Joshua didn't know any better, he would have thought that the reason for Scott's silence was that he had been sitting pondering his own question.

"Usually?" Joshua replied. "A very sick person. Which is why I need you to tell me everything. It may not be too late to get whoever did it some kind of help."

"So rehabilitation?"

"That's right."

Scott seemed to think about this for a second. "I really didn't see anything, you know. The blinds were drawn the whole lesson. The only reason I saw it is because I always open them for Mr Hemming."

"That's okay," Joshua said, clasping his large hands together. "I wouldn't expect you to have seen whoever did this. This is a routine procedure, to make sure that we didn't miss anything. All I need is a statement from you."

*

James Franko was in the process of packing up his desk when the phone rang. A long standing compulsion of his, he let it ring for five seconds before picking up.

"Lyefield Police, DCI Franko speaking."

"This is Chief Superintendent Braithwaite, from the Lindum Office," the voice on the other end of the line said.

He sounded old and authoritative. Franko guessed Braithwaite to be around the same age as him. He pictured him with an appearance older than his years, with thinning grey hair and turkey jowls.

"Good afternoon Superintendent, how can I help you?" He forced a polite tone. Franko didn't want to get caught up in political and bureaucratic bullshit, but a call from a superior wasn't something that was wise to ignore.

"I just received a call from one of your Officers, regarding a case that just arrived at our station."

Initially Franko expressed confusion. Ordinarily his men only collaborated with the station in Lindum on matters that required forensic assistance. Being a relatively small force they didn't have access to a laboratory, so it made sense to use the facilities of the much larger station in the city.

Then he remembered: David Stafford sat in his office the day before, insistent determination on his face; recognising the signs, praying to the heavens that it was anything but that, yet at the same time gripped by a nostalgic thrill.

His mouth grew dry.

Please God, don't let it be the cats...

Franko didn't let his concern show in his voice. "Which Officer?" he asked.

"A Constable David Stafford."

His heart quavered, kicking at the inside of his chest.

"And he called you?" the Detective confirmed. He took a deep breath, not caring if Braithwaite heard. "Let me guess... Mutilations. Almost definitely feline."

"How did you know that?" the superior Officer questioned, a curious tone prevalent in his voice.

"It was brought to my attention very recently that David Stafford has been looking into a number of cases of missing pets," Franko explained. "Dozens of cats have gone missing over the last few weeks. I told him to work it in his free time so, if anything came of it, we wouldn't be scrambling for information."

"It sounds like you expected something to come of it," Braithwaite said, immediately picking up on the subtle urgency in Franko's voice.

"I didn't want to assume, just cover my bases. Look, it'd be easier for us to have this conversation in person. Maybe tomorrow? I hate talking over the phone."

"Only if you tell me what's going on."

"This is still early days so I didn't want to jump to conclusions. I'm telling you this now, in confidence, but I'm asking you not to panic. I might still be wrong, for all we know." He closed his eyes and began to pace, moving about his desk and stretching the tether of the phone cord. "The way this looks... We're probably dealing with a dangerous psychopath."

Pausing for a second, he could hear Braithwaite breathing heavily down the line, as he listened intently.

"They're probably a fledgling; still young and experimenting. It's how it starts. Now... If we can track this, we might be able to get them help. Catch it early and enter them into therapy or a mental health program, before anyone gets hurt."

"And you're sure about this?" Braithwaite finally said. His voice wavered ever so slightly, as he attempted to process the situation. It was so subtle, most people would have missed it.

Franko, however, wasn't most people.

"Listen, sir," he started, a reassuring air about his tone. "We are damn lucky to have caught this as early as we have. You can thank David for that. At this stage whoever it is is still learning; developing. But if we let this fester and don't do anything about it now, a lot of people could end up getting hurt."

For a brief second, memories of an Islington flat flickered across Franko's vision. The handiwork of The Butcher.

"Please, trust me on this one."

Again, Braithwaite took a moment to himself. After a while he spoke; a weight behind his voice. "Can you come here now? I'll call Constable Stafford back as well, and he can join us."

Franko's sleeve bunched under his arm as he checked his watch. The thin gold hand moved around the face, ticking away the seconds. It was coming up to four o'clock. The nurse would be with Sarah until at least five. If he called home soon, he would be able to ask her to extend her shift until he got back.

"Only if it's right now," he answered. "And I can't stay for more than an hour."

"That's perfect," the Chief Superintendent replied. "I'll see you soon." Then he hung up.

As he slotted the phone back into the receiver, Franko flipped his eyes closed and sighed. An uncomfortable tingle spread down his arms.

He caught himself wondering how many years it had been. How long since he had left the Murder Squad. Hopefully it wasn't too long. Hopefully, his senses were still sharp enough.

Walking over to the glass that separated him from his subordinates, Franko observed his translucent reflection. He looked worse than he felt. Everyone had noticed it, but few knew the reason why. He wasn't good at hiding his feelings, and currently wore his emotional frailty like some kind of disfiguring feature. Before he left, he would quickly dip in to the bathroom and splash some cold water on his face.

He moved back to his phone and called home, telling the nurse about the change in circumstances. The matronly voice of the woman told him not to worry, reassuring him that it was okay, before putting Sarah on the phone. Her voice was weary and tired, but she sounded better than she did the day before, and for that Franko was thankful.

Following a soft exchange of 'I love you's, he set about his routine to head out. He left his office and headed down one of the corridors, leading off of the central space.

After returning from the bathroom, rubbing his eyes, he took a second to himself, to collect his thoughts.

Franko snatched up his coat and keys, and began to make his way out of the station, to the car park. A cloud of smoke caught him in the face as he pushed through the heavy double doors. A pair of uniformed Constables were stood inside the alcove, smoking.

Setting his face into a harsh glare, Franko dispersed the cloud with a wave of his hand, and continued on his way. He hated cigarettes. Cancer sticks, he used to call them. Ever since Sarah had received her diagnosis, however, he had pointedly avoided using the phrase. It just didn't sound right; like he was trivialising her illness.

The picture of Stephanie and his grandchildren, hanging from his rear view mirror, swayed slowly as he closed the door of his private car. Their smiling faces brought him back to reality. They were some of the few people that were able to alleviate the tumultuous feelings that regularly gripped him. Them and Arthur.

He didn't have any pictures of Arthur. Franko's son hated having his picture taken. Every time he had been immortalised on film, his hand obscured his face. Sarah had often told him to keep them, however Franko didn't believe in framing a photo of his son's palm. At least, that's what he always said before Sarah got sick. Two weeks after she had gotten the results, Franko had snapped a picture and put it on the night stand, on her side of the bed. It was still there, now.

Franko's mental image of the framed picture was interrupted by another sharp flash of memories. Polaroids, taken of young boys. At the time, Arthur was the same age as them. The Detective had locked his son in the house for two weeks.

He jammed his keys into the ignition.

Pulling out of the car park, his mind was filled with theories and prospects for the future. About how this time it would be different. Not like The Butcher. Not at all.

Don't worry, Nick, he thought. *This one is coming back alive. This is one that we can help.*

Chapter 10

"I can't believe you got taken 'down town'."

Pru was laying back on her bed, phone hooked into the crook of her neck. Her brown eyes focussed on one of the numerous posters tacked to the ceiling of her bedroom. The image of a band, all dressed in black, reflected in the dark of her pupil.

"Tell me about it," Scott's voice said, from the other end of the line. "It felt like I was in some kind of bad cop show. It was intense."

"It's good that they were concerned enough to drive you home," Pru replied, attempting to find the bright side of the situation. "Especially considering how shaken you were. Poor baby."

Like usual, her words were harsh, but not without reason. She had long ago figured out that the best way to get Scott to open up was through derogatory humour; specifically directed at him. Anything other than that, especially sympathy, would result in him locking up what he was actually feeling and burying his emotions. Pru wanted to avoid that as much as possible. He needed to talk. If not, she knew he would start to dwell on it.

"I don't think it was concern," he replied. "More like obligation. It's what they were supposed to do, so they did it. Plus it's not like any of this is actually to do with me, I just found the thing."

Pru noted a shudder in his voice, as Scott recalled what he had seen.

Again, she opted for humour. "Wouldn't it have been great if it was, though? We have been talking about how you needed to spice up your rep."

"Well it's plenty spiced now. Any more and it'll be fucking over-seasoned. It's on its way to it already. Do you know how many people I've had messaging me, asking about it all?"

"Tell me numbers all you want, I'm not going to be impressed. It's what you do with them that interests me."

"Such wit. Did you come up with that all on your own?"

"Maybe." She started to play with a lock of her hair, twiddling it between her fingers and holding it close to her face. Squinting her eyes, Pru noted a number of split ends and forced herself to fight back a groan.

"It's not as if anyone knows anything about it, either," Scott's static-charged voice continued. "All they saw was me being taken away in a police car, with one of the guys from Tech Support, and a Caretaker."

"Yeah I've been meaning to ask about that."

"Apparently they saw it too," he explained. "On the security cameras."

"Didn't quite get the full experience like you, then?"

"Not at all. I swear I could practically smell the thing..."

Pru attempted to form a mental image of what Scott had seen, but consistently managed to draw blanks. He had given her a brief description, however it was severely lacking in detail. No matter how hard she tried, the limited information stopped her imagination short. She considered asking him for more details, but soon dismissed the idea. It was wise not to push him. For all she knew, Pru could dredge up some kind of horrible repressed memories and rattle him even more.

"So any concerned messages from a certain someone?" she asked, changing the topic yet again. "You know, if you play your cards right, you could really milk that sympathy angle."

"I've said it before, I'll say it again: You so should have been born with a dick."

"Nah," Pru grunted, hefting herself up. Now on her feet, she walked over to the full-length mirror, hanging between the two windows. Through the glass, she could see a blue Corsa drive past her house. "Dan's too delicate. If I had a dick, I'd end up breaking him." Pushing the flat of her hand over her forehead and sweeping back her fringe, she inspected her skin for blemishes. "Plus, it totally wouldn't suit me. What with the tits and all."

"What tits?" Scott asked, pointedly.

"Rude."

"True," his voice shot back.

As they talked, Pru caught herself breaking into a smile. No matter how many times they repeated the same rhythm of conversation, it always felt so effortlessly natural. Like it was predetermined, stitched into the very fabric of the universe, for them to be in each other's lives. Scott was the only person who she could be completely honest with. She had told him things that she wouldn't dream of telling anybody else. It was a given. They had been, and always would be, together. An inseparable double act.

"I'm glad you've still got your wit," Pru said, past the grin. "I was scared that it'd be shocked out of you."

"What can I say, I don't scare easily."

"So I'll be coming round to pick you up for the party tomorrow?" she probed, half laughing as she spoke.

"You know I honestly thought that you would drop that. Considering my traumatic experience and all."

"I'm not nearly that kind."

They both broke into similarly jovial snickers. Voices overlapped across the phone line, their tones so similar anyone listening in would find it difficult to distinguish between the two.

"Look, I'm going to grab myself something to eat," Scott said, phasing out the laugh as he spoke. "I'll talk to you later."

"Okay, Mr Willard," she flapped, mockingly. "Talk to you later."

*

His thumb blipping against the red phone icon, Scott hung up and let out a deep breath. Pru always displayed a miraculous knack when it came to lifting his spirits. She had always been that way.

He could vividly remember looking up at her face, watching Pru's eyes crease as she burst into a boisterous belly laugh. In the corner of his peripheral vision, he could just about make out the twisted joints of his dislocated fingers. Scott recalled not even registering the pain. Her laugh had been infectious, filling his head and intercepting the sensation.

Back when Pru's grandparents were still alive, they had lived next door to Scott's family. It was how he had first met his future best friend. At three years old, she popped her head over the top of the fence and demanded an introduction. They were practically inseparable ever since.

Scaling said fence was how Scott had the accident. When he was seven, he attempted to climb the structure, in response to a dare. After reaching the top, the fingers of his left hand slipped between the wooden joining and, as he came down the other side, were pulled from their sockets.

He still had a scar across his ring finger. While the others were merely dislocated, that one was almost torn off. Scott was lucky that the doctors in A&E were able to save it.

It was the only thing about him that Pru didn't mock. He figured it was because she still felt responsible for it. Despite her forefront and sometimes crass attitude, Pru was surprisingly sensitive when it came to the people she felt close to.

It was because of this that he hadn't told her about the note.

Even though she would have claimed the contrary, Scott knew that Pru would be worried.

He held the folded paper between the tips of his finger and thumb. A prickly heat crawled across his skin, sweat beading on the back of his hand.

The stationary was plain and mass-produced. Off-white copier paper, similar to the kind Scott used to print at school. It had been folded once and slipped into a too big envelope. The pen used was likely a fountain pen, leaving behind tiny droplets of black ink. Etched onto the sheet, the script was impressively neat. Scott found himself reminded of a calligraphy booth, set up in the school's entrance hall, during the last open day.

The message was short and simple:

Did you like my present?

Scott initially assumed that whoever posted it had gotten the wrong address. Then he realised that there was no postmark. No stamp. There wasn't even an address on the envelope. Just his name. "Scott Willard". In the same looping writing as the message.

It didn't sit right with him.

Something about the way it had been delivered. The note had clearly been passed through the door by someone who knew where he lived; someone who knew him. Then there was the timing of it. Right after he had gotten back from the police station. After he had seen that thing. If it was a joke, sent by his friends, then it wasn't a particularly funny one.

He considered, in a fleeting worry, calling the police. The thought was soon dismissed, however. Scott decided that he was working himself up about nothing. He thought of Kyle, of his strange and sometimes sick sense of humour. Considering that, it was almost definitely something of his doing.

Beginning to make his way to the kitchen, Scott kept his eyes trained on the floor. Louis had a habit of weaving his way between Scott's legs while he walked. More than once, Scott had ignored his feet and taken a tumble down the stairs.

As he cooked, he made a point of feeding the cat as well. It made sense to do it while he was in the kitchen. He also liked that he had company for a meal. Even though his companion wasn't human, it was still comforting knowing that he wasn't alone as he ate. This was the third day he had spent alone in the house and the loneliness was starting to set in.

Swallowing the emotion, Scott distracted himself by stirring the small pot of chilli. Beans and chunks of tomato moved in and out of view, swimming through the stewing ground meat. He watched them, mesmerised by the motions.

He didn't like feeling overly sentimental; admitting that he missed his family. It made staying behind that much harder. An entire week still remained until they all returned home, and Scott didn't want to spend that time moping about and getting himself down.

Once they inevitably returned, Scott knew that he would feel stupid for missing them in the first place. The twins had more than enough attitude to spare and, at thirteen years old, were growing progressively worse. They were even starting to get on each other's nerves. They had managed to share a womb yet were currently incapable of spending more than an hour in the same room together. He didn't like it. He preferred the way it was when they were younger, back when they had been the adoring little sisters, and him the doting older brother.

At least that was how he chose to remember it.

The truth was, most of his affection, during his younger years, was directed towards his mother. He was a mummy's boy through and through. Even at seventeen years old Scott was still close with her. While he was perfectly self-sufficient, as evidenced by his lone presence at home, his mother always made a point of doing almost everything for him, when she was around. Washing, ironing, and cooking. All for her son.

Scott got all of his best features from her. His mother had the same hair; the same nose. The same striking hazel eyes.

He often thought that, had he been born a girl, he would have been just like her. His mother's double.

As he thought about her, his nose twigged a nostalgic scent. Imagined or otherwise, it was definitely his mother's smell. Lavender. She used to put small burlap bags of it under Scott's pillow to help him sleep.

Smiling to himself, Scott took the pot off of the hob and plated up his meal. Dipping down to scratch Louis behind the ears, he traversed the kitchen and set the dish onto the table. Snatching up the cutlery he started to eat.

However, no matter how much he ate, he couldn't rid himself of a strange feeling in his gut. It felt like an empty space; a void inside his stomach. He could feel the acid bubbling away, sloshing around.

Out of the corner of his eye he looked down at the plain white stationary, emblazoned with black calligraphy. The feeling that Scott had gotten when he first read the note returned. He felt nervous.

Chapter 11

Across the street from the Lindum Police Station, peppered across an empty lot, the framework of a building had been erected. Scaffolding clung to the outside and tarpaulin lay across the ground, gleaming like plastic water. Overlooking the site a crane leaned over, pecking downwards like a mechanical bird. A labourer was leaning against the side of the machine, thumbing through a paperback. Looking up, over the top of the book, he watched as DCI James Franko stepped out of his car.

*

The first thing that David noticed about Chief Superintendent Thomas Braithwaite's office was how unfathomably cold it was. Despite it only being late April, the senior Officer had cranked his air conditioning up so high that the room was practically sub-zero in temperature. An uncomfortable chill slicked over the back of David's neck, setting him on edge. The sharp twinge of cold raced across the enamel of his teeth.

Clenching his fists repeatedly, to clear his anxiety, he felt the sticky sensation of nervous sweat gripping his palms. Behind his ribs, his heart quivered.

The Chief Superintendent was positioned behind his desk, an expectant look on his face. A trim man of sixty one, his face left the impression of frailty, yet his frame bore a wiry strength to it. Grey hair, still full and thick, had been combed out of his face and parted along the edge of his widow's peak, at a seven-to-three ratio. When he smiled, his snaggletooth peeked out past his lips.

"Constable Stafford." Braithwaite's voice, again, contributed towards the illusion of frailty. While still commanding and direct in tone, it wavered in subtle undercurrents that could have suggested illness. "Thank you for coming to see me on such short notice."

David had to bite his tongue. The Chief Superintendent was already preparing to stand at the forefront of the investigation; to take credit for whatever kind of success they had. Braithwaite was making it seem as if the urgency of the meeting had been his call, rather than David's. It rubbed him up the wrong way, annoyance prickling across the surface of his skin. What made it worse was the knowledge that, should anything go wrong, the superior Officer would not hesitate to jump ship and pin it all on him.

Nodding, so that his mouth didn't betray him, David took the offered seat and listened.

"We did very well to notice this all as early as we did," the Chief Superintendent began, waving his hand as he spoke. "But what we need to do now is stay on top of it."

He didn't like the way Braithwaite kept using the word "we". It felt like he was being annexed into a forced comradery; like all of the hard work he had done off of his own back was being trivialised.

Just as he was about to say something, Franko entered the room.

David immediately felt his limbs lock up and his back straighten, like he had jammed his finger into an electrical socket. He sat bolt upright.

Having not been informed of his superior's invitation to the meeting, Franko's sudden appearance set David on edge. Despite being well into his thirties, he felt like a naughty child, caught by their parent or teacher while doing something wrong.

David could practically hear the gears grinding together as the DCI robotically moved about the room.

"James!" Braithwaite exclaimed, standing and making his way around his desk. He moved with his hand outstretched, like the nose of a shark sniffing for blood. "Thank you for getting here so quickly!"

"Franko," the DCI corrected, refusing the handshake and nodding towards his superior.

He had no time for false pleasantries; no time for the typical "How do you do's" of polite conversation. Franko wanted to explain the facts, set up a plan of action, and leave. Despite the nurse's assurance that he could take as long as he wanted, Franko didn't like to burden her. He wanted to get home and take care of Sarah himself.

Worse still, there was something about the Chief Superintendent that Franko hated immediately.

Braithwaite's breath smelt of Listerine. A chemical freshness, from where he had washed his mouth out mere moments before their meeting. Franko held his breath and sat down next to David.

Franko had, correctly, assumed that the Chief Superintendent was doing his utmost to impress him; to put his best foot forwards. Lower in rank though he was, over the years James Franko had developed a reputation within the British Police as one of the best Officers in recent history. He had even appeared on a number of True Crime television programs, discussing several high profile cases he was responsible for closing. The most notable of these was that of The Islington Butcher.

"It really is a pleasure to have you here," Braithwaite continued, moving back around his desk and sitting down in his high-backed leather chair. "I've had a bit of time to think about what to do, since our conversation over the phone, and I think I might have a few ideas."

He didn't seem anywhere near as shaken as he had sounded on the phone. Franko thought that his superior almost looked excited.

David noticed it too. Braithwaite seemed all too eager to leap headfirst into an investigation. Like he wanted to make a name for himself.

"With all due respect, sir, I think we should save the ideas until later," Franko said. "Right now we're just here to give you the facts. Isn't that right, David?"

Barely used to his commanding officer addressing him by his first name, David just about caught the question, managing to nod just in time.

Holding his hands up, Braithwaite relented. "Sorry, sorry. I didn't mean to get ahead of myself."

"David." Franko turned towards his subordinate and tilted his head to the side. "Why don't you tell the Superintendent what you've found?"

"Everything?"

"Everything."

Swallowing a breath, David flitted his eyes back and forth between the two higher-ranked Officers sat around him. Braithwaite hovered expectantly, leaning over his moat of a desk, waiting for a response. Franko watched him patiently through his tired eyes, his pupils making small mechanical movements. He imagined the DCI's brain as a giant processing unit, his eyes the scanner. Warmth spread over his skin as the lasers of Franko's eyes analysed him.

"Alright..." David began, slowly. "I'll tell you everything that I've found."

Chapter 12

Scott awoke blurry-eyed to the sound of his alarm clock. Reaching out to shut off the device, he found his arm moving sluggish and slow. He had barely gotten a wink of sleep, and his nerves were shot. While he knew that the message was probably nothing, the nervous feeling that it gave him, combined with the memories of what had happened at school, caused his brain to steamroll on through the night, ensuring that he stayed awake for as long as possible.

Reaching the bathroom, he examined his face in the mirror. He didn't look good. His eyes were weary, drooping bags hanging beneath them, and he looked pale.

Splashing ice cold water onto his face, to hopefully remove the worst of his sleep-deprived appearance, Scott rubbed at his eyes and set about his starting his morning routine. He washed, dressed, fed the cat.

The only thing he didn't do was eat.

Overnight, the perturbed thoughts had unsettled his stomach. Food, he thought, would only make it worse.

As he locked his front door behind him, Scott took a second to glance down the road. In spite of the long passed onset of spring, the sky was a murky grey. Pastel clouds crawled across the skyline, and a chilling breeze cut between the hedges and fences of his neighbours. Pink blossoms, clinging to trees like bunches of cotton candy, almost seemed to have had their vibrancy drained from them, their colours muted and pale. Cars crawled along the road and, across the street, Scott could see a girl from his school on her phone, waiting for her friends.

Stepping out of his front garden and closing the gate, he checked the time on his watch and began to make his way down the path, his shoes tapping against the tarmac. Looming over him, the houses that flanked the street threw shadows down on the road, adding to the gloom of the overhead clouds.

The street on which he lived resided in the middle of an upmarket housing estate, located in the far west corner of Lindum and, as such, the residences were all relatively modern. New builds over the course of the past fifteen years had expanded the city, providing a number of jobs for anyone skilled in labouring, as well as a progressively increasing number of properties. Land formerly part of the countryside had been eaten up by the numerous developments, however some still remained, running along the far west edge of both Lindum and Lyefield. Several small cottages were situated in the enduring fields, at least a mile and a half from the edge of the estate on which Scott lived, providing a quaint and picturesque view that drew potential buyers to the complex.

Scott could just about see the cottages as tiny dots, through the gaps in the eclectic mix of semi-detached buildings.

Having been constructed over the course of fifteen years, the estate was slightly muddled when it came to the designs of the houses. Every five or so properties, the general appearance of the buildings changed, reflecting the style of housing design from when they had been constructed.

Walking down the road, out of the estate and towards his school, Scott felt like he was walking back in time. Screen doors, deep alcoves, rounded arches, walls, fences, hedges, paths, stairs. Every conceivable feature of a home met him as he turned off of Lexington Avenue and onto Hyperion Way.

Pru met him, sat on top of a low red brick wall that marked the end of somebody's front garden.

"Damn man, what happened?" she said, pushing herself up onto her feet in an exaggerated fashion. "You look like death."

"Thanks," Scott replied, starting to walk. "You know, you always did have a knack for making me feel better about myself."

"Hey, I'm just telling you the truth," Pru said, joining her friend at a brisk pace. "Who knows? You might have rolled out of bed this morning and come straight here, unaware of just how bad you actually look."

Despite the insults, Scott smiled. "So, what, you're telling me you're providing some kind of public service?"

"In as many words. Now you know, you can avoid people and spare them what you've inflicted on me."

"By which you mean-?"

"Your face, yes."

Pru beamed out a cheerful grin that, as always, managed to lift Scott's mood. Infected by her attitude, he almost completely forgot about the stormy feeling that had clung to him all morning. The warmth of her atmosphere had washed it away, cleaning it off of him like a hot shower, and draining the dregs down the plughole.

"You're quick today," he said, complimenting her wit. "I mean, I'd rather it wasn't directed at me, but you know. Props."

"Why thank you," Pru said making an elaborate rolling gesture with her hand. "I tip my hat to you."

"You're not wearing a hat."

"Oh come on, Scott!" She laughed and shoved his shoulder, hard. "Use your imagination!"

"Alright, alright," he replied, chuckling and righting his legs, to stop himself from stumbling into the road. "So, come on, give it up. Why are you being so nice, today?"

"Nice?" Pru half scoffed, half laughed. "And here I thought that I was insulting you."

"With you it's the same thing," Scott smiled.

Eyeing her best friend out of the corner of her eye, Pru pushed a lock of hair behind her ear. Her four, now exposed, piercings glittered in the morning light. "You know, I just thought that with everything going on, you kind of needed cheering up. But if you're going to complain about it…"

"No, no," he reassured, smiling pleasantly. "Don't stop. Really."

"Come on," she grinned, linking arms with him and setting off at a brisk pace. "If you want something to look forward to, just think: Tom's party is tonight."

"Ode to joy," Scott replied, sarcastically.

"Oh come on, you're looking forward to it really! Trust me, a night out is just what you need."

"Yeah, but last time-"

"Last time you got really really drunk and slept with some random girl," Pru interrupted, brushing aside the issue brashly. "You woke up the next day, realised what you'd done and freaked out. Listen, I like to tease you for it, but right now maybe that's just what you need. Take your mind off of all this stress you've been under."

"So what you're saying is I need to sleep with someone?"

"I'm saying you need to get fucked," she replied, crassly. "Whether it's fucked drunk, or fucked *fucked* is up to you."

"What would I ever do without you?" Scott lifted one eyebrow and broke into a grin. "Such wisdom."

"Oft spoken from the mouths of babes," she quoted, airily.

"Yes, but you're not a babe." His blunt response was accompanied by a smile.

"I beg to differ!" she laughed. "Dan is always calling me babe!"

"Wrong kind of babe, babe," Scott replied, joining his best friend, with a chuckle.

Just as Pru was about to respond, she glanced back over her shoulder, momentarily pausing. Her train of thought stopped short. She had just seen something.

"Hey, speak of the devil," she said, smiling. "And after all that talk of what you need to get over this."

Scott glanced down at her, from his taller standing height. "What?" he asked, slightly perplexed.

"Take a look behind us," Pru grinned.

Scott looked back, down the road. At least a hundred yards back, seemingly making a point of hanging back, was a girl. Short, with blonde hair, Scott recognised her instantly. It was Alice.

But that's not right... he caught himself thinking. *She lives in the opposite direction.*

*

David arrived at the Lindum Police Station, a cordial of confused feelings clinging to him like sweat. The musk of apprehension filled the inside of his car, lingering in the air and swimming about his head.

The previous afternoon, after relating everything he had discovered to Braithwaite, he was almost taken off of the case. The bastard of a Superintendent actually had the nerve to 'thank him for his services'. He had even leant over his desk to shake David's hand.

It was Franko who saved him from being just another footnote on the investigation papers. David had never been so surprised. His mouth may have even hung open, for all he knew.

"I actually think it would be for the best if we kept David on this. I know he's not a Detective, but he was sharp enough to figure all of this out, when no one else did."

Braithwaite had agreed only under the condition that David was partnered with one of his Detectives. They would be based out of Lindum, until the case was closed, and would report directly to him. Franko would also be serving as a consultant.

David figured that the reason the Chief Superintendent had agreed to let him stay on was so that he would have a patsy; someone to shift any blame onto in the worst possible scenario. He also sensed that Braithwaite, to a certain extent, admired Franko. Or at the very least wanted to be like him. The older man had seen the case as an opportunity to make a name for himself, and the best (or rather the most effective) way to do so was to remain in Franko's good books.

David was thankful for that.

Reversing into a free parking space, he glanced over his shoulder at the entrance to the building. Light shimmered across the glass of the sliding doors in a white liquid shine. As opposed to the quaint charm of the Lyfield station, the Lindum branch of the police service felt clinical and detached.

Moguls of emotion sprang up inside him as he made his way towards the disabled access ramp, which led up to the doors. The feelings came in waves: Excitement dropping into dread. He was anxious to begin his official investigation; his first brush with CID. However, he was less than thrilled to be working under Braithwaite. Worse still was the prospect of a new partner. While he was generally well-liked in his own station, David had little experience with the Lindum Officers. Detectives were notoriously territorial, they didn't like anybody stepping on their toes and intruding into their cases. Him coming from another station would almost certainly aggravate the issue.

Showing his warrant card to the woman behind the reception desk, David was greeted with a friendly smile. Sliding through the gap in the glass shield, his office identification was passed to him, his own picture staring up at him through a frozen expression. The Lindum station utilised magnetic locks on most of their doors, so the ID card would also serve as David's keys, during his time there.

"You'll be just down the hall," the woman (who's name tag identified her as Linda) said, pointing him down a branching corridor. "They set up the incident room for you all last night. I think some of our Detectives are in there already."

Picking up the ID and thanking Linda, David started to make his way down the hall. Blood pulsed through his skull, throbbing under his skin. He could smell copper, from where the vessels in his nose were struggling to contain the rushing blood.

Paula had told him not to worry; that this was all a good thing. After he had presented her with the massive bouquet of lilies, she had sat on his lap practically the entire night, their conversations punctuated by kisses. In between a flurry of pecks, she had made the extra effort to convince him that he would get along well with his new comrades (and if anyone had a problem with him, she would call up Julie and have her beat some sense into them).

Arriving at the door to the nerve centre of the investigation, he closed his eyes and took a deep breath. Touching his card against the sensor, an electronic beep resounded in his head; the light flashing green.

David's expression hardened as he laid eyes on what was obviously a joke dreamed up by several of the Lindum Officers. The case board, at the head of the room and tacked with numerous pictures of cats, had been given the header **"Pussy Hunting"**.

Squaring his jaw, David swallowed his anger and breathed out through his nose. Scanning the room, he spotted a single occupant, sitting in the corner.

Detective Sergeant Timothy Rawlings sat at his desk, leaning so far back in his chair that he was practically horizontal. His broad frame stretched out the stitching of the tweed jacket that he wore, the buttons of his shirt receiving similar treatment as they struggled to contain the breadth of his muscular chest. His iron grey hair was long, hanging in thick curly locks and resting against his shoulders. A quick glance downwards revealed to David that he was wearing odd socks. Not the 'fumble in the dark and grabbing two of a similar colour' kind of odd either. The one on his right foot was red, while the other was bright green.

David hoped and prayed to all the Gods he could think of that this was not his new partner. His mouth grey dry, like it was stuffed with cotton wool. His hopes, however, were dashed entirely as the peculiar man spoke.

"You the poor schmuck they decided to pair with me?" he asked, looking up at David and giving him the once over. His voice was husky and gravelly, years of smoking having practically destroyed his vocal chords.

He nodded and hesitantly held out his right hand. "David Stafford."

"Rawlings." He slid himself out of the chair and gripped the new arrival's hand tightly.

David could feel the Detective's thumb pressing firmly into the back of his hand. Catching a whiff of the large man, now that he was close enough, David recognised the scent of nicotine cut with coffee.

He was glad that Rawlings had introduced himself using his surname. He was one of the few people in the world that did not suit his given name. In no stretch of his imagination could David ever envision the man in front of him being called Tim.

Now that he was up close, David had the opportunity to study his new partner's face. His features were blunt and hard; a strong jaw, hidden by grey stubble, wide cheeks, and a broad nose. Beneath his thick brows, Rawlings' eyes bore the most extreme case of heterochromia David had ever seen. His right eye was a light blue, flecked with brown, while the iris of his left eye had been split evenly at a diagonal angle. One half was brown, while the other was hazel.

"Heard that you've been looking into this mess with the cats all on your own?" Rawlings asked, turning his back on David and moving to sit back down. "Hell of a thing that, giving up all your free time on a hunch... Not many people would have."

"Would you?" David asked, simply. He was still assessing him; analysing the man. His response would be a good indicator of what type of man he was.

He realised in a flash that this was exactly what Franko would have done. A pulse of discomfort raced through his system.

"Depends," Rawlings grunted as he collapsed back into the reclining leather seat. "Depends on a lot of things actually... How many, who asked... If I was bored at the time."

David started, taking a step back. His expression must have been that of stunned shock, as the Detective immediately picked up on it. Rawlings' lips twisted into a smile.

"I'm just being honest," he said. "If we're going to be working together, I might as well just throw you in at the deep end. It'll save you time trying to figure me out down the line. Or whatever it is you were doing just now. Watching me. If you want to know anything just ask. I don't like staring. Creeps me out, so knock that shit off right now or I swear to God I'm going to thump ya'."

Taken aback by the man's directness, David blinked several times before averting his eyes and apologising.

"Don't worry about it," the large man continued, sweeping one hand back through his hair. "I didn't ask ya' to offend me, and it's not like you did it on purpose." He indicated a chair and desk parallel to his own. "Come on mate, take a seat."

Making a point not to stare at the odd individual, David made his way to his new desk, the stunned sensation of their introduction addling his brain. Never before had he met a man quite so (for lack of a better word) odd. And brash. And yet, in spite of his forefront nature, still so difficult to figure out.

Looking over at the Detective Sergeant's desk, and forcing a special effort to avoid flicking his gaze up at Rawlings' mismatched eyes, he attempted to find something, anything that could help to humanise him. Make him relatable.

He found it. Tucked behind the monitor of Rawlings desktop, framed in pine, was a small photograph.

It was a picture of a cat.

Chapter 13

I was five the first time she hit me. I still can't remember what I'd done, but I know that I deserved it. Mum would only ever hit me if I deserved it. That's what she always told me.

It hurt. A lot. I cried a lot too. But that only made her hit me again.

I can't remember much about it, but what I can remember are the colours. I can always remember colours. Mum was wearing a blue jumper. Her nails were painted a similar shade; an off ocean blue. I can remember them shimmering as they raked over the skin of my cheek. When I looked in the mirror, my skin was flushed rose and the scratch glared out an angry vermillion.

After that first time, it started to happen more and more. Mum would hit me for any reason at all. Sometimes even without a reason. Because I deserved it.

Eventually I became inured to it.

Daddy taught me that word. It means you get used to it. And I did get used to it. It was normal. If Mum thought I had been bad, then I was punished.

I agree. It makes sense. If you are bad, then you are punished. Corrected, so that you don't do it again.

But sometimes I did do the bad things again. Even though I knew that they were wrong. Because I wanted to see the colours again. The beautiful shades of pink and purple and red. Especially the red. It made me think of fields of roses. I would imagine digging them up, gripping the barbed stems and feeling the pain as they pricked me; the blood bubbling out between my fingers matching the petals. I dreamed about giving them to Mum and saying I was sorry for being such a bad girl.

One of the houses near us had a rose bush in their garden. Every time we drove past, I considered opening the door. Flinging myself out and making my dreams reality.

It was a hot night in June when I finally decided to commit to my fantasy. To make it real. I can't remember how old I was. Mum had left the window in the living room open, so after I crept downstairs I climbed out.

The walk took longer than I expected, but when I got there it was worth it. The earth was soft under my fingers and the thorns were just as sharp as I imagined. However, I regretted doing it at night. The moonlight bled all of the colour away; the red of the roses and my blood looking black. But I still knew it was there. I could feel the colour clinging to me.

When I got back the wind had blown the window shut. But I didn't care. I didn't want to sneak in. I wanted Mum to see what I'd done. So I knocked on the door.

Mum was furious.

I was covered in brown mud and crimson blood. Filthy.

A dirty little beast. That's what Mum called me as she grabbed me by the hair and dragged me inside. I dropped the roses on the way, but by the time I realised I was already upstairs.

I remember being confused. She hadn't hit me yet, which was completely wrong. Rather, she dragged me down the hall and put me in the bath. But it was strange. Once she had torn my clothes off and put me in the tub, I sat there naked thinking: Why isn't there any water?

That was when she went and got the kettle.

Chapter 14

"She couldn't have been following me." Scott flicked his eyes over towards Kyle Ballard and chewed on the corner of his lip. "Right?"

"Why don't you just ask her?" Kyle grunted, rubbing at his eyes and falling back in his chair. "It's too early for me to deal with your crap."

"It's twelve in the afternoon," Scott replied, pointedly.

The dark-skinned boy let out a low groan and scrunched his face up. Lifting his forearm over his face, he attempted to shut out the morning light and tilted his head back even further.

"That's what you get for staying up till two in the morning every night," Scott said, jabbing one finger through the air, towards Kyle.

"Can't I even get a bit of sympathy?"

"What, when you're refusing to help me, or even answer my questions? Not a chance."

"Ugh." Sitting upright, Kyle turned towards his friend through his dark brown eyes. "Fine. I give you advice and you leave me to nap?"

Scott quickly glanced around the room. They had a free period, so other than themselves, only two other students were currently inhabiting the space. "Deal. But if a teacher comes, I'm not waking you up."

"Deal. Look, I know you saw what you saw, but so what? So she was walking to school from the opposite direction. How do you even know that she was following you? Maybe she was staying at a friend's house last night. Maybe a relative lives down that way."

Scott decided not to bring up the fact that Alice had been walking alone, instead letting Kyle finish his speech.

"Maybe she was following you," he continued. "Why are you acting like it's a bad thing? It's good. It means that she likes you, in case you hadn't figured that out anyway, you fucking genius." Kyle pointed at Scott in a matter-of-fact manner. "It means that you're in there. It means that you can actually have a good time tonight. And if you don't like her after that then no harm no foul. She still has a good night."

"Are you seriously telling me to do the 'fuck-and-chuck-'?" Scott asked, pulling an unpleasant face.

He should have known better than to ask Kyle for advice. One of his best friends, though he was, Kyle was notoriously uncaring towards women. Whether it was the way he was raised or just something innate about him, he viewed them as little more than objects for his own or others' amusement. It was a side of him that Scott both hated and found strangely intriguing. He couldn't quite wrap his mind around how, in this day and age, an attitude like Kyle's still existed.

Needless to say, Pru hated him for it. She tolerated Kyle because he was friends with everybody else. If she could get away with it, Scott figured that she would never say so much as a word to him.

"Yes," Kyle replied, bluntly. He started to pick at his fingernails.

Scott grimaced internally as he remembered his last ill-fated party hookup. "Well you've been helpful."

Kyle raised an eyebrow. "Really?"

"No."

Watching his friend shrug and return to his laying position, Scott's mind trailed back to the image of Alice, hanging back as she slowly kept pace with him and Pru. While he couldn't clearly make out her face, he was sure that she had been watching him.

He thought about what exactly that meant. And more importantly how he felt about what it meant.

Alice liked him. A lot. That much was clear to him now. While he had initially been oblivious to her advances, his talks with Pru and the recent incidents when he had caught her watching him forced Scott to re-evaluate his perception of her. Alice was forward. She was making no bones about how much she was into him.

And now she's, what? Following me? Watching me? Maybe she's been doing it for a while? It could be that I've only noticed it recently because of everything that's been on my mind.

His brain flashed across the grotesque sight of the corpses. The lone eye staring up at him. Bubbles of nausea swam through his stomach.

Reaching out, Scott grasped the plastic water bottle set onto the table and downed a big glug. It succeeded in settling his stomach, but reminded him of just how empty it was. He was starting to regret not eating breakfast.

Attempting to clear his mind of the memory, he focussed in on the situation with Alice. About how he had decided to leave it all until the party and find out how he felt then. Wait for her to make a move, and see in the moment if he reciprocated the feelings. He was starting to regret that too.

He had History last period, and she sat next to him. With the thoughts of her following him still fresh in his mind, Scott was sure that the situation would be awkward.

It didn't help that the more he thought about her, the more he focussed on her features. His mental image was forcing him to zero in on all of the most appealing aspects of her appearance. The glossy locks of her hair, like liquid honeycomb; the smooth edges of her almond shaped eyes; the gentle swell of her bust; the gradual flare of her hips. Scott knew that after thinking about all of this as much as he had, he wouldn't be able to tear his eyes away from her.

He didn't want to look like a creeper. Not knowing what to say, and being certain that he was going to stare, however, ensured that he was firmly on track to looking like a slack-jawed gawker.

And he still wasn't sure about how he felt.

She was good looking, but that didn't necessarily mean he wanted to be with her. And the following; the watching. He didn't know whether to feel flattered or uneasy.

Girls were complicated.

Life was complicated.

He considered taking the coward's way out. Leaving school early and heading home. Taking the time to prepare himself mentally for the party. Time to compose himself appropriately before the onslaught of people. He had already had enough of them that day; strangers coming up to him and asking him about why the police had taken him to the station. Scott had already answered the same questions twenty times before Kyle and Jack had told them all to fuck off.

The teachers would understand. After what he had been through the day before, a number of them were surprised that he was even at school.

Checking the time on the wall-mounted clock, he ticked through the options in his head. Lunch period would be in ten minutes. After that, he had another free period, before History last thing.

Scott made up his mind.

He could afford to miss History.

*

Pru was laying back on one of the few sofas that inhabited the Sixth Form common room, when she got the text from Scott.

"Gone home. Needed a break from it all... Don't miss me too much okay? :P"

She knew that it would happen sooner or later. Scott had a problem with overthinking things and getting himself worked up, and while he was never normally one to skip school, Pru understood that the memories of the day before, and the pressure of the Alice predicament were getting to him.

Shifting her laying position, Pru sank further into the cushions and started to type out a reply. The sofa was far too soft, giving her very little leverage to prop herself up and reply quickly. The springs had long since been removed by the overly safety-conscious faculty, making it so that anyone who dared sit on them sunk so far into the structure that they were practically squatting on the floor.

After hitting send, Pru tucked the phone back into the pocket of her jacket and snatched up a discarded tabloid paper from the floor. The bright yellow letters of "The Mayfair Star" glared down at her, forcing Pru to squint ever so slightly. The majority of the front page had been taken up by the image of a local Lindum celebrity. Stacee Swift (her preferred pseudonym) was an alternative model, brought to fame by a number of high-profile and highly publicised relationships. At the bottom of the cover, a pure white headline had been plastered across the width of the paper: "Swift Exit!" Subheading: "Stacee leaves Zayne for new famous face!" Footer: "Find out more on Page 5."

Flipping to the corresponding page, Pru laid eyes on a number of images of the model; none of which had anything to do with the associated story. She caught herself admiring the numerous tattoos that covered Stacee, and wishing that she had the money to invest in some of her own.

God willing, if she had the means to do so, Pru would have covered her entire back in ink.

She could imagine revealing them to her shocked parents; so desperate to remain supportive of their daughter, but ultimately shackled by their own conservative upbringing. Pru broke into a quiet laugh. Her boyfriend Daniel would also have a few things to say if she ever committed herself to the needle. He had made a point several times of saying that he wasn't a fan of tattoos on girls. It was the one thing that she was slowly working towards changing about their relationship. The only person close to her that would genuinely applaud her decision would be Scott. He had always been a firm believer in doing what made you happy, and telling anyone who didn't like it to go and screw themselves.

Pru hoped that going home to sort himself out would make Scott happy. He needed it. She hoped that, by the time she swung by his house that night in her Dad's car, he would have cheered up.

An almost motherly need to help him rose up inside of her. A mental image of her patting Scott on the head and hugging him passed in front of her eyes. Within a matter of seconds, however, she had laughed it away. She knew what he responded to; what made him feel better. And it wasn't babying.

"Hey babe."

Daniel Sallinger sauntered through the doors to the common room, at the head of a gaggle of students, and raised a hand to wave at his girlfriend. Sinking down into the sofa next to her, just as Pru moved her legs out of the way, he leaned over and planted a quick peck on her.

"Sup hot lips," Pru shot back, grinning.

"Not bad, not bad. How's your day been going so far?"

"What, you mean in the two hours we've been apart?" She forced a swoon, throwing her head back comically. "It's been agony! Darling, I don't know how I could go on any more, without you in my life!"

"Again with the sarcasm," he laughed.

"It's what I do," Pru replied with a smile.

Looking over at her, Dan pulled an exasperated face and sighed; all the while fighting to keep a smile off of his lips. "Why do you read that shit?" He pointed at the tabloid paper and shook his head.

Glancing down at her copy of The Mayfair Star, Pru started to laugh. "Hey I don't read it all the time. Just when they do articles on Stacee." She hurriedly flipped back through the pages, until she arrived at the photos of the glamour shoot. "Look at her! Isn't she gorgeous?!"

Dan joined her in a chuckle. "Yeah, but the articles are garbage. I mean, look at this..." He reached out and took the paper, thumbing through it until he arrived at a text-ridden page. Clearing his throat, he readied himself to read the headline. "Everybody was Kung-Fuel Fighting. Fight breaks out in ESSO Petrol Station."

Pru burst out laughing. "Oh come on! That's hysterical! Besides, it's just a local paper. Nowhere outside of the valley even sells it. It's not like it really needs cutting-edge journalism."

"They spelt 'fuel': F-E-W-L, Pru. It may not be The Independent, but I'm expecting at least some standards."

Snatching back the paper, to observe the typo, Pru maintained her smile. "Yeah, but this is a Jessie Goodwin article. He always spells stuff wrong."

"That's not an excuse," Dan replied, with a grin. "Ask Scott. He'll agree with me."

"Can't, he's gone home."

"Shit, is he alright?" Concerned, Dan sat up and looked down at his girlfriend through sympathetic eyes.

"He's better," Pru said, staring off into space as she spoke. The digits on her left hand starting to fiddle with one of her numerous earrings. "I wouldn't have blamed him for taking the whole day off, after what happened to him yesterday."

"That's not good..." Dan said, scratching at the side of his spiked brown hair. "It must have really gotten to him then?"

"I don't think so," she replied, finally looking up at her boyfriend. "Like... I know he's affected by it — he'd be nuts if he wasn't — but he's taking it better than I thought. Honestly I think the only reason why he's gone home is because he doesn't want to see Alice just yet."

"Really?"

Pru wagged a finger and chewed the inside of her cheek. "I know how he thinks."

Chapter 15

Peeling into the car park of Lindum Police Station, St. Claire swung his car into an empty space and stared out of his window. It seemed bigger than he remembered. The last time he had visited the station was over two years ago, before it had been renovated. He knew that it would be larger, however compared to the quaint appearance of his own Lyefield station, the building looked titanic in size.

A cardboard box sat on the passenger seat next to him, the various knick-knacks staring up at him, around white flashes of paper.

David had called him earlier that morning and asked St. Claire to bring him a number of things from the office. As he was already making the trip, he decided to include a number of familiar trinkets from the Constable's desk, to make his new environment feel more like home.

He was happy for David; glad that his fellow officer was breaking into the criminal investigation side of policing. However, he couldn't help but feel slightly envious. Only a few days earlier, he had told David of his intentions to take the Detectives examination, and now here he was, being invited to work on a case. In Lindum no less.

He traversed the tarmac, clutching the box to his chest, before approaching the doorway. The sliding doors parted with a gentle hiss, allowing him entrance.

The inside of the building was just as gaudy and in your face as the outside. There was chrome and glass everywhere; clean white walls punctuating the ever-present glimmer of light. Large bright lights had been set into the ceiling, at periodic intervals, ensuring that every inch of the corridors and entryways were illuminated.

A pretty middle aged woman, sat behind the reception desk, beckoned him over.

"Good afternoon, love," she said, the crow's feet stretching from the corners of her eyes creasing as she spoke. "Is there anything I can do for you? You're looking a bit lost."

"Yeah," he admitted, smiling bashfully. "I'm here to drop off a few things for a friend; David Stafford." Reaching down with his right hand, he clumsily fished his warrant card out of his pocked and flashed the credentials.

"Oh, the new Officer!"

St. Claire nodded, over the lip of the box that he had tucked beneath his chin. "Yeah. Where can I find him?"

"Just a second," she smiled. "I'll give the boys in the incident room a call, and let him know you're here. They'll need to buzz you in, because we use maglocks on the doors." She leaned over the desk and pointed down the hall, towards another intersecting corridor. "The room is just down there."

"Thank you."

The door to the case room was opened by a bespectacled young man of twenty five. His hair was unruly, and the stubble clinging to his jaw was short and patchy. Breaking into an "aw shucks" shit-eating grin, the man let St. Claire in.

"Nice to meet you," he said, keeping the smile and pointing at a free desk for him to set the box down on. "DC Simon Wilson. Thanks for bringing that stuff for David, we've been super busy here. Swamped really. And because he's so ahead of us, we couldn't have him rushing off just to pick up a few things." As he finished, he laughed slightly.

Wilson moved in a listless fashion, subtly bouncing on the spot, shifting his weight from one foot to the other. His sentences were overly cheerful, and he placed comical emphasis on particular words. The whole ordeal was spotlighted by his hands, moving erratically with a single finger raised, in the shape of a gun.

This was a man who's wife would call him "hubby" unironically. St. Claire hated him instantly.

He forced a smile and lifted the box higher. "That's okay; Dave's a good pal. I couldn't exactly say no."

As he spoke, St. Claire scanned the room for his cohort. There were fewer desks than he thought there would be (four to be specific), and all were set up with a monitor and littered with paperwork.

David was sat at the far end of the space, on a desk parallel to a large bear of a man. As David noticed him, he got up to walk over. The grizzly, however, spoke first.

"Who the hell is this?"

Stunned by the blunt statement, as well as the gravelly tone of the voice, St. Claire hesitated for a second and fumbled his words. "Ex... Excuse me?"

"In case you haven't noticed, this is an Incident Room," Rawlings continued. "My incident room. So you better have a damn good reason for coming here unannounced."

Again, he was stunned. The man was rude. Overly so. More than that, he was wheezing so much that he seemed close to toppling over. His voice had been so ruined by cigarettes, that St. Claire was surprised that he didn't see a mist of smoke slip out of his lips as he spoke.

"Jheeze Rawlings, give him a break," Wilson laughed, sighing as he put his hands on his hips. "He's just here to drop of some stuff. Anyone listening would have thought that he had spat on your mother's grave."

"My mother isn't dead," Rawlings replied, bluntly. Turning away from the trio of officers, he returned his attention to the half-peeled orange on his desk.

"Sorry about him," David said, taking the box from St. Claire. Apologetically cocking his head to the side, he indicated Rawlings with a quick flick of his eyes. "I'm still getting used to him myself. He's... An acquired taste."

Across the room, Rawlings either didn't hear them or ignored the comment. Preoccupied with the orange, he slipped a slice into his mouth and continued absent-mindedly scrolling through something on his desktop screen.

"You're telling me," St. Claire muttered.

"He's not so bad," Wilson chuckled, pushing his black frame glasses up his nose. "You just need to realise that he doesn't mean what he says. Well, most of the time anyway. He's not particularly good with people."

"I've noticed," St. Claire replied, glancing over at the large hairy man. "So... How are things going here?"

"Dave just got through briefing us. Told us everything that he'd found out and man I've got to say I'm impressed. We're talking about eventually setting up a canvas. Nothing definite at the moment, but once we narrow down where the most cats are going missing from we can start going door to door."

"So how long is that going to take?" The Lyefield officer eyeballed Wilson. "Narrowing it down, I mean."

"It would've taken a lot longer without the bodies," David said, setting the box down on his desk and turning back around to face the other men. He folded his arms across his chest. "Whoever this is didn't seem to care about us finding out whose pets they were. They left the name tags and collars on them. You'd think they would have taken them off. Damn near skinned the cats, but left the tags on. Doesn't really make sense."

"Could be trying to lead you in the wrong direction?" St. Claire suggested.

"We've thought about that too," Wilson explained. "Just to be sure, we're cross checking the names with all of the missing lists."

St. Claire allowed himself to feel impressed by the progress and efficiency. Despite his immediate dislike of Wilson, and the brash nature of Rawlings, he couldn't deny that they were good at their jobs. Undoubtedly why they had been put on the case. And why they were in CID to begin with.

Another quick look around the room, and he realised that there was a fourth desk.

He pointed at it. "So who's missing?"

"Oh?" Wilson grinned and flicked his eyes over the workspace. "That's my partner. Babs. She's out at the moment making calls to all of the lost pet services and animal rescue centres."

"Sounds like you've got yourself a good new team." St. Claire fired the compliment over to David, who accepted it with a silent smile.

He could see his friend's emotions as clear as day. Determination was shining behind his eyes. Hope clung to his features. David needed this. He needed to be right; to solve the case. Whether it was to prove it to himself, or someone else, he didn't know. All St. Claire was sure of was that failing after all of his hard work would ruin David.

I hope to God they're as good as they seem, he thought. *I want you to catch whoever is responsible for this.*

Chapter 16

Daddy has always looked after me. Comforted me when Mum went off the rails and snapped. He would tell me that it was okay and hold me close, making me promise not to make her angry again. And yet even when I did, and when I got punished, he would always treat me the same. He wouldn't punish me for crying.

Whenever she used the kettle, he would rub aloe on my skin and bring me ice. The chill always stung a bit, but that just meant that it was working. It always turned my skin the most wonderful shade of pink; so bright that it almost seemed to glow and bleed out into the air.

He would coo gently as he lathered it on and once he was done, he would stroke my hair and kiss my forehead.

Daddy always made me feel loved.

And so when I was seven and he came into my bedroom, I welcomed him in.

He laid down on the bed and cuddled me, and I could feel his warm breath on my neck; the scratch of his stubble. He smelt like aftershave. A musky and heady scent, like worn leather. Even now, when I smell that, I think about him.

It hurt when he forced himself inside me, but it was okay. When he brushed away my tears, he told me that it was supposed to. Hurt that is.

Love hurts.

I can see that now.

That's why Mum always hit me. Always punished me. It's because she loves me.

That's what love is.

And I can feel it again now. Love. The same as with Daddy.

I met a boy. A wonderful boy.

The way he looks at me, with those gorgeous hazel eyes, sends tingles all over me. Like my body is full of bees. My heart feels like it's vibrating and my skin prickles like I've been stung.

I talk to him sometimes, but it's never enough. It feels like ice is being jabbed into my heart every time he walks away and leaves me. So I've been following him for a while.

Nothing obvious, of course. Just from a safe distance. And every time I see him, I feel like my body is on fire. Like gasoline has been poured down my throat, soaked into my hair, and I've been set alight. Sometimes I think that if he were to touch me, I would crumble into charcoal.

It terrifies me, but thrills me at the same time.

I often find myself wondering that if he did touch me, if his skin were to graze against mine, what colour I would burn.

I bet that it would be beautiful.

Chapter 17

The doorbell rang just as Scott was stepping out of the shower.

He just about heard it over the gargle of water vanishing down the plug hole; the soap being sucked down the pipes in a nautilus spiral.

His damp feet slapped against the tiles as he ventured out in search of a towel. Steam parted around him as he moved, licking at his limbs and condensing in the hairs on his arms and legs. Wet hair stuck to his forehead, the sharp points of his fringe jutting out from his brows and in front of his eyes.

Snatching up the linen, he wrapped it around his midriff and quickly ran down the stairs.

Pru was a lot earlier than he thought she would be. The party didn't start until seven, but most people wouldn't start arriving till at least eight. Checking the clock in the hallway, on his way downstairs, Scott realised that it wasn't much past five o'clock.

He reached the front door just as the bell rang a second time.

Opening it, without a second thought, he expected to see Pru. What he was, instead, presented with was a short girl with honey blonde hair.

Alice.

Suddenly horribly aware of just how exposed he looked, Scott instinctively flinched backwards in an attempt to cover his naked chest. A million thoughts charged through his head at once, like an uncontrollable stampede. His heartbeat knocked against the inside of his head, like a multitude of rapidly quickening hoof strikes.

He wanted to know why Alice was there. Why she had shown up unannounced on his doorstep. But, most importantly, how on earth she knew where he lived.

"Um," she said, attempting to make light of the situation as her eyes raced over his body, like she was drinking in the sight of him. "S-sorry about this Scott... I, uh... I didn't mean to just show up like this..."

Alice was stammering, clearly nervous and scrambling to find the right words. She was usually far more charming; more upfront and flirtatious. Her eyes, however, never once left him. They were curiously steady and intensely focussed. Set into her clear blue irises, her pupils were dilated.

"I just-... You weren't in school this afternoon, so I thought that I would bring you the homework from Mr Smyth's lesson." Her plump lips formed a smile around the words, exposing the white enamel of her teeth. "You know, so you don't fall behind."

Unsure of what exactly to say, due to the salvo of thoughts assaulting him, Scott broke into a forced smile and managed to umm out a thank you. Reaching out with his right hand (all the while making sure his left kept a firm grasp on the towel at his waist), he took the paper sheets from Alice. Ink rubbed off on his damp fingers as he gripped them, staining his skin. Bringing the digits up to his face, to examine them, he caught Alice out of the corner of his eye wetting her lips with the tip of her tongue.

"So..." she hesitated as she noticed Scott looking at her. Still her eyes didn't leave him. "I... I hope that you're okay. After yesterday, I mean. The police just took you away and it freaked a lot of people out."

"Yeah, I'm alright," Scott replied, setting down the papers and scratching the side of his still wet hair.

The awkward feelings that he had been trying to avoid by leaving school started to creep up inside Scott. Concerned though he was about her knowledge of where he lived, he could feel his vision moving over her body and latching onto the curves of her figure, like Alice had magnets hidden inside her clothes.

Through the white material of her shirt, he could see that her stomach was tight and toned. Her waist was pulled in neatly, and her hips flared out ever so slightly.

Suddenly realising that he was starting to stare, Scott corrected himself and returned his vision to her face. He could feel himself growing stiff and needed to calm down. The last thing that he wanted was to make the situation even more awkward.

"That's good," Alice said, smiling and winding her fingers together behind her back. "You're dealing with it really well. I don't think many people would be so okay after seeing a load of dead bodies like that."

Scott started to nod before a thought struck him. It started as a curiosity but rapidly grew into something more.

How does she know about the dead bodies?

At school he had made a special effort not to say exactly what it was that he had seen. He didn't want people to know, certain that if they did they would ask more questions and force him to relive it again. And yet Alice knew.

"Hey, Alice, how do you-"

He was interrupted as Louis, back from a romp around the garden, made a dash through the front door. Reflexively, Alice scooped the cat up, just as he moved between her legs. Lifting the feline, she hugged him to her chest.

"You've got a cat," she laughed, nuzzling her nose into Louis' head. "I love cats. My Mum won't let me have one though. What's his name?"

"Uh, Louis."

"Well aren't you just the cutest thing," Alice cooed, scratching the top of the cat's head before lifting one of his paws. "And all your paws are white. It's like you're wearing little shoes!"

"Watch he doesn't bite you," Scott said, a slightly concerned tone to his voice.

"It's okay," she replied. "Cats like me." Pressing her nose into the gap between Louis' ears, she addressed the cat. "You wouldn't bite me, would you?"

"I- Uh- I'm sorry Alice, you've kind of caught me a bit off guard here," he suddenly said, gripping his towel tighter and sweeping his hair out of his face. "I don't want to be rude, but I'm kind of dripping all over carpet here. Not to mention, I'm pretty much naked right now."

"More of a second date thing, huh," Alice smirked as she set Louis down on the floor. Standing back up straight, she laughed softly and permitted herself another fast glance over his body. "But you're right, I should get going. So... I guess I'll see you tonight then. Right?"

A curious feeling knotted Scott's stomach. It was something that he couldn't quite put his finger on. For some strange reason he felt nervous.

Dismissing the feeling, he again forced a smile. "Sure. I'll see you tonight."

As the blonde girl departed down the garden path, Scott closed the door behind her and took a deep breath. Leaning back against the structure, he shut his eyes and tensed his jaw.

Seeing Alice was every bit as awkward and confusing as he had thought it would be. It was why he had decided to go home early. Worse still, the feelings that the encounter had left him with were so muddled and enigmatic that his brain felt like it was going to explode from the strain.

The inside of his forehead throbbed, the dull ache spreading down across his brows and settling on his eyes. It felt as if the thoughts storming through his head were attempting to punch their way out from inside his skull.

How had Alice known where he lived?

The more he dwelled on that question, the more he was convinced that Alice had been following him. She must have trailed him home one day after school to see where he lived. Use it as an excuse to eventually talk to him and start conversations. That must have been what had happened today. Having not shown up for his History class, Alice seized the opportunity to show up at his house.

In a way it was sweet. That she was so into him that she was finding excuses to talk to him; to see him. It was nice of her to bring him the homework that he had missed.

Nevertheless, there were ways of going about things. This was different from hanging around in the hallways at school, waiting for him. It was borderline stalker territory.

The situation at the door left Scott feeling overwrought. He didn't know what to expect at Tom's party. No idea how he would feel when Alice inevitably made her move on him.

Rubbing one hand across his face, he grunted and made his way back upstairs.

I guess I'm just going to have to take it as it comes. Stop being such a coward and make a decision. But... I'm really not looking forward to it.

Chapter 18

Helen Raleigh lived in a world of hopeful curiosities.

Jovially intelligent, cuttingly sarcastic, and with a glancing touch of ADHD, she found herself in a perpetual state of listless boredom. There was only so far that the teasing of her fellows could take her, only so many remarks that she could drop before they had enough and, inevitably, turned on her.

Even flirting with members of the opposite sex was beginning to lose its lustre. While she enjoyed the attention, her opinion of the conversation was never particularly high. Lower still was her mood, following the disappointingly short-lived romp with most potential suitors.

Men never quite seemed to *get* her.

Helen figured that it was something to do with the kind of males that she attracted. Whether it was the air that she held about herself, or simply the way that she looked, she only ever attracted two extremely definable categories of guys.

First, and by far the more prevalent of the two, were the 'peacocks'. They strutted about, parading their good looks and expecting (demanding) praise. That isn't to say that Helen found the arrogance unattractive. On the contrary, it stirred something inside of her that hooked her attention and demanded release. The only problem was the aftermath. Guys with faces like that typically had IQ's the same as their shoe size, leaving any semblance of conversation all but dead on arrival. There was also the fact that the majority were extremely selfish lovers and, whenever the thought did enter into their head to pass a piece of the pie her way, they would use a set of flashy (yet ultimately ineffective) moves that they had undoubtedly learned from pornos. They were uncomfortable and designed more to make them feel accomplished, than for Helen to glean any form of release.

The second category she preferred, however not by much. These were the intellectuals— the hipsters. The kind who wore black framed glasses, waistcoats, and fedoras. They trimmed their beards and carried boot polish, to shine their leather shoes on the fly. The pretension hung thick in the air and, in spite of their smarts, the conversation was still stifled. Bearing such strong liberal opinions (and being convinced that such was the only one to be considered, through nothing more than politically-correct entitlement), Helen's own views were little more than phlegm, clinging to the repartee. They regarded it in the same way one would observe their own snot in a handkerchief, before discretely disposing of it. And when they did eventually make it to the bedroom, they treated her like she was made of glass. Being treated with respect was nice, but not in that kind of situation.

Helen wanted to get fucked, and nobody seemed to want to do it right.

And I doubt anyone here would even know how... she thought, bitterly.

Having returned home from university earlier that day, Helen had found her parents gone and her younger brother in the midst of preparing for a party. With all of her local friends away, and bearing the begrudged sense of duty of an older sister, she had decided to stay and chaperone. At least that was what she had told Tom.

Truth told, she had missed these kind of parties: The daunting sense of nerves, knowing that everybody you had ever said hello to at school would be showing up; the hopeful lust that gripped you knowing that, by the end of the night, you would at least find someone to lock lips with; the worry that, due to the noise, the police would inevitably be called. It appealed to her nature, causing something expectant to stir inside her.

Gripping the cold glass of the bottle between her fingers, she brought the rim to her lips and threw her head back. The pulse of bass throbbed in her ears. Across the room, the amp set against the wall vibrated over the floor.

Pushing her digits back through her hair, she set down the beer and flitted her eyes around the room. People were clustered in small groups, preoccupied with their own barren conversations, seemingly making a show of excluding her.

After all, who would want to talk to someone so starved for social interaction, that she would crash her little brother's party?

Tilting her head back, Helen closed her eyes and emitted a half-hearted sigh from between her lips.

"Something tells me you're not exactly enjoying yourself right now."

The voice came from behind her, splitting the roar of music and slipping its way into her ears.

Cool air wafted over the smooth skin of Helen's exposed arms, plucking up goosebumps, as a figure stepped through the sliding patio doors behind her. He was tall, but not overly broad. She could sense his body heat behind her, giving her a general idea of his build.

"What can I say, I'm not really feeling welcome," she replied, grinning as she turned to face the new arrival.

"Now I can't imagine that. Though I'd be lying if I said I didn't understand. I'm feeling a bit out of place myself."

He broke into a friendly smile and looked down at her. His teeth were bright and neatly straight, arranging themselves charmingly. Light brown hair fell messily around his face and shining from beneath matching brows were a pair of striking hazel eyes.

So, she considered saying. *Which are you? Peacock or hipster?*

What she actually said, however, was: "So have you got a name to go with that attitude?"

"Scott," he replied, scratching the side of his head bashfully. "Willard. How about you?"

"Helen," she said, picking up her bottle and taking another swig. "I'm Tom's sister."

Scott laughed. "Really? I've got to say, that's a surprise."

"And whys that?"

"Well not to sound rude, but Tom's far from the best looking guy. And —well— you're the opposite."

"I think there was a compliment in there somewhere," Helen laughed playfully, pushing her hair behind her ear.

"Trust me there was," he replied, returning the laugh. "Though now that I know who you are, I am curious about why you feel unwelcome. This *is* your house."

"If you were having a party, would you want your brother or sister to show up?"

"Point taken."

"So you've got siblings then?"

"Do you usually analyse people like this, or is it just me?" Scott asked, raising one eyebrow and taking a sip of the Budweiser gripped between his fingers.

"I'll let you figure that out. You want to take this conversation outside? I'd hate it if you missed the chance for a good comeback, just because you couldn't hear what I was saying."

"Sounds like a plan."

Exiting through the sliding glass door behind Scott, the pair ventured out into the garden. Overlooking a long and narrow patch of grass, they stood by a low wall that bordered the stone patio. All around them, pockets of people chattered amongst themselves, smoking. A sickly sour scent hung in the air as, down the garden, a detached group passed around a joint. Stood off to the side, leaning against the garden fence and nursing a small plastic cup of alcohol, a girl was busy texting her friend.

"So why is it that you feel out of place?" Helen asked. "Stud like you, I thought you'd be the life of the party."

"Stud, huh?" he chuckled once to himself. "Sorry, but you're not even close... I dunno, I guess I feel out of place because I'm kind of sick of people."

"Then why are you talking to me? Does that make me special?"

"Well, sick of people I know. And as for you... What can I say, I guess I felt like I found a kindred spirit."

Helen grinned and raised an eyebrow. "That a fact?"

Pressing the translucent brown bottle against his lips, Scott swigged a large gulp of beer before nodding. "You seemed like you needed someone to talk to. God knows I do."

"Why not your friends?" The young man had piqued Helen's interest. His responses were fast and confident, like he was used to her form of back-and-forth banter, and he gave off an air like he was more mature and older than his years.

Scott Willard was a rare find. Someone that Helen felt could actually understand her. Understand the intricacies of her personality and not become offended by the tiniest little thing.

It also didn't hurt that he was easy on the eyes.

"My best friend is here," he replied, running his fingertips across a scar on his left hand. "But at things like this she tends to hang around with her boyfriend. And like I said: I'm kind of sick of people. I mean, best friends are the exception, but she gets that I'd prefer being on my own over hanging out with her boyf'."

"That's fair," Helen smiled. "So I guess this means that I get the honour of keeping you company?"

He chuckled again. Lines creased out from his eyes as he did so. Helen realised, with a flush, that when Scott smiled he did it with more than just his mouth. His entire face smiled, and she liked that. A lot.

"You could say that," he grinned. "If you want, that is. I'd hate to think that you keeping me company would be a waste of you time. If you have better things to do, please, feel free."

"No, it's okay. I like talking to you. And anyway, it's not like I had any better options, did I? Or did you somehow miss everyone else avoiding me like the plague?"

"You know, I did catch that. Honestly, because I'd only actually seen the back of your head, I thought they were avoiding you because you were, like really, really ugly."

Helen burst out laughing.

Scott's smile broadened. "I'm glad to see that I was wrong."

Recovering from her sudden flash of giggles, Helen eyed him with a sidelong glance. "You know most other girls would have slapped you for that."

"Well something tells me you're not like most other girls," he replied.

"Are you always this smooth, or is it just the booze talking?"

"Trust me," he said. "I'm not smooth at all. I'm like fucking sandpaper. If you were anybody else, this conversation would already have gone up in flames."

"But didn't you just say I'm not really like other girls?" Helen paused to take another drink from her bottle, before setting it down on top of the wall.

"That I did."

"See. Really it just goes to show how smooth you are that you picked the one girl here that would appreciate your conversation. You're good."

"You know, if I didn't know any better, I would say that you were flirting with me."

"If you didn't know any better, huh? Who's to say that I'm not?"

"Me." He laughed again and took another drink. "I don't flirt. Sick of people, remember?"

Something about the unassuming way that he was oblivious to her advances thrilled Helen even more. He wasn't like the guys that went out of their way to try and impress her. Scott seemed genuine. He was talking to her because he enjoyed the conversation, not because he was trying to get in her knickers. It was a welcome change.

Just as Helen was about to speak again, the blaring voice of her younger brother interrupted their conversation. Tom, as drunk as the night was dark, staggered out of the back door of the house and tripped once on the frame. Sprawling out as he went, his arms flailed wildly in an attempt to steady himself. He was, thankfully, caught by a number of his own guests and hoisted into an upright position. There was blood on his face, dripping out from the corner of his mouth and down his chin, in a line as thick as a thumb.

"For fucks sake," Helen muttered, eyeing Tom disapprovingly. "Sorry about this, Scott, I'll be back in a second."

As the hazel-eyed boy casually reassured her, Helen marched over towards her younger brother. Hooking his arm over her neck, she steadied him and hissed into his ear. "What the hell have you done this time? And why are you bleeding?"

All she got was a burbled and disoriented response. His breath stank of vodka and cheap cider.

"He was dancing on the table in the dining room," one of the party guests said, offering their assistance before Helen brushed them off. "One second he was fine, and the next he'd fallen over."

"I think he kneed himself in the face," another added.

Perfect... Helen thought, bitterly.

Hoisting her brother up higher, she started to practically drag him back towards the house. "Come on, you heavy shit. Time for bed."

Turning her head and calling over Tom's arm, Helen directed her attention back towards Scott. "I'm just going to put him to bed. Don't go anywhere, alright?"

*

As he watched Helen lug her younger brother inside, Scott caught himself breathing a sigh of relief. The last thing that he expected was to find someone that he could just —just— talk to, without any kind of sympathy of morbid curiosity.

He was sick of the forced bonhomie of everyone that knew him. Too many people had asked him about what he had seen, all the while maintaining a sad smile. Like they wanted him to feel better, but were still gunning to find out exactly what had happened. Niceties were just a means to an end.

The only person that wasn't like it was Pru. And even then, Scott felt like it wasn't enough. Especially at the party. He didn't want to seem like a lost child and cling to her the entire time. It would be weird and would have gotten him nowhere. He needed to talk to someone; have a conversation that didn't automatically start with the phrase: "Are you alright?"

Helen, so far, had been everything that he was looking for. In many ways, she reminded him of Pru. The quick wit and the teasing nature of her conversation was something that he was more than used to. In fact, it was something that he enjoyed.

Perhaps the night wasn't going to be so bad after all.

He had left his house and sat in Pru's father's car feeling nothing but dread. In spite of all of Pru's reassurance, he could think of nothing worse than going out that night, especially considering the awkward liaison with Alice at his front door. Now that he was actually committing to his attendance, his mind had whirled into overdrive and every curious and uncomfortable feeling he had ever felt about Alice returned full force, slamming into him like a wrecking ball. Yes, she was attractive. Yes, she was good conversation. But that was where it ended. Now that he was on the spot and under the pressure of committing to a decision, he couldn't imagine having a relationship with her. Not with all of the uncomfortable feelings plucking at him. It wasn't a slight against her (at least this was how he rationalised it), rather that he knew that Alice wasn't right for him.

All that was left was to tell her.

Unfortunately, since Scott had arrived at Tom's house at just after eight, he had yet to see her. Now that it was closer to half past nine, he was wondering if Alice was even going to show up at all.

He had looked for her, initially, however after half an hour he had grown sick of wading through the sweaty bodies of people inside the house and retreated to the garden. There (he hoped) he would at least have some time away from all of the inebriated rubberneckers.

That was when he had seen Helen, through the glass of the patio doors.

Seemingly making a point of standing separate from everybody else, the way that she held herself was what had first caught Scott's attention. Rather than slouching awkwardly, her back was straight and her shoulders thrown back. A confident air had clung to the girl despite the fact that (until he had nutted up and gone over to her) she had been stood alone for half an hour.

He admired the confidence that it took to stand isolated in the middle of a party and not seem affected by it. Helen was comfortable in her own skin and enjoyed her own company.

Having watched her for close to thirty minutes, Scott had decided to finally go up and talk to the girl. Impolitely excusing himself from yet another asinine attempt at concern, he approached Helen through the sliding doors. At that point the fact that he had only seen the back of her head was irrelevant. What she looked like had no bearing on his desire for conversation with a like-minded individual.

As it stood, however, he was pleasantly surprised when she had turned around.

Much like her younger brother, Helen's hair was dark and curly, falling in thick locks around her face. Her skin was a pale olive tone and her eyes were bright green, the contrast catching Scott's attention and holding him transfixed for the majority of their conversation.

Watching her disappear back inside the house, Scott found himself eyeing the backside of her jeans. Catching himself, he attempted to suppress the blush spreading across his cheeks.

Scott, usually oblivious to the advances of girls, and hesitant to act on any kind of romantic situation, felt something grow inside him. Something that he hadn't felt in a long time. Elusive and fleeting, it danced through him quickly, leaving him dazed and light headed.

He wanted to get to know Helen better. He wanted to see more of her.

Perhaps, he thought, *this could be where things start to get better.*

Had Scott had even the slightest idea of what was coming, he would have realised just how wrong he was.

Chapter 19

Dumping her younger brother into his bed and leaving him to writhe in drunken patheticness, Helen let out a long breath and pushed her hair out of her face.

Uncomfortably shifting from foot to foot, Helen kept an eye on him for several long moments to make sure that he didn't vomit. Before long, however, she decided to vacate the premises.

She hated being in Tom's bedroom. The space smelt musky, the result of an overfull wash basket and a lack of ventilation.

Closing the door behind her, Helen paused and directed a number of party guests away from the room. A gaggle of Tom's friends, who had followed her upstairs, hung around the hallway, lingering and flitting about like flies.

Turning towards them, she sighed half-heartedly. "He should be alright for now, but one or two of you should probably watch him. Make sure he doesn't drink anymore or throw up. Right?"

The closest two nodded, just about managing to direct their response at her before she quickly departed.

Helen was confident that her brother's friends could look after him. And if they didn't then, as far as she was concerned, anything that happened to him wasn't her fault. Little brother be damned, he wasn't her responsibility. Especially seeing as he had done it to himself.

Plus, Helen was eager to get back on her way. Get back to Scott and finish their conversation.

Maybe even finish something else.

Talking to hazel-eyed young man had filled her with an excited flutter. Eager need and expectation throbbed through her womb. Be it the alcohol or simply Scott's charm, she knew what she wanted. It was just a case of if he wanted the same.

But there are ways of testing that, she thought.

Hurrying into the bathroom, Helen quickly peeled off her top and unhooked the clasp of her bra before stuffing it into the airing cupboard beneath the sink. Settling into a casual standing position, in front of the mirror, she pinched her nipples, tweaking them into stiff nubs. Satisfied by the effects, she swiftly redressed before again examining herself in the reflective glass. Two rigid peaks stood at attention, visible beneath the fabric of the shirt.

Pushing through the swarm of bodies, Helen descended the staircase and began to scan the crowd for Scott's face. As had been the case for the majority of the night, almost everyone made a pointed effort avoid meeting her eye. A number of girls sat around the dining table, sipping bottles of luminous blue alcohol, while a crowd of boys tried with all their might to impress them. Stood in the corner, a girl tapped away at her phone, no doubt drunk-texting a boy that she liked, while across the room a small group were talking amongst themselves.

The cool air plucked at her nipples, hardening them even more, as she slipped out the back door and into the garden.

He was exactly where she had left him, sat down on the decorative patio wall.

"You know, I was actually worried that you wouldn't be coming back," he said, with a grin.

"Come on, do you really think I would do that to you?"

"Honestly, I don't know what to think," Scott replied, the corners of his eyes narrowing discerningly. "I did only meet you half an hour ago. Really, I don't know you from Adam."

"Who's this Adam?" she teased. "Anyone I need to watch out for? I'm not much of a fan of competition."

"I don't think you need to worry about anyone," he said, rising. "Plus, between you and me, you're much prettier than him."

Helen fanned her face with her hand and laughed. "Oh my, Mr Willard. You're flattering me."

"At least I'm doing something right." He took a drink from the plastic cup clasped in his fist. The strong scent of spirits wafted off of his breath and into the air.

"Moving on to stronger stuff?" she asked, indicating the vodka.

"Well, you know... Gotta spice things up a bit. Plus, I'm going to need a bit of liquid courage if I want to get anywhere with you."

"Are my ears deceiving me, or did you just admit that you were going to try it on with me?" Helen laughed. "That takes guts. What if I don't feel the same? Hm?"

"Then I really must be seeing things," Scott replied. "Because it looks to me like you took off your bra." He smiled coyly and flicked his eyes down her shirt, before returning them to Helen's face. "Admit it," he added, playfully. "You're trying to seduce me."

Helen's olive cheeks tinged pink. She wasn't used to being so blatantly called out on her advances. "I might be."

"Come on," he said softly, putting down the cup and taking off his jacket. "You know you didn't have to do that to get my attention. Here. You can have this." Passing Helen the light brown workman's jacket, he pointed at her chest and laughed. "You look like you need it. Those things could cut glass."

Helen laughed and slipped on the coat. Inhaling sharply, she quickly breathed in his scent. "You're very forward."

"It's better than being backwards."

Again, she found herself softly chuckling. "Funny too."

"I try."

"You succeed."

Sitting back down on the wall, Scott patted the stone surface beside him. "Care to join me for a sit?"

"Don't mind if I do."

Sliding the seat of her jeans onto the nodose surface, the material creased along the inside of her thighs. A restricted feeling clung to her lower half, tightening the coils of her muscles.

Looking up at Scott, her green eyes traced the line of his jaw and settled onto the thin line of his lips. She kept her eyes on them as he spoke.

For over an hour they sat and talked about delicious nothings. They could have been talking about anything in the world and it wouldn't have mattered. Their conversation flowed smoothly, meandering effortlessly through the vibrant fields of interest and attraction, with no indication of an approaching coast.

In the recesses of her mind, Helen thanked her brother for throwing the party; for telling his guests to ignore her. For had he not, she would never have been approached by Scott.

When he put a hand on her knee, her entire body shivered. Shifting, Helen attempted to cover the unintentional reaction by acting as if she were cold.

Scott noticed the motion and beamed softly. "I'm really happy I met you tonight."

God, he knows exactly what to say, her mind rolled as Helen reached out and gripped the cup that Scott had set aside. Bringing it to her lips, the burn of vodka swam past her gums before dropping down her throat.

She wanted to kiss him; to wind her fingers through the soft brown locks of his hair and knot her tongue inside his mouth. She wanted to run her hands over his chest, before slipping them behind his back and cupping the mound of his ass. He had good legs and an even better bum. Helen could see it through his tight blue jeans.

A dry sensation gripped her mouth, like it had been stuffed with wads of cotton. Moving her tongue about her teeth, moisture returned just in time for her to reply. "I'm really glad I met you too."

Again he flashed that killer smile, and she knew that she was done. She wanted him.

*

Alice Goodacre stepped towards the patio doors, just in time to see it happen.

Her feet locked up, like they had been trapped in a pit of tar, and the corner of her eye twitched; throbbing like a tiny heart.

She watched as the girl (the girl *wearing his jacket*) looped her arms around Scott's neck and stuck her tongue down his throat.

For a brief, hopeful instant Alice expected Scott to push her away. To hold the girl at arm's reach and explain that he liked someone else. But he didn't. He leaned forwards and stroked the side of her face with his fingers, tracing the edge of her ear gently.

Incredulous rage flared inside her chest, igniting an ether of jealous spite.

Alice could do nothing but watch, dumbstruck, as the pair rose and moved about the garden, joined at the lips. They sauntered hungrily, entwined in each other, before disappearing through the back door and into the house.

Following them with her eyes, Alice felt acid course through her veins.

Scott and the girl ascended the staircase and vanished into an empty bedroom, shutting the door behind them.

Chapter 20

A brisk chill had fallen on Lindum overnight. Out of season frost clung to the windscreens of cars and dew hung from the blades of grass in half-frozen beads, like icy marbles. Dark clouds swarmed overhead, turning over one another as if fighting for poll position to empty their depths on the landscape.

Scott gripped the bedsheets and wound them tightly around him in a dazed effort to stave off the cold. The window was open and the frosty air breathed over the naked skin of his arms and back.

Warm air suddenly washed over the nape of his neck. The smooth sensation of skin wound around his body and settled on his chest, burning like hot fire.

He could feel her laying behind his back, nuzzling her face into the crook between his shoulder blades.

Helen was still asleep.

Slowly, the night was coming back to him. Scott could remember meeting Helen. Talking to her extensively. He could remember kissing her; how deliciously soft her lips were as they bruised against his. Fragments of images entered his mind of climbing the stairs and slipping into her bedroom. Falling together onto the sheets and embracing.

A warmth spread through his chest.

Turning over, Scott wrapped his arms around Helen's shoulders and held her body close to his. Past the outline of her shoulder, he could see a digital clock set onto her bedside dresser. It read the time as just past seven in the morning.

He needed to be at school in an hour and a half. Nothing if not punctual, Scott considered rising and getting ready to depart. However, something made him want to stay. He didn't want to wake Helen. More than that, he enjoyed the feeling of her laying beside him; her body heat radiating over him. It made him feel comfortable and secure, despite his naked exposure.

Helen's soft breathing faltered for a moment as he touched his forehead against her own and shut his eyes. Gradually, stirring sleepily, she awoke.

"Morning," Scott said gently, with a smile.

Still partially submerged in the haze of sleep, Helen slowly opened her eyes and took several seconds to respond. Laying eyes on his face, a tired smile formed on her lips.

"G'morning..." she muttered, closing her eyes again and slipping her head into the crook of Scott's neck.

"Someone's affectionate," he chuckled, stroking her hair and hugging her close.

"Piss off," Helen laughed into his collar.

"And for a second I thought, I was going to wake up with someone nice," Scott replied, joining her in laughing.

"I'll have you know that I'm a delight," she responded, pulling back and staring into his eyes. "Besides, I don't think you're in a position to insult me. You did just wake up in my bed."

"An honest mistake, I assure you. I must have been sleep walking."

"Is that a fact?"

"Uh-huh."

"So you're telling me I imagined us screwing last night?" she teased.

"You must have done." His tone was mockingly incredulous. "I'm more of a second date kind of guy. There's no way I would go to bed with a girl I just met. Unless, of course, they were special."

"You really are a smooth one, aren't you?" Helen chuckled, giving him a slight shove. "Anyway, don't you have school to get to?"

"I might do."

"And what does that mean?"

"It means I'd rather stay here with you," he said, with a grin.

Watching a faint blush spread over Helen's cheeks, Scott leaned forwards and kissed her.

Returning the kiss, Helen firmly pressed her hand against his chest. After several seconds, she pushed him away. "Go on. Go. I don't want you to be late."

"Trying to get rid of me, eh?"

"Just being realistic," she smiled. "Besides, I have to head back to uni today. I only came back for a day, to get my washing done and visit the folks."

A brief flutter of loss flapped through his heart. He had expected his time with her to last longer. The thought hadn't even entered his peripheral that just after meeting her, Helen would already be on her way. His eyes drooped ever so slightly.

Helen must have noticed the look on his face. Kissing him on the cheek, she smiled. "I'll definitely see you next time I'm here." She held up three fingers in a sort of salute. "Scout's honour. And..." Pushing up from the bed, Helen reached uncomfortably over Scott, for her bedside table, and snatched up her phone. "I'll even give you my number."

"Your real number?" he teased.

Helen laughed. "Of course my real number! Here..." Grabbing Scott's phone from the pocket of his discarded jeans, she typed in her number and passed it back to him. "Test it, if you don't believe me."

"It's okay," Scott smiled. "I believe you."

"Now go on!" Helen insisted, swiping her curly hair out of her face. "You'll be late!"

Climbing out of the covers and into the cold morning air, Scott laughed and quickly dressed. "Okay, okay!" Smoothing down his shirt, he turned back to the bed and cocked his head to the side. "Promise me that this won't be the last time I see you though."

Helen took a second to compose herself. The disarming charm of his smile had again smacked her full force, leaving her momentarily stunned. "I promise."

Feeling her eyes on him as he left, Scott gave a brief wave and smiled contently to himself.

The next time he would see her couldn't come soon enough.

Chapter 21

Stafford and Rawlings had to race a storm to the train tracks. A call had come in early in the day about a potential dump site, forcing them to move fast lest they be washed from the scene.

Upon their arrival, the rain was just starting to spit down.

Iron tracks split the ground, hard brown and flecked with splashes of orange rust. All around, small grey stones had been scattered, interrupted occasionally by a flash of green where grass had managed to sprout through. Bordering the transport line, at the bottom of parallel slopes, were a number of bushes. The parasitic shrubbery had grafted itself onto the erected fences, winding through the thin links of metal.

The leaves had been disturbed, in a section roughly a meter and a half wide. Somebody had taken a pair of cutters to the fence, clipping the thin metal diamonds one by one until a sizable hole was opened. Snaking down towards the empty space, from the tracks, a thick line of crimson red glared up at the officers, like a pair of tightly-pursed painted lips.

And, laid on the tracks, was a mound of mangled cat corpses.

"No doubt about it," David said, crouching down beside the pile. Around his feet, the plastic bags that covered his shoes shimmered in the light. "This is definitely our guy."

Rawlings hung back, holding a gloved hand in front of his nose and mouth to fight back a gag. "Jesus, don't stand so close to it."

Confused, David looked up at his new partner and lifted one eyebrow. "Are you serious?"

Rawlings averted his eyes. "It's disgusting."

"Aren't you supposed to be a Detective?" David asked. "I'd have thought you'd be used to this."

He scoffed. "No. I mostly deal with rape, and drugs, and-"

"*Murder?*" the Constable persisted.

"Stabbings," Rawlings replied, bluntly. "And shootings. Not... *Disfiguring* things." Quickly moving his mismatched eyes back to his comrade, he glanced over him. "How come you're so okay with it?"

"I usually work traffic collisions," David explained. "I'm used to seeing mangled bodies like this."

"Whatever..." Turning his attention away from his partner, Rawlings started to question the National Rail employee stood behind him.

Forensics Investigators had already arrived and were in the process of erecting a tent around the site, to protect it from the weather. The scene was quickly whipped up into a frenzied atmosphere. Photographs were snapped, police tape was strung out, and evidence was bagged and tagged.

As everything around him moved at lightning speed, David stayed crouched, staring intently at the cat corpses. His eyes begged them to reveal their secrets: To tell him exactly what had happened; to scream at him who had killed them.

All of a sudden, a thought flashed through his mind.

"Why did he make the dump here?" he called over his shoulder, at Rawlings.

The excessively hairy man abruptly turned away from the rail employee, leaving her stunned at his rudeness. "What?" he asked, gruffly.

"Why were the cats dumped here?" David reiterated. "At the school they were left there because our guy knew the routine; knew that he wouldn't be caught. That's how we know there's a connection to the school. But why here? What's the link to the train tracks?"

"What makes you think there is one?"

"Because it's out in the open." He stood up and indicated the scene. As he did so, the rain started to come down even harder. Lashing down onto the tent now covering them, the water roared over the top of their conversation. In response, David raised his voice. "What about this place made him pick it? Why risk getting caught like this?"

"Maybe he wanted to stop the trains?"

Rawlings bowled out the phrase so suddenly, David was momentarily taken aback. "What was that?"

"The train. He probably wanted to stop it."

"But why would he-?" David stopped short and directed his attention to the National Rail employee. A subtle urgency gripped his voice. "What's down the line from here?"

"One direction is a straight route to Highwich," she replied. "But that's a twenty minute drive."

"And the other way?"

"Lyefield station. But why does that matter?"

"Is the station manned?" Rawlings asked, sharply.

"Sometimes," the woman replied. "Usually only by one guy though. It's not really used that much. It's a tiny station. Only five people get on from there a day. At most." She suddenly stopped to think. "Actually..."

David lowered his brows. "Actually, what?"

"It might be more today..."

"And why's that?"

"There are repairs happening at Lindum this weekend. Some of the lines out of there are closed, so passengers may have to get replacements from other stations. Lyefield is one of them."

Rawlings abruptly departed, heading straight for his car. Giving chase, David ran up behind him, into the pouring rain. "What are you thinking?"

"I think they wanted to get someone alone. Stop the train, no one comes to the station."

"Really?"

"It's what I'd do."

Chapter 22

The station attendant smirked down at Helen as he passed her the ticket, eyeing the valley of her cleavage in a stare that lasted far too long.

Snatching the orange stub of paper out of his hand, she pulled an unattractive face, like she had just stepped in dog mess. Helen was in a foul mood and the never-ending slew of bad luck that had hit her that day didn't seem to be letting up at all.

When gathering up her things, for her trip back to university, Helen discovered that one of Tom's intoxicated party guests had decided to use the clean laundry hamper as their own personal sick bucket. Forced to stay behind and do almost all of her washing again, she had arrived at the station too late to catch the train back to London from the Lindum Station. Not that it would have mattered. As she got to the station, Helen discovered that planned repairs were being conducted on the line from Friday through to the Sunday. Crammed inside a too-small replacement bus, she was forced to traverse the countryside and get a train from the much smaller station on the outskirts of Lyefield.

Mostly unmanned and several decades old, the Lyefield station didn't even have a ticket machine. Constructed from browning yellow bricks, it was little more than a concrete platform, bordering rusted iron tracks. Graffiti had been sprayed onto a number of the walls, yet nobody had bothered to clean it off, leaving it to wither and fade. Set into the middle of an otherwise empty field, bordering a seldom-used country road, it was so out of place that it almost hurt.

Then there were the employees. Or rather the employee. Ever since Helen had arrived, stepping off the bus on her own, he had done nothing but stare at her. She could feel his oily gaze slicking over her, to the point where she could almost see a visible shine on her skin. It made her feel uneasy and wrong.

Worse than the leers of the spotty attendant, the atmosphere at the train station was downright miserable. Grey clouds swarmed overhead, churning about themselves and rumbling, threatening a biblical downpour.

She hoped that the train would come before the rain started.

Leaning against the only wall on the platform, Helen watched the station employee retreat back to the warmth of the free-standing stone office building. For a brief instant, she regretted not being nicer to him. If it got her out of the cold and potential rain, she could afford a false smile.

As she stood and thought, a dull ache spread through her body, reminding Helen of yet another stroke of bad luck. Spreading through the bottom of her abdomen, the ache caused the muscles in her stomach to tense up and cramp. Her "friend" had arrived early.

Jesus Christ, uterus, she thought, rubbing one hand over her stomach, tenderly. *So I didn't get you pregnant! No need to throw a fucking temper tantrum!*

Helen didn't like taking the pill, because of the way it messed with her hormones, but whenever her time of the month struck she always considered going back onto it. The only good thing about having her period was the relief that she got knowing that she wasn't pregnant.

The laundry list of bad things was far longer. It made her feel tired and annoyed; far more of a bitch than she usually was, and that was saying something. She also felt hungry, a side effect that was not good for her diet, and the way her hormones were, eating the way that she wanted would almost certainly cause her to just get pissed off at herself. The pain was bearable, but not by much, and the persistent ache wasn't something that painkillers were very effective against. Worst of all, however, was how turned on it made her feel. It grossed her out. The fact that the time when she felt the most undesirable, the time when she least wanted guys to touch her, was when she felt the most up for it.

An image of Scott invasively slipped into her mind: The glimmer of light that danced behind his hazel orbs; the way that his face crumpled when he smiled; the feeling of his weight on top of her; his arms wrapped around her body from behind; the warmth that he left in the bed that morning, after he had departed.

A tingle stirred in her underwear.

Face flushing red, Helen cursed herself under her breath and gritted her teeth.

The last thing that she wanted was to make herself hornier than she already was. Thinking about him was only making it worse.

She also didn't like the fact that she was mooning over a guy. Fluttery, girly feelings annoyed her. Pining over him and getting herself hot and bothered over a guy she had just met (and a friend of her brother's at that) made her feel stupid. Like she was less like herself than the day before. Helen wasn't the type to crush on someone; that's what she had always been like. Anything she did contrary to that caused feelings of self-deprecating annoyance to brew within her.

Even so, something about Scott kept her coming back to the thought of him. Be it his personality, his appearance or even an innate air about him, Helen found Scott Willard irresistible. It was why, for one of the few times in her life, she had given him her real phone number.

And, God, she wanted him to use it.

Or (even more against her personal taboo) Helen could be the one to text him.

Pride be damned, she wanted to.

Digging into the pocket of her jacket, Helen's fingers wound around the cool, glassy surface of her smartphone. After a moment's hesitation, it was out in the open air.

Without warning, a fat drop of rain fell from the sky and exploded against the screen. Flinching back in surprise, Helen hugged the device to her chest, to save it from the moisture.

Within moments, the heavens had opened. Rain cascaded down upon the fields, thrashing against the tiny station and soaking the concrete. Puddles grew larger and larger before connecting and waterfalling down onto the tracks.

Frantically stuffing the phone back into her pocket, Helen scrambled for her suitcases. Traversing the platform, for the attendants' station, she rapped against the door.

After several seconds, there was no response. Banging again on the wood, Helen called out. "Come on! Open up!"

The acne-ridden face of the National Rail employee came out to meet the open air as the door swung in on weathered hinges. "Wadda'ya want?"

Hair close to soaking, Helen swept her fringe aside. "Shelter? What the fuck else?"

"Ya' see the sign?" he grunted, jabbing a finger towards the metal sheet, tacked to the wood. "Employees only. No can do."

"Come off it! It's pissing it down out here!"

"Not my problem."

Incredulous rage gripped her. Her vibrant green eyes narrowed into daggers. "Well then what am I supposed to do?"

"Stand in it till the train comes, I guess."

"And when the fuck is that? It was supposed to be here ten minutes ago!"

The attendant scratched the side of his head, scattering a snowfall of dandruff onto the shoulders of the navy fleece that he wore. "Dunno. Got a call in a little bit ago. Apparently the train's been delayed. Something on the tracks."

"You've got to be kidding me."

"Sorry love."

Without another word, he shut the door.

Finally giving in to her anger, Helen furiously balled her fists and shouted. "Twat!"

Snatching up her things, Helen pushed the suitcases flat against the wall of the small building, before doing the same with her back. The only option left to her was to hope that the overhanging lip of the tiles would provide at least some shelter.

Time passed in silence, save for the hiss of rain and the roar of an occasional passing car as, for several minutes, Helen seethed to herself. In the back of her mind, a slew of guttural insults polluted her brain. Expectation rose inside her every time she heard the creak of wood, as she prepared to release the manhole cover of her mouth and sling verbal sewage at the spotty bastard.

All of a sudden, the sound of a car horn perforated the air.

Glancing over towards the road, Helen spotted the cherry red outline of a Nissan Micra, through the filter of rain. The driver beeped the horn a second time.

Ordinarily, Helen wouldn't have ventured over. The car, however, was familiar. She had seen it parked outside her house the night before. It also didn't hurt that it was a potential escape from the rain.

Dragging the cases over, she arrived at the car just as the owner opened the passenger side door. Sat in the driver's seat was a teenage girl.

"You look soaked," she cried. "Come on, you can put your stuff in the back!"

Smiling her thanks, Helen loaded the cases into the back seat before sliding into the front of the car and shutting the door.

"Thank you so much!" Helen said again, pushing her damp hair away from her eyes. "You really didn't have to stop."

"It's okay, you looked like you needed a break," the girl replied, smiling.

Now that she was up close, Helen realised just how pretty her saviour was. Petite and looking much younger than she probably was, she recognised her immediately from the party.

"You're Tom's sister, right?" she continued, looking Helen up and down. "Where are you going?"

"I was supposed to be getting the train to London," Helen sighed, half-smiling with relief, now that she was out of the rain. "But Lindum station is having repairs done, so I had to come here."

"Oh no, that's not good!"

"You're telling me. Now I have to switch at Lincoln and again at Newark. The Lindum train usually takes me straight there, but now it's all just one big fucking mess."

"At least this train won't be long now?" the girl offered, hopefully smiling.

"Fat chance," Helen scoffed. "Apparently it's delayed because something's on the tracks. Probably just a fucking stick or something."

For a second, the girl pulled a concerned face, before brightening up suddenly. "Wait did you say you were going to change at Lincoln?"

"Yeah?"

"I'm actually heading that way myself," she said. "Not all the way, but I can drop you at Highwich. The station there at least has a canopy to stand under."

"Oh my god, really? Are you sure?"

"Of course!" the girl insisted. "It's only twenty five minutes down the road. Plus, I'm already going there to see family."

"Thank you so much, you're a life-saver!" Helen gushed, blinking hard to stop tears from welling in her eyes. "That's so nice of you! And- You're helping me so much and — I'm so sorry — I don't even know your name!"

The girl smiled and offered her hand. "My name is Alice."

Chapter 23

David was in desperate need of coffee. The storm that was still descending had soaked him through to the bone, the wind plucking at the moisture in an icy chill. Coffee, he hoped, would help to warm him up. The least that it could do was help rid him of the lousy taste in his mouth. It would also give him something to focus on, besides the case. Something to hold in his free hand, to occupy even a modicum of his attention.

After driving to the Lyefield train station, they had found nothing there. It was exactly what David was hoping to avoid. An empty station was a trap of duality. On one hand it could mean that it was just another day, just another disused location. The other possibility was far worse. Whoever the Cat Hunter was trying to get on their own was long gone.

Initially, he had held out on the hope that he was just being paranoid. His brain screamed that there was no evidence to suggest that whoever was responsible for the mutilations would suddenly jump to kidnapping, or even murder.

Unless they were triggered by something.

The station attendant was beyond useless. He remembered there being a girl on the platform, carrying suitcases, however he was at a loss for a name, and the description of her was vague. She had paid for her ticket in cash, so there wasn't even a record of her debit card. Apparently all he heard was the honk of a horn, and then the girl was gone.

Either the girl had been picked up by somebody, or their psychopath had kidnapped her.

It added another layer to the investigations; another route that needed attention. They would have to sit on it and wait for a missing person to be reported. And until that happened, they had to operate as if both possibilities were true.

The cafe that David and Rawlings were now sat in was a greasy spoon affair; plastic chairs bordering minimalistic tables, ordained with condiments. Dotted about the space, patrons tucked into their breakfasts, wolfing down plates full of bacon and beans before washing them down with mugs of tea.

His newly ordered coffee warming his hand, David sat and watched the rivulets of rain pour down the window.

Opposite him, Rawlings was midway through mutilating his Full English. Having broken the yolk of his fried egg, he had mixed the yellow with the juice of his tinned tomatoes before carving up the various meats and hash browns, and mixing it all into an undefinable pink mess. Reaching out, he snatched up a bottle of Worcester Sauce and a shaker of pepper.

Part of the reason why David was observing the window was so that he didn't have to look at it. Watching the Detective eat made him feel sick.

"We'll start canvassing later today," Rawlings muttered, momentarily setting down his cutlery to wipe around his beard with the cheap paper napkin. "Once the rain dies down." He picked up the knife and fork, and again began shovelling food into his mouth. "I don't want to be stood out in that again if I don't have to."

"Where are you thinking of starting?" David asked, turning back towards his associate, before attempting to form a barricade out of condiments and mugs, so that he didn't have to look at Rawlings' breakfast.

The bulky man waved his knife around dismissively. "Earlier I would have said near where the cats disappeared from. Today? Around here. The houses closest to the train station. See if anyone saw anything suspicious."

"There aren't any houses near the station," David retorted. "Not for a good half mile. Even less near the tracks, where the dump was made."

"Check the traffic cameras then," Rawlings shot back, speaking around the mush of meat in his mouth. "And you better not tell me there aren't any on the roads, or so help me I'm going to scream."

"Not many," David said. "But there are some. Here's hoping whoever we're looking for got spooked. It'd make things so much easier if their license got snapped for speeding."

"I doubt it," the Detective offered, unhelpfully. "Whoever's doing this is comfortable, and knows what they're doing. I don't think they'd get caught by something as stupid as a speed camera. Still, it doesn't hurt to check. I want to be thorough." He finished his breakfast and set down the cutlery, before tapping his index finger repeatedly against the table. "Tell Wilson and Russell when they get here."

With that, he stood and moved to leave.

David flustered for a second, not expecting the sudden departure. "Hey! Hey! Wait! Where are you going? You're my partner, you can't just run off like this."

"I'm also the lead on this," the DS shot back, bluntly. "I need to get back to the incident room." Lifting one hand, he indicated his watch. "It's nearly twelve o'clock. I'm always at my desk by twelve thirty to type up my notes for the morning."

"Always?"

"Yes, always," he replied, in a matter of fact manner.

"Then how am I supposed to get back to the station?"

"Wait for Wilson, he should be able to drive you. I need to type up my notes."

David exhaled slowly, to compose himself. "You need a hobby."

"I have a hobby," Rawlings replied, simply. "I collect animal skulls."

The odd statement remained hanging in the air long after the Detective Sergeant departed. It dangled on a thin and unsteady wire, emulating David's discomfort at it. But, despite the sinister implications of the statement, the uncomfortable feeling was different than the one he got from the cat killer. It felt more like Rawlings had over-shared a deeply personal secret.

He would question his new partner about it later.

At that moment, however, he needed to draw up a distinctive plan of action; choose a starting point and plan his moves from there. He wanted something to give the other two Detectives, upon their arrival.

Settling on delegation, he pulled out a notebook and began to scribble down shorthand. Simon, he decided, would review that traffic camera footage. Even after only a day together, David could tell that he was good with the details. Examining the footage would suit him nicely. The best task for Babs was one where she could exercise control; get people to move the way that she wanted. It was because of that that David opted to leave her in charge of the site, and the Scene of Crime Officers.

That leaves me and Rawlings to canvas houses... he thought.

Joy... his mind added, sarcastically.

There was also the report to Braithwaite that was due to be sent to the Chief Superintendent on Monday morning. Something that he had yet to even start. Franko had also requested a copy. His superior wanted a concise, detailed write up of all the information that David had amassed prior to his official assignment.

It made sense, yet David still resented him for it.

He'd been doing that a lot as of late. In spite of how curiously supportive the ageing DCI had been, David couldn't help but feel as if he was being tested. Scrutinised under the maximum magnification of Franko's microscope-like vision. He felt exposed and vulnerable.

His thoughts of his boss were interrupted as Simon Wilson and Barbera Russell walked into the cafe. The duo sat down opposite him and smiled their greetings.

Detective Constable Barbera Russell was a slight woman in her thirties, standing at not much over five foot tall. She was wearing a form-fitting navy dress, beneath a trim jacket, and heels. She had good legs, and the outfit showed that. It also showed the roll of a muffin top, looping over the hem of her underwear.

Babs was nice enough, however there was something very particular about her that David found increasingly annoying.

"Hey David. Where's Tim?" The way that she spoke rubbed him the wrong way. Her voice was strangely child-like, despite her age. She placed emphasis on the wrong words.

"Gone," he replied, sipping from the mug of dark black coffee. "Apparently he had to type up his notes."

"That sounds like him," Wilson said, leaning back in the cheap plastic chair and looking up at the large acrylic menu, displayed over the front counter of the cafe. "He's got a routine. The problem is you don't fit into it yet."

"It's not his fault though," Babs added. "It's a big problem for him. He can't control it, so don't make him feel bad."

Despite the infantile way that she weighed her words, David sensed something serious in her choice of phrase. "I'm guessing there's a story here?"

"Babs thinks he's on the spectrum." Wilson railed it out in such a matter-of-fact manner that he was momentarily stunned.

"Really?" David asked, leaning forwards in his chair. He had suspected that something was different about Rawlings. Now it seemed he was getting confirmation.

"Yeah, midway between Genius and Absolute Fucking Lunatic."

Unsure of whether to take the statement as a joke, he fell back into his seat and exhaled sharply. "That's not funny, you know."

Wilson's mouth curled into a smile. "I was only half joking. He's not diagnosed but we've seen enough people like him to know. His hitching post stands somewhere between Aspergers and Obsessive Compulsives."

"He's really good at his job, though," Babs drawled. "I think better because of it. Because he can, like, see things different from the rest of us. And he focuses on some things more."

"Yes, but just because you focus on something more doesn't mean you're seeing everything," David replied. "You can get tunnel vision."

Wilson, upon hearing the statement, merely shrugged.

"So David," Babs interjected. "What happened down at the tracks?"

"Just another dump," he replied. "Similar to the school; no witnesses. But..."

"But?" Wilson probed.

"Rawlings thinks he did it to stop the trains, to get someone on their own at the station. He says that's what he would have done."

"Of course he did." Wilson raised a finger to excuse himself as he went to the counter and ordered his own breakfast. When he returned, he continued the conversation. "Look, I'm not saying it's not a good theory. But we don't have any evidence that that's the case. And even if we did, what would we do with it?"

"There was a girl at Lyefield station," David retorted. "The attendant said he heard a car horn, and after that she was gone."

"Again, what are we supposed to do with that?" Wilson repeated. "Without a missing person's report, there's no way to even know if they're missing. Whoever it is could have just been picked up by a friend. Rawlings very well may have been right, but where does that get us?" Stirring sugar into his tea, he leaned back and stared at Stafford pensively. "You expect us to go door to door and ask: 'Excuse me, but is there any chance someone you know was abducted by a psychopath?' Come on."

David merely sighed and took a sip of his coffee.

"I know it doesn't sit right with you," Wilson continued, sympathy finally passing onto his face. "But there is nothing we can do about the girl at this point. If something comes of it — Oh, thanks love — If something comes of it, then you can bet we'll be the first people on it. So at least find some comfort in that. I mean, what little you can." Glancing down at his breakfast, he turned the plate 90 degrees and picked up a bottle of ketchup. "What we need to be focussing on is the cats. Follow the path of destruction back, and we'll find the source."

"I'll be canvassing later today with Rawlings," David said. "Talking to the owners of the cats that were killed or hurt. Hopefully we'll find something that we can use; see if they remember anything."

"Good call," Wilson said, taking a bite out of his bacon sandwich.

"Rawlings also had an idea to check the traffic cameras in the area, see if they spotted something. I figured you'd be up for giving that a shot?"

Wiping tomato sauce from the corner of his mouth, Wilson nodded his approval.

"Barbera, something tells me you're good at direction. How'd you feel being the one to oversee the crime scene?"

"Only as long as Murray from Scene of Crime is there," she smirked. "I could watch those buns of his all day."

"Well I didn't catch any of their names," David admitted, returning the smile. "But there was a certain attractive young man in overalls. Red hair?"

"Oh yes," Babs grinned.

Chapter 24

The scratch of graphite against paper ground out sharply as Scott took notes. Flicking his eyes between the board at the front of the room, and his notebook, he chewed at the inside of his cheek.

His diligent note-taking, however, was little more than a front. Inside his head, Scott's brain was awash with a cordial of different thoughts and feelings. An imperfect emulsion of intense distractions.

The pencil beginning to wander, Scott caught himself doodling in the margin of his book. A malformed circle stared up at him, sending his mind momentarily back in time. For a split second, he was looking down at the mutilated eye of a cat.

Blinking hard, he forced the thought out of his head, before another intense feeling welled up in the cavity behind his ribs.

Scott shifted in place and laid one hand down on his thigh. The lump of the phone in his pocket reminded him of Helen.

His back still stung from where her fingernails had cut deep trenches into his skin. The pain was a sweet sensation, though. It reminded him of the amazing night that he had spent with her. Made him think about just how much he wanted to see her again.

Unable to contain himself, he had text her during his first free period on the Friday morning, only to get no response for several hours.

When she did reply, it wasn't exactly what he had been expecting, though not altogether unpleasant.

Helen, Scott had discovered, texted in full sentences. There was no abbreviation of words, nor omission of punctuation. Initially, it had come across as overly blunt. Scott wasn't used to seeing full-stops and was at first concerned that he had said something wrong. Before long, however, he discovered that this was just another of the girl's individual idiosyncrasies.

They had talked all weekend, without any sign of letting up.

Even as Monday rolled around, he still found himself periodically checking his phone just in case he missed the tell-tale vibration that indicated an incoming message.

Pru was already teasing him for it.

"Scott and Helen, sitting in a tree. F-U-C-K-I-N-G!"

Although she would never admit to it, Scott knew that his best friend was over the moon. He had found someone that he could connect with in more than just arbitrary conversation; someone that made him happy.

She was the one saying that he needed something good to come along. And Scott agreed.

After the incident with the cats, the stressful situation with Alice, and not to mention being left home alone, he needed something good.

Helen was that something.

Scott was beyond relieved that Alice hadn't shown up at the party. If she had, he never would have had the opportunity or the nerve to talk to Tom's sister.

Smiling to himself, as he erased the circle jotted onto the paper in front of him, Scott glanced over the room at Tom Raleigh. His curly hair had been bunched together and pushed out of his face by a dark blue bandana.

He really couldn't see much of Helen in him at all.

Although I guess that's a good thing, he thought, with a smirk.

As the bell rang to signal the end of the period, he began to gather up his belongings. Stuffing them into his bag, Scott straightened up and was just about to leave as Tom and a blonde boy named Paul Castell passed him by.

He caught them in the hallway. Half jogging up behind Tom, Scott raised his voice slightly to be heard over the murmur of the crowd.

"Hey Tom," he said, falling into step beside the curly haired boy.

"Hey man," Tom replied, breaking into his typical goofy smile. "Sorry I didn't catch you Friday, decided to give school a miss. Hangover was a motherfucker."

Scott laughed briefly. "It's okay. I was, uh, actually meaning to have a word with you. I tried to catch you before class today but-"

"I turned up late," Tom chuckled. "Story of my life. So wat'cha wanna talk to me about?"

"Well, I uh — I guess I didn't plan this too well — I wanted to talk to you about your sister."

"Oh so you're the guy that dragged her off to bed at the party."

The statement was so sudden and unexpected, Scott felt his ears turn red. The blood spread across his forehead, scattering warmth across his face in the wake of the blush.

"Look," Tom laughed, clapping one hand against his friend's shoulder. "I'm not mad or anything. It doesn't really mean much to me at all. Shit, I don't even see her ninety percent of the time anyway. And that's when she's at home. So don't expect the whole protective brother crap from me." His smile widened. "Just promise me one thing."

"Okay?"

"That if you ever come over, you stay out of my room." Tom chuckled and jabbed his elbow into Scott's ribs.

"Well that depends if you still keep crates of cider under your bed. I mean, I've gotta drink something."

The curly boy laughed louder than before. "You cheeky fucker!"

*

Despite Sarah's assurance that he was great with kids, Franko was thankful that he hadn't listened to his careers advisor at school, and become a teacher. While the role of a Detective was far from the least stressful position in the world, babysitting children who weren't his own was a process that ground heavily against Franko's already worn sense of patience.

The reports from Stafford and Rawlings currently sitting on his desk were the epitome of what tested him the most.

Obvious mistakes irked him, and he wasn't about to go out of his way to hold anyone's hand.

While Stafford's work was impressive, Franko had noted several problems with the write-up of his investigation, until his official assignment onto the case. However, even in spite of the annoyance, this was something that he could ultimately forgive. Stafford wasn't a Detective, no matter how much he enjoyed playing as one, so the DCI could afford him some of the shortfalls that came with his formatting.

The real problem was the Detective Sergeant.

Having read through the documents, Franko decided that Rawlings was functionally illiterate. He had a broad enough vocabulary to know and understand the meanings of complicated words, yet he spelt them phonetically.

It didn't instil Franko with much confidence that this was the man leading the investigation.

However, results were results. And if Rawlings' track record was to be believed, Franko would have to concede. Spelling and grammar mistakes aside.

Taking off his glasses, the ageing Detective pinched the bridge of his nose. Tracing the outline of his nose as he exhaled, his dark brown eyes stared out of the glass wall that construed the front of his office.

St. Claire was still hunched over his desk, flitting through paperwork at a rapid pace. Just watching him made Franko sweat. He vaguely remembered a time, years past, when he was as driven as the young Officer. Since then, he had learned to take his time; work at a pace that suited him.

That would be something that St. Claire would need to learn too.

Placing his glasses back onto his face, Franko returned his attention to the pages set down in front of him.

"So you've decided to interview the owners of the cats..." he muttered under his breath as he read. "A good starting point..."

But if they were to get anywhere significant, they would need more people on side. Franko wanted to catch the unsub before they escalated, and there was only so fast that they could move with a team of four. Interviewing was arduous enough.

Rising, he moved over to his office door and called across the communal office. "Chambers, St. Claire! Can I have a word with you both?"

He sat as the two Uniforms entered his office, and motioned them both to sit. Watching them, he slowly moved his fingers in a steady and mechanical fashion, the tips drumming into the wood of his desk.

The older woman and young man sank into the chairs across the wooden moat. St. Claire's youthful features bore a look of intrigue, while beneath Julie's botoxed forehead, her eyes were sharp.

"How busy are you both at the moment?" His eyes moved quickly, surveying their expressions. They both held an air of restrained curiosity. "St. Claire, I know you're pulling a lot of overtime at the moment to take in lieu. And I know you're looking for some time off for the summer, Chambers. So what would you both say to helping out Stafford on his case?"

"The one with the cats?" Julie asked.

"Yes. It doesn't sit right with me having so few people working on it. Worse still is that the DCS is basing the investigation out of Lindum. Don't get me wrong, their facilities are much better than ours and as a central location it works well for response times. But at the end of the day Stafford was the one who caught this, and I don't want the Lindum Station taking credit for my Officers' hard work."

He noticed a twitch of a smirk play across St. Claire's lips. The young constable clearly agreed with him.

"So if you're up for it, I want you two to head over and provide support. Correct me if I'm wrong, but as far as I can see, all you've got on your plates is paperwork. You're capable Officers, and you've got time to spare. All I'm asking is you help Stafford out in any way you can, until his case closes. After that, consider this my approval to take as much time off as you want. Just don't take the mickey with it. Sound fair?"

"You're being strangely civil today, sir," St. Claire replied with a grin.

"Watch it, or I'll forget that I'm in a good mood," Franko shot back.

"What exactly would we be doing, then?" Julie made an effort to try and lower her paralysed brows as she spoke.

"You'd be extra feet on the ground," Franko replied, turning towards the woman. "At the moment they're interviewing all of the cat owners in Lindum that have reported a missing or injured animal. I want you to give them a hand with that; help them cover more distance quickly. Past that, you'll be doing anything that's needed. If a lead needs chasing urgently and Stafford's team can't cover the manpower, I want you to pick up the slack."

Julie seemed to ponder the offer for several seconds. Beside her, St. Claire remained uncharacteristically restrained, as if he were waiting for the more experienced woman to make her decision before he weighed in.

Clasping his hands together on the desk, Franko waited patiently.

"Okay," Julie finally replied, nodding once. "It's a deal."

St. Claire too voiced his agreement, and Franko dismissed the pair.

He was left sitting in his office, pensively listening to the rotary click of his ceiling fan.

Braithwaite be damned, he wanted people that he knew and trusted on this case. People that he saw potential in.

It took a particular kind of person to stare evil in the face; to be swallowed by black and come back out whole.

Franko believed in evil. He believed in darkness; in phantoms, demons and monsters. He had seen them. The only problem was that they weren't supernatural in nature. They lived beneath the skin, hiding in plain sight. Wearing the meat of decent, loving people.

The problem was that, ninety nine times out of a hundred, evil wasn't born. Evil was forged and tempered through years of systematic abuse. You needed to approach it with sympathy and compassion.

Nicholas had told him that; back when he was a part of the MET's Murder Squad.

He hoped to god that whoever the Cat Hunter was, they weren't a part of the other one percent.

The portion of murderers born with a piece missing. The killers without the capacity for empathy and remorse.

Franko had once interviewed a six year old boy who had smothered his baby brother in his sleep. When asked why he did it, the child simply replied that the crying of the baby annoyed him.

The Detective could still remember the cold void in the boy's eyes. There was no remorse there. In fact, there wasn't much of anything. In the child's eyes he could see an absence. A kind of black hole that swallowed anything that dared encroach upon it.

Even years later, thinking about a person like that sent a shiver down Franko's spine.

Somebody devoid of guilt was capable of anything.

Chapter 25

"Thank you, Natalie. If you think of anything else please make sure to give us a call. Tell your parents the same too, when they get back from shopping, okay?"

David waved briefly as the young girl closed the door behind him.

Walking down the narrow path away from the entrance to the property, the Constable groaned to himself and scratched at the side of his head. Parked to his left, on the gravel driveway, he passed by a red car.

Almost four whole days of interviewing, and they had turned up jack. The visit to this countryside cottage was just another in a long list of dead ends surrounding the mystery of the Cat Hunter.

Rawlings was already sitting in the car, parked just past the heath to the left of the property. When it became apparent that the teenage girl that called the cottage her home had almost nothing to offer them, the burly Detective had dismissed himself and returned to the vehicle.

Glancing around briefly, as he made his way back to the car, David afforded himself a view of the scenery. Perched on the top of a pasteurised hill, three miles from the nearest estate, the residence provided the Officer a clear line of sight towards the far west corners of Lindum and Lyefield. Various designs of houses, from the staggered builds, were clearly visible in coloured bands in the midst of the closest housing estate. If he squinted his eyes, David could just about make out the distant roof of St. Matthew's Comprehensive School.

He thought back to the first dump. The force that had toppled the dominos, leading to his official assignment onto the case.

Twisting his lips, David knocked his tongue against the roof of his mouth as he slid into the passenger side of Rawlings' car.

"You finally done?" Rawlings asked, not even waiting for his partner to lock in his seatbelt before twisting the key in the ignition.

"It's called being polite," David snipped back, quickly fastening himself in as the car peeled away into the country road.

The Detective half grunted and turned down the country road. A subtle tapping sound filled the inside of the vehicle as the side clipped the branches of the shrubs that bordered the property.

"So where to now?" The burly Officer's mismatched eyes flicked briefly over David.

Crossing the Hunt family off of his printed list, David moved his attention down to the next name on the list. "Next is Odette Lewis. She lives about one mile from here... The records we got from the Vets show that she has six cats. Two of them were reported missing a little over two weeks ago. I called ahead this morning to let her know we were coming, all I got was her son on the phone. She hasn't got a mobile. Her son came with her to report it, so his was the contact number. He said not to expect to get much from her, though... She's nearly ninety."

"If she's that old, why the hell is she living all on her own out in the middle of nowhere?"

"Her son didn't say. Maybe she thinks she's capable? Doesn't want to ask for help?"

"Perfect."

"Hey you better be nice to this one," David replied, bluntly. "Honestly, I don't know how you get anything done with the way you ask questions."

"I don't like it when people don't spell things out," Rawlings retorted. "Why should I have to work out what people mean?"

"That's your job isn't it? To detect?"

After that remark, Rawlings ignored any further attempts from David to converse with him. Internally cursing his tongue, the uniformed Officer occupied himself by staring out of the window at their destination. In the background, he could hear the stilted synthetic voice of Rawlings' SatNav. David had long since learned that, regardless of how simple the journey was, the Detective Sergeant could get lost following a straight line.

Aside from the remote location, Odette Lewis' bungalow was perfectly suited to accommodating a senior citizen. Only having one floor, it saved the woman the troubles typically associated with stairs. From the looks of things, the floor plan seemed small, minimising the distances she needed to walk. The garden was just the right size for her to potter around in, without it being too much of a chore.

As they pulled up, David spotted a veranda swing along the North-facing side of the house. He imagined the elderly woman would sit there to read and admire the scenery.

Traversing the paved slabs leading up to the front door, David took a deep breath and hoped that his companion would at least be somewhat pleasant.

Bracing himself, he knocked on the door. Flecks of red paint cracked and stuck to his knuckles.

After several minutes of no answer, David knocked again. "Mrs Lewis?"

Still no reply from inside the house.

"That's weird..." he muttered, turning to the side and indicating the driveway. "Her car's still here. She should be home." Grasping the door handle, he rattled the knob only to find it locked.

"Maybe someone took her out?" Rawlings offered, unhelpfully.

"Or maybe she had a fall?" David suggested, pointedly. "We should at least check to see if she's alright. How about we each take a side and meet at the back? Look through the windows and see if we can see anything. Then we try the back door. If after that we get nothing, we come back later. How does that sound?"

Rawlings huffed dismissively at the suggestion before begrudgingly setting off around the southern perimeter of the house. As he walked, he pulled out a pack of Marlboro Red and sparked up a cigarette. The cloud of smoke followed him around the corner.

Christ, you would have thought I'd spat in his fucking coffee...

Turning to his right, David came up to the sole window that occupied the front of the house. Peering through the white netting on the other side of the glass, he observed a modest kitchen. From the little he could see, everything appeared in order.

Moving around the corner, he passed the swing and looked through the North-facing window. Inside he could see a sitting room, or at least a room that had once been such. It was cluttered with furniture: a dining table, several accompanying chairs, three armchairs and a large old box television set. Mounted on the wall to his right, David could see a fireplace; the mantle above it set with photos of children.

As everything seemed rightfully in its place, David was about to move on.

But then he noticed the smell.

Sickly pungent, it was a foul mix of faeces and decay. The instant it invaded his sinuses, he had to suppress a gag. Cutting into his senses, within moments it was all that he could focus on.

The seal around one of the double glazing windows must have been improperly fitted. Otherwise, the scent wouldn't have leaked out at all. David thanked the heavens for poor craftsmanship.

Hurrying around the back of the house, he found Rawlings absent-mindedly picking a scab concealed by his beard. The cigarette in his free hand flicked ash down onto the ground.

He began a half interested question. "Find anyth-?"

David cut him off urgently as he made for the back door. "Did you notice the smell?"

"The what?"

"The smell — The fucking smell!" David gripped the handle and turned, relieved to find it unlocked. "Mrs Lewis this is the Police! We're coming in!"

"Hey! We can't just burst in without probable- Holy mother of fuck!"

The moment the back door opened, the Detective was nearly floored by the smell. Stagnant and rotting, the odour was so thick it was like the air was filled with tar.

Bursting through the door, David hurriedly looked around the spare bedroom only to find his worst fear realised.

Laying on her side in the middle of the room, was Odette Lewis. So far was she into decomposition, her skin had turned red and her fingernails had begun to peel off. Around the body, the air was rife with the smell of death.

"For fuck sake..." David choked out, tears welling in his eyes. Taking a step back, he gritted his teeth and shook his head. "You fucking son of a bitch..."

Still half retching, Rawlings clamped one hand over his nose and mouth and stepped up behind his partner. "Jesus Christ... How long has she been here?"

"Probably since she reported her cats missing." Turning, David left the room. "Fucking- I... I didn't think it they'd go this far!"

Rawlings followed him back out. "Who?"

"The fucking Cat Hunter!"

Flitting his attention between the open door and David, Rawlings pulled a confused expression from behind his hand. "What are you-?" He stopped short as he noticed something through the doorway. So focussed had he been on the body of the old woman, that he had completely missed it.

Dumped in a pile, on the far side of the room, were Odette's four remaining cats.

They had been torn limb from limb.

Chapter 26

The Coroner moved his hands slowly over the body, probing for signs of resistance. Beneath the skin, the contents moved slowly, like a plastic bag full of pulp.

"She's been dead for at least a week," he muttered, peering through his glasses and rotating his jaw slowly. Removing one latex glove, he scratched the short hairs that clung to his cheek and readjusted the cotton buds stuck into his nose. "Judging by the stage of decomposition, probably longer. The skin has already turned red, meaning the blood is decomposing. And just going off of the smell, I think it's safe to assume that the organs are already liquefying."

"Liquefying?" Rawlings asked, almost making a point of not looking at the corpse.

"You ever seen The Wizard of Oz?" the Coroner asked. "You know that one scene with the Witch? "I'm melting! I'm melting!" Decomp is pretty much just like that. But slower."

The scruffy Detective retched and turned away from the scene.

"Thanks for that," David fought out, suppressing a gag as he clamped one hand over his mouth. "That used to be my favourite movie."

"Sorry," the Coroner half smiled.

"So you're saying she's been here for more than a week?"

"Near enough. If you want a definite answer, though, I'd need more time to examine the body back at the morgue."

Rising from his crouched position, the Coroner rubbed the side of his bent neck.

Broad set and just over six foot two, the Lindum Coroner was an imposing figure that a number of Officers were slightly afraid of. A dull yet piercing blue, his eyes stared out from beneath a pair of thick dark brows and moved steadily. Matching the still movement of his eyes, his actions were deliberate and slow; weighted heavily. As if bowing under the weight of his stature, or perhaps a result of years looking down at bodies, his spine bore a noticeable curvature to it.

Looking up at the Coroner, David squinted his eyes out of sympathy for the poor woman laying beneath them. "Any idea on cause of death?"

"From what I can see, COD was blunt force trauma to the side of the head. The corpse has a contusion along the left side of the scalp, just above the ear. It looks like she fell and hit her head on the corner of the dresser here. Now whether the fall was natural or whether she was pushed, I won't be able to tell unless I examine the body more closely."

A white flash briefly illuminated the body, as one of the SOC Officers snapped a photo to be used as evidence. Afterimages of colour remained in David's vision as he averted his eyes from the exposure.

All around the room other Forensic Investigators, all wearing disposable hazmat suits, busied themselves cataloguing evidence and dusting for fingerprints.

One such Officer, in the process of extracting a print from the doorframe, was brushed aside as DCI Franko entered the house. Over his shoes he wore plastic bags matching those that clad the feet of David, Rawlings and the Coroner.

Darkness hooded his eyes, as if the high-beams of his vision had been set to dim. The clockwork that moved his joints seemed unusually stiff and restrained, briefly planting the thought into David's head that he should have invested in a can of WD-40.

The machine that was the Detective Chief Inspector seemed to be failing ever so slightly.

And then there was the expression that he wore. It was an emotion that David never thought that his boss would have been programmed to have. Grief.

Approaching the lower-ranked Officers, Franko slowly shook his head. "I thought we had more time than this..."

"Clearly we didn't," Rawlings replied tactlessly.

David made a point of positioning himself between his boss and his partner. "We had no way of knowing. And who knows? It might come back that Mrs Lewis' death was an accident. She came home and found her cats like this, and was so shocked she had a fall. Stranger things have happened."

Franko attempted a half smile, as thanks for the effort to console him. "That's nice of you to say." Dark eyes clicked around the room. "But you're wrong. There's signs of a struggle. Here, here and here..."

Following the motions of Franko's eyes, David noted various evidence of a disturbance.

"And if decomp wasn't so advanced, you'd probably find evidence of bruising on her wrists."

"I'll bet I could still find something now," the Coroner interjected, stepping forwards and nodding slightly.

"Well this is a pleasant surprise at least," Franko replied, letting out a relieved breath as he finally noticed the Coroner.

"Don't sound too happy to see me. It might ruin this "hard as nails" image that you have going for you now." The corners of his eyes creased sympathetically. "How's Sarah?"

"More of the same. I'm trying not to get my hopes up."

Noting the exchange, David retreated a step in an attempt to blend into the background. He didn't know who Sarah was, but judging by how Franko had answered the Coroner's question, David could tell that the subject was sensitive.

"So..." the Coroner continued, snagging onto the tether of the previous conversation. "Why do you think Mrs Lewis had to die?" He crouched down next to the corpse and balanced on the balls of his feet.

David watched Franko's eyelids flick closed, like the shutter of a Polaroid camera. When they snapped back open, they reflected Odette's entire form in a crystal reflection.

"More than likely our cat killer was here for the occupant's pets," Franko said, barely moving as he spoke. "She probably walked in on our unsub and disturbed them. They didn't expect her to come home when she did, and panicked. This kill wasn't planned."

"So you're thinking he ran after it happened?" David asked, staring sidelong at his superior. "If he didn't mean to kill her, and was spooked, that's a good sign, right?"

Inexperienced in Major Crimes as he was, David was attempting to grasp at anything even remotely tangible. He hoped that if their killer had panicked then they would have left behind evidence or made mistakes. He hoped that if they had panicked then that meant the killer was still somewhat human; still capable of remorse and regret.

"They didn't run."

"What?"

The DCI's hard voice snapped him out of his train of thought with a sudden jolt.

"I said that our unsub didn't run..." Franko pointed at the pile of cat carcasses in the corner. "There's something off about that."

Rawlings, who until then had been hanging back, with his hand clasped over his mouth, injected himself back into the conversation. "What do you mean something is off?"

"How many cats did Mrs Lewis have?"

David stumbled his words slightly as he spoke. "Um, s-six. But two were reported missing."

"Didn't you notice?"

Franko didn't get a response. The room's other occupants stood in silence and waited.

"They stayed and watched her die... And then later they came back and continued what she had interrupted. There's eight cats over there."

Chapter 27

I've never exactly been the same as the other kids. I could never understand why they were nice to me; why they would care if someone else was crying. It's not that I was incapable of crying or laughing. Not at all. I just needed a reason to do so.

Hurt me and I cry. That much was true.

Laughing was a different matter. I didn't laugh very much. Unless I was told why I should do it, I wouldn't. Because there wasn't a reason.

It's not that I was emotionless. I just didn't see the point. After all, why would you cry if nothing makes you sad? Why would you laugh if you didn't find anything funny?

I realised that I wasn't "normal". Pieces were missing.

That's why I started to act.

It wasn't because I felt left out, or because not being normal made me sad. No. It was just easier this way.

When you are a hollow person, you build up layers so that nobody suspects that you're empty inside.

But when I met him, I found something to fill me. To put in place of the missing parts. He made me feel real; more than just a flesh and blood marionette, responding to the social strings. The first time he talked to me, I felt like I was going to laugh, cry and scream, all at once.

Once a year our school sets aside a day for creative outlets, called Arts Day. It's almost always in June, but that year it was particularly hot.

All of the other students had taken off their blazers, but I had left mine on. It was around the time Mum had started using the fork, so I couldn't let anyone see my arms. I didn't want them to feel sorry for me.

"Aren't you hot in that?"

That was the first thing he said to me.

Looking back at it, I know that it wasn't much. But it meant the world to me.

He was concerned about my wellbeing. Worrying about me. The way that he looked at me with those eyes made my heart seize up.

I could practically feel my pulse come to a stop as my blood throbbed through by body.

Up until that point, the only other person who asked me things like that had been Daddy. But this boy felt different.

I don't know how to describe it; just that it was alien to me.

When I tried to reply, I don't think I even managed a complete word.

But he just laughed off my ham-fisted response with ease.

The way that he spoke was confident and self-assured, slipping easily through my stammers and fumbles. He was a knife slicing through the conversational sea. And it was wonderful.

I had been stood by the calligraphy booth. Mum insisted on teaching me how to write in correct script, so it was the only place I could have gone to, despite not being part of the club.

He asked me about it all, but before I could reply the bell interrupted me, and he went on his way.

But I never forgot it.

The sound of his voice, the look in his eyes.

He cared about me. More than anyone I had ever met in my life.

That's why it hurt so much. Seeing that jezebel kissing him. Pawing at him with her hands.

She didn't deserve to touch him. To be so close to him.

I felt like I had been pulled apart at the seams; spilling my organs across the floor, dousing the ground with acid and bile.

After I collected myself, I knew what I needed to do.

Drugging her was easy. It was just a case of spiking the drink I offered her with sleeping pills.

The hard part was carrying her without anyone seeing.

When she woke up she pleaded with me to let her go, but at that point her words were nothing more than white noise. Even now I can't remember them.

I watched as she licked her lips, as if to lubricate the lies.

So I cut out her tongue.

It's always surprised me just how moist living things are. Little more than sacks of fluid once punctured. You slice the membrane and out it pours; the liquid red. Waterfalling. I never expected there to be quite so much. Never expected how quickly she would bleed out.

I got the duct tape and sealed her mouth, so that she could drown on the blood.

Chapter 28

"Arsehole!"

Slamming her hand into the steering wheel of her father's car, Pru leaned out of the window and swore loudly at the passing silver Honda. The sound of her horn split the air and eclipsed her curses.

"Fucking twat-bag!" she gasped, pulling her head back into the car.

"Jesus, calm down," Scott laughed, glancing nervously sideways at his best friend. "No need to get so aggy."

"He just cut me off!" Pru snapped back. "I missed the junction; you *know* what that means."

"Um, we stay on the motorway?" he replied sarcastically.

"At 5pm!" she continued. "We're going to hit the traffic coming off of the industrial estate. *Evolution* moves faster!"

"Anyone ever tell you you've got mad road rage?"

Turning her eyes away from the road, Pru shot him a hard glare that prompted him to mockingly hold his tongue. Laughing under his breath, Scott curled the corner of his mouth into a grin.

"I catch you smirking again and I'm going to stop giving you dating advice."

"I think you'll find I don't need your tips anymore," Scott said, pulling out his phone and waving the screen at Pru. "Look. Texts and everything!"

Pru chuckled. "Aww. Have you graduated to putting little 'x's at the end of your messages yet?"

"Piss off."

"I'll take that as a no then." Changing lanes, Pru kept her eyes on the road as she spoke. "It's been a long time since I've seen you this into someone. It's nice."

"Look at you getting all sentimental on me."

"I'm what kind of mental?"

"Oh my, you're so funny." Again, Scott's voice took on a sarcastic tone.

"Pretty too," Pru grinned, flicking her hair ostentatiously and gasping. "And smart? I mean- Don't even get me started."

"Sorry, I haven't noticed. Eyes for another and all that."

"Lucky girl."

"Do my ears deceive me, or did I just hear you compliment me? Miracles never cease!"

"Hey, I've complimented you before!"

"Really?" Scott teased. "Name one other time."

Gaining a distant look in her eyes, Pru stared out of the windscreen. A pensive expression plucked at her face. She watched the cars ahead steadily advance along the carriageway.

"It was a Tuesday..." she said, her voice soft and completely deadpan.

His voice vibrating with laughter, Scott turned towards his friend and shook his head. "You really had me going there for a second."

Joining him with a jovial tone, Pru pushed her dark hair behind her ear with one hand as she spoke. "No, but seriously. Do you remember when we got put in the same Form class in Year Eight?"

"What, when you punched Connor Neagle in the face?"

"I'm not talking about that." She indicated and turned back into their original lane. "But he deserved that. He was an arsehole."

"He was also almost two feet taller than you."

"And this is also totally off track from what I wanted to talk to you about." Her dark eyes momentarily moved to him, so that he knew not to interrupt. "Remember Miss Tasker got us all to introduce ourselves to the group?"

"I told her I wanted to be a Mechanic, like my Dad." He thought back to the scene of the classroom. Of the little girl stood at the front, in a blazer two sizes too big, with dark bangs covering her face. "And you said that you wanted to be one too. So that you could work with me."

"Everyone laughed," Pru completed, turning slightly red as she reminisced. "And Jack Burns asked if we were going out."

"You gave him the dirtiest look I think I've ever seen," Scott laughed. "Scared the absolute shit out of him. Huh... There seems to be a running theme here with you and boys."

"What, that I hated them? Well, all of them except you. But... Do you remember what I said after, when Tasker asked me why?"

Scott didn't respond. He didn't need to. He could remember it clear as day.

"I said that I wanted to work with you, because you were the coolest person that I knew."

A dull hum filled the inside of the car as Scott's phone vibrated. Even before checking the screen, he knew who the text was going to be from.

Helen's name filled the centre of the illuminated screen.

"Well what are you waiting for, stud? Gets to replying."

Flicking his pupils over the message as he clicked out a response, Scott spoke over to Pru. "So whereabouts are we meeting everyone?"

"Dan said outside Krispy Kreme's. Opposite the cinema."

Parkridge Shopping Centre lay fifteen miles North of Lindum, off of the third motorway junction (which the pair had missed). It overlooked a number of the fields and valleys and was a regular haunt for the teenagers of Lindum and the surrounding towns and villages. It wasn't large by any stretch of the imagination, but it was the best that they had in the area. Three stories tall, it bordered the industrial estate and housed a number of shops ranging from clothing boutiques to technical paraphernalia, as well as a sizeable cinema. Busses ran regularly out of the city centre to the retail park but were rarely trusted to arrive on time.

Pru had been beyond happy that she had secured her Father's car for their outing.

"Okay, cool," Scott replied. Noting the time at the top of his phone, as he finished his reply to Helen and sent the message, he turned back towards Pru. "We're already five minutes late. Here's hoping Kyle doesn't get into too much trouble when I'm not there."

"You're hoping he doesn't buy tickets to a horror film?" Pru teased, trying to cover her concern for Scott. While he seemed to have forgotten finding the mangled cats, she still decided to err on the side of caution. She had only been half joking about Kyle. The last thing Scott needed was to see some kind of gruesome slasher flick; especially when he had seen the real deal first hand.

"Trust me, in Parkridge he can get up to way worse than that," Scott replied. "Last summer he glued mirrors to the toes of his shoes and walked around looking up girls' skirts."

"That's sick."

"Yeah, but at the same time you've gotta admire the inventiveness of it. Hey, it's at least a bit more intelligent than the time we-"

"-spent all day running up the down escalator, and down the up escalator," Pru finished, chuckling. "Why the hell did we do that? God, we're such idiots."

Joining her in a boisterous chuckle, Scott felt their conversation slip into silence.

Pru was the only person that he could do this with. Sit and enjoy their company, while at the same time being devoid of conversation. The sensation was calming and relaxed, giving him some time to switch off and take some time to appreciate his best friend.

He was glad that she supported his interest in Helen. God knew, if Pru didn't approve then he would have never heard the end of it.

Not to mention, Scott wouldn't particularly want to date someone that she didn't like; someone that couldn't get along with his best friend.

The sound of Gerard Way's vocals punctuated their silence as Pru's favourite album hummed from the car's sound system. Reaching the final track on the disk, it looped back to the beginning and slipped into the instrumentals of the first track. Having long since memorised the beat of the song, she began to rhythmically tap her finger against the rim of the steering wheel.

All around them, the other cars had slowed to a crawl as the northbound motorway descended into traffic. Rattling along next to them, a rust-coated van loaded with metal piping matched their pace.

It was still another two miles until they reached the roundabout that they needed to take.

Outside of her peripheral vision, Pru could hear Scott humming along to the music. Feeling herself starting to smile, she joined him.

The tone changed and the second song kicked in with a heavy guitar riff.

Voices rising, the inside of the car was soon filled by the sound of their tone-deaf duet.

"~Haaaaave you heard the news that you're dead~"

Chapter 29

James Franko felt the thrum of the engine pulse through his fingers as he twisted the key in the ignition. The purring of the car cut short and he was left sitting in silence in the car park of the Lindum Morgue.

A sandstone brown single-story building, it stood at odds to the monolithic buildings of the city around it, yet somehow managed to perpetuate a more intimidating appearance.

Pulling his phone out of his pocket, Franko checked to make sure that it was on full volume. Serious though the case was, if something happened to Sarah while he was gone, the nurse would need to get in contact with him. He couldn't afford to miss any potential calls.

Satisfied that he would be able to hear the phone, Franko slipped it back into his jacket and looked back out of the car window at the morgue.

A subtle sense of dread plucked at him.

He needed to speak to the Coroner; to discuss the findings and examine the body of Odette Lewis himself. However, that wasn't the problem. So used was he to seeing the dead that, much to his shame, it barely affected him at all.

What he was dreading was seeing David Stafford.

So determined was he to expose the potential Detective to the world of murder investigation, Franko had invited him along to sit in on the examination and talks with the Coroner. An action that he found himself regretting.

Franko hated appearing vulnerable. He didn't like seeming as if he needed sympathy. Yet, as of late, that's exactly how he was feeling. The longer Sarah's illness went on, the more he felt as if he was projecting an air of weakness. So he attempted to cover his emotional vulnerability with a cold and hard mask.

David, however, was extremely sharp.

He wasn't sure if his mask would fool him. It had been slipping a lot as of late, so he decided to arrive early and give himself time to prepare.

Locking his car, he entered the morgue through the automatic sliding doors. The rest of the journey to where Odette Lewis currently lay passed with a lucid distance. He could barely remember walking down the hallway or through the doors.

A curious thought settled on him, questioning whether his loss of time was a result of the building's nature. Did the dead, whose time had been stolen from them, regain it by taking that of those who visit them?

The pale linoleum of the floor squeaked beneath the soles of his leather shoes. Momentarily glancing down, his eyes picked out a smudge of rubber, from the wheel of some kind of cart.

Around him a heavy chill choked the air, from the refrigeration unit used to keep the bodies below freezing. A cloud of smoke escaped his lips as he breathed.

Staring past the vapour, he could see the Coroner at work on the body of Odette Lewis.

Looking up over the cadaver, the large man ceased the movement of his scalpel before placing the instrument down. Dark red blood decorated the silver surface of the blade.

"Any news?" Franko asked, pulling himself out of his daze.

"It looks like the government is looking to cut funding to the NHS," the Coroner replied, matter-of-factly, as he snapped off his latex gloves. "Again."

"I meant about Mrs Lewis. Do you have any news on Mrs Lewis?"

"You were right about her being pushed. We're lucky she was so old. Brittle bones. The corpse has cracks and bruising along the ulnas, like they were grabbed. The direction and position indicate that she was pushed. If someone had grabbed her to stop a fall there would have been dislocation of the joints too. No sign of that, though."

"Okay, good. Well, not good. You know what I mean."

"Rough day?" the Coroner asked, looking down at Franko from his taller standing height. Despite his stooped posture, he found his eye line level with the iron grey of the Detective's hair.

"Rough week."

"It's Monday."

"I meant last week," Franko half muttered, pawing at his face to rub his eyes. "Sorry, I've been really distracted recently. Sarah's been in remission for three weeks now."

The Coroner broke into a bright smile. "Surely that's a good thing, James? That's wonderful news!"

"You'd think so..." He ignored the cheer and averted his eyes, opting instead to stare down at the mottled and discoloured body that lay between them. "I just can't seem to settle. The nurse is with her in the days, and I'm still taking care of her at night, but-... I don't want to get my hopes up. Not in case there's another relapse."

Blue eyes narrowing in sympathy, the Coroner removed his glasses and tucked them into the breast pocket of his lab coat. "How about the kids? What do they think about it all?"

"Stephane's just glad that it's gone for now. She's been bringing the grandkids over a lot recently, so that's good at least... Andy looks a lot like Sarah. Same smile." A deep and loving expression filled Franko's face. "Tommy looks more like his Dad, though. He started Primary School back in September. Almost finished his first year."

"From where I'm standing it all looks pretty good," the Coroner chuckled, in an attempt to cheer his friend up. "I don't want to jinx you or anything, but things are looking like they're on the up and up. Hell, I bet Arthur is even visiting."

"He's come over from Manchester a few times, yeah. Back when Sarah first got sick, he took the dogs. Said that it wouldn't help me, having to look after them too. They seem to like it at his."

"See," the large man persisted. "There's nothing to feel down about. Just take things as they come. I'm sure it's all going to work out in the end. Things always do with you."

Franko didn't respond immediately, instead opting to place his hands on the chilling metal of the table. When he did reply, his voice was weighted and steady. "Listen. Don't mention any of this in front of David, okay? I want him focussed on this case, not feeling sympathy for me, alright?"

The Coroner only nodded a response.

Glancing up at the wall-mounted clock, he knitted his brows together and checked the time. "Speaking of your guy, shouldn't he be getting here soon?"

"Not for another five minutes. I told him to get here for half past."

"Didn't want him to see you down and out?"

"In so many words..." Franko muttered, half-heartedly. "I just don't want him getting distracted from the case."

The Coroner smirked. "Sounds to me like you're grooming him."

"What, like Nick did with me?" For the first time since he entered the morgue, Franko allowed a smile to tug at his mouth. "No, no... Not David. He's ambitious; he'll get there on his own. St. Claire on the other hand... He's the one I've got my eye on. It's just a shame he's not the one that caught this case."

"I bet that hasn't stopped you from assigning him to it anyway."

"He needs all the help he can get."

"Who, David or St. Claire?"

The conversation suddenly stopped short as David arrived, pushing through the heavy swinging doors. Draped over his shoulders he wore the provided white coat, and he had already pulled on his Latex gloves.

Despite the sombre and serious mood that hung over him, Franko could feel a subtle air of anticipation around David. He was clearly excited for his first consultation with the Coroner, regarding a murder investigation.

"Sorry, sorry," he apologised. "I'm really late, aren't I?"

"You're not late," Franko replied, stopping him with a calm tone. "I was just early. You haven't missed anything; we've just been catching up."

"That's exactly right," the Coroner smiled. "I haven't even told him the COD yet."

"Oh, okay," David breathed, relieved. "So..." He took a breath and looked down at Odette's body. "What was it that killed her?"

"Subdural Haematoma," the large man stated in a matter of fact manner. "After being pushed, the victim caught her head on the corner of the dresser. The blow to the head ruptured a number of veins other than these around the contusion, causing brain damage." He indicated a deep purple spot on the scalp, darker than the rest of the decomposing skin, above Odette's ear. "She would have seized up within minutes, and died a few hours later. Horrible way to go."

Franko watched the younger Officer's mouth twist into a grimace.

Following on with procedure, in an attempt to take David's mind off of the harrowing nature of the crime, the DCI indicated a number of plastic tubes, set off to the side. Placed onto a steel gurney, the clear surfaces caught the overhead lighting in a liquid glare.

"I take it you lifted some evidence from the body?"

"Before I washed her, yeah. The Scene of Crime lads had already bagged the clothes, but I found those when I combed through her hair."

David grasped one of the cylinders and lifted it up, peering at the contents. "Hair?"

"That's right. And it didn't belong to Mrs Lewis. Wrong colour. It's also the wrong length."

"Could it have come from the son?" Franko asked.

"No," David added. "Her son has grey hair. Buzz cut. This is much too long. And brown."

"So best bet, this came from the killer." Looking back over at the Coroner, Franko nodded his appreciation. "Good work."

"Don't thank me yet. Only one of the hairs has a tag on it. And even then, if their DNA isn't on record, you're one-way blind."

"Still, we have DNA," David said, optimistically. He set down the tube and turned back towards the body. "Which means we'll be able to eliminate any suspects we pull in."

"Come back to me when you have any suspects to eliminate," Franko said, his voice flat and steady. "But..." He took a break. "You're right. And you know... It never hurts to look on the bright side every once in a while."

Chapter 30

Pulling up outside Scott's house, Pru slowed the car to a crawl and checked the oncoming lane, before swerving into an empty space beside the kerb. Rolling into place beneath a recently lit lamppost, the entire car was swathed in a dull orange glow.

Taking her right hand off of the wheel, Pru reached up and started to pick at the corner of her mouth. Remnants of BBQ sauce, evidence of their meal at the Parkridge TGI Fridays, still clung to the corners of her lips.

"Thanks for the lift," Scott smiled, shifting in his seat in an attempt to access the clasp of the seatbelt.

"Don't mention it," she replied, sucking on her finger before turning the stereo down. "It's not as if you could've walked back."

"Well I could have," he laughed. "But it would have taken fucking hours."

Nodding towards the front of her friend's house, swamped with shadow, Pru lowered one eyebrow. "When do your family get back?"

"This Sunday, I think," Scott replied. "Or next Monday. Either way, they're getting back really late or really early."

"Are you going to be glad when they're home?"

"Maybe," he silently grinned. "I'd be lying if I said I didn't miss them... At least a little bit."

"Do you think your sisters miss you?" Pru asked, an ever so slight amount of humour present in her voice.

"A little bit. I'm pretty sure they miss the cat more, though."

"Speaking of..." Pru squinted her eyes and peered through the darkness, towards the front door. "He's laying on your porch."

Scott tutted under his breath and followed the line of her eyes. "Damn him... He'll go out of the flap on the back door, but he'll never go back in through it." Patting down his pockets, he made sure that he had everything before exiting the vehicle. "Little arsehole," he added.

Rolling down her window to wave, Pru called after Scott as he made his way along the garden path. "See you tomorrow!"

"By the corner, yeah?"

"Yeah, same as always."

Stooping to scoop up the cat, Scott heard Pru's car rev slightly before peeling away and vanishing down the road. The distant sound of the engine blended with the muffled purr escaping Louis as Scott slipped his hands beneath the feline and cradled him in the crook of one arm.

Fishing into his pocket for the house key, with his free hand, Scott took a deep breath as he stared down at the ground. As he did so, Louis twisted uncomfortably in his grip, in an attempt to wiggle free.

Turning slightly, to readjust his hold on the cat, Scott's eyes momentarily flicked down the dark street.

Ice licked at the nape of his neck.

Someone had just walked over his grave.

An off sensation knotted his stomach. A feeling, like he was watching a horror film and waiting for the jump-scare, gripped him with a dull intensity.

Scott briefly remembered a September evening, sat on Pru's sofa watching The Haunting in Connecticut. The pair had switched off all of the lights and turned her Dad's sound system way up. Midway through the film, Pru had gotten up to use the toilet. When she returned, he hadn't heard her sneak up on him.

He remembered an uneasy feeling settling on him, in the moments before Pru grabbed him.

The same sensation curling around his stomach, Scott dashed his eyes around the empty street. As far as he could see, he was alone. However that did little to quiet his nerves. Rather, it enhanced them.

Quickly slipping through his front door, cat slung under one arm, he plunged the key into the lock and bolted the entrance behind him.

Even as he dropped Louis and started to remove his shoes, Scott could feel a deep unease welling in the chasm of his stomach. Despite the door locked and latched behind him, he felt as if a presence was lurking over his shoulder.

He felt on edge. Like he was balanced on the edge of a knife.

He felt like he was being watched.

When the cat pawed at his leg, he almost jumped out of his skin. Lurching backwards, he felt Louis' claws plunge through the material of his jeans and sink into his calf.

"For fuck sake, you stupid cat!" he swore, loudly. "You scared the shit out of me!"

Louis only offered a meow in response. He clearly didn't care. Cocking his head to the side, he stared pointedly up at Scott.

"What, you want food?" he asked, not even expecting a reply. "Come on then, let's get you some biscuits."

Moving towards the kitchen, he instinctively switched on every light as he went, illuminating the darkness of the empty house. Echoing back at him, the sound of his footsteps perforated the still air.

Arriving in the illuminated kitchen, he opened a cupboard before pulling out a box of cat biscuits. Setting the cardboard container down upon the counter, he closed the door.

Again, ice ran down his back.

Scott could have sworn that, after closing the cupboard door, he saw something peering through the darkness of his back window. Barely an afterimage, it was gone before he registered it.

Padding slowly across the tiles, he leaned back from the window, before grasping the cord of the blinds and rolling them into place. Shutting out the night, Scott threw his attention around the room; paranoia still clinging to him like an icy sweat.

Heading over to the back door, he took a deep breath and checked if it was locked.

Chapter 31

My whole life, Daddy was the only one that cared about me. That understood me. Near the end, touching was the way he showed it.

Touching made everything better.

It was a way to show how much he loved me, without Mum finding out. Without her hearing us.

We didn't need words to say that we loved each other.

The way that it hung there afterwards has always fascinated me. I always think about slicing it off and hanging it on my wall. So that when I'm feeling sad, I can give it a comforting tug.

I think, one day soon, I might do just that.

Of course, Mum wouldn't approve. Should she discover the decoration, I would almost certainly receive some kind of reprimand.

It wouldn't be the kettle and the bath; that's only for the times when I get dirty or make a mess. She only uses the fork on my arm if I do something wrong at the dinner table.

Probably, I would end up locked in the closet.

Once it's empty that is.

Recently, things have been taking up space.

Not that I've had much time to pay attention to that. I have been much too busy with him.

I have been seeing him a lot more recently. Every time I lay eyes on him, it's like the first time all over again. A tingling burn spreads through my body, every time he locks eyes with me.

Like electricity.

It reminds me of a time only a year ago. Or was it two?

I was passing by a field on my way home from school, when I saw the cows. A dense and punctuating brown in a field of emerald green. I remember thinking about how sturdy they looked. About how difficult it would be to kill one.

In an attempt to climb into the field, I accidentally touched the electric fence. Just like when he looks at me, I remember the pulsating shock ripping through my body. I could taste my fillings.

Completely alien to me, the sensation filled me with a feeling I had never experienced before. So I grabbed it again. And again. And again.

That's how he *makes me feel. Every time I see him, it's like I'm experiencing that new sensation again.*

He's warm. He's strong. He's safe. And I crave him. I need him close to me; as close as my own skin. I have delusions of diving into his mouth and wearing him like a suit; shielding me from the cruel spite of the world.

So that's how I know.

It's not just Daddy anymore.

Daddy isn't the only one who cares. He cares too. He understands me.

And I want him to touch me as well.

Chapter 32

Shifting listlessly against the cushions of his sofa, David struggled to find a comfortable position. A dull throb of pain radiated out from the middle of his spine, ensuring that wherever and however he sat, he would be unable to rest easy. He had been stood up for far too much of the day and now his body was making him pay for it.

Even worse, the freezing temperatures inside the morgue had stiffened his muscles, leaving them tightly knotted and unyielding.

He hadn't felt this worn down in a long time.

David had been thankful upon his return to the Lindum Station. While he had been out, discovering a body and sitting in on the autopsy, St. Claire and Julie had been plucked from obscurity in Lyefield and assigned to help him on the case. The fact that Franko had even considered that he would appreciate some allies left him with an altogether warmer feeling towards the DCI.

Less thrilled with the development, however, were the Lindum Detectives. As far as they were concerned, David's colleagues were just yet more Uniforms sniffing around above their pay grade. Rawlings had been livid.

David grunted and swallowed down a mouthful of tea. "Fuck him..."

He was glad that St. Claire was part of his backup. The younger man had been a good friend for a long time. He could always count on him to have his back, offering the occasional sarcastic remark to add levity to even the bleakest of situations. And dedicated? The word didn't even begin to describe the drive the man had.

And not just in terms of his work. Whenever St. Claire set his mind on something, he wouldn't give up until he got what he wanted. He was like a hound, out for blood.

David could vividly remember his comrade, back when they had first met. It was around the time St. Claire had first shown an interest in his future girlfriend.

Jess worked in the local council at the time, and David had been partnered with St. Claire while Klajdi was on sick-leave. They were preoccupied with chasing a paper trail in the council's traffic department when St. Claire first spotted her. Stunningly good looking, even dressed in the work-provided fleece, she caught the young Constable's attention the second she entered the room, and he wouldn't leave her alone until she agreed to go for a drink with him. He followed behind her, as if tethered to her clothes. Brainless and out of his depth. Focussing single-mindedly on nothing but her.

Much like in his professional life, St. Claire's persistence paid off. The pair had been together ever since.

The thoughts of his comrade's romantic life elicited a smile from David's mouth. It spurred on thoughts of his own love; of Paula's calming comfort.

She was the only reason why he was still awake. Late though it was, he decided to receive her, once her shift was over.

Since his official involvement in the case of the missing cats, Paula had been nothing but supportive of him, urging David on to do well in the investigation. To prove himself capable of Detective work.

If he spent every day of the next few weeks letting her know how much it meant to him, then it still wouldn't be enough.

Snatching back up the coloured pages of the tabloid paper beside him, he thumbed through the pages of The Mayfair Star; the sound of a game show playing in the background, from the television. The local papers had already caught on to the story of Odette Lewis' murder and the national probably wouldn't be far behind, given the sensationalist spin the tabloid he currently held had put on it.

Jessie must have tripped over himself trying to get this printed in tonight's edition, David thought, thumbing through to the page almost entirely covered by a photo of Odette's house. Several police cars were depicted outside, practically framing the blue and white tape strung across the front gate.

As his eyes dashed over the text, he noticed a number of spelling mistakes and false claims. Particular notice was paid to the "grizzly nature of the murder", despite the fact that the police had yet to release an official statement.

Exactly as David predicted, printed beneath the story, the credited journalist was none other than one Jessie Goodwin.

Born and raised in Lyefield, Goodwin was the bane of the local police forces.

Earning fame a number of years earlier as an online journalist, the man had drawn attention to himself through a number of controversial articles "exposing" celebrity misdemeanour. During the peak of his popularity, by nothing more than sheer chance of luck,

Jesse had managed to snap a photograph of a well-known recording artist, engaging in an illicit affair with his wife's sister. He had sold the picture for a small fortune. Shortly after, he had been approached by the owner of a local tabloid paper offered a job writing for their celebrity columns.

Where he truly drew interest, however, was in criminal procedure. Using his new platform as a jumping point, the young man had begun to stick his nose where it didn't belong. Namely in the business of the Lyefield and Lindum Police Forces. Whenever he caught a whiff of any particularly interesting case, he always made a point of writing about it as much as possible; the truth or otherwise.

Too numerous to count where the times when the journalist had inadvertently tarred Officers with his writing.

David's thoughts left the journalist at the sound of his front door. The rustling of clothes as Paula slogged down the hallway, following an arduous shift, reached him in the living room; the sound slightly muffled by the low hum of the television. Expectantly sitting up, he put down the paper and met his wife with a smile.

Paula returned the grin and collapsed onto the sofa beside David. Her eyes were slightly hooded with the need to sleep.

"Long day?" he asked, reaching out and stroking her leg with his fingertips. As he made contact, David felt the familiar electric sensation spark through his limbs.

"Stressful..." Paula replied, closing her eyes and leaning her head on David's shoulder. "Some idiot fell into the wine shelf today. Literally, it was everywhere."

"That doesn't sound good..."

"The glass was the worst," she continued. "And the smell. It was like I was in the middle of a brewery."

David merely hummed in response, not wanting to burden her with the details of Odette's Lewis' murder. In the back of his mind, he figured that if it came down to smells then he easily had Paula beat.

Nuzzling deeper into the crook of her husband's neck, Paula breathed in contently. "Thank you for waiting up for me."

"Well I couldn't miss out on seeing you," he smiled in reply. "Even if you do seem to be dozing off."

"Five more minutes," she mumbled, throwing her arms around him as her laugh was muffled by his broad chest. "You're sweet, though."

Laughing, David looped his arm around her shoulder.

"I'll have to make it up to you tomorrow," Paula continued, sleepily. "Dinner tomorrow night. Not the same as usual, though... Something special."

"How about a pudding?" David asked, not caring much about his blood sugar.

"I could make you a blondie? Salted caramel."

"Is that an offer of baked goods, or are you going to dye my hair? Because I'd prefer one over the other."

Paula finally opened her eyes again. "Either or. Whichever you'd prefer. I think I'd be pretty good at accommodating either."

Crow's feet extended from the corners of David's eyes as he smiled. Broad and genuine, his expression was filled with love. "Is there anything you can't do?"

"I'm really bad at strip poker, and I dance like I'm on drugs. Bad ones."

"Is that an admission of guilt, Mrs Stafford?" he asked, teasingly. "I might have to take you down to the station."

"Take me somewhere else, and we can work it out," Paula replied. Then she kissed him.

Chapter 33

Waking in a chilling sweat, Franko's sleep-addled vision swept across the pitch black of the room, before settling on the dense outline four feet to his right. His brief panic subsided as his ears tuned to the sound of slow and regular breathing. Sarah hadn't woken, even during his stint of restless sleep.

The visions seen in his dream crawling back into the recesses of his mind, Franko quietly slipped out of the bedsheets and traversed the room; making his way to the window, for a breath of air.

Leaning out into the night, Franko stared upwards and breathed in. The sky seemed to stretch on endlessly; a uniform and featureless black.

The street lamp that typically illuminated the road outside was out; something the local residents had often complained about to the council. Franko had once been included in that number, but in that moment he was thankful for the dark. His recurring dream (or rather, nightmare) found its horrors not in the fear of the unknown, but in the terror of the seen. Shadows were Franko's friends, helping him hide from the stark horrors living in his head.

While most of the dream was patchwork — pieced together from information he had gathered later or at the time — the truly terrifying images were those that he had witnessed himself. The grim thoughts and fragments, locked in the recesses of his mind, found form in his dream.

And it was always the same scene.

*

The Butcher had come to London and carved himself a nice piece of meat.

Veal was in season; a prized cut taken from the flank being the prime piece of the day. The Butcher had written it on the wall, lest he forget the order.

The blood, having been drained long before he did his work, did not bother The Butcher much. The metallic smell, however, still clung to the air like a humid red mist. He could almost taste the iron, as if he were licking his own carving knife.

Sunlight glittered behind the blade as he cut the meat, shimmering pink off of the flesh and slicing a line of red through the skin. His hands, once clean and pale, were punctuated with red, and stained crimson.

As he worked, he wrote notes. Letters to accompany that day's orders.

The veal wasn't all that was on the menu. Liver, kidneys and sweetbreads had also been ordered. A loin too had been cut earlier in the day.

A big order, he had to be sure that everything was of the highest quality. His patron would not accept any half measures. The meat had to be perfect.

The sweetbreads were in The Butcher's hands when he realised something was amiss. A slight redness, paler and yet more pronounced than the stain of blood, and a noticeable swelling. Small nodules decorating the organ.

Now Detective Sergeant James Franko stood over the veal, watching as Nicholas crouched close to it.

"Pancreatic cancer," he said, solemnly. "There was something wrong with the meat."

To the side, Dean Price illuminated the worktop with the flash of his camera. Everything was sharpened into harsh, visceral detail.

Swinging his vision around the room, Franko's eyes swallowed the scene. Incomprehensible symbols, painted in blood (now dry and flaking brown), littered the walls. Within the myriad of cyphers and pictograms, Latin phrases jumped out at him. The curtains had been ripped from the rail, most likely in a rage, and every photograph in the room had had the faces obliterated by harsh white gouges. Every piece of furniture, save for one, had been overturned...

And, laid upon the coffee table, missing flesh from his thighs, his organs ripped from his body, Charlie Miller stared up at Franko through dead and unseeing eyes.

He was only seven years old.

*

Pulling another cool stream of air down his throat, Franko closed his eyes and tried to blot out the dream. Tried to stop it from lurching back to the front of his mind, to knock against the inside of his skull.

Not wanting to wake Sarah, and content in hiding in shadow, he didn't turn the light on. Instead, he made his way across the room and disappeared into the darkness of the landing. Franko traversed the hallway and descended the stairs, climbing down into a denser black and almost losing his footing as he missed the bottom stair and plunged his foot into the void.

Catching himself on the banister, he took a second to compose himself. Pausing at the foot of the staircase, he felt the flutter in his chest slowly subside.

Franko moved silently through the darkness, and into the kitchen. The soles of his feet padded gently against the cold tiles, a chilling sensation creeping up his limbs.

He poured himself a glass of water and drank slowly. The cool liquid settling his stomach, Franko set down the glass and closed his eyes. The images of Charlie Miller were gone, replaced now by thoughts of cats. Living ones, thankfully.

The Cat Hunter returned to his mind, in place of The Butcher. He had initially hoped that they would be able to catch them, before the killings escalated into the deaths of human victims. He hoped that the death of Mrs Lewis would be the only one; prayed that it had been an accident.

But he was not so optimistic to confuse hope with belief.

Filling another glass, Franko turned and made his way back to his bedroom.

The space was sparse, yet punctuated with large solitary furniture. Sarah had her own bed, so that her husband's often restless sleep didn't wake her. There was a slight gap between the two cots, so that they could reach across when they craved each other's touch.

Set upon the dresser beside her bed were several boxes of makeup. Even given her illness, Sarah still afforded to look nice.

"If I don't take pride in how I look, how can I expect you to?"

That was what she had told Franko, one morning. She had been weakly applying rouge to her cheeks, to make sure that she still had colour to her face, before she headed to her chemotherapy appointment. His response came easily.

"You'll always be the most beautiful woman in the world."

Setting down the glass of water on the dresser, Franko stopped to smile down at the sleeping face of his wife. Even in sleep she wore the shawl around her head and, given the recent cold weather, it kept her warm in the chill of the night.

As his eyes settled gently on Sarah, Franko's heart suddenly lurched in his chest.

She wasn't breathing.

Taking a hasty step forwards, Franko reached out with one hand to check her pulse. Before his fingers made contact with the smooth skin of her neck, however, a flutter of a breath escaped Sarah's lips.

Franko let out a breath that he didn't know he had held. Relief washed through him like a wave.

Settling down into his own bed, he sat upright and continued to watch Sarah sleep. He couldn't bring himself to return back to sleep. Both out of fear of the dreams, and the worry that his wife would need him.

Franko remained awake, his vision tuned on the dark outline of Sarah. As he watched, he counted the small ministrations of her breathing.

Chapter 34

Scott held his phone under the desk, shielding it from the attention of his teacher as he quickly dashed out a reply to Helen. Not that he needed to hide it. With a few minutes remaining until the start of the History lesson, Mr Smyth was preoccupied with attempting to link his laptop to the projector at the front of the classroom. Every so often, his characteristic Birmingham drawl would drone across the room.

Smiling to himself as he blipped his thumb against the "send" icon, Scott prepared to slip his phone back into his pocket when he noticed movement in his peripheral vision. Whether it was due to his recently acquired feelings of paranoia, or something altogether more sinister, he felt a shudder prickle across his neck.

Alice Goodacre settled down beside him, into her assigned seat, and began to unpack her textbooks and stationary. Elaborate in its disorganisation, the contents of her bag soon littered her desk.

In addition to the chaotic way she was unpacking her belongings, Alice's attire also seemed geared towards drawing as much attention as possible. She wore a short sleeved red and white polka-dotted shirt, and a tight black pencil skirt. Her bright blonde hair had been curled into ringlets and bunched around her head, bouncing as her hands moved erratically about the desk.

As if waiting for Scott to say something to her, she momentarily flicked her grey eyes over him.

It was then that Scott realised something: He hadn't seen Alice at all, since the day of the party, when she had turned up at his front door. He wasn't even sure if she had been at school on Friday or Monday; the only lesson they had together being History on Tuesdays and Thursdays.

Turning fully to look at Alice, Scott attempted to fight the awkward feeling that drew across his nerves, like a bow across violin strings.

"How've you been?" he asked, cringing internally at his attempt at conversation. "I haven't seen you around school. Or at — uh — Tom's do. Have you been sick or-...?"

Scott stopped mid-question as he lost the ability to form words. A bumbling string of phrases, he had done little to dispel the strained tension he felt in the air. In fact, he felt as if he had just made it worse.

"No, no," Alice half stammered in reply, shifting in her seat to face him. Resting on a pile of notes, her hands momentarily trembled as if from nerves. "I haven't been ill-... Well I have. Sort of. I mean... I did go to the party on Thursday, but I think you might have missed me. I turned up pretty late."

Her eyes flicked about as if trying to latch onto something, or rather in an attempt to avoid meeting Scott's.

"Yeah, um... I'm sorry about missing you. I don't know what to say really. I think by the time you got there I was-"

"With Tom's sister?"

Despite the fact that Alice had interrupted him, her voice didn't have an angry tone to it. Or much of a tone at all. Scott was surprised by just how restrained her expression was when she had spoken.

Scott didn't have a reply for her. He sat, desperately wracking his brain in an attempt to think of something to say.

"It's alright," she continued, attempting a light-hearted air. "It's not like I'd called dibs or anything. I was just too late, right? It's my own fault for not making it earlier. I mean my parents are-" Alice stopped momentarily as she caught herself. "It's just bad timing. Naomi didn't get with Leon either."

The change in topic threw Scott for several seconds. Perplexed, he only managed to blurt out a questioning "huh" of confusion.

Alice's face plucked into a mirthless smile. "Me and Naomi had this bet, or agreement, or whatever, that we would both... Well... Both try with the boy we liked, at the party. Like, we'd only do it if the other did. It's silly."

This time Scott's face dropped into a sad and apologetic expression. "I'm sorry."

Alice again attempted a humorous and airy tone. "It's okay. You didn't know."

"Still..."

"Don't. Please." The same half-hearted smile gripped her face. "Anyway, you really like this other girl. And I get that, it's not your fault. Besides... If it really bothered me that much I would have just locked you away somewhere. You know, to keep you away from all those other girls."

Her attempt at humour was forced and strained. Scott smiled out a reply but, again, didn't know what exactly to say.

*

The next two hours passed at a crawl. Whether it was the awkward tension between himself and Alice or the droll and tiring way that Mr Smyth taught his lessons (or perhaps a mixture of both), by the time the second bell rang, to signal the beginning of lunch, Scott couldn't get out of the classroom fast enough.

Hurrying through the hallways at a strong pace, Scott left the building and made his way to his group's daily meeting point. So eager was he to get out of the class, he managed to arrive early, despite typically being one of the last to arrive.

His fast pace an attempt to put as much distance between himself and the stilted atmosphere of the classroom, Scott moved in a listless and distracted way. His footsteps, typically uniform and rhythmic, fumbled in an odd pattern that betrayed the stress jackknifing through his brain.

Avoiding the grass verge, fearing the damp grass would ruin his trousers, Scott sat down on the bordering wall that ran alongside the stairs leading to the Athletics court. From his perch, he stared over the school and attempted to place his friends. He was disappointed, however, to find that none of them were in sight.

Pulling his phone out of his pocket, Scott was surprised to see that he had no messages from Helen. That was very strange. Despite her off texting habit of messaging full paragraphs, punctuation and all, she was always prompt with her responses. Or she had been over the past five days.

Maybe she's in a meeting with one of her tutors... Scott hypothesised, scratching at the side of his head as he slipped the phone back into his trousers.

Leaning back, he cocked his head to the side and stared up at the sky. Solid white clouds, punctuated by whispers of grey, crawled their way along overhead, spurred by the chilling wind that plucked at Scott's clothes. His hazel eyes darted around the grey and white blanket, in an attempt to locate even the faintest sliver of blue.

But clear skies never came. Everything remained dull and muted; a varying pattern of greyscale.

He wasn't sure why, but the sight of the clouds filled him with an odd sense of trepidation. A disquiet that swam through his system, chilling and unsettling him with the slick strokes.

When Scott finally turned his attention back towards the school building, he spied Jack Gibson crossing the grass and heading for him. Usually at their designated meeting point well before anyone else, Jack distorted his baby blue eyes into a confused expression. Lifting his hand in a half-hearted wave, Scott beckoned his friend closer and began to talk long before Jack arrived at the grassy verge.

"You're a bit late today."

"Fuck off," Jack laughed in reply. "You're just early. What happened? Smyth finally give into the stress and leave you with a sub?"

"Nah." Scott scratched at the side of his head. "He actually let us go on time though, which is a change. I guess I must have just walked fast to get here."

"More like sprinted," Jack teased, finally sitting down on the opposite wall, bordering the other side of the concrete stairs. "I've seen you walk; you're a plodder."

"I keep up with Pru alright when we walk in in the mornings."

"And she ambles." Jack unzipped his backpack and pulled out a sandwich, wrapped in cling film. Tearing through the plastic, he stuffed one half of his lunch into his mouth.

"So what you're saying is that both of us are slow, and that's why I never noticed?" Scott asked, playfully.

Jack hummed out a response through the cheese and ham wedged into his mouth.

Scott tutted and, in an attempt to steer the conversation away from why he had been moving so fast, settled into the mundane. "Did you hear the new Angeldown song?"

Shaking his head and swallowing, Jack wiped the corner of his mouth with his thumb. "Any good?"

"It's alright," Scott replied. "Nothing amazing, but it's better than most of the stuff on their last album."

"It feels more like they're going back to the first record then?"

Scott reached for his pocket as his phone vibrated. "Eh, more like a combination of that and the second."

Glancing around absent-mindedly, as he fished out the device, he spied a figure stood outside of the main school building. Static and unmoving, Alice's expression was impossible to read at the distance. Waiting for her own gaggle of friends, she stood alone, phone in hand.

When she moved her gaze onto him, Scott instinctively turned his attention away, to the device in his palm.

The liquid screen of his touchscreen lit up with a chemical sheen, as it came to life in his hand. Swiping his finger across the cool and slick surface, his eyes reflected the harsh glare of white as his messages were opened.

Several lines of Helen's long and articulate response filled the screen.

A comforting ease flooded him, in a wave of content. Their correspondence brought back memories of their time together, of the calming effect of her conversation. Her witty responses to his words.

Even thinking about her brought a smile to his lips. Helen's dark curly hair and olive skin were things that he regularly thought about over the course of his days. Her bright green eyes and sharp features a constant presence in his mind.

Pru had even commented on how much happier he had seemed since meeting Helen.

Scott's fingers danced over his phone as he responded, a peaceful smile clinging to his face.

*

Across the open stretch of grass, Alice continued to watch him.

Chapter 35

David knocked his tongue against the roof of his mouth, as he set the phone down on its receiver. Across the room, lounging behind his desk, Rawlings crumpled up a sheet of paper and tossed the wad into the wire-mesh bin next to the door. Barbera sat at her own desk, fingers clacking away at the keyboard as she typed up some kind of report. Opposite David, taking up the entire south side of the large central desk of the incident room, St. Claire and Julie were hunched over paperwork. Wilson was out of the office on a coffee run, having collected everyone's orders a half hour earlier.

It had been three days since the discovery of Odette Lewis' body, and progress in the investigation was moving at a crawl. That isn't to say that there had been no progress at all. However it was beginning to dawn on David that, perhaps, the majority of Detective work was nothing more than a mixture of educated guesswork and patience. Not that he was adverse to the notion. David's natural patience was extremely broad.

The thing that was bothering him about the slow advance of the investigation was the tension that pervaded the air in the incident room. While he himself was less than thrilled about working with Rawlings, David at least recognised that the man was a competent Detective. His obsessive nature alone meant that, despite his numerous character flaws, he was at least efficient in his work. St. Claire and Julie, however, failed to see that much. They thought him arrogant and slow-witted.

David counted his blessings that they were all currently busy and working. Had they not been, then he was almost certain that there would be some kind of argument. At the very least an exchange of snide comments.

The brief reprieve was more than welcome.

David's eyes moved up to the clock mounted on the wall. It was almost four o'clock. Detective Chief Inspector Franko would be arriving soon for a progress report on the case. Though David doubted that he would be very interested in what they had uncovered and obtained.

The DCI hadn't seemed right recently. Something about the way he held himself and spoke betrayed a strange hesitance. As if he were terrified of finding the culprit, for fear of what they would turn out to be. Because he knew all too well what kind of person would do these things.

He hated seeing him like this. Seeing how vulnerable and exposed the situation made him. By all right and logic, he should have enjoyed it, but something strong held him back. Until that point, he had been far from Franko's biggest fan. He held a particular distaste for him, perpetuated by how painfully human he made him feel. Franko had made him feel inadequate; too bogged down by emotions. And now David was seeing those elements of himself in the DCI. And he hated it.

Once again picking up his phone, David prepared to dial another number, in an attempt to take his mind off of Franko.

He was interrupted when St. Claire reached over the table and tapped him on the forearm.

"What's this I'm seeing about a missing girl?" he asked, squinting his eyes and pointing down to the sheet of paper in front of him.

"Maybe missing," David corrected, putting down the phone. "Rawlings," he nodded his head towards the burly Detective, "thinks that our cat killer dumped the cats on the train tracks to stop the trains. To get someone on their own. Because nobody really travels out from Lyefield station."

St. Claire knitted his brows together. "Right?"

"When we got there, the station attendant told us that there had been a girl on the platform," David continued. "One minute she was there, and the next she wasn't. He said that a car might have picked her up, but he couldn't be sure what kind."

Holding one hand up in front of his mouth, St. Claire rested his elbow on the table and hummed pensively.

"But..." David leant back in his chair and folded his arms over his broad chest. "Because no one has been reported missing, and because we couldn't get an accurate description of the girl, we haven't been able to follow it up."

"Don't you think it's strange?" St. Claire suddenly asked.

"Don't I think what's strange?" David repeated back.

"That there haven't been any missing cats reported in the past six days. The cats in Mrs Lewis' house were killed more than a week before you found her body; the same with her. So why... Why hasn't our perp been active since last Friday, when they made the dump on the train tracks?"

"You think something is keeping them busy?" David asked, lifting an eyebrow. "Like our missing girl?"

St. Claire nodded. "That or they've gotten bored and given up."

"No. No, not this one... He wouldn't get bored. If anything, he'd escalate. Try his hand at something more dangerous."

"Like a person," Rawlings said, from across the room.

Fishing into the satchel next to his desk, the Detective Sergeant pulled out a tangerine and started to peel the fruit. As he spoke, he slipped wedges into his mouth.

"Things like this are either a slow build, or they escalate quickly."

"But they already killed Odette Lewis," St. Claire replied. "They can't really escalate more than that."

"That was an accident," Rawlings said, picking a fleck of white membrane out of his beard. "The next one won't be. Plus... Something's keeping him occupied. I'd wager it's the girl that's missing."

"So you're sure someone is actually missing?" the Lyefield officer asked.

"No solid evidence yet," the burly man replied. "But that's not to say he didn't use the cats on the tracks for something. And, like I said to David... It's what I'd do."

David watched as St. Claire eyed Rawlings cautiously. The way that the large man spoke often gave credence to the idea that, had he not been a police officer, Rawlings would have made a pretty good criminal.

"Not much we can do about it though," he continued. "Not until we at least have a missing person's case to go off of."

Caught in the middle of a half-hearted sigh, David heard Wilson breeze into the office through the door behind him.

"Good afternoon gentlemen." He nodded at Babs and Julie. "Ladies." Setting down the cardboard cup holder, he began to dish out the coffees. "Anyone want to bring me up to speed?"

His light-hearted tone elicited a grunt from Rawlings, as he grabbed his beverage. "Fuck off Wilson."

St. Claire had to fight back the urge to laugh. His distaste for the two men was so strong that he was left teetering in the middle of a comedic limbo.

Noting his friend almost literally biting his tongue, David stifled a chuckle. It wasn't often that he saw St. Claire holding back from speaking his mind. Even in front of Franko, the young Constable was strangely loose with his words. His sarcasm was biting, to the point that many often misunderstood it as being mean-spirited.

David figured that the only reason why St. Claire hadn't so much as said "boo" to the Detectives was to ensure that they would be able to work together without issue. Arguments did very little for work ethic, even less so considering they were visitors in the Lindum station.

"I've got a question," Julie said, raising one knobbled and boney finger. Until that point, she had stayed silent for most of the day. Even as she spoke, her eyes remained fixed to the page in front of her.

Wilson sipped his coffee and wiped the corner of his mouth. "Go on."

"Don't you get smart with me," Julie snapped, finally looking up and locking eyes with the young man. "I'm not above giving you a smack 'round the 'ed."

While St. Claire at least had to good grace to restrain his tongue, the same could not be said of Julie.

Wilson recoiled from the sharp tone and grimaced out an apology.

"That's better," she continued, returning her attention to the paper set down on top of the table. "Now... What I had a question about was this boy. Scott... Willard."

"Who?" David asked, leaning over the table and peering at the paperwork.

"It says here that he was the one that found the first dump site."

"What, at the school?" Wilson walked up behind the elderly woman and looked down over her shoulder at the photo of a young man paperclipped to the corner of the documents. "Oh, I remember this kid. I think... Joshua interviewed him about what he saw."

"Did no-one do a follow up interview with him?" Julie asked, bluntly.

Pulling up another tab onto her screen, Babs began to quickly trawl through the witness statements. "I'm sure we did. We chased up the IT Technician, and the Caretaker..." Her pupils bounced across the page. "The Teacher..."

"Well?" The older woman raised her voice and called over at the female Detective.

"It's not here..." Babs hummed. "That's strange. Maybe he just slipped through the cracks. I mean we have been pretty swept off of our feet lately, what with the other dump on Friday, and the body on Monday."

"Yes but it's Thursday now," Julie snapped.

"Why does it even matter?" Rawling asked, finishing his tangerine and pulling a face.

"Because... Doesn't this here seem a bit odd to you?" Her finger settled onto a line of handwritten text. "The place where the cats were dumped is a blind spot from everywhere in the school, except for this one window which is right on top of it. The window also only has the blinds closed when that specific Teacher uses the room... Which is for exactly one hour, once a week."

"Yeah, so what's your point?" Rawlings muttered gruffly. "All that lets us know is that the Cat Hunter knows the school and the routine. Something we already knew."

"This Scott boy," Julie continued. "He said in his statement that every Wednesday, he is always the one that opens the blinds."

Realising what Julie was getting at, David opened both of his eyes wide. "You're thinking if the perp scoped out the site beforehand, maybe the boy noticed something!"

"And he might not even know it."

It was at that moment that Detective Chief Inspector Franko entered the incident room. Mechanically closing the door behind him with a slow and practiced motion, the slow grind of gears rolled out of his clockwork joints. His mahogany eyes were red and bloodshot from lack of sleep.

"I hope you all have something for me," he said.

Chapter 36

Scott was half dozing in front of his television set when the doorbell snapped his eyelids open. He felt a heavy weight on his chest and glanced down to find Louis asleep just under the well beneath his Adam's apple. Swearing under his breath, he slowly moved his hands up before rapidly grabbing the cat and scooping it off of him; terrified of the feline's claws.

Ambling to the entryway of the house, he rubbed his eyes and peered through the dimming afternoon light as he opened the door. What he was met with was not what he expected.

Stood in the alcove of Scott's porch was a man in a grey suit. Broad and rugged, he had close-cropped hair and a friendly face, offset by a blunt nose. Either side of his head, his ears were slightly puffy; evidence of years playing rugby. At a guess, Scott placed him in his mid to late thirties.

"Scott Willard?" the man asked, probing for the name as he leant in towards the entrance to the house.

"That's me," he confirmed, keeping his hand on the door handle beside him. "Who are you?"

The man broke into a friendly and charismatic smile. It was the kind of self-assured grin that the captain of a sports team would wear when recruiting new players. "My name is David Stafford, I'm an officer with Lyefield—sorry, Lindum— Police."

Scott's mind lurched with the memory of blood. Mutilated cat corpses momentarily dominated his vision; the sight of the single cloudy eye staring up at him.

"Is this about the cats?" he asked, hesitantly.

David noticed the wavering in Scott's expression and switched his own to a more sympathetic face. "Yes, it is. I'm sorry for springing this on you all of a sudden, but there was something that I wanted to check with you. And I figured you wouldn't want to come all the way down to the station just to answer a few questions."

"Yeah that makes sense," Scott muttered. "Um, did you want to come in?"

"Is that okay?" David asked, leaning in and peering around the entryway. "I don't want to interrupt anything."

"Don't worry," the young man replied, beckoning him inside. "I wasn't in the middle of anything, and my family are away at the moment."

Closing the door behind him, David cocked his head to the side. "On holiday?"

"Yeah, my parents and my sisters."

"I hope you haven't been left on your own too long," David joked with a smirk. Pulling his hands out of his pockets, he followed the boy down the hallway and into the living room. "When are they back?"

"Sunday or Monday, I can't remember which. It's either late at night or early in the morning." Scott sat down on the sofa and directed the Officer to the armchair on the opposite side of the room. Leaning forwards, he rested his forearms on his knees. "So what was it you wanted to ask me? I'm more than happy to help in any way I can."

"Thank you, I'm sure you will." David again smiled, however this time it seemed far more sincere. Scott felt himself instinctively relax.

Lifting his hands, David wrung his digits together and took a breath. His eyes set solid beneath his brow and behind his irises, Scott could see him thinking through the questions; deciding which to ask first.

"You said in your statement that you always open the blinds, after your lesson with Mr Hemming. Is that right?"

"Yeah, that's right. We're usually in a different room, but on Wednesdays we change. So because it's only one period, he always just shows video clips."

"And the blinds are closed because...?"

"His projector isn't too good, and the light from the window ruins the image. So he shuts the blinds."

"Do many people know this?" David asked, again leaning in towards the boy.

"Most people that take psychology, and quite a few teachers. But other than that, not really."

The Officer placed his elbows on his knees and steepled his fingers under his nose. His eyes stared off at nothing in particular, as he thought through the information Scott had given him.

"And you always help him after the lesson?" he asked, suddenly.

"Yeah."

"*Always?*" David repeated, emphasising the word.

"Yeah, every week. I have a free next period, and Hemming is usually in a rush, so I do things to help him out. Open the blinds, pack up the projector. Those sort of things."

"Okay, okay..." David once again gained the same faraway expression to his face as he thought.

Watching the Officer think things through caused Scott's own thoughts to jump back to something that had bothered him, the day that he had discovered the cat corpses: The note passed through his door. He wondered why it had been delivered on that day; who had delivered it; what the "present" it referred to was. A disquieting unease rippled through his stomach.

Just as he was about to raise his concerns with the Officer, David spoke and interrupted his train of thought.

"All of those times you closed the blinds, did you ever see anything strange?" he asked. "Anything at all. It could be something small, or something you felt didn't mean anything at the time. It might be you saw someone hanging around the area that shouldn't have been there, maybe even a feeling you remember having. Can you remember anything like that?"

Distracted from his prior unease, Scott lost himself in thought. He tried to think of anything at all that stood out about the brief instants in which he opened the blinds of the classroom, but consistently drew blanks.

"No, no... Nothing that I can-"

He stopped short as he suddenly latched onto a memory. Like a single loose thread jutting out from a neatly-sewn shirt. Once he noticed it, it remained prominent in his mind, and was impossible to ignore. Tugging on the thought, his memories began to unravel.

"Wait... It might be nothing, but... There is one thing I remember."

"That's good," David smiled, in response. "Anything— everything can be of help."

"Well, one time I rolled up the blinds, the same as usual... And there was someone out there."

"And that's strange?"

"Yeah... Yeah. You can only really get to that spot if you go through the bushes that run alongside the fence. It's right at the edge of the school grounds too, and the field is on the opposite side. So kids don't go there."

His interest piqued, David made no effort to hide the intrigue on his face. "Do you remember what this person looked like?"

"It was a girl," Scott replied. "I remember the long hair... Not much else though. They were mostly covered by the trees, and they ran away before I got a good look... Plus... This was like two months ago."

"Can you remember the hair colour at least?" David prompted.

Scott squinted his eyes, as he attempted to pull detail out of the memory. All he found, however, was the vague image of a shape darting through the bushes.

Disappointment etched onto his face, Scott apologised. "Sorry, I can't remember."

"That's okay." David's mouth wound into a sympathetic expression. "Even what you've told me today is helpful. Anything, no matter how little it may seem, can always help."

Scott smiled back and averted his eyes, turning them towards the door. With a start, he flustered briefly and rose to his feet. "Sorry, sorry, I should have asked earlier. Did you want a cup of tea or something? Coffee?"

The officer laughed and sat back in the armchair. He was caught out by the boy's politeness; not expecting a teenager to be that welcoming. "Uh, yes. Tea will be fine, thank you."

"Actually," Scott said, as he moved for the door. "I'm sorry if this is asking a bit much, but there's something I'm a bit worried about. I was wondering if you could take a look at it and tell me what you think."

His interest piqued, David stood and followed the young man out to the kitchen. "Sure, what is it?"

"Sorry if it's nothing," Scott said, picking up the neatly folded piece of paper from the worktop, "but I got this letter through my door last Wednesday. It had my name on it, but no stamp... So someone must have come here and posted it themselves."

Taking the clean white sheet, David unfolded it and examined the neatly looping handwriting. The script was impressively written; something that he took note of. As he read, a vague flutter of familiarity gripped him, as if he had seen the peculiar writing style before. However, gone in an instant, he brushed off the feeling of recognition. "I don't see anything out of the ordinary," he admitted. "Secret admirer? Young lad like you must have all the girls after him."

Scott smiled bashfully as the statement prompted his thoughts to return to Helen. Despite the pleasant thought, however, the nature of the note still left him feeling uneasy.

"I don't know... Barely anyone at school knows my address. And... I guess because I got it the same day I found the cats, it just made me nervous. Like I said, it's probably nothing."

Despite voicing his assurance of an overreaction on his part, Scott still couldn't shake the nervous feeling in his stomach. He hoped that telling the Officer would at least help settle his concerns. Even if it only resulted in David telling him that he was being paranoid.

However, instead of rebuking his nervous concern, the Officer gave him advice.

"If your intuition is telling you something, then trust it," he said. "Then if something comes of it, at least you were prepared. And if not, at least you get a pleasant surprise." David set the note down on the dining table in the middle of the room, as Scott put the kettle on to boil. "Now I'm not saying you definitely need to be worried. But if you do feel like you need help with anything, just give us a call. Okay?"

Scott broke into a grin. "I thought it was the Police's job to reassure people. You basically just told me to watch out for stalkers. And call 999 if I get too scared."

"Well I'm not exactly on the clock at the moment," David chuckled. "And I did tell you not to be worried. I just gave you a bit of sound advice."

Pouring the boiling water into the two mugs, Scott stirred in the teabags and moved for the sugar pot. "Milk and sugar?" he asked, over his shoulder.

"One and a little bit of milk," David replied.

As he finished the tea, Scott handed the mug to David and continued the conversation. "So intuition... Is that why you're here, asking me about the cats after hours?"

"Something like that," David said, sipping the brew. "I guess it's the reason why I'm on this case in the first place."

The way the older man spoke belied the true nature of his work. It was something bigger than what Scott had seen at the school. He could see it in David's face and the way that he held himself when talking about the case.

"It's more than just the cats at the school, isn't it?"

"You could say that," David replied, setting his mug down on the kitchen table, beside the note. "There have been some... strange things happening recently."

"And you're trying to find out why?"

"As best I can," he said, with a grin.

Drinking from his own mug, Scott peered over the rim and again studied the Officer's expression. This time, he saw something else. A fierce determination that gripped every feature of his face.

The silence of the room was suddenly cut by the vibrating of David's phone. Pulling it out of his pocket, he inspected the message and smiled.

"If you don't mind, I'd like for you to come to the Station tomorrow," David continued, turning his attention back to Scott. "After you finish school. Just to fill out an official statement, with everything we spoke about tonight. And anything else you might remember, in the meantime."

"Yeah, yeah, that's fine," Scott replied, setting down his tea and leaning back against the worktop.

Pulling a card out of his pocket, David handed it to Scott. "And if you need anything, or come up with anything after that, then give me a call. Alright?"

Scott nodded and placed the business card down on the worktop behind him.

Leaving the mug still half full of tea on the dining table, David smiled and excused himself. "Sorry for interrupting your night. I've got to get going now; the wife is waiting up for me. Thank you for the tea."

"Don't mention it," Scott replied, following him to the door.

"And again... If you need anything, make sure to use that number. Okay?"

Scott smiled and waved the Officer off. "Thank you. I will."

Waiting until David had gone, Scott watched the older man clamber into his car and drive off into the gloom of the afternoon.

The meeting with the Officer had been strange and sudden, catching him completely off-guard. He didn't expect the police to follow up on the incident with the cats. Didn't expect to have the memories of the mutilated corpses dredged up again.

Then there was the memory of the girl vanishing through the bushes. Something about it seemed strangely familiar. Despite the fact he had not seen the girl's face, or even managed to distinguish her hair colour, Scott felt like he recognised her. However, that could have just been his mind playing tricks on him for all he knew.

As the red brake lights of the car vanished with the distance, Scott turned back on himself and moved to close the door behind him.

Movement flashed in his peripheral vision.

Quickly whipping his head around, he tried to place the origin of the shadow, but it was far too fast to distinguish. Just like when Pru had dropped him home on Monday night, he felt a shiver run down his spine. Bolting back into the house, he locked the door behind him.

For a brief instant, he considered calling David and asking him to come back.

Grinding his teeth together, Scott cursed himself for feeling so vulnerable and banished the thought from his mind.

He walked to the kitchen and turned the business card upside down.

Chapter 37

Friday morning broke slowly, the grey light seeping through the clouds and settling on Lindum in a hazy blanket. A fog had formed in the hills during the night, crawling down through the housing estate and lingering in the streets, covering everything in a grim layer of damp.

Scott felt the moisture clinging to his clothes as he left his house and locked the door behind him. Beads of dew formed in the strands of his hair as he walked, and cold prickled between the goosebumps on his arms. Traversing the pavement, his feet danced around the newly-formed puddles, in an effort to save his trouser legs from the water.

His watch, the face filmed with a layer of condensation, told him that he was running on time — the same as every other day.

Looking up from his wrist, his attention swept the street, identifying a number of students wearing the uniform of his school. Two boys walked side-by-side on the opposite side of the road, passing by a girl busy taking a picture of herself with her phone, while ahead of him another boy walked along, with his hands stuffed into his pockets.

As he walked, Scott thought about his meeting with David Stafford the night before. Despite agreeing to head to the Police Station after school, he felt a strange sense of hesitation towards the prospect. While he did want to be of help in any way that he could, something held him back from wanting to go. Perhaps it was the prospect of reliving the memory yet again.

Not wanting to talk about what he had seen was the whole reason why he had avoided almost everyone he knew at Tom's party, a week earlier; the reason why he had spoken to Helen, over the plethora of familiar faces. And as such, not wanting to talk about it had, so far, proved rather profitable.

Pulling out his phone, Scott smiled as he identified Helen's usual "good morning" text. Responding with a message of his own, he arrived at his usual meeting place and lifted his hand in a wave to Pru.

Rounding the corner and seeing her best friend looking down at his phone, Pru laughed and jabbed him in the ribs with her elbow. "Texting your giiiiirlfriend?" she asked, teasingly lengthening the word.

"Might be," he replied, finishing the message and pocketing the device.

"How is Helen, anyway?"

"She's good," Scott said, with a smile. "Lectures are same as usual, and coursework is fine. She's been talking to me a lot about things she's been reading, and they all seem pretty interesting."

"That's good to hear," Pru replied, a content expression passing across her face.

"How was your night?" Scott asked, turning the question back onto her. "You and Dan went out somewhere, right?"

"Just to Parkridge again. We went around to a few of the shops; had a look at some things. He's fishing to see what I want for my birthday. Problem is he's not very subtle about it, bless him."

"Did you at least give him some good hints?"

"Concert tickets," Pru laughed. "Not exactly something you can buy in a shop though, so last night was kind of pointless." Keeping her humorous tone, she flipped the conversation back onto Scott. "So how about you? You doing alright since I last checked in? Any strange goings on, or just another night in the life of Scott Willard?"

"I had the police round for a visit... So that was fun."

Pru's eyebrows traced an arc on her forehead, as they lifted into surprise. "What did they want?"

"It was about what I saw last week," Scott replied, scratching at the side of his head. "One of the guys on the case came round to check and see if I'd missed anything. I answered a couple of questions, but he wasn't there long... Wants me to come back to the station after school to fill out another statement."

Pru bit at the inside of her cheek, pulling it in in concern. "Do they think you saw something important?"

"I don't think so. I think it's more just that they want to cover everything. Be thorough, you know?"

"I guess so," Pru hummed. "You gonna be alright? Or did you want me to pick you up and make sure you're safe?" Her voice took on a teasing tone, as she tried to cheer him up through their own personal vintage of sarcasm.

"Only if you make sure not to go inside," he quipped back. "God knows what they have on you. You might wind up in a cell."

"Oh ha ha," Pru laughed, mockingly, as the pair strode through the school gates and formed part of the swarming crush of bodies.

"You know one of these days I might take offence to the things you say about me."

"Get in line behind me," he laughed. "For every one thing I say to you, you know you've got a truckload more."

"I'm afraid I have to plead ignorance on that," Pru flapped, airily.

"Plead anything you want, you know it's true."

"I can assure you that it's not," she replied, half-chuckling. "I am a pleasure and a delight. No idea when I could have said something offensive to you."

"Alright Mother Theresa. Or would you prefer Ghandi?"

"Either's fine. Just as long as you're acknowledging the truth."

Breaking off from the crowd, the duo entered the school building on their left through a wide set of doors and began to move through the hallway.

"So what time do you think you'll be finished tonight?" Pru asked, continuing the vein of the conversation from earlier. "Just so I know what time to pick you up from the Police Station."

"I dunno..." Scott replied, hesitantly. "I don't think I'll go right after school. I'll be there probably closer to five. Just so I have some breathing room."

"So you want me to take you home at six?"

"Yeah, that sounds good," he said, with a smile. "I don't think I'll be there for a whole hour, but six sounds best in case it overruns."

"Well if you need me earlier, just drop me a text."

"Thanks for that... You didn't need to offer that."

Pru laughed and looped her arm around his neck. "I know that. Something tells me you needed it though. Not that you'd ever admit it."

She was right. Never typically one to ask for help, he had secretly hoped that she would offer to drive him home. Not because it was far, or he thought that he would be tired, but because he knew he would need to see a friendly face. Something to take his mind off of the memory of the cats that the statement would dredge up.

"Oh no," Pru chuckled, craning her neck up to peer over the students that littered the hallway. "Here comes trouble."

Wading through the crowd, his thick mop of curly hair bouncing as he moved, Tom Raleigh was slowly making his way towards the pair. Initially moving to meet the young man with a smile, Scott's expression faded as he noted the sombre look on Tom's face.

Typically light-hearted and jovial, he now bore a restrained look of concern.

"Are you alright Tom?" Scott asked, knitting his brows together as the other boy approached. "You look a bit down?"

Tom hesitated as he moved within arm's reach of Scott, and flicked his eyes nervously away. "Hey, sorry if this is a bit weird but... You haven't heard from my sister, have you?"

Scott stopped for an instant and pulled a confused expression. "What?"

"I know it's stupid to ask you," Tom carried on, "but my Mum is really worried. The last time Helen messaged her was Thursday and she's really freaking out. She doesn't text home that much, but it's been a while and Mum hasn't heard anything. I tried calling her myself but I didn't get an answer. Dad didn't either."

"Oh, yeah," Scott flustered and pulled out his phone, waving it about as he spoke. "We started messaging Friday, and it's been pretty nonstop since. I didn't know she wasn't talking to you guys, though. Do you think something happened? I can ask her if you want."

"Thanks man." Tom broke into a slight smile and swept his hand back through his long corkscrew curls. "I figured they probably had a falling out or something. And me and her don't really get on too well, so I guess it makes sense why she didn't pick up when I called." He laughed once, his face finally starting to brighten somewhat.

Despite his assurance, both when they had first spoken on Monday, and just then, that he and his sister weren't exactly close, it was clear to Scott that Tom had been worried about Helen. Finally hearing that she was at least talking to Scott seemed to have lifted his spirits.

"Yeah, yeah," Scott said, punctuating the lull in conversation with a delayed statement. Unlocking his phone, he pulled up the messages and prepared to type out one to Helen.

"Whoa," Tom laughed. "Paragraphs or what. Who even texts like that?"

"Yeah, your sister isn't exactly normal is she," Scott replied with a chuckle.

"What? Helen doesn't text like that."

The statement was short and offhand, but something about it sent a pulse through Scott's body. Almost as if he had gripped the end of an exposed wire. His spine stiffened and his body lurched bolt upright.

"Huh?"

Tom pulled out his own phone and searched through his own messages. "I said Helen doesn't text like that. Look. Fucking emojis everywhere."

"No, no, that isn't right," Scott laughed nervously. "She sends paragraphs. Full punctuation and everything. Has done since I got her number on Friday. Look."

Rapidly, he swiped his finger down and cycled back through the seemingly endless stream of messages.

"Jheeze, you two talk a lot," Pru teased, over his shoulder.

"Shut up," he laughed, dismissively.

"That's really weird," Tom commented. "Maybe she gave you the wrong number and you've been texting someone else? Shit, I mean it's happened before."

"Nope," Scott said. "I watched her type it in and everything. Here, give me your phone. I bet you it's the same number."

The two compared the digits and stared down at the crystal screens of their phones. As Scott predicted, the numbers were exactly the same.

"Huh..." Tom muttered. "I'll be damned..." He looked up at Scott and shook his head slightly. "Never thought I'd see her type like that. Maybe it's something you brought out in her." He laughed ever so slightly. "Either way, it's weird and I don't like it."

"Do you want me to text her, then?" Scott asked, readying his thumbs over the touchscreen.

"If you could, please," Tom smiled. "Even if it's just asking her what's going on. That way I could at least tell Mum something."

Scott nodded and tapped out a brief message. No sooner had he done so, the small tick icon indicating that the message had been "seen" appeared at the bottom of the screen.

However, while Helen's responses were usually fast, Scott was left waiting for a reply.

Even when he went to his Form Group for registration, Helen hadn't gotten back to him. He told himself that she must have had to go to a very important lecture and that she couldn't reply. As of Second Period, he thought that maybe she had forgotten to send him a text back. He decided to prompt a reply by sending her another message reading simply:

Are you alright?

Lunch came and went, and he still hadn't heard anything back. Lost in his own thoughts and theories, he barely paid attention to his friends. Their words were white noise, coming to him as if through some kind of thick filter.

Scott began to grow concerned.

Within the span of an hour, he sent two more texts. Self-conscious and not wanting to appear clingy, he restrained himself from sending any more.

He ended the school day walking home, his phone burning a hole in his pocket, and a sinking feeling tugging at his stomach.

Chapter 38

His feet dragging limply across the path, Scott ambled distracted back towards his house. He walked almost the entire journey in silence, only speaking up and breaking from his distracted stupor to bid Pru goodbye.

Offering him a friendly smile and reminding him that she would pick him up later, Pru waved him off and disappeared down her own turning.

The rest of the way, he barely moved his eyes. Shock still and facing ahead, they were glazed with distant thoughts. He saw things, but didn't necessarily take notice. The pigeons that fluttered their way along the drains, fishing for discarded food, might as well have not existed. The same could be said of the cars that passed him; the silver, black and blue paint flashing by and barely existing to him, save as a reflection in his hazel iris.

The puddles from that morning remained, despite no further rainfall during the day, yet he did not dodge them as he had done on his way to school. Instead of dancing around them, to save the cuffs of his trousers, he instead walked straight through, scattering a cluster of water droplets up his legs.

Finally reaching his front gate, he permitted himself a quick glance down the street. Empty save for the cherry red Nissan Micra parked against the kerb across the road, the street didn't hold his attention for long.

Scott slipped the key to his front door into the lock and kicked off his shoes.

His mind so addled by thoughts of Helen, he barely paid any notice to where he was going, and promptly walked into the banister to his staircase. Swearing loudly, he rubbed tenderly at his side and shook his head.

He needed a shower. Hot water to help clear his head and wash of the nervous sweat that had built up during the day.

Then he would head down to the Police Station and give his statement. Hopefully by the time he was done, Helen would have gotten back to him. And if not, he would still at least be greeted by a friendly face.

He considered asking Pru if he could spend the night at hers.

It would be nice to have a meal not cooked by himself, or fresh from a packet, and he hadn't seen her parents in a long time. They were good people; always treating him like another member of the family. He had even gone on holiday with them, a number of years before.

Trudging up the stairs, and unbuttoning his shirt, he reached for the light switch. As the day had dragged on, the previously grey clouds and fog that had veiled Lindum had transformed into a dense and sinister black. The upstairs windows of his house facing away from the setting sun resulted in almost the entire top floor of his residence being dwarfed in shadow.

The lights didn't come on.

Still half distracted, Scott tried the switch two more times before he realised the power was out.

No power meant no hot water.

And no hot water meant no shower.

Running back down the stairs, he moved for the kitchen. The fuse box was located inside a cupboard, around the bend of the L-shaped room, beneath the slope of the ceiling where the stairs cut into the structure.

As he moved, he heard a faint dripping sound. The steady rhythmic splashing pervaded the air, pricking up Scott's senses. Figuring it to be the tap, he made a mental note to check it once he'd reset the fuses.

Ducking down under the incline of the ceiling, Scott reached out and gripped the handle of the small cupboard door. As soon as the wooden barrier swung open, a pungent smell hit him full smack in the face. Strong and suffocating, it carried a metallic twang to it, like freshly cut copper.

Scott's eyes widened in horror.

"Louis...?"

Hung by the tail, from the right angle of one of the stairs, his cat swayed in the air. His fur drenched in coagulated crimson blood, he barely resembled himself anymore. His legs hung at odd angles, jutting out from his body and bending in ways that shouldn't have been anatomically possible. Bent backwards and twisted almost completely around, Louis' head stared back at Scott through bulging, accusing eyes.

Choking on a breath, Scott felt tears well in the corners of his eyes. More than anything else, confusion flooded his system. He couldn't understand what was going on. How this had happened.

He felt sick.

So gripped by the horror of what he was seeing, Scott didn't register the sound of footsteps approaching him from behind. Soft and light, they pattered over the tiles of the kitchen floor.

He only began to turn when he felt the warmth of body heat behind him.

But by then, it was already too late.

Fireworks exploded in his vision as something incredibly hard smashed into the back of Scott's skull. His body locked up and tensed, the neurons in his brain firing off a burning pulse down through his limbs. Pain roared through his face and red creeped into his vision.

Toppling sideways, everything came to him as if in time-lapse. One second he was standing, half turned away from the alcove; Louis' broken body in his peripheral. The next, he was laying on the floor; the image of shoes dominated his tinted vision.

A warm, sticky, sensation crawled around the side of his face and he realised that he was bleeding.

Attempting to lift himself, Scott felt the strength leave his arms.

Five seconds later, he had blacked out.

Chapter 39

Flicking absent-mindedly through his notes, David attempted to fill the empty space left in the wake of Rawlings' departure. Clocking out at half four, the burly man hadn't even bothered to say goodbye when he traversed the room and left through the panel glass door. Poor at conversation, though he was, the man was at least some form of company.

Now, without him, the incident room was empty. Wilson and Babs were out chasing a lead, and St. Claire and Julie had long since gone home. David was left on his own, contemplating the case and waiting for Scott Willard.

Through their conversation the night before, David decided that he liked the boy. He reminded him a bit of himself when he was younger. More so in confidence than in other personality attributes. Scott didn't mind talking to people, and seemed to relate well through conversation. It was something David had always thought of as a good quality in himself, and was happy to be on the receiving end of it.

Even more positive was the fact that the young man seemed more than willing to help them out in any way that he could.

David was thankful for that.

Other evidence and dump sites aside, he had a strange feeling about the school as a choice of location. It was the first place chosen by the Cat Hunter as a set piece in their horrific drama, and that was significant. Any aid he could gain from Scott could be more than helpful. Even if it didn't seem that way at first.

In an earlier meeting with Franko, he had been told: "Evidence is only relevant if you look at it with the right eyes. Something that seemed insignificant before could turn out to be exactly what you were looking for."

Checking the time on the clock above the door, David placed himself at almost five o'clock. The boy would be arriving at the station soon, to give his statement — if he hadn't already. He considered heading down to the front desk, either to meet him or to at least check he had been seen to.

Casting a brief gaze over the evidence board, his eyes picked out incomplete lines; residue of erased board marker. They were all that remained of the previously erased title.

"Pussy Hunting"

If he hadn't been so invested in the case, he would have almost found it funny.

Rising, he traversed the room and hit the green wall-mounted button, to disengage the magnetic lock. His footsteps rang down the corridor, regular like the rhythm of a metronome.

David reached the entrance to the station in good time and poured himself a paper cup of water, from the cooler next to the reception desk. Due to the overhead clouds, the lights in the entryway had all been switched on, leaving everything with the faint glow of artificial illumination.

Asking if Scott had arrived yet, he was met with a polite shake of the head from the girl behind the counter.

Figuring that the young man must have been running late, he settled down onto one of the squat sofas in the waiting room and conversed with the receptionist, all the while periodically checking the time.

His wait was long, and time passed at a crawl. The forty-five minute wait felt more like several hours. By the time it was nearly six o'clock, David rose to his feet and began to make his way back to the incident room.

Through the glass of the front doors, he saw movement and expectantly moved towards them. Upon his arrival, however, he did not see the young man he was waiting for. Instead he saw a car, driven by a young woman with dark hair, pull up outside and settle into an empty parking space.

*

Prudence Harding swung her car into an empty space outside the Lindum Police Station. Curling her fingers around the key, she killed the engine and lay back, staring through the windshield. Opening the window a crack, she allowed the cold air to wash over her skin.

Pru loved cold weather. She always had done. The freshness of a cool breeze was stimulating and calming to her. Even in the winter Pru always slept with her window open a crack.

Scott had always been the opposite. He preferred hot weather and more temperate climates.

She'd always argued against his preference, consistently stating that it was easier to warm up than to cool down. If you were cold you need only put on more clothes or turn up the heating. Being too hot was a different matter. Worse still, heat made you sweaty and sticky; something that Pru hated.

Closing her eyes, Pru thought of other things about her and Scott that were different. She couldn't think of many. Ever since she had first met him, over her Grandparents' fence, they had always been so similar it was almost eerie.

If anything was different about them, it was how they reacted to things.

Scott was sensitive and easily shaken by things, but when it came to recovering and dealing with it, he was stronger than anyone she knew. While, on the other hand, Pru was harder to hurt. The problem was that when it did happen, she didn't know how to deal with it and get over it.

They helped to balance each other out. To give their opposite exactly what they needed, when they needed it. To help each other through their issues.

That was how she knew, with utmost certainty, that Scott would be able to make it through giving his statement. Even given the mood he was in after Helen started to ignore his messages. He was resilient and tough. Even when he didn't like to think so himself.

Clicking her eyes open, Pru checked her phone for the time.

Having just turned six o'clock, she figured that Scott would be finished soon. And if he did look shaken, he could always come to her house and stay the night. When she asked her Dad to borrow his car, so that she could pick Scott up, he had offered the invitation. Her parents were good like that. They cared. And Scott was like the brother that she never had.

If her parents had their way, then she probably would have been dating him.

The thought elicited a slight smile across her thin lips. Whenever anybody suggested anything of the sort, she always had the same reaction. She admired Scott, and she loved him. But she wasn't *in love* with him. Pru figured that the same was true for Scott. They had a connection, but it wasn't the romantic kind.

Not that anyone looking from the outside would think something different. They bickered like an old married couple.

A side effect of her knowing Scott for so long, and being so close to him, was that they both knew exactly what to do to wind each other up. The one thing she couldn't stand him doing was when he would dislocate the fingers on his left hand.

After an accident in their childhood, he had nearly lost the ring finger on his left hand. The resulting scar was something that he joked was like their own kind of wedding ring. That, Pru found funny. It helped her feel better, despite knowing that it was because of her that he had been hurt. What she didn't like was that he had since been able to pop the digits out of their sockets at will. It grossed her out and sent a chill down her spine every time he did it.

Just thinking of it caused her to unconsciously flinch.

Keeping her phone unlocked, she looked back through photos of them together. In most, Scott was covering his face with his hand, or hiding behind his hair. One in particular made her laugh.

She had used a marker pen to draw "tattoos" down her arm. When Scott asked her what she was doing, Pru had pinned him and used the same pen to draw whiskers onto his face. Before he had a chance to stop her, she had snapped the photo.

Recovering from the unexpected laughter, Pru looked up at the Police Station in front of her. Cool electric light seeped out of the mostly glass structure and fell on the car park, illuminating her car in a pale glow.

His shadow etched into the entrance, she watched the form of a man pacing back and forth across the entryway.

She checked the time again.

6:15pm

"Come on Scott..." she muttered under her breath. "Where are you...?"

Chapter 40

Scott awoke to a find himself face down in the middle of a dimly lit room. The rough carpeting beneath him scratched at his cheek, and a dull pain throbbed across the back of his skull.

As he attempted to lift himself up, he found his body sluggish and heavy. His limbs ached and moved slowly; the joints stiff. It felt as if he hadn't moved for hours.

Trying to raise his head, Scott felt a sharp twinge of pain race across his scalp. Reaching back with his left hand, searching for the source of the pain, he wound his fingers through the locks of his hair. They felt damp and sticky, clumping together and clinging to his digits.

"What is this...?" he muttered, his mind as slow as his movements. "Sticky..."

As Scott's fingers grazed along exposed and tender flesh, he winced in pain.

"Hurts..." he groaned, flinching back from the contact. "Someone... Someone hit me...?"

Scott's head swam as he struggled to right himself into a sitting position. He felt disoriented and vacant; almost as if it wasn't him controlling his own body.

His eyes still not having adjusted to the dull gloom around him, he squinted and attempted to place himself. He didn't recognise a thing.

Fear and unease began to well up inside his clouded mind. It felt as if he were falling, and he didn't know when he would hit the ground. He felt as if he had just tripped over and was trapped in the limbo of not knowing if he was going to catch himself or fall on his face.

Again, pain shot through the back of his head.

Desperately trying to figure out where he was and what was going on, Scott attempted to think through everything that he could remember. He remembered arriving back at his house. He remembered the lights being out. So he had gone to the fuse box, and that was when he found the-

"Cat...!" he gasped. His stomach churned and his throat burned. Vomit dared to surge up and out of his mouth, but he fought it back.

Retching once, Scott bent forwards and held his left hand up in front of his mouth. The instant his skin touched his lips, he was hit by a strong smell. Deep and musky, it carried a metallic twang to it. It smelt like a bag full of old copper coins.

Removing his hand, he peered down through the half-light at his digits and identified a dark liquid shine.

"Blood..." he muttered, as if he didn't really believe it himself. His voice was slow and jaded. "Oh... From... My head..."

The longer he sat, the more his anxiety grew. The fog was gradually lifting from his mind, and the clearer it became the more his terrified feelings built.

Scott had no idea where he was. Nothing about the room was familiar. His head hurt and his hands were starting to shake. His breathing began to speed up and grow ragged. He could feel the beating of his heart grow faster and faster; every pulse of his blood sending a sharp shot of pain through the wound on the back of his head.

This had something to do with all the strange events that had been occurring. The peculiar feelings he had been having; like he was being watched. Everything that the police officer had told him to trust his intuition on. The cats disappearing, the strange note, the seemingly unfounded feelings of paranoia.

Even in such a stressful situation, his intuition told him that much.

As the fear clouded his mind, he struggled to figure out who was behind it. Who would do something like this? His thoughts fell into a void; scattered images and fragments of conversations filling Scott's head. Everything was jumbled, everything was distant, everything was passing him by and leaving him stumped. Everything except the pain that he was feeling.

Almost as if by sheer chance, he caught onto something. Like he was falling into a deep ravine and through luck alone had managed to grab at a branch extending out of the rocky wall. Scott remembered an episode of an American crime show, though he had long since forgotten the name. One scene in particular played over and over again, until he could practically recite the words:

'The perpetrator is almost always someone close, someone overlooked. They're pleasant and charming and when they're

eventually caught, you always hear everyone that knew them saying how shocked they were; how it could never in a million years have been them that was responsible.'

"If it meant that much to me, then I would have locked you up somewhere."

Alice's words from three days earlier slipped through his mind, like water leaking from a faucet.

As he relived the memory, every bad feeling Scott had ever felt about the girl returned full force. Every strange comment she had ever made; every time he had caught her staring at him; every time he had looked over his shoulder and found the girl seemingly following him; the time she had turned up unannounced at his house. All of it led him to the conclusion that she was behind this.

A burning urgency tore through him, racing through his limbs at lightning speed and vibrating, as if his entire body were filled to the brim with bees. He needed to get out, escape the unfamiliar surroundings, and flee. The only question was how. There were no windows, only one door, and given the situation it was more than likely locked. He didn't even know where he was.

Scott placed his hands flat on the floor to steady his swaying body and again felt the dull scratch of carpet. Carpet. Carpeting meant a home, somewhere residential. Good for him; it meant that if he did manage to escape, he wouldn't have to go far to get help. That is unless this was one of the cottages that lay nestled into the countryside that bordered both Lindum and Lyefield. If he was being detained in one of those properties, it meant crossing at least a half mile of countryside before he came across another residence.

Assuming that he was able to escape at all.

He staggered to his feet, but soon felt something hard slam into his knees. Much to his lucid surprise, Scott realised that it was the ground and that he had fallen. His legs were unsteady and full of too much sensation, the loosening blood flooding his limbs.

Gasping in a large lungful of air, he tried once again to stand. He was unsteady at first, but soon managed to anchor his feet and right himself.

Stumbling forwards, he made for the door ahead of him. It was slow going, each footstep taking far longer than it should, but in the end he made it.

Resting one hand on the door handle, to prop himself up, Scott was stunned as the door gave way and swung away from him. Perhaps owing to the gloomy half-light, he had assumed that it was locked. To the contrary, it was even open.

The prospect of freedom fluttered in his chest and gave him hope. Hope that he could escape whatever wretched place he had found himself in.

Slowly stepping forwards into the maw of the blackened hallway, Scott reached for the wall. Capable though he was of standing, pins and needles had begun to take over his legs, and he could feel the muscles starting to stiffen and cramp. Once or twice he staggered, but his hand managed to find purchase against the plaster of the wall. It was enough to steady him. To keep him upright.

It was then, as he pulled himself back to balance, that Scott noticed the sound. Grainy and distant, he could barely identify it over his own heavy breathing. But it was there all the same.

Escaping through the crack of an open door ahead of him, was music.

His senses now returning to him en-masse, Scott's head grew clearer. His feet found their bearings on the ground, and the haze that formerly gripped his mind was beginning to lift.

With the revival of his senses, so too did his hearing sharpen. And, before long, he was able to distinguish the music that was playing.

He knew the song well. It was one of his mother's favourites. But something about the context left him feeling wrong inside. As if the content didn't match the tone.

Now closer to the door, the sound of Jackie Wilson's soulful voice was all he could hear.

The words struck at him and left him terrified.

Because if they were right, then he knew exactly why he was there.

Let me tell ya, your love (your love keeps lifting me)
Keep on lifting (love keeps lifting me)
Higher (lifting me)
Higher and higher (higher)
I said your love (your love keeps lifting me)

Keep on (love keeps lifting me)
Lifting me (lifting me)
Higher and higher (higher)

Thinking of nothing more than shutting off the music, Scott swung open the door and stepped into the room.

There were no windows, and the light fixture in the ceiling bore no bulb, leaving the room illuminated only by a small lamp set down in the far corner. Beside it, plugged into the same electrical outlet was a small CD player (no doubt the source of the music) and a set of speakers.

However, that is not what Scott took notice of.

Dominating his vision, as if it bore some kind of magnetic force, was the chair. Set in the dead centre of the room, it swallowed his attention.

Because, sat on this chair, was a person.

A girl.

A girl with honey blonde hair, and eyes like the sea after a storm.

Alice Goodacre sat facing him, her arms bound to those of the chair by a pair of belts. Red ringed her throat, staining her pale skin and bridging the gap between her jaw and the cut.

He could see her windpipe.

Icy fingers gripped his heart, seizing it and freezing the air in his lungs. The thought of not being able to breathe leapt in his head. His vision blurred and he started to tremble uncontrollably.

Scott realised, to his further terror, that he was having a panic attack.

Falling forwards, he blindly reached out. Clamping down on Alice's arm, he was horrified to find her skin cold and clammy.

His thoughts tumbled into a void as fear overtook his system. Black took over his eyes, and breaths came to him short and sharp.

As if a million miles away, he could still hear the echoing of the song.

Scott blacked out.

Chapter 41

It was only recently that I came to the realisation that I wasn't the only one at fault. I deserved the punishment, yes. And because of that I took it, expected it when I did things wrong. Even Daddy accepted punishment. Whenever he would make mistakes Mum would hit him; much the same as she did to me.

But Mum never accepted when things were her fault. When she made mistakes, and did things wrong, who was there to reprimand her the same way that she did me?

Nobody.

And that wasn't right.

I remember coming home from school, the same way that I always did. I walked through the new housing estate, past his house, and caught the bus at the end of the road. The route had recently been changed, so the journey was quicker than I was used to. The bus wound through the roads of the countryside and swept past fields and bushes and trees. More than anything I remember how astoundingly and vividly green everything was that day. How bright and strong the colours felt as they danced through my nerve endings. Perhaps they knew; knew that I was about to find clarity in everything. The colours were telling me what to expect when I arrived home.

I saw him coming out of the door as I walked up the lane towards my house. His shirt was untucked and he had a smear of pale lipstick on his neck, poking up from out of his collar. I stood and watched as he bundled himself into his car and waved through the windshield. Waved at my Mother, who was stood in the doorway to our house. Her usually immaculate hair was tussled and messy, and her skin was a hot and searing pink.

Mum being home this early was nothing out of the ordinary; she worked part time so this must have been one of the days that she had off. But it was the presence of the man that I found strange. I had never met him before, and I thought I knew all of my parents' friends. After all, they didn't have many.

Waiting at the end of the driveway, I stood just out of view, behind our hedge and watched him leave in his car. Once I was sure that Mum had gone back into the house, and the man was a good distance away, I stepped out and entered our house. Mum would have gotten angry if she had seen me lingering and not introducing myself. It would have been rude. So I didn't say anything, for fear of getting into trouble and having her hit me again.

It was later at dinner that it happened.

Daddy had gotten back from work shorty before the meal and was busy setting plates down on the dining room table. As usual I helped him, not saying a word. Mum always told me that good girls were seen and not heard.

She asked Daddy how his day had been, and what work had been like. I can't quite remember what he had replied with, but I know that it was something mundane. Nothing out of the ordinary.

It was when he asked what she had done that day that everything changed.

"Nothing much," she had replied. "I didn't go out at all, and was on my own all day."

The urge to speak dwarfed my fear of a beating.

"What about that man that I saw earlier?" I asked, innocently.

As Daddy was about to ask what I was talking about, she appeared in the dining room. Silhouetted by the doorway to the kitchen, she was every part intimidating as she was beautiful. Her face was set like stone as she told me there was no man there earlier.

Again, my mouth ran away from me. "No," I said. "I saw him. Why are you lying Mum? You always tell me that I shouldn't tell lies."

She hit me so hard and fast that I didn't even realise what had happened at first. It was the hardest she had ever hit me. It wasn't like all of the times she struck me before. She had always hit me with an open hand, but not this time. This was a punch. I saw her balled fist in my peripheral vision as I fell back against the table.

Mum told me not to open my mouth again.

How dare I call her a liar.

But she was. She had told Daddy that no one had come to the house that day, yet I had seen the man leaving.

I was used to pain, so I stood back up. I told her to stop lying; that I had seen the man come out of the house and drive away. He had waved at her when he left. I **saw** it.

Before I understood what happened, I was on the other side of the house. I still don't quite know how I got there. I don't remember crawling the distance. One moment I was leaning against the dining room table, and the next I was curled into a ball in the corner of the living room. My arms were held crossed over my head, offering whatever kind of feeble resistance they could.

Mum was still hitting me. Punches rained down, mixed in with slaps and the occasional kick. The shrieking sound of her voice was shrill and full of venom, like an injured animal.

I didn't understand what was going on.

When you were bad you were punished. I was used to that. Even when I didn't think I had done something wrong, Mum would hit me. But I had always known, deep down, that I deserved it.

But not this time.

This time it was her that had been bad. Mum had **lied**. *Yet she was hitting* **me**.

Why?

By the time her hands closed around my neck, I was already half out of it. Lucid thoughts swam through my head and I phased out of consciousness. I felt something warm overtake me, and the pain slipped away.

For a brief moment I entertained the thought that I was dying.

It was a nice thought.

I wondered what it would be like to be dead. To have all of your nerve endings shut down, leaving you with only blackness.

I always liked black. It felt cool and comforting.

When I came to, I felt strangely weightless. My vision was filled with the sight of my Mother looming over something, her arms held out, pinning someone to the floor by the throat. I realised with only minor surprise that it was me.

I'd read about something like that before; an out of body experience.

Intrigued, I stood and watched my own face turn the most beautiful shade of blue. Originally I planned to observe myself; to see if I could witness my own death. But what ended up drawing my attention was my Mother.

Her face was bright red, and sweat was soaking her skin. Heavy breaths shook her body, from the exertion of strangling me. The tendons in her neck were raised and taut, like a length of piano wire, and the muscles in her arms were trembling.

For the first time, I saw my Mother for was she was: Human.

My entire life, she had been a persistent and dominating force. Less a person and more an idea. Like some kind of God. It was by her will that I had come into the world, and likely would be by her will that I would leave it. She had been absolute and infallible.

But not anymore.

I saw the frailty of her. How painfully **ordinary** *she was.*

The lie that she had told all of a sudden made sense. She was afraid of being punished, so she had lied. She did it so that she could avoid the consequences; just like I had done in the past.

That was why she was beating me. Why she was choking me.

Because she knew that she was wrong.

I returned to my body when Daddy ripped her off of me.

The pain I had escaped hit me all at once, searing through my body like someone had filled me with hot oil.

My throat was burning, and every breath was a struggle. My right eye was swollen shut, and my vision was filled with a delicious red. A warm and sticky sensation trickled down my chin, and I realised that blood was flowing from my mouth. My side felt like someone had jabbed me with a red hot poker, leading me to believe that my ribs were broken.

Through my crimson vision, I watched as Mum turned about herself and clawed Daddy across the face. She was still shrieking; though her voice was completely incomprehensible to me.

Once she broke out of his grip, she turned back on me and moved to continue the beating...

But stopped short.

An unfamiliar expression passed over her face. Never before in my life had I seen her pull a face like that.

I have since seen that face a lot, and looking back on that moment now, it fills me with such a sense of power that I can't even accurately describe it.

My Mother had been afraid.

It was only for an instant, but it was there all the same.

And the reason why she wore that expression... Was because I was laughing.

I had seen through her. I knew that she was, like me, just another weak human. The revelation left me reeling with thoughts.

Before I had struggled to express myself; to accurately interpret even my own emotions. But the thought of my mother being just like me stirred something deep inside me. It was just so ridiculous.

For a long minute I sat on the floor, covered in blood, and laughed.

Chapter 42

Taking the tight and compact corners of Lindum's city centre with practiced ease, Pru's face was illuminated by the orange glow of street lights. Dots of illumination, from the numerous windows and electronic signs, reflected in her pupils like stars in the night sky.

Overhead, the dark clouds continued to churn and swirl. Thick and foreboding, they blanketed the city and blotted out the light of the moon. Sheet lightning flashed through the gaps in a brilliant white burst, drowning the area in light. Not long after, the rumble of thunder cascaded down from the sky, echoing through the valley in which Lindum sat. It reverberated off of the surrounding hills, bouncing back into the city and shaking the streets. Rain threatened to rear its head in a downpour that would have made Noah reconsider his choice of boat. Wind swept the roads and rocked Pru's car, as it collided with the side, and beneath her hands the steering wheel threatened to be turned off course with the motion of the wheels.

Tightening her grip on the wheel, Pru toyed with the switch for the windscreen wipers, in anticipation of the rain. Her foot lifted slightly, easing up on the accelerator, and her body tightened in expectation.

A nervous sensation radiated out of her chest, tingling down her arms and up her neck, heating her thoughts.

Pru had waited in the car park of the Police Station for 45 minutes, and tried calling Scott three times, before leaving her car and heading through the doors to the front desk. What she was told left her confused and more than slightly anxious: Scott had never arrived for his interview. Attempting to call him again, his phone had taken her straight through to voicemail. Something wasn't right.

Even as she left the town centre, her father's car battling the wind for control, her system was awash with unease.

Not showing up for an appointment wasn't like Scott. Neither was him not messaging ahead any change in plans. If there was one thing that Pru could count on about him, it was his punctuality. She could practically set her watch to him. So when she was told that he never arrived at the police station, it left her more than slightly worried.

So much so that she ignored the turning that led to her own house, and began to make her way towards the road that Scott lived on.

A concerned and motherly instinct welled up inside her. She had to make sure that Scott was alright. And if he wasn't answering his phone, then the only way that she could do that would be to go to his house and see him in person. Only then would she be able to dismiss the nerves that were bubbling up inside her stomach. Only then would she be able to sleep easy.

Moving her steering wheel in a steady and practiced motion, she swung the car down Scott's road and slowed to a crawl. Looking for a space to pull in and park, Pru's eyes fell on the front of the house.

The first thing she noticed was that the front door was open.

That, combined with his absence at the station, and the fact that Scott hadn't been answering his phone, left Pru with a chilling feeling of dread.

Quickly and clumsily pulling into the closest space, she got out of her car and hurried over to the open door. The lights in the house were out. Inside the depths of the darkness, a strong and pungent aroma brewed. Sickly and metallic, like rusty metal.

Pushing her way into the house, not bothering to take her shoes off, Pru whipped her head around.

"Scott?!"

Her voice, normally so boisterous and loud, sounded small and scared. She didn't even recognise it herself.

Her fingers fumbled for the light switch, and the harsh click rattled in her head. The lights didn't come on, leaving her drowned in darkness.

"Scott?!"

This time the name came through clearer. The fear was still there, but now it was accompanied by an urgency.

Pru pulled out her phone, and switched on the flashlight setting. Everything was covered in a pale and milky glow.

As her eyes adjusted to the abnormal light source, Pru took several uneasy steps forward. The sound of them rattled off of the walls and returned back to her, setting her on edge and leaving a chill racing over her teeth.

Another crash of thunder shocked her into a stupor. Her hairs stood on end and her body lurched bolt upright, like she had grabbed hold of an electric fence.

Stumbling once in surprise, she reached out of the bannister of the staircase and just about managed to steady herself.

Her eyes finally acclimated to the light, Pru advanced deeper into the house.

The living room offered nothing; empty save for the television and the furniture.

Something about the empty house left Pru with an instinctive feeling of dread. Like she was trapped in some kind of horror film, and was the unsuspecting victim, unwittingly wandering into the claws of the monster. Another chill raced down her spine, as she took a step into the kitchen.

Clear of any unfamiliar presences, the kitchen was a similar story to the living room.

She was just about to turn and check the rest of the house, when something white caught the light of her torch. Small and rectangular, it was set carefully onto the worktop, purposely centred on the structure.

Her curiosity taking over, Pru walked over to the counter and picked up what turned out to be a business card.

Constable David Stafford
Lyefield Police

Pru's eyes danced over the text, illuminated by her phone, and settled onto the number, inscribed at the bottom of the card.

Maybe this was who he was supposed to be meeting at the Station... she thought. *But then why does it say Lyefield Police, instead of Lindum?*

Moving to set down the card, Pru briefly glanced down at the floor-

-and spotted blood on the tiles.

Under the pale light of her phone's torch, it looked black.

Fear knotted her stomach. She audibly took in a sharp breath and stepped back.

Following the trail of viscous black spots, her eyes came to rest on a wide pool. Just around the corner of the kitchen, it began beneath the sloping ceiling belying the underside of the staircase.

Hesitantly following the stains, Pru leaned around the corner and peered into the darkness of the cupboard.

As she laid eyes on Louis' mangled, hanging form she nearly threw up.

Fumbling with her phone, she ran back to the counter and picked up the business card.

Without a moment's hesitation, she dialled the number for David Stafford.

Chapter 43

For the second time in (what he assumed was) a number of hours, Scott Willard rose from dazed and distant unconsciousness. This time, however, he was not met with the ache that accompanied the movement of disused joints. No. This time, he was unable to move his limbs at all.

He realised, with vague surprise, that he was sitting up.

Scott was sat on a high-backed wooden chair, both of his wrists bound to the narrow arms by a pair of leather belts. His legs, also secured to those of the chair, felt weak. Almost like they weren't his own; the amount of time spent in the sitting position having resulted in all of his blood pooling in his feet and numbing the limbs.

His addled mind, foggy though it was, jumped immediately to death. Seeing Alice in almost the exact same position earlier assured him of that. He was going to die, away from his family. Separated from his mother and father and sisters by thousands and thousands of miles, by fields and forests and oceans and mountains, he would be killed without ever having the chance to say goodbye. That is if he was killed straight away.

If.

The mere concept of the word "if" terrified him. The presence of the word left an entire world of possibilities open to him. "If" meant that there was something between life and death, and Scott knew exactly what that was. Between life and death lay torture. And torture could last a long time; potentially forever. That was the point of torture, to stave off death for as long as possible, but keep the pain.

Fear leapt up inside him, causing his stomach to somersault. The organ felt like it was going to surge whole up his throat; the painful lump cutting of his oxygen. He began to frantically struggle, in an attempt to free himself.

Tears welled in his eyes, and an urgent note escaped his lips in a high pitched keening. Instinctively opening his mouth to scream, Scott had to restrain himself from crying out. Screaming was bad. Screaming meant alerting whoever had him that he was awake. That he was ripe for whatever sick game they had in mind for him.

Swallowing the wail, he closed his eyes and tried to calm the frantic pounding of his heart. The last thing he needed was another panic attack.

Breathing. That was important.

Slow breaths.

The silence around him was agonising. Suffocating and muffled, almost as if Scott was submerged in water. The sound of his own breathing came back at him as if through a filter of cotton.

A dark spot on the carpet gripped his eyes like a vice, and he knew instinctively that the stain was what presently remained of Alice. A lump bounced in his throat and an overwhelming feeling of guilt crashed into him. Anger at himself, that he could have ever suspected her, burned at his body.

Or perhaps that was the beginning of muscle atrophy.

Again attempting to move, Scott rocked from side to side. However, with his legs bound as they were, he was unable to anchor himself correctly. The strength necessary to tilt the chair never came, and he was left helplessly wriggling and fighting against the restraints.

So preoccupied with his attempt to escape, Scott was caught off guard as the door ahead of him swung open. His heart leaping in his chest, he sat bolt upright. Bullets of sweat prickled from his temples.

Stood in the doorway of the room was a young woman.

Lithe and unassuming, she couldn't have been much older than fifteen. Her hair was such a dark shade of brown that in the shadows it appeared black, and her skin was pale and without blemish. Her jaw was sharp and defined, cutting the air like the edge of a knife. The blade of her chin pointed down narrowly, giving her face a distinctly heart-like shape. And, set beneath a pair of thin and elegant brows, eyes tombstone grey flicked over Scott's face, beadily alive to his reactions.

The most striking thing about her appearance, however, was not any defining feature that she bore. No. What struck Scott the most, was that he knew her.

In fact, he saw her every day.

The girl who stood across the road from his house, every single morning. He had always assumed that she was waiting for her friends. But now he knew different. Now he was sure. She had been waiting for *him*.

He recalled a scene. The school Arts Day.

A younger girl was stood by the calligraphy booth. Despite the sweltering weather, she still wore her blazer. Discomfort clung to her in much the same way as her own perspiration. And yet she didn't discard it. Rather she was clinging to it, like she didn't want to take it off. Scott remembered thinking that she looked sad. He remembered the way that she had smiled, when he spoke to her. It looked wrong, almost as if she didn't quite know how it was done. But he could tell that she appreciated it all the same: The fact that he had stopped to talk. Like she needed it.

Smiling in the same curious manner as she had done when they first met, the girl cocked her head to the side.

"Hello Scott," she said, her voice cracking as if from lack of use.

His mouth lost the words. Information overloaded his brain, wiping out his ability to speak. In Scott's mouth, his tongue had turned to mush.

"Sorry," the girl continued, laughing in a practiced and calculated motion. "I never told you my name, did I? This is really embarrassing; I mean I know so much about you and you don't really know anything about me."

Kneeling down in front of the chair, she moved her face close to his and stared deep into his eyes.

"I'm Natalie. Natalie Hunt."

He caught her name, but was still too distracted to respond. Now that Natalie was up close to him, his nose caught whiff of a strange scent. Sharp and acidic, it overtook his senses.

"I am sorry that I had to do this," Natalie said, knitting her brows together in a showy display of empathy. "I just... You came home early and- No... No that isn't right. I turned the power off so that you would find my present. I think I must have panicked. Or I got too excited." She began to babble, as if unsure of her own words. Still practically nose-to-nose with Scott, her eyes gained a peculiar distance to them, as if she were viewing her memories in real time. "I think I just wanted to be alone with you. To take you back to my house. That's what you do with boys you like. That's what Daddy told me, at least. And today... Today is special."

"You like me?" Scott finally managed to utter, the words cracking past his lips. His throat was dry from lack of use, his voice coming through half-formed and weak.

"A lot," Natalie replied, her pupils once again finding focus and tuning to his face. "For a long time."

Standing, Natalie turned away from him and closed the door. Fiddling with the light switch mounted beside it, she hesitated before flicking on the lights.

His eyes adjusting to the sudden illumination, Scott's vision settled on Natalie's attire for the first time. She was wearing a black t-shirt, and jeans of a similar colour. Dark stains swiped across the thighs of her trousers, from where she had wiped something off of her hands.

He noticed a red stain along the side of her right pinkie.

"You're bleeding...?" Scott said, before he could catch himself.

Following Scott's line of sight, Natalie lifted her hand and inspected the blood.

"It's not mine," she replied, simply.

The dismissive way that she spoke left him with a sick feeling as he remembered Alice, bound to the chair, with her throat slit. Again, he fought back the urge to throw up.

"Alice's?"

There was an urgency to his voice that belied his fear.

Natalie's face ticked noticeably. She hadn't expected his use of the name. It didn't fit with her quixotic hopes for their meeting.

She moved faster than he expected her to. Lunging across the room, the small girl struck him hard across the face with the back of her hand. Despite her small stature, the swing carried far more force than Scott had anticipated, his head shocking backwards and bouncing atop his neck.

Tasting blood on his tongue, Scott realised that she had hit him hard enough to tear his cheek against his teeth. He needed to be careful with what he said. Given the situation, and her sudden outburst, even the slightest thing he said wrong could result in something much worse.

Again, the image of Alice's bloody throat flashed into his mind.

"It's cat blood," Natalie said, her voice mellifluous and pleasant. Her expression returned to its former calm, yet somewhat calculated, state.

In an attempt to placate her, Scott played along. "From my present?" he asked.

Just saying it made him feel disgusting. It brought back memories of the note, passed through his door. Made him think of how she must have dumped the corpses at the school, as some kind of perverse gift to him. And done the same with Louis.

Scott felt sick. The sensation like maggots crawling under his skin returned, the sparse contents of his stomach churning violently. Scott had always liked cats. Something about remembering them and knowing that they must have been in a situation mirroring his own disturbed him far more than it had done before.

It occurred to him, peculiarly, that maybe Natalie liked cats as well. Well... Parts of them, at least.

Either not seeing the nausea that had twisted itself around Scott's mouth, or choosing to ignore it, Natalie brightened noticeably. "Yes! Though I'm going to have to go and get some more soon. I really want you to try it yourself. It's just... Something about it. I can't even describe it."

Striding back over towards him, she hesitated for a brief second, before nervously easing herself down to sit on his lap. Feeling the warmth of her legs on his own, Scott shifted his position as best he could. He found himself thinking about how absurdly light she was.

Scott recalled his aching joints, from when he had first awoken. He realised that, in order to move him, she must have dragged him by his limbs. The stopping and starting must have put strain on the sockets.

Looping one arm around his shoulders, Natalie rested her head in the crook of Scott's neck. Once again, he smelt the same strong odour. It seemed to seep out of her pores and lingered in the air, like sour pheromones.

When she spoke, however, her breath smelt of mint.

"You share the things you love with the people you love," she said. Her voice lowered, and she whispered into his neck with hot breath. "I never thought I'd be able to do that with you. Share things, I mean. I never even thought that we'd be this close... The only time I ever even touched you was last Tuesday, when you brushed past me on your way into school. I think... I think that's when I knew. That I needed you."

Scott swallowed, unsure of what to say. He needed to gauge her reactions; get a good feel for what she was saying and how he had to react. Slip ups would get him hurt. Or worse.

She kissed him once on the neck. As Natalie's lips brushed his skin, a chill coursed through Scott's body, plucking up goosebumps.

"I thought I'd lost you, last week," Natalie continued, her voice taking on a hard edge to it, despite its softness. "When I saw you at the party... I watched you outside, talking to her. Then inside... Going upstairs." Her hand, looped around his neck and resting on his back, suddenly tensed. The hard prick of fingernails dug at Scott's skin. "But it's okay... Because something good came out of it. I got to talk to you. Well... Send you messages at least."

Ringing through his mind with the clack of wood, another piece of the puzzle fell into place. That was why Helen hadn't been talking to her parents. Why her texts to Scott had been so different to those she sent to Tom. Why she had stopped talking to him, after he had mentioned her parents.

For the past week, Scott hadn't been talking to Helen. It was Natalie.

But then how did she get her phone...? Scott thought, terror in his mind's voice.

"What did you do?" he asked, this time aloud.

A jaded look passed over Natalie's face, as she sat up and stared into Scott's eyes. "Drugging her was easy. So was getting rid of her. The problem was cleaning up after. Mum would have been furious if she had found out."

"What happened?" he repeated.

That was when Natalie shut down. The jaded look remained on her face, but took on a curious hardness. She rose to her feet and turned her back on him.

Making for the door, she moved in a slow and mechanical fashion.

"I'll be back soon," she said, ignoring Scott's question.

Walking out of the room, she shut the door behind her. All the while, Scott tried to call after her, but received no response.

He was left alone in the room, painfully aware of his restraints.

Once again, the fear took over and he began to tremble.

Chapter 44

David sharply whipped his car around in a tight U-turn and sped back towards Lindum. Displayed on the crystal screen of his dashboard, the hands-free phone symbol blipped out of sight as the call was disconnected. Gripping the wheel, his palms were soaked with a chilling, clammy sweat.

He should have known that something wasn't right when the boy hadn't arrived at the Station, for his interview. Scott didn't seem like the kind of person to go back on an agreement. Him not arriving should have been enough of a red flag; especially considering the boy was currently at home alone.

Memories of the note that Scott had showed him invasively drummed through his head.

Did you like my present?

A powerful feeling washed over him. A peculiar sense of uncertainty. David had missed something. Something extremely important.

The girl that had just called him said that Scott was missing. That there was blood in his house, and the lights were off. That she had found a dead cat hanging in the airing cupboard.

This wasn't some kind of ridiculous coincidence. Scott was the one that found the dead cats at the school. The fact that there was now one in his house set off every alarm in David's head. Worse still was that he was now missing. Red flashed in his vision and the ringing rippled through him, causing his hands to tremble.

Lightning flashed overhead, the sonic boom of thunder not far behind. Black clouds churned in the sky, threatening a maelstrom.

Reaching out, David tapped against the touchscreen mounted on his dash and dialled Franko's work phone. The synthetic sound of the ring filled the silence of the car and rattled inside his eardrums.

Franko always let his phone ring for five seconds; a long standing compulsion that David was well aware of. Ordinarily, he didn't care about the delay, but now every second felt like an hour. Fear and anxiety numbed him to time, leaving him hating the electronic sound that seemed to drone endlessly in his ears.

"Franko."

His superior's voice eliminated the tone, and pierced the inside of the car.

"James, it's David," he said, forgetting courtesy and addressing the DCI by his first name. "I... I've caught on to something. It could be nothing, but... If I'm right; if this is what I think it is, then... This could get really bad."

The DCI spoke with a restrained urgency that David had never heard before. His usually slow and mechanical voice lost its hard edge and rolled quickly down the line. "David, I need you to calm down. Tell me what's happened."

If he had been panicking, David wasn't aware. But Franko had sensed something in his voice; enough to switch his tone and try to get the situation under control.

"Sorry..." he replied, taking a breath and blinking hard.

White again flashed in his vision, as lightning struck overhead. The deafening crash of thunder punctuated David's speech.

"I just got a call," he continued, only realising once he started to speak how on edge he was feeling. Emotion burned and bubbled in his stomach. "From a girl; she said her name was — damn, what was it? Pru? Pru — She said her name was Pru Harding. Her friend is the boy I briefed you on: The one that found the first dump site. He was supposed to come in and give us another written statement, but never arrived. She was supposed to pick him up from the station, but when he didn't show she went to his house. Lights were off, and the door was open. She went inside and-"

"He was missing," Franko said, interrupting him. If David didn't know any better, he would have suggested that there was a tiny note of fear in the DCI's voice.

"Yeah, no trace," he replied, his voice again growing anxious. "More than that... Shit, James, she found a dead cat. Hung in the cupboard under the stairs."

"Shit."

David realised that this was the first time he had ever heard James Franko swear. The presence of it unnerved him, making him all too aware of the situation. It confirmed his fears and suspicions, kicking his senses into overdrive. His vision tunnelled and all that he was aware of was the road in front of him. White lines raced over the blacktop, blurring until they merged into one continuous grey trail.

"I'm on my way there now." Even as he spoke, he was only vaguely aware of the words.

"To the house?" Franko asked. "Okay. I'll call up the Lindum station, and get them to send some uniforms over. And the Scene of Crime team. You call your partner, tell Rawlings to meet you there."

The thrum of the engine roaring in his ears, David just about made out Franko's voice. "Okay, sir."

"I'll be heading over myself in a second," he continued. "And David..."

"Yes sir?"

"Be careful." Franko's words were firm but reassuring. Like he were a concerned but encouraging parent. "And call Rawlings."

The DCI hung up, leaving the dial tone lingering in the cold air.

Thunder and lightning, closer this time, shook the car. Still, however, the rain didn't yet fall. The clouds dared not release the storm that was brewing, seemingly waiting and biding their time.

He turned off on the right, and drove over the next intersection before finally hanging up the phone and dialling Rawlings' number.

The disgruntled DS answered on the second ring. "What do you want?"

In the background of the call, David could hear the teeming of a large crowd, accompanied by the clink of glasses. Not particularly raucous, the setting was still alive with atmosphere; something that he was shocked that the burly and disgruntled individual would be a part of. Rawlings was more than likely in a pub. Somewhere local if David was lucky. He prayed to God that the Detective would still be sober enough to drive.

"I'm sorry about this," David said, making little effort to sound apologetic. "But something's come up. Something big, to do with the case. I need you to meet me at the address I'm about to give you."

"I just got poured a fucking ale," Rawlings replied, harshly. "I haven't even had a chance to take a sip yet!"

"Better for us, it means you're still in a fit state to drive."

"Tell me again why I need to come out?" the voice, ruined by cigarettes, asked. "Because if you don't give me a good reason, so help me I'm downing this pint."

"You know you said about the Cat Killer kidnapping the girl at the station?" David began, in an attempt to play to his partner's vanity.

"It's happened again tonight. The kid who found the first dump site has gone missing. And there's another dead cat at his house."

Rawlings didn't reply straight away. He seemed to be taking the time to think about it, to get his bearings on what he wanted to do.

"Rawlings?" David said, raising his voice and pushing his comrade for a response.

"Alright! Alright!" he blustered. David heard the rustling of clothes as the large man rose to his feet and began to pull on his coat. "I'll meet you there. What's the postcode?"

David reached across his handbrake and into the bag that lay sprawled across the passenger seat. Fishing into the contents, his fingers clumsily gripped his notepad. Eyes still on the road, he used his left hand to thumb through the pages, until he reached a six digit line of text.

"LM3 9XY," he said, finally looking away from the windshield to read the characters.

"Okay, got it," Rawlings replied. He didn't even say goodbye when he hung up.

Killing the phone line, David reached out and turned down the radio. The sound was distracting; the harsh music setting him on edge, and the obnoxious voices of the radio hosts grating against his nerves.

Turning down into the new housing estate, he ignored the distant dots of light, from the cottages that decorated the countryside.

Chapter 45

Detective Sergeant Timothy Rawlings pocketed his phone and swung a hard gaze around the pub, from his mismatched eyes. The public house was already teeming with patrons, as was typical of a Friday night, even considering the fact that it wasn't far past seven o'clock. The smell of hops filled the air, from the locally brewed ale, and mixed with the scent of nicotine that clung to the clothes of the men that made the bar stools their home. Dull orange light radiated from the hanging overhead lights, leaving everything with a warm and earthy tone. Above the bulbs, dense oak cross beams supported the high ceiling and allowed the room a rustic appearance.

His long iron grey hair catching the light like fire on metal, Rawlings finished pulling on his coat and grunted in disappointment. A full pint sat beside him on the bar, the pale frothy head pristine and clear. He had yet to take a single sip.

While it was true that David's lead was promising (even more so considering it was based on Rawlings' own theories), the prospect of staying and finishing his beer tempted him more than once. The pub was hosting a local ale festival, and the beer might not have even been there the next day. He had been waiting a long time to try it. Just looking at it sat there was making his mouth water.

Squaring his beard-lined jaw, Rawlings ripped his eyes away from the glass and began to make his way towards the exit.

"Hey, Timmy! Where you going?"

Jim Mitchell, the landlord of The King's Arms, dwarfed the room not through any form of charisma or aura, but through sheer physical size. So rotund that he almost had a radius, Jim was the size of a transit van and as bald as an egg. He wore a flannel shirt so huge that it looked like someone had stretched a patchwork marquee over his body.

Waving over to the detective, his massive hand bore a dark shade of red to the skin, his expensive gold watch cutting off the circulation.

"Work," Rawlings grunted in reply, shrugging his huge, muscular shoulders.

"Work?" Jim parroted back, half mocking and chuckling. "Since when have you ever left the Arms to go back to work?"

He was right. Rawlings spent every Friday night in the pub and, as far as Jim was aware, he hadn't missed a day in fifteen years. Antisocial though he was, the burly Detective was a creature of habit. He would sit in his seat at the bar, knocking back pints of Wychwood ale and absorbing the conversation around him. And once he was there, he wouldn't leave until almost exactly eleven in the evening.

"Since now," Rawlings shot back. "I need to chase a lead on something."

Again the landlord's form shook with a boisterous belly laugh. "You're chasing a lead? Jesus, Timmy, anyone would think you were actually a police officer!"

"Fuck off," the Detective replied, bluntly.

"Come on," Jim said, waddling across the room to him. "You haven't even had one yet. Look, you've just left your pint on the bar. You know we got that in today from the Brewers Fair?"

"If I have one, then I won't be able to drive." He pulled a pen out of his pocket and began to write on the back of his hand. The angular letters of the postcode rolled onto his skin, before he could forget what it was. "Look. That's a Lindum postcode. I can't exactly walk there, can I?"

"We're not that far," Jim replied, dismissively waving one hand. "We're barely in Lyefield, you can walk that."

"I thought I told you to fuck off, Jim?" Rawlings retorted, a vague flicker of a smile finally forming on his lips.

"Alright, alright," the landlord said, grasping the untouched pint that the Detective had left on the bar. "Tell you what: You make it back before 11 and I'll buy you a drink." He downed half of the pint. "No, make that two. How's that sound?"

Rawlings pondered the proposition for a moment, before making up his mind. "Deal."

"Don't be too long though," Jim grinned. "We'll miss having our regular gargoyle sitting at the bar."

The broad, hairy man again grunted and made a move for the door, checking the postcode scrawled onto the back of his hand, with messy writing. Pushing out of the heavy wooden doors, the cold night air hit him in the face, shocking him into an awake alertness.

Pulling up the collar of his thick jacket, Rawlings dashed his peculiar eyes down the rural street, in an attempt to place his car. The chill licked at the exposed skin of his face, and the dense storm-filled air beaded moisture in the hairs of his beard and choked in his throat. He could smell almonds in the air, and he knew that a storm was coming. As if in response to his thoughts, lightning split the sky in a jagged white line.

Rawlings turned his eyes upwards and watched the black clouds fight for position. The devil was chasing them from over the horizon, whipping at them with lightning, and screaming with the deafening boom of thunder. The clouds trembled in fear, as if afraid to release what they carried down on the landscape, and he knew that when the rain did come, it would be thick and fast.

In anticipation, he dipped his head down and lifted his shoulders up, as like he was shielding his neck. An expression of distaste etched itself onto his face. He hated the rain, and there had been far too much of it recently. It left him cold and wet, and the sensation of peeling off wet clothes was one of the worst feelings he could think of.

The very thought of standing in the rain, giving a crime scene the once over, was only made more tolerable by the prospect of finally getting somewhere with the case. The investigation had been a pain in the arse, only made worse by the people he was expected to work with. While David was at least tolerable and (despite the fact he would never admit it) he got on well with him, Rawlings couldn't stand the other two Lyefield Uniforms. They rubbed him the wrong way, sniffing around where they didn't belong. James Franko be damned, he didn't trust Julie and St. Claire further than he could throw them. If he were in a bind, he knew that they wouldn't have his back. He doubted that they would even know what to do. They'd probably never faced down more than a speeding motorist.

What would they know about staring down a murderer? he thought. *How would they react to being stabbed? Not well I'd wager.*

Rawlings had been stabbed before. A number of times.

The first was when he was twenty five. A coked out thug had taken a screwdriver to him, when he was trying to squeeze information out about his dealer. Had he not lifted his hand in time, Rawlings would have lost an eye. He still had a scar on his right hand, between his second and third metacarpals, from where the tool had pierced him.

Rawlings had also been stabbed with a kitchen knife. Again chasing a lead on a drug ring, he had barged into an apartment on the upper east side of Lindum, and interrupted a heroin deal. He could still remember the girl sat in the corner, her eyes grey and vacant and her skin waxy pale. Even across the room he could see the single bead of blood, swelling from the crook of her arm. It was the sight of her that had distracted him and let the fucker in the overalls get the drop on him. The knife had entered through the side of his abdomen and sheared a gash across his right kidney. Despite the searing pain, and sparks of scotoma in his vision, he had managed to floor the kid and wrestle the blade out of his hand. His partner later told him that he broke the boy's jaw, and dislocated his left arm.

The third time was again with a knife. That one wasn't as bad as the other two. A teenage prostitute hadn't taken kindly to his attempts to get her off of the street. She took exception to him grabbing her by the arm, and had stabbed him through the forearm with a pocket knife; no doubt carried for protection from her more pushy and dangerous customers.

He still considered the wound from the screwdriver the worst. The main reason was because it was blunt, and it takes a lot of force to stab with a dull instrument. The second reason was because, as it penetrated his hand, the makeshift weapon had been turned off course. Levered by the angle of the screwdriver, the bones in his hand had been broken. It felt like a red hot poker burning through his flesh.

Rawlings admired the smooth skin left by the scarring as he gripped the handle of his car door. He felt like it added character to his large, strong hands.

Settling in behind his steering wheel, he slammed the car door and cranked up the heating to full-whack. His engine roaring to life, Rawlings pulled out of the space that bordered the footpath and began to make his way out of Lyefield.

Lifting his left hand, he tapped away on the illuminated screen of his SatNav, periodically checking the postcode against the digits scrawled onto his hand. Rawlings was notoriously poor with directions, even requiring the satellite device to make his way to work in the mornings, the twenty years he spent driving almost exactly the same route having done nothing. The tiny screen fixed to his windshield was a godsend.

Taking the country lanes with small, compact turns of his steering wheel, Rawlings made for the western edge of Lindum. From his position, driving into the valley in which the city dwelled, from the north, he could see the lights of the new housing estate.

As he drove, he thought of David. Of how his new partner would greet him, upon his arrival at the house.

Probably playing up to what's going on, Rawlings thought. *He's so green he might as well piss grass. Probably will try and get up close to all of the gory bits. Suits me fine... Less for me to see then.*

Fishing a packet of Marlboro from the glove compartment, he shook loose a cigarette and lit it with a cheap plastic lighter. Not daring to open his window, through fear of a sudden downpour, he was soon swamped in a dense veil of grey smoke. Flicking ash into the tray he had glued to his dashboard, the large man slipped the cigarette back into his mouth and turned up the volume on the SatNav.

As the synthetic female voice recited the directions to him, Rawlings wondered if the trip out to the house would be worth it.

Chapter 46

Pru was lingering in the entryway of Scott's house when she saw the headlights of the car pull up. The white beams of illumination rounded the corner so fast that the shock of the light caused her heart to momentarily seize in her chest.

After calling David Stafford, from the number on the card she had found, Pru had waited in the porch of the house for the Officer to arrive. Having seen one too many crime dramas, she was overly careful to avoid touching anything, conscious of preserving fingerprints. She hadn't even shut the front door.

To a certain extent, a part of her still couldn't believe that what was happening was real. The events carried a strange detachment to them, as if she were watching it all unfold through a television screen.

The distance she was placing on it helped Pru to remove herself from the situation. In the crime shows the culprit was always caught, and as long as she believed that was how the events were unfolding, then Scott would return safe.

A broad man in his thirties stepped out of the car and hurried up the path towards the house. His face bore a look of concern, tinged with fierce resolve.

"I'm Officer Stafford," he said, slowing his pace as he moved within arm's reach of the doorway. "Pru, right? Are you okay?"

Somewhat coming out of her daze, she regained enough sense to nod her head. The man offered her a reassuring smile that reminded her vaguely of her father.

He looked different to how she imagined he would, when they spoke on the phone. The Officer was taller and broader than she expected, with an older looking face that didn't match his youthful voice. His large frame was filled out, though not in a doughy way, and his arms and chest had a strength to them. Wind beat at his jacket and shirt, but he resisted it easily, stood like a pillar in a storm.

"Do you want to sit in my car?" David asked, hesitantly taking a step forwards. It seemed like he wanted to pat her on the shoulder, but restrained himself from coming into contact with her.

Pru shook her head quickly. Some kind of powerful force kept her in the house, willing her to stay. She felt as if leaving to sit in the car would be like betraying Scott. An overwhelming urge to quickly explain everything overtook her. The faster the Officer got the information, the sooner he would be able to find Scott.

"I need to show you," she said, turning to delve deeper into the darkness of the house.

"Wait," David called out, with an urgency that made her freeze in place. "I think it's for the best if you at least stay here by the door. There's more officers on their way to talk to you, and the crime scene guys won't be far behind. You don't need to go back in there."

Turning and looking into the Officer's eyes, Pru saw something in them. A comforting concern that put her at ease. He clearly didn't want her seeing the cat again. She realised that he was trying to shield her from the horror of her discovery, and that touched her.

The chilling darkness at her back spurred her forwards, while the comforting warmth David seemed to radiate drew her in, and before she knew it Pru was outside.

"Is Scott going to be okay?" she suddenly asked, surprising even herself with the weakness in her voice.

David smiled and cocked his head to one side. "He's going to be fine. Don't worry... We'll find him."

His tone sounded unsure, but his words were enough to at least somewhat calm her. Pru felt her shoulders slack, as if a weight had been removed from her. It was only then that she realised that she had been trembling.

The realisation that her emotions were so frail struck her in the chest and stunned her for a second. Pru had always prided herself on her ability to remain calm, to be the one that always helped everyone else with their problems, and kept a straight face when her own rolled around. She was known, among both her own circle of friends and her associates at large, as someone you could rely on in a crisis. But now the concept seemed laughable, the use of the word "crisis" to describe anything but the current situation both mocking and insulting. Nothing could have prepared her for anything like this.

Gripping her in its current, the wind grew teeth and tested them on her arms, biting at her and prickling up gooseflesh. Pru's body shuddered, a shiver different from her prior terrified trembling.

In the distance, the harsh flash of sirens strobed through the gaps between semi-detached buildings, casting beams of blue light down on the street. The glare of the lights contrasted with the darkness, making the shadows seem as black and dense as ink.

"See," David smiled again. "The others are almost here. Everything's going to be okay."

A deep appreciation caught her, welling up in her chest. Pru knew that comforting her was David's job, but it was still comforting all the same. The reassurance was something she deeply needed, and was so glad that he was there to help her.

The headlights of cars appeared at the mouth of the street, casting light in beams that intersected the orange glow of the streetlights.

As the first neon green and white cruiser pulled up, a large dark-skinned man stepped out of the passenger side and made his way quickly into the garden.

"I'm Sergeant Joshua Akinfe," the man said, curtly addressing David directly. "Has anyone been inside yet?"

"No, just her," he replied, looking up at the bulky form of the uniformed Sergeant. "I was waiting for everyone else. SOC would go mental if I went in without gloves or shoe protectors."

"The boy that's missing," Joshua continued. "Did I hear it right when the report said that it's Scott Willard?"

"Yes," Pru blurted out suddenly. "Scott's missing!" Her words sounded infantile and pleading, but she didn't care.

"Jesus..." the big man said, grimacing. His lips pulled back, and light flashed off of the surface of his gold tooth. "I was the one who interviewed him, back when he found the bodies."

"You didn't notice anything strange back then?" David asked.

"No," Joshua replied. "I was a bit worried when he told me he was at home by himself, but nothing past that. Definitely didn't expect anything like this to happen."

David hummed and nodded slowly. After pausing for a second, he turned towards Pru and looked down at her. "Pru... I'm going to need to have a look at the scene. I want you to stay here with the Sergeant's partner, okay?"

Her hand caught his sleeve before she was even aware of it. Words, pleading and childish, formed in her mouth. "Please don't leave me."

It killed her pride to say it, but even looking on her words in hindsight Pru didn't care. David's was the first friendly face that she had seen, and just having him nearby calmed her.

David exchanged glances with Joshua. The Sergeant knitted his brows as a frown touched his lips. Whether he didn't notice it or didn't care Pru was unsure, but within a moment, David was smiling again. A warm and comforting curl of the lips, hugging his teeth.

"Okay," he said, with a nod. "I'll stay here with you for a little while longer. And while I do that, how about you call your parents? Have them come and pick you up. You don't have to give a statement or go to the station until you're ready."

His kind words again touched her. They made her feel at least somewhat at ease, and filled her with a deep appreciation. In spite of the cold night air, and the looming threat of rain, she felt warm.

Something wet streaked a line down her cheek, and Pru knew that she was crying.

Chapter 47

The muscles in Scott's arms and legs were searing with the swelling burn of lactic acid, as he feebly rocked back and forth, in an attempt to topple the chair that he was bound to. His right hand was turning slightly pink, from the restrictive clasp of the belt, and he had long since lost feeling in his feet. An uncomfortable tightness spread through his stomach as his sitting position put pressure on his bladder. Moving slowly around his mouth, his sandpaper tongue snagged against his moist cheeks.

He wasn't sure how long he had sat there, but it felt like an eternity. An insurmountable amount of time, spent pondering his own death. Planning and attempting his own escape.

If he got the *chance* to escape.

Despite how unhinged Natalie seemed, Scott sensed a dark intelligence in her mind. It was as if something powerful were swimming inside her head; churning and growing, feeding off of her imagination. He heard the sonic boom of thunder from outside the house and imagined lightning sparking through her mind, firing like supercharged neurons inside Natalie's head. Disturbed though she was, the girl was smart enough and careful enough to have taken him in the first place; to have taken both Alice and Helen, without anyone realising.

Scott's memories of the girls caused a coil of self-disgust to wind through his stomach. Constricting like a serpent around his organs, the guilt shot an ache through his heart. If it hadn't been for him, then they wouldn't have died — wouldn't have been *killed*. Natalie's obsession with him was dangerous, and his closeness to the girls (both perceived or otherwise) was what had driven her over the edge.

If they had never met him, then the girls would never have been taken, tortured and killed. It was his fault, and he would never forgive himself for that.

However, it was because of that guilt that he needed to escape.

He needed to get away, and *apologise* to their families. To tell them how desperately sorry he was, and to spend every day of the rest of his life making it up to them.

Continuing to rock feebly in the chair, he tried to regain at least some sensation in his legs. He considered screaming, but soon dismissed the idea. It would do little more that alert Natalie to what he was trying to do. There mere fact that she hadn't gagged him made him realise that there wasn't anyone around to hear him, even if he did cry out.

Scott's attempted escape was cut short as Natalie finally returned to the room. So distracted by his own thoughts, Scott hadn't even heard her walking down the hallway.

Opening the door quickly, the lithe girl dropped a plastic shopping bag on the floor, and stood staring at him for a moment. As the bag hit the floor the contents rattled with a metallic clink that sent a shiver down Scott's spine.

Looking up at the girl, Scott again took the time to observe her expression. Listless and with an air of vacancy, she stared down at him with an unpractised smile on her lips. Her striking features stood at odds to her emotionally stunted expression.

Natalie Hunt was beautiful, and yet not in the way that many would expect. Like shards of crystal that glittered with sparkling light, she was captivating, yet still — ultimately — broken.

"Sorry I took so long." Her voice had a nervous edge to it as if (and more than likely because) she were speaking to a crush. "I was just getting some things ready. I... I really didn't mean for this to turn out this way so... So it needs to be perfect."

"It's okay," he replied in a steady and practiced voice. "I know."

Natalie's mouth twitched into the now familiar abused smile. She bashfully flicked her eyes down towards the floor and locked her fingers together in front of her chest.

As she did so, Scott remained silent. Too afraid of what the unpredictable girl would do next, he tried his best to remain calm. He needed to make sure that when she did speak he wasn't too riled and strung out that he said the wrong thing. The last thing he wanted was for her to snap. The very concept terrified him, and he was all too aware of where it would lead if he prompted that kind of response from her.

Seemingly remembering something important, Natalie flustered and crouched down next to the plastic bag she had dropped when she entered the room. "Sorry, sorry... I completely forgot. I... I got a surprise for you."

The words gripped Scott's heart like an icy hand, but he managed to force a smile.

It froze to his lips in paralysing terror, as Natalie pulled out a knife.

"I saw the scar on your hand," she said, indicating the shimmering flesh looping Scott's left ring finger. "And I thought it looked like..." She blushed fiercely. "Like a wedding ring."

His eyes shooting down to the scar, Scott remembered almost losing the finger as a child. He remembered the pain he felt as the digits of his hand slipped between the boards of the fence and jammed in place. He remembered how all of his other fingers had been pulled from their sockets...

But most importantly he remembered how, ever since, he was able to purposely and easily dislocate them himself.

It was a sick party trick that he often performed to gross people out. By positioning his fingers in a certain way, and suddenly moving them, he was able to pop them out of place so that his fingers hung limply from his palm.

A brief flicker of hope fluttered in his chest.

If he were able to dislocate his fingers, there was the chance that he could pull his left hand loose from his restraints. He knew, from the now purple shading of his right hand, that the belt restraining his left wrist was the looser of the two. It was just a case of popping his fingers out of their sockets and pulling his hand free.

The problem was doing so without Natalie noticing.

An evil glint of metal pulled his attention back to Natalie.

The knife was closer to him now. Lingering in the air in front of his face; sleek and silver and wickedly sharp.

A vision entered his head of her plunging the knife into him. Slashing his skin and baring the gore of his body to the open air. As the fear took him, his straining bladder twinged in pain and a sliver of urine escaped.

Noticing Scott's expression, Natalie dropped the knife and took a step closer again. "Are you okay Scott?" When she received no reply, Natalie leaned in and analysed his face intently, through darting grey eyes. Seemingly coming to a conclusion, she dropped her voice to a whisper. "Do you need to go to the toilet?"

Scott didn't say a word. He couldn't find his voice to speak. Whether it was the embarrassment of wetting himself in fear, or due to the fear itself, his tongue was unable to form words.

Instead he nodded, quickly.

Suddenly stepping back, Natalie stood up straight. "Wait right there."

Without another word, she turned around and disappeared quickly out of the room.

Seizing the opportunity, Scott hurriedly anchored his left thumb in the socket before jerking it rapidly to the side. With a sickening locking sound, the digit came loose and fell onto the arm of the chair.

Just as he prepared to do the same with his index finger, however, Natalie reappeared in the doorway. In her hands she held an empty milk bottle.

Laying eyes on the container, Scott's mind shut down in disbelief.

She's not... he thought.

Crouching down in front of the chair Natalie set down the bottle and reached out for Scott's belt. Her hands moved clumsily, as if she were overcome with nerves, but soon she had it unfastened. Next she set to work on the buttons of his trousers.

Shifting his hips around, he tried to impede her progress. Having her hands down there made him feel uncomfortable and violated. The very idea of her touching him in such an intimate area made him feel wrong and afraid.

Despite his struggling, Natalie managed to unbutton his trousers. One hand settled on his hip, her fingernails digging in and holding Scott in place with a surprising strength, as the other delved inside his boxer shorts and came to rest on his penis.

A horrible sensation of vulnerability smashed into him as she squeezed down on his smooth skin. Much to his shame, he felt himself unintentionally hardening, and he fought back the urge to cry.

Pulling out Scott's member, Natalie's eyes lingered in fascination for several moments, before she lifted the empty bottle and slipped the tip inside.

"There you go," she said innocently, finally releasing him and holding the bottle with two hands.

Scott clenched his teeth and fought against every urge that he had. Even after everything that he had been through, peeing in front of this girl was out of the question. Doing so would strip him of his last shreds of dignity. He already felt horrible and disgusted, and doing that would only make it worse.

"I thought you said you needed to go," Natalie said, her voice raising slightly. Despite still being soft, there was an ever so slight aggressive edge to it. "Did you *lie* to me?"

His eyes now closed, Scott took the cue from her voice and imagined her picking up the knife. Tears beaded in the corners of his eyes and fear overtook him.

Terror trumping his dignity, he finally let go and pissed into the bottle.

When he was finished, Scott opened his red tear-filled eyes and breathed heavily. His heart was hammering in his chest and he felt like he had just run a mile. Stress seared his nerve endings and he began to tremble.

"There we go," Natalie said with a smile.

Setting down the half-full three litre bottle, she prepared to return him to his trousers when she stopped. Biting her tongue between her lips, she ran one hand gently over his shaft and gave him a quick stroke, before seemingly coming to her senses.

Even as she buttoned his trousers back up, Scott felt sick. The contents of his stomach churned, and he had to fight back the urge to vomit.

He didn't even notice that she had picked up the knife again.

"Now that's done with..." she continued. "I can show you my surprise."

Turning his attention back to her, and seeing the knife, Scott's thoughts immediately turned to torture.

However, in that moment, the girl did something that he didn't expect.

Taking the knife to herself, Natalie dragged the blade around the ring finger of her left hand. Digging the edge in so deep that Scott was sure she would cut the finger off, she parted the skin and revealed bone and muscle. Crimson blood flowed from the wound and splashed against the carpeted floor.

"What are you doing?!" he blurted out, unable to contain his horror.

Breaking into a smile, Natalie strode back to the chair. Laying her hand down on his left hand, luckily not noticing his dislocated thumb, she wound her fingers around Scott's own in a bloody clasp.

"Now we both have one," she said. "It's like I said: It's like a wedding ring. That's what you do when you love someone."

Without warning, she reached out with her right hand and slashed the knife over the skin of Scott's left forearm. Pain shot up the limb like a bolt of electricity and locked his muscles in place. A scream formed in his throat and escaped his lips in a harsh cry.

Natalie just continued to smile. The same dead-eyed, deluded smile. "Sometimes love hurts, Scott. That's what Daddy used to tell me. And I love you a lot."

Grinding his molars together, Scott inhaled a deep breath and shuddered with the exhale. Swallowing the pain, he focussed on his left hand. Natalie had since released it, leaving both it and the belt slick with blood.

It was his only chance.

"So, what about your parents?" Scott asked, trying to sound casual, in spite of the pain that he was feeling. He was grasping at straws, trying to find grounds to distract her. As long as Natalie was looking at him, there was a chance that he would be caught trying to escape. No matter how careful he was, there was no way he could slip his restraints while he was the centre of her attention.

Natalie gained a distant expression to her face. She cocked her head to the side and stared at Scott through glazed eyes, as if she didn't quite comprehend the question. "My parents?" she parroted back.

"Yeah," Scott confirmed, nodding his head and insisting. Noticing her eyes trained on his face, he used this opportunity to inch his dislocated thumb past the bloody leather of the belt. "Your parents."

The corner of Natalie's eye twitched. Wound around the handle of the knife, her fingertips began to tingle; the sensation spreading through her body at lightning speed. Blood rushed to her head and she could practically feel it bubbling up and filling her skull. If she didn't know any better, she would have sworn that Scott could see the meniscus of the blood rising across her eyes. "Dead." she replied, simply.

She said the word casually, without a hint of sorrow or remorse. Scott got a sinking feeling in the pit of his stomach that something had happened to Natalie's parents, or rather that *Natalie* had happened.

That was when she started to babble. The words tumbled from her mouth in a continuous stream of consciousness, like marbles dropping to the floor. "They got everything that came to them, after what they did to me. They wanted me to be perfect, I had to be perfect;

I had to be what they expected, and when I wasn't the punishment came, and the punishment meant the water and the closet and- and- and that darn fork. And Daddy would tell me that it wouldn't happen anymore, every time, but it did and-... and it happened so much he stopped saying that it wouldn't, but he still told me that he loved me — Daddy always told me that he loved me — but Mummy couldn't know, and when she did there was the water and the closet over and over and over and over!" Disoriented fragments of her life entered Scott's head and flickered in front of his eyes, as she spoke. "I just wanted them to stop, to know how it felt when they did those things to me!"

Storming over to the other side of the room, Natalie flung open a door set into the wall. Spewing from the tiny space a sour, tepid smell assaulted Scott's senses. He gagged and fought back the urge to vomit again. A dull buzzing filled the air, along with a wet rustling, like thousands of tiny objects were squirming across a damp surface. Evidence of flies and maggots burbled out of the closet, and as Scott's eyes adjusted to the darkness of the storage space he was able to make out two vaguely humanoid objects. These were the third and fourth dead bodies Scott had seen in all of several hours and they still filled him with a sickening and vile sensation.

Natalie slammed the door, shutting out the horrific sight, yet the smell remained, lingering in the air and clinging to Scott's clothes. A crawling feeling tingled over him, almost like he was surrounded by the maggots and they were wriggling over his skin.

"I just wanted them to understand," she continued, the jaded look on her face only seeming to become more pronounced. "I was sad that I had to do it at first, but now... Now I know that they deserved it! For all the times that they hurt me! For all the times that they told lies!"

For the first time since he had awoken, bound to the chair, Scott noticed something about Natalie. It was her arms. He hadn't realised it before, but her forearms, visible now that she had rolled up her sleeves, were covered with puncture wounds. The majority had healed and scarred, however a number of them still bore darkened scabs.

"Fuckers..." he found himself gasping under his breath. Even in spite of all the horrible things that she had done, Scott found himself feeling sorry for her; hating how her parents had treated her; figuring that she wasn't born like this, she was created and moulded into what she was. Through years of systematic abuse.

"Yeah, the fuckers deserved it," the girl said, turning to the side and flicking her eyes over the blood that smeared the walls.

Scott was stunned at the presence of the swear. Even dazed as he was, he knew that it wasn't normal, despite how natural the word sounded coming out of her mouth. Up until this point, she had been using synonyms of dirty words, substituting phrases. He realised with a sudden jolt that she was mirroring him. Natalie had heard him use the word and was working it into her own vocabulary, in an effort appear more like him. It was what hopeless people did on dates; copied the behaviour of the other person, in a vain attempt to become more appealing.

"Do you want to know how I did it?" she asked, taking a step closer to him and clasping Scott's right hand with her bloody digits. Her eyes, staring deep into his own, were glazed and still, like tempered glass. "It wasn't as easy as you'd think."

Scott swallowed hard, feeling his Adam's apple bounce in his throat. Yet he did not dare look away from her eyes. Her gaze was so intense and focussed that it bore into his skull.

"Mum told lies," Natalie continued. "Too many lies. So she had to be punished. I waited for them to fall asleep, and went into their room at night. Daddy always had a lot of belts, so I used those to tie them to the headboard. Mum had to be first. She needed to be first. Stabbing her the first time was harder than I thought... But after she woke up, the struggling made it easier. The only problem was how long it took." A horrifying expression of wonder took over her face. "Do you know how long it takes to stab someone thirty seven times?"

Scott felt his heart kick and thrash in his chest. His breathing quickened and came in short, panicked gasps. The inside of his forehead throbbed, the dull ache spreading down across his brows and settling on his eyes. It felt as if the thoughts storming through his head were attempting to punch their way out from inside his skull.

"Daddy woke up while I was doing it... He kept screaming and screaming at me. I couldn't get him to stop. So in the end, I had to cut his throat. I didn't mean to kill him. I just... I just wanted him to stop screaming." A shuddering smile formed on her face. "But now I know that he deserved it too."

Scott tried to speak, but the words never came. Horror gripped him like a vice and refused to let go.

The expectation of her next words crashed through his mind like a tsunami. All of his other thoughts were swept away, leaving only a desolate void of fear behind.

Just as Natalie opened her mouth to speak again, however, something happened that Scott did not expect.

There was a knock at the front door.

Chapter 48

Franko arrived just as Pru's parents collected her from the scene. He watched as the mother peeled away in her blue Honda, the teenage girl in the passenger seat, while behind the father departed in the car that Pru had no doubt driven to the scene. Stepping out onto the pavement, the ageing DCI stared at the two cars as they disappeared down the end of the street.

Massaging the heels of his palms into his eye sockets, Franko turned his vision back onto the house. Police tape was already strung across the front garden in a blue and white barrier, forming crosses in his vision. Scene of crime officers swarmed the garden, moving in and out of the building, their forms covered entirely in hazmat suits, masks and plastic goggles.

The sea of activity repulsed him, forcing Franko to linger momentarily beside his car. He flashed back to a crime scene in North London, thirty years past. He hoped against hope that this wouldn't end the same way.

The walls built around his life were starting to break apart, and he was terrified of what might spill through, should the cracks widen enough.

Franko pushed his way through the crowd, turning aside the quixotic theories of the uniformed officers as he went. He had little time for the ramblings of the uninformed masses; regarding them in the same way you would an overly optimistic child. Looking back at them, he wondered if there was just something fundamentally different between himself and them: a disconnect between the brain and the mouth where words arrived before conscious thought kicked in. The minds of others just seemed so distant from his own that there had to be something different in the way they perceived and experienced things. Franko often wondered strange things like that. Like if blind people dreamt in sounds, or if the deaf thought in signs.

Bagging his shoes and snapping on a pair of latex gloves, he delved into the depths of the house. Temporary light fixtures had been set up inside, until the forensics team had finished dusting the fuse box for prints, and collecting trace from the under-stairs cupboard.

Tampering with the box at this point, to restore power to the house, would have compromised evidence.

Leaning out of the way of a woman, swamped in an anti-contamination suit, Franko briefly flicked his eyes downwards at the small plastic bag held in her hands. No doubt some kind of fibrous evidence collected from the kitchen.

He found David Stafford and Simon Wilson stood around the dining table, in the kitchen. Each of them wore gloves, shoe protectors, and sombre expressions. While David bore the twisted look of uncomfortable pessimism, he noticed something else on the face of the Detective. The curdled expression on Wilson's face was so pungent that Franko unintentionally associated him with off milk. Spoilt, sour and ruining his day.

"-doubt that she saw anything. He was probably long gone by the time she came to check on him."

Franko caught the tail end of one of David's sentences as he entered the room. He also heard the response of one of the forensic specialists.

"I think you're right," she replied, her features all but hidden from view. As she spoke, her eyes seemed to overcompensate for the lack of defining features on show, giving her an almost cartoonish air. "The blood on the floor has completely dried. Coagulation happens quite quickly, but not that fast. At a guess I'd say the room's about 20 degrees, maybe a touch colder."

"Meaning that it's been here for at least an hour," Franko cut in. "If we take it that the girl called David right after arriving and finding the scene, she can't have arrived more than a half hour ago. That's still thirty minutes out... At least. I agree with David, she didn't see anything."

Wilson turned quickly to face the DCI, just barely managing to discard the annoyed expression that had previously donned his face. Upon closer inspection, a faded smudge of lipstick swiped a line from the corner of his mouth. No doubt from his wife. Franko quickly made the connection and realised that the new development must have ripped him mid-date from his wife.

Too bad... he thought, steeling his gaze so as to not wear his thoughts on his face. *You think you're the only one who's got somewhere better to be?*

The last thing Franko wanted to be doing was staring down evil. In a perfect world he would be at home with Sarah, making sure that nothing happened to her. Being there for her in case she needed him. He took a small comfort in the fact that Stephanie and the grandkids were with her. At least Sarah was with family, instead of just being handed off to the nurse.

Mechanically, his eyes flicked down to the floor and spotted the hard brown of dry blood, smeared across the tiles.

His heart hitched momentarily in his chest, as he thought about the boy that lived in the house — the boy that was missing. He wasn't with family.

"Has anyone thought to contact his parents?" Franko asked, pointedly staring at David.

"Someone should be calling them now," David replied, his words catching on the hook of his nerves.

"He left his parents' mobile numbers when he gave his first statement," Wilson added. "As well as the number of the hotel they're staying at."

"Okay, good. What about canvassing the street? I saw uniforms outside, but are you making use of them?" Franko knitted his brows and stared long and hard at David, analysing his response for areas of fault.

"Priority was securing the scene. We set up a perimeter around the house, and we've got a couple of guys on standby in case the press show up. Once more of our guys arrive, though, we're going to start door to door. Probably won't have to, though... All those gawkers outside, someone must have seen something." David's top lip curled in a grimace of distaste. "Nothing's private anymore..."

A feeling similar to pride momentarily passed through Franko. After working to groom David into something akin to a lead Detective, he was finally starting to act like one.

He also noted the younger man's use of plural pronouns. Franko knew all too well that the coordination of the effort was David's own, yet the Constable didn't even think to use it as an opportunity to promote himself. He cared about the case — about the victim — not some kind of forced attempt at sprinting through the ranks.

He hummed his approval and turned his vision on the kitchen. Very little was out of place (if he were to ignore the mutilated cat hanging in the airing cupboard). There were no signs of a struggle past the blood pool on the floor, and the cast off from whatever weapon had been used to subdue the victim. Everything was eerily calm and in place.

It was at times like these that he wished Dean Price was still alive. Retirement be damned, if he could Franko would have called him and pleaded for him to drive the four hours from London. Forensic extraordinaire and self-proclaimed "human magnifying glass", Dean could have found a needle in a stack of needles; more than that, he could even tell you exactly when and where it was made.

Instead, he had to put his faith in the Lindum forensics unit. So far, it seemed, they were at least thorough and competent enough to justify that faith.

"Any theories on what happened?" Franko asked, beginning to pace around the room.

"Well..." David began. "Sorry if I'm sounding a bit too much like Rawlings, but this smells of a trap." He pointed up at the lights, then to the fuse box as he explained. "Whoever took him cut the power to make sure he came to the fuse box. Then they used the cat as a distraction to get the drop on him."

"Probably came up from behind, using the blind spot of the corner," Wilson added. "Must have hit him with something fucking hard to knock him out."

"All of which tells us whoever did this knows the layout of the house," Franko continued, his voice heavy. "They managed to kill the cat, cut the power and hide ready for the trap before he got home from school. They couldn't have done it this smoothly without having been here before. That or they're extraordinarily lucky."

"They may be lucky and well prepared," the forensic specialist added, her voice cutting through the darkness like a blade, "but they're not very strong. Look at the blood smears. He was dragged. Not very consistently either. Whoever took him stopped and started a lot."

"I don't know whether to find that comforting or not..." David muttered, under his breath.

"Don't," Franko answered. "Find it comforting, I mean. Strength is relative; the fact that they're not physically strong doesn't change a damn thing. They're still dangerous. Don't forget that." Stepping back and looking over the three people in front of him, Franko addressed them as a whole. "What else have you found?"

David walked over to the dining table and picked up a folded piece of paper. He held it gingerly by corners as if worried that, in spite of his gloves, he might somehow contaminate it. "This."

Carefully unfolding it, he displayed the contents to the DCI, as Wilson shone his torch on the sheet.

"Scott had this passed through his door the same day that he found the first dump site," David explained. "My guess is he didn't report it because he thought the two were unrelated. I even thought so myself, when he told me about it yesterday. But now..."

"Now we know that this is almost definitely from our perp," Franko muttered. "Fantastic."

"So we know now that he's been the target from the beginning?" Wilson asked.

"More than likely, yes," Franko confirmed. "But something doesn't seem right... They started off with the cats, and truth told it probably should have stayed at that. But this is a rapid escalation... Someone like this doesn't suddenly go from animal mutilations to kidnapping. There's got to have been some kind of trigger." He took a deep breath, and held it for a moment. "I just hope to god they haven't killed anyone yet." An image of Odette Lewis rose up inside his head. "Intentionally, I mean."

He indicated David and Wilson, and motioned for them to follow him. Moving to exit the kitchen, he moved his hands about as he spoke. The methodical mind-set was beginning to take over, and he could feel his mind clicking through the various steps and stages of his process.

"I need you two to start going door-to-door," he began. "Have the uniforms help you, so you can cover more ground quicker. Use as many of them as you need. When you're done with the street, re-convene at the house, and by then the scene of crime guys will have finished processing the scene. Wilson, I want you to call your partner. Have her start checking traffic cameras, and see if they picked up anything."

Reaching the doorway, Franko looked up and out of the house. Whipped from the clouds by the lightning, rain had finally started to descend on the landscape. Thick and fat drops crashed down on the street, drowning the onlookers and officers both. A stream had already formed in the road, running downhill before being swallowed by the guttering. The forensics unit, in the middle of erecting a marquee in the front garden, sped up their efforts into a furious pace, so that any trace evidence left in the garden wasn't washed away.

Eyes darting down the road, between the cascading sheets of rain, Franko observed the crowds of people, as if looking for someone.

Turning his back on the downpour, his eyes fell on David once again. "I thought I told you to call your partner?"

"I did," David said, knitting his brows in confusion. "Right after I called you that was the first thing I did."

Franko hummed pensively. "Strange... He should be here by now."

"Yeah..." Wilson joined in. "Where the fuck is Rawlings?"

Chapter 49

Masum Khalid was running late.

The dry cleaner had been late in finishing his suit, meaning that his trip home resulted in him meeting the swarm of storm-induced traffic streaming both to and from the middle of Lindum's City Centre. After sitting in the gridlock of cars for more than an hour, he finally managed to make his way back to his apartment, in the South East end of the city.

An opulent neighbourhood, teeming with studio apartments, he had moved into his three bedroom flat three years earlier and never felt more at home. Stylish in the clinical, minimalist sense, Masum's decoration and design was composed almost entirely of sleek black and white. His garage, where he parked his soft-top BMW Z3, was built in below the space, and only accessible by key card. Much like the rest of the estate. Usually, he liked that. The fenced-off area afforded him a sense of exclusivity that could seldom be found in the rest of the city. Now, however, it was more than a small issue.

In such a rush to get home from the dry cleaners, he had left his access card on the main desk of the establishment. Not wanting to return through the traffic, he had to phone one of his neighbours to let him in. The time it took him to realise his predicament, and for his well-intentioned neighbour to arrive and unlock the gate, was enough to fill him with more than a touch of anxiety.

Masum was already late by at least an hour, and now that time had been added to by twenty minutes. If he didn't hurry, he was going to miss his meeting.

Checking his watch, as he abandoned his convertible on the kerb outside of his building, Masum swore under his breath. It was nearly eight o'clock. The fact that it was a Friday night also didn't help to improve his mood.

Hurrying up the stairs, he fished his keys out of his jacket pocket, the dry-cleaned suit bundled under the other arm, and entered his apartment. Passing through the kitchen, and taking a brief glance at the landline phone on the counter, he was relieved to see that he didn't have any answer phone messages.

Yet.

His investor likely wouldn't forgive him, if he were late.

Somewhat of a local celebrity (at least in his own mind) Masum was the owner of at least four restaurants in the greater Lindum area. Specialising in Indian and Bangladeshi cuisine, he was attempting to form what could eventually become a successful and recognisable brand.

At least that was the plan, if his investors decided to play ball.

The meeting was scheduled for nine o'clock in his first, and highest rated restaurant. **"Masum's"** was located in Parkridge Shopping Centre, fifteen miles north of Lindum, just beside the industrial estate. One of the most high-class establishments in the Centre (in his opinion) Masum's father had opened the restaurant while he was still in school, and had given it to him following his graduation. Not satisfied with one establishment, he had taken it upon himself to re-invest all of his profits and open another restaurant in Lindum's city centre. This was then followed by a takeaway, and so on.

The prospect of being able to branch out further from the valley in which the city and its subsidiary towns were located made his hands itch in anticipation. A true businessman if ever there was one, Masum was more than eager to further expand his brand.

Showering quickly, Masum hurriedly moved around his apartment, shaving as he went. The last thing he wanted to do was ruin his business model by being late to one meeting.

Fate, however, didn't appear to be on his side.

The main route to Parkridge was along the motorway. However, given the time of night and the fact that it was a Friday evening, he was almost certainly going to hit the traffic coming out of the industrial estate. That would eat up at least an hour that he didn't have.

Checking the time again, this time on his steel wall-mounted clock, he saw that it was now closer to quarter-past-eight. Swearing again, he hurried back to the bathroom and lathered his hair with product.

Giving himself the once-over in the mirror, Masum made sure that he looked just right before quickly running to dress in his newly cleaned suit.

A somewhat large man, his weight spoke less of sloth and gluttony, and more of opulence and fortune. Well-fed, with glossy black hair and strong, powerful shoulders, he had boyish features and friendly eyes. His cheeks now free from stubble, he sported a van-dyke beard.

As he dressed, his ears twigged to a heavy thumping sound, almost as if a group of people were running over his roof. Still in the process of tying his tie, he moved to the window and grimaced when he laid eyes on the downpour. It would only exacerbate the traffic situation, and people had a bad habit of driving stupid when it rained.

Again checking the time, he pulled on his jacket and snatched up his phone, wallet and keys before practically running out of the door and pounding down the stairs of the complex. Leaping down, from halfway up the flight, he flung open the front door and dived into his car.

Making up his mind, Masum decided to avoid the motorway altogether. The traffic situation was bad enough, but rain on top was not a good mix.

His best bet, if he were to arrive on time, would be to take the country roads and loop into Parkridge from the North West.

Chapter 50

Natalie heard the knock at the door, the dull thumping sound coming at her as if through an invisible filter. At first, she mistook it for the sound of her own heartbeat. Just standing as close as she was to Scott, her pulse was so fast that she could feel her entire body trembling, as if she were about to erupt into some kind of joy-induced seizure. It only stood to reason that she would be able to hear the beat of her heart.

Almost nose-to-nose with Scott, she watched as he registered the sound. His pupils dilated in response to the knock, expanding and swallowing light. Knowing that he was staring at her, and seeing her own reflection ringed in the darkness of his pupil, Natalie felt her breath hitch in her throat. As she inhaled, she caught a faint wisp of Scott's scent; musky and coppery. Blood flushed to her cheeks in a pink blush, and she could feel her head grow hot. A slight dizziness took her and she fought to stay poised, drunk off of his presence.

Again the knock came from the door, and she was snapped from the daze.

Her right hand, holding the metal grip of the kitchen knife, tensed and tightened. Emanating from the weapon, a comforting sensation eased through her.

Around Natalie, everything seemed to crawl into slow-motion. Options and thoughts swam through her head, as she considered what to do in the situation.

There was someone at the door. That much she was certain of. Who exactly it was she had no idea. Her house rarely had visitors, save for the postman and the man that checked their water meter, and she doubted that it would be either of them. After all, it was far too late at night. That left only two options: either it was a stranger, or it was the man she had seen her mother with.

A powerful force took over her as she considered the possibility.

Either way, something had to be done. This was *the* night. The special night that she had spent endless hours planning and preparing for. Scott was there, her competition had been taken out of the picture, and everything was running smoothly. Everything was going exactly as she hoped it would.

Everything except the knocking at the door.

It bothered and distracted her, taking her attention away from what was important. Even when her bloody fingers had hold of Scott's own; even with his face practically inches from hers, it was all she could think about.

She considered ignoring it. She considered leaving well enough alone and pretending that no one was home. But that wouldn't work. The lights in the front room were on, and the car was in the driveway. Meaning that she would have to answer the door, lest her absence arouse suspicion.

But then what?

She would have to just turn them away; tell them that whoever they were looking for (more than likely her parents) were currently out, and would call them when they got home. After all, that had worked when the police had knocked on her door a few days earlier.

Releasing her grasp on Scott's hand, she straightened up and turned around. Only vaguely aware that she was still holding the knife, she closed the door to the room behind her and ventured down the hallway. Her footsteps echoed through the dimly lit space and pulsed in her head, their effect similar to that of the rap on the front door. Coming to the end of the hall, she turned left and began to climb the stairs out of the basement. Natalie's pace was quick and brisk, but in her mind time was moving at a fraction of its correct speed. After what seemed like an hour she reached the top of the staircase and moved out of the door that opened into the kitchen. Absent-mindedly sliding the bolt into place, she paused for a second before traversing the clear linoleum floor. Through the archway leading into the kitchen, she could see rain through the living room window, the thousands of droplets illuminated like stars by the headlights of a car on her driveway.

For the third time, she heard the banging of knuckles against wood, as the uninvited guest knocked on the door. Filtered by the barrier, her ears recognised the distant sound of someone swearing.

Reaching the door, the bloody fingers of her left hand unlatched the deadbolt before winding around the doorknob. Cold air smashed her in the face as she swung the structure open, shocking her senses into needle precision. The musty smell of rain assaulted her nose, and in the distance her eyes picked out a thread of lightning, stitching the sky. The white flash was intense enough to send a shiver through her body at its purity, and when the thunder followed it sounded like the deafening crescendo of the final act in an opera.

The air, charged by static from the storm, was sticky and thick. Taking a slow breath, Natalie had a hard time filling her lungs with the heavy hair. Flicking her eyes closed for a brief second Natalie saw afterimages of the lightning, dancing in angular shocks of purple and red. When she opened them again, the colours remained in her eyes, holding stark against the white of the lightning. Instinctively she thought of blood and bruising, her heart again beating faster at the thoughts.

A large figure moved into her line of sight, blocking out the brilliance of the storm and intrusively dominating her vision. Darkness fell on her as she looked up into the shadow cast by the silhouette.

An ominous feeling washed over Natalie, causing her hand holding the knife to tremble. Fear and anxiety plucked at her heartstrings, like the fingers of some cruel God playing her like an instrument. Thunder rolled in her ears, like a percussive slam of bass, and lightning flashed like the crash of a cymbal.

"Hey," the figure said, in a voice ruined by cigarettes, a note of confusion in its undertones. "I know you."

Chapter 51

Rawlings turned the corner of the country lane with a clumsy, unpractised tilt of the steering wheel. Ahead, his headlights parted the darkness, illuminating the scenery in varied flashes of green. Hedgerows, banks and trees tore past him as he sped up, prompted by the speed limit displayed on the liquid crystal screen of his SatNav. His mismatched eyes flinched closed beneath his dark brows as a flash of lightning seared the landscape.

"In four hundred yards, you will have reached your destination." The synthetic female voice of the satellite device dictated the final order of his journey, just before thunder shook the frame of the car.

Confused by the direction, Rawlings checked the screen before again sweeping his vision across his surroundings. Currently powering along a country road, in the middle of the fields that bordered the western edge of Lindum, he was as far removed from civilisation as was possible. Contouring the side of a hill with his route, to his left the lights of the new estate fringed the horizon, like distant stars.

Maybe the boy lived in one of the houses dotted about the countryside? That would certainly explain how he had gone missing, without anyone noticing.

What Rawlings took issue with, however, was that he wasn't hearing any sirens. He couldn't even see the flashing neon of cruiser lights. Given the time that David had called him, surely there had to have been at least some uniforms there already.

Apparently not.

The road he was currently on was the epitome of the phrase "silent as the grave". Indeed, save for the occasional boom of thunder, he heard nothing. For a brief moment Rawlings considered the idea that a particularly loud clap had temporarily deafened him.

Rounding yet another corner, he finally laid eyes on a house.

Perched midway up the hill, at the end of a long gravel driveway, the house was a humble redbrick affair. Sloping steeply, the roof was thatched and was spotted with a pair of window, set into opposite halves of the house. Originally built as something akin to a bungalow or cottage, the house more than likely had a sizeable basement, with the attic being converted into extra upstairs rooms. Beneath the canopy of the angular roof, the front door had been painted a deep royal blue. A large evergreen took up residence in the front garden, its fur leaves shaking violently with the thrash of the wind, while at the end of the drive was a cherry red car. Seeping through the front window, the lights were on.

"You have arrived at your destination."

Something about the property seemed familiar to Rawlings. More than likely, he had driven past it at some point in his life, on his way to another scene.

Pulling up the driveway, he left his headlights on as he stepped out of his car and traversed the space to the front door. Knocking on the door, flecks of blue paint peeled off and stuck to his knuckles.

Wind tugged at his heavy overcoat with strong, icy fingers, threatening to rip it from him. A chill licked at the nape of his neck, and he shifted uncomfortably on the spot.

Rawlings waited for about a minute before he knocked a second time.

That was when it started to rain.

There was no build up, no brief spatter or shower as a prelude to the storm. The heavens opened and rain lashed down thick and fast. Within a second, Rawlings' thick iron grey locks of hair were completely soaked and sticking to his forehead.

Hurriedly turning sideways, Rawlings flattened his back against the wall of the house. Reaching out with this left hand, he rapped backwards on the door for the third time. Turning his head sideways, he attempted to peer through the window, in an attempt to locate the owner. As his head extended, a fat drop of rain slapped against the back of his neck and rolled down between his shoulder blades.

Swearing under his breath, he pulled his body flat against the building once again, to escape the rain.

A blade of light suddenly cut across the gravel as the front door was opened. Releasing a relieved breath, at the prospect of escaping the rain, Rawlings stepped sideways into the doorway and prepared to introduce himself to the occupant. If the girl had phoned David, after finding a dead cat, then she would likely still be in shock. He needed to approach the situation gently.

Looking down at the figure in the doorway, he opened his mouth to speak, but the words stopped short. Lightning and thunder erupted behind him, throwing the features of the occupant into harsh detail. The face that met him was not one traumatised by the horror of stumbling across gore, but rather one of inquisitive curiosity. The girl was short and petite, with sharp and well-defined features. Her skin was milky pale and her hair was dark and contrasting. But it wasn't her features or expression that stopped Rawlings short. No. It was something else. Something glaring that he did not expect.

"Hey," he said, his words finding ground as realisation settled on his mind. "I know you."

It was true. Rawlings had seen this girl before. Now that he thought about it, the house was familiar too. He had been there, and spoken to this same girl, recently.

He remembered doing the rounds with David, earlier in the week. Going to the houses of people that reported their cats as either missing or injured. This house was one of them, and the girl that currently stood in front of him had been one of the pet owners. The reason why this particular girl stood out so much to Rawlings was all because of timing. Hers had been the last house the pair visited, before they found the body of Odette Lewis, just down the road. The girl had told them that her parents weren't home, so they had left the property without going inside.

Wrong house... Rawlings realised, mentally kicking himself for his poor sense of direction. *Shit. I need to call David.*

"Yes," the girl replied, with a slow and level voice. "You were here on Monday. I'm sorry, but Mum and Daddy aren't home again."

"No, sorry, sorry..." Rawlings flapped, lifting one hand and waving it about. Shrugging his shoulders upwards, he attempted to shield his neck from the rain and breathed out heavily. "I think I must have the wrong address. I, uh-"

He stopped short and paused. Rawlings was just about to excuse himself again, when he noticed something strange. Something that screamed at every police instinct that he had.

Blood.

Bubbling from around the knuckle of her left ring finger, it was soaking her digits and dripping down onto the floor, where it expanded into a steadily growing puddle over the floorboards. Rawlings immediately knew that it wasn't an ordinary cut; it was far too deep and far too thin. Even looking down at her, he could see that.

"Excuse me," he said, taking a step into the door way. "Is your hand alright? It looks like you cut yourself."

The girl's face twitched noticeably. Rawlings noted that. He also noticed how her expression spontaneously morphed into a strained smile. "No, no. I'm fine!"

That was a look that he recognised all too well. Typically seen on wives all too familiar with the back of their husband's hand, it was the dismissive smile of a victim. And it set off alarm bells inside Rawlings' head.

Something wasn't right.

"Are you sure?" he asked, leaning back slightly so as to not appear intimidating. "If it's bad you might need to go to the doctor."

"I said I'm fine!"

The knife came from Rawlings' left. At first he didn't see it. It suddenly appeared mid-air, as if through time-lapse photography.

She must have been holding it in her right hand, blocking it from view with the inwards-opening door.

The Detective felt his pulse speed up as adrenaline flooded his system. He could see the knife coming, predicting its trajectory. She was aiming for his neck.

Rawlings' mind whited out. He had no idea why the girl was attacking him. The mere concept seemed ridiculous and alien, shutting down his thoughts and leaving his mind numb and full of static.

His body, however, reacted automatically.

The blade was already far too close for him to stop it, disarm her, or even dodge. Prompted by instinct, Rawlings' left arm shot up.

The cold bite of metal burned his throat as the blade punctured the skin of his neck. Blood soaked his windpipe and coppery droplets burned the inside of his lungs. Pain seared through his nerve endings and fireworks exploded in his vision.

But by that point he had already reacted.

His left fist slammed into the girl's face with all the force of a sledgehammer. Skin ripped from his knuckles as her teeth were shattered on impact. Enamel scattered across the floor and blood burst from the crushed cartilage of her nose. Not expecting the sudden retaliation, her head shot back and her feet were whipped out from underneath her.

The force of the punch knocking the girl back, Rawlings felt the knife rip itself out of his neck. Pain assaulted him and his limbs shut down. Legs giving way beneath him, Rawlings collapsed forwards and fell on top of the girl.

His heartbeat roaring in his ears, fire took his body and afterimages of colour burned in his vision. Blood flooded his throat and his left lung started to cramp with a hot heaviness as it filled with fluid. Darkness began to creep in from his peripheral.

Rain, coming in thick and fast, streamed through the doorway and fell upon Rawlings' back, yet he didn't care.

Because he couldn't feel it.

Chapter 52

Natalie Hunt regained consciousness almost as quickly as she lost it.

For a brief instant she had no idea of where, or even who, she was. The only thing she was aware of was the explosion of pain searing across her face. Dispersing out through her body, it left her with the contradicting feeling of a searing numbness. The ground vanished underfoot as her legs swung up, and her stomach jumped up into her chest. Falling backwards, her eyes placed a scattering of tiny marble-like shards flying through the air. In a moment of vacant surprise, she realised that they were her teeth.

Her head hit the floor, a sharp shot of pain ripping down her spine. Her fingertips twitched from the shock and her right hand released the knife, sending it spinning across the wooden floor.

Opening her mouth, to take a breath, she instead let out a guttural cry of pain as the Police Officer collapsed on top of her. Air was forced out of her lungs, and she felt her ribs strain almost to cracking point, under the sudden increase in pressure. The weight crushing down on her stomach burst in her abdomen and vomit dared to surge up and out of her throat.

However, even as all of the pain bloomed in her body, something else roared into the forefront of Natalie's mind. Before even her lucid sense of self returned from unconsciousness, it pulsed through her system.

Hatred.

Visceral and acidic, it seared through her veins and burned along her nerve endings. Firing through the synapses in her brain, the hatred gripped her system and shuddered through her body.

She hated the man. Hated him with a purity unlike anything she had ever felt before.

He had hit her. Punched her in the face.

Despite her familiarity with pain, through her mother's education, never before in her life had Natalie felt pain quite like what was radiating through her face. It was the punch of a full grown man, and a large one at that. So powerful was the punch, it had completely shattered her teeth and broken her nose. The pain was so severe that it was all that she could think of.

Thrashing her arms out, Natalie attempted to pull herself upright but found her progress impeded by the weight of the man on top of her. Screaming in rage, she began to slam her hands into his head and shoulders, clawing at his hair and exposed skin in an attempt to rip his body off of her.

Finally managing to shift slightly, she lurched sideways and grabbed at the handle of the knife. Grasping it on her third attempt, the blade swung up through the air and plunged into the Officer's back.

Screaming again, Natalie used the handle of the knife as an anchor and began to roll the man off of her. Strain burned in her arms from the effort and, past the blood that now smeared her mouth and nose, her once white skin turned red.

Now turned onto his back, the Officer's punctured throat stared up at her like an evil eye, as she scrambled to her feet. A second later, a vicious and spiteful kick drilled into his side.

Natalie was getting ready to hit the man again when she suddenly stopped, her body locking up as if her joints had all spontaneously stopped working. Her mind seized with a jolt as she realised something, the asperity of the thought stopping her in place.

Scott was still downstairs.

She had left him alone, to answer the door. That wasn't part of her plan. It wasn't the night she envisioned. Everything was all wrong.

She needed to get back to him. To get things back on track and carry on with the night. The right way.

Slowly, almost mechanically, Natalie turned away from body of the Policeman. Rain streamed through the open door, and she didn't even think to close it.

*

A deep thump, as if something heavy had landed on the floor above him, rattled in Scott's ears. Dust shook loose from the ceiling and settled on Scott in a grey mist.

For the most part, however, he ignored it. Whatever was happening upstairs felt a million miles away. Too far away from him to even bother acknowledging.

All that mattered was escaping.

Pulling back with his bound left arm, Scott again tried to wrench free his hand. His thumb dangling loose, he tried to squeeze his hand past the bloody leather of the belt. His wrist passed through with little resistance, however by the time the belt reached the knuckle of his thumb, it had already ground to a halt. Even with the digit dislocated, his hand wasn't narrow enough to pass through the restraint.

Choking on a breath, Scott gritted his teeth in frustration. Tears formed in his eyes and sweat beaded on his face.

Desperation took over and he began to violent tug on his limb. Each jolt of his body sent a pulse of pain through his arm, as the empty socket was slammed into the leather restraint. But still, he failed to slip free.

Breathing desperately between clenched teeth, spit flew from his lips and spattered against his bound arm.

Leaking through the ceiling, he heard a scream, shortly followed by another.

He didn't have long. He needed to break free.

The struggle resumed in earnest. Over and over he pulled on his arm, desperate to move it even one millimetre. His fingertips had turned red and were beginning to tremble.

After what seemed like an age, his hand moved. Only slightly, but it definitely moved. Tears sprung up in Scott's eyes, and he almost cried with happiness.

Taking a breath and swallowing his tears, he prepared to resume his escape-

When the door opened.

Natalie strode into the room, covered in blood. Soaking into her face and across her chest, the fluid had stained both her clothes and her skin, filling the room with the pungent metallic scent that Scott was now so accustomed to. Her hand holding the knife was moving sporadically, twitching and jumping as if it had a mind of its own. Her nose, now broken, hung at an odd angle across her face and dripped a waterfall of red over her ripped top lip. When she smiled her shattered teeth peeked past her bloodied lips, jutting unevenly from the torn gums, glinting viciously with blood, like the mouth of a shark.

"Sorry I took so long," she said, her voice warped by the blood that had flooded her sinuses. "I didn't mean for there to be so many distractions today."

Chapter 53

It started off as a feeling; a vague sense of intuition. First coming to him as he wrote details in his notepad, it arrived as he watched the trail of ink appear behind his pen. Ordinarily he would have ignored it, but the more time he spent thinking about Scott the more it glared at him.

David had just finished on his third house when he turned back, leaving his accompanying uniformed officer behind. Rain lashed down on him, soaking him through and washing away the unnecessary thoughts. The more it beat down on him, the clearer his theory became.

"I thought I told you to go door to door!" Franko called over to him, from his position beneath the marquee covering the front garden. "What's the problem?"

"Sorry, sir!" David replied. "But there's something I need to check! Do we still have that note on site? The one I said was passed through the boy's door last week?"

Franko lowered his brows in one slow, clockwork movement. "What about it?"

"I'm not sure yet. It's just a feeling. It hasn't been taken back to the lab yet? I need to have another look at it."

"I think it's still here." He waved over to one of the figures wearing a plastic suit. "Is the note still here? The one from the kitchen? Don't look at me like that, we're not going to take it out of the bag. We just need to look at it." He glanced back at David as he stepped out of the rain and under the protective canopy. "You just need to look at it, right?"

"That's right, sir." He swiped one hand across his face, wiping moisture out of his eyes. "I just... I've missed something. I need another look at it. I feel like I've missed something."

Franko took the plastic sheath from the forensics specialist and handed it to David. "What is it?"

Eyes flicking over the looping text, David licked his lips and held his breath. "I recognise this handwriting!"

"What do you mean, you recognise the handwriting?" Franko asked, his voice bearing a hesitant edge to it, as if he didn't quite believe what David was saying.

"I mean I've seen this somewhere before," David repeated. "This way of writing. Normal people don't write like this. It's too distinct to be a coincidence."

"Where have you seen it before, Stafford?" The DCI's expression was level, but his voice belied his true feelings. David could hear the hopeful expectation; something that he never thought he would hear coming from his typically robotic superior.

"In... In the reports of the missing cats," he said, tripping over his words. "On the records taken by the Vets, the owners had to fill in forms with the pets' names, and all of their details. That's where I've seen this before!"

Franko's spine straightened, his body growing rigid. "Do we still have those?"

"Back at the station, yes."

"Right," Franko said, beginning to walk towards his car, and signalling for David to follow suit. "You're coming with me. We need to go through those reports."

Turning to venture further down the road, David fished in his pocket for his car keys, when the intensity of his superior's voice stopped him short.

"Where are you going?"

Confused, he paused and struggled to say even the most simple of responses. "Um, m-my car?"

"No, we're taking mine," Franko shot back. "Yours will keep. We'll come back for it later. There's no sense in taking two cars, when we need to get back fast. I also need you to talk me through these reports. It's easier than doing it over the phone."

"O... O-Okay..." he stammered, walking back towards Franko's car, as if on autopilot.

"Hey!" Wilson suddenly shouted, from down the road. "Where are you going? What about the door to doors?"

"Something's come up!" David replied, raising his voice to be heard over the thrash of rain. "I need to get back to the station and check something!"

"What do you mean "something's come up"? In case you haven't noticed, we have a missing kid here!"

"I'm well aware of that," Franko said, sharply. "But if this is what David thinks it is, we might actually be able to find him. You stay here and continue with the door to doors. I'm leaving you in charge of the uniforms." Turning, he opened his car door and paused before climbing inside. "And if Rawlings isn't here in five minutes, call him again! We need him right now!"

Without another word, Franko got into his car and slammed the door. Following suit, David only offered Wilson a hesitant shrug before he joined his superior in the car.

As soon as David clicked his seatbelt in place, Franko sped down the road, weaving in and out around parked cars. Stunned by the speed of the DCI's driving, he flattened back in his seat and grabbed hold of the door handle. Perhaps influenced by his superior's age, at just under sixty years old, David's perception of Franko did not include the notion that he was a particularly fast or aggressive driver. The current situation, however, forced him to re-evaluate his views. He wondered, for a moment, what else he had mistakenly judged Franko on.

Quickly looking around the inside of the car, David's curiosity motivated him to search out details about the DCI's life. The only thing of substance he found was a hanging picture, dangling from beneath the rear view mirror. Sealed inside plastic and smiling down at him, the faces of a young woman and two little boys swung back and forth through the air. Two of them had the same nose as his superior, and all of them bore identical mahogany eyes.

"So this note," Franko said, cutting into his attention with a swift stroke of his voice, "and how it matches one of the reports. What's your theory? What do you think it's telling us? I'm trusting you on this one, so you need to give me everything. And don't worry... When this breaks and we catch them, if your theory is what leads us there, you're getting full credit. Braithwaite be damned, if you earn it you're getting it."

His words stunned David. Never did he expect Franko to be so supported. He knew that the DCI appreciated a good work ethic and results, but the offer to give him full credit for closing the case came completely out of left field.

Scrambling, he tried to organise his thoughts and theories into a coherent sentence. "Okay, basically-"

"No, not basically," Franko cut in. "Give me everything. Don't scrimp the details or simplify it."

"Okay... What I'm thinking is: Whoever wrote that note and put it through Scott's door also filed a report about a missing cat. The handwriting is far too detailed and specific; not many people write like that. Calligraphy like that, you need to be trained in."

"So why would our unsub file a missing cat report in the first place?" the DCI asked, playing the devil's advocate. "Maybe this person just happened to have lost a cat, and also just happened to be an admirer of this Scott boy? Stranger things have happened. What makes you so sure there's a connection?"

David didn't understand the use of the term 'unsub', but he replied all the same. "The note was passed through the door on the same day he found the corpses. The timing is too suspicious; it's why we took the note in as evidence, in the first place. It had to have been from the Cat Hunter. As for the missing report... They wrote it to throw us off their trail. After all, why would we investigate someone who has done that? Logic would dictate that the killer would want to take attention away from themself, not draw more onto them... And that's exactly why they did it. To throw us off their trail."

A proud smile touched Franko's lips. "So why send the note to Scott in the first place? If they're as forward-thinking as you claim, they must have realised that we would be able to match the handwriting to the report."

"Not necessarily," David replied, conviction burning in his chest as he stared out of the drowned windshield at the nightlife of Lindum City Centre. "Either they couldn't help themself, and had to send it, or... Or they didn't expect Scott to keep the note."

"So..." Franko said, momentarily taking his eyes off of the road to stare at David. "What are we expecting to find, when we get back to the station?"

David broke into a confident smile. "A missing cat report, written by our killer... Complete with a name and address."

Chapter 54

Looking down at Scott, bound to the chair, Natalie broke into her best estimation of what a smile should look like. Given her mutilated mouth, however, this was no easy task. Her bloody lips snagged against the jagged enamel of her broken teeth, further ripping open the torn flesh. She felt a warm dribble of blood roll down her chin, drip into the air, and splash against her shirt.

Catching his gaze, a nervous wave of passion undulated through her body. Her heart fluttered into a fast rhythm, the sound of blood ululating in her ears like the distant cry of night birds. A shiver of pleasure caught the tempo and rippled under her skin, causing her hand holding the knife to jump and spasm.

She watched as Scott's jaw dropped low, and his bloodshot hazel eyes scanned her malformed face.

"Natalie... What did you do...?"

Hearing Scott use her name, Natalie felt something stir inside her. A peculiar feeling that she couldn't quite place. A bead of moisture formed between her legs.

"I answered the door," she replied, fighting back a blush at her own indecency. "We don't usually have visitors so it really surprised me. But he's gone now, so it's okay. We can carry on where we left off."

Sauntering over on unsteady legs, Natalie set the knife down on the floor by Scott's foot and paused for a second. The desire to straddle his lap filled her, and for a brief moment she wrestled with herself over whether or not she would do it. She didn't want to come across as too forward — too slutty. Daddy had always liked her to be demure and submissive, so at first she considered leaving well enough alone and simply crouching beside him. However a memory leapt up in her mind, and banished the notion with its presence. Natalie remembered the girl (she couldn't quite remember her name) lunging at Scott and shoving her tongue down his throat; and she remembered how Scott reciprocated. He liked forward girls. Girls who knew what they wanted.

Easing herself down onto his lap, she splayed her legs either side of his torso and slipped them beneath the arms of the chair. Her crotch bottoming down on his own, heat bled through her womb and she just about managed to suppress a throaty gasp.

"I just wanted this to be perfect," she said, her solicitous cooing deformed by her smashed nose. "Today's a special day. It's why I needed you here."

Wrapping her arms around Scott's head, she nuzzled her chin into his hair and inhaled his scent. No sooner had she done so, another wave of heat washed through her body. His face pressed into her breasts, Scott's hot breath trickled through the material of her top, the sensation stiffening her nipples into hard buds.

Swallowing her need, Natalie leaned back and looked down at Scott. "You're all I ever wanted. Today... Today I couldn't even think about spending it without you. It's supposed to be special."

"What's special about today?" he asked, shifting slightly to the side; the zipper of his trousers rubbing against her sweet spot.

Natalie cupped his face in her sticky, bloody hands and lowered her face in front of his. "It's my sixteenth birthday."

Then she kissed him. Jagged teeth scraped along his lips and blood trickled from the corner of her mouth as her torn tongue probed into his mouth. Tasting him for the first time, Natalie felt her body begin to drift in weightless bliss.

Tears of happiness formed in her eyes when she finally pulled away, and shallow breaths shuddered her chest. Propelled by the urge to feel him, she began to run her hands over his body, tracing the contours of his collarbones before moving up his neck and over his face. The sheer closeness of him sent her mind reeling, leaving her dead to everything else. In that moment, she felt a beautiful red passion wash through her like a tropical sea.

Seemingly catching his breath, Scott again shifted to one side. Eyes not once leaving her face, his voice wavered slightly as he spoke. "S-so... What did you want to do for... For your birthday?"

Love exploded in Natalie's chest as she heard the question. She had never been asked that before, not even by her Daddy. Tears burst from her eyes, diluting the blood that smeared her face, and another tremble rocked her body.

"I..." She stopped for a second to compose herself; to quash the sudden flood of happiness that had burst inside her. "I want to dance with you."

Failing to see the flash of hope that passed across Scott's face, she gently lifted herself off of him and crouched on the floor.

Excitement took hold as she reached out with bloody fingers and began to unbuckle the belts that secured his legs to those of the chair.

As she did so, words trickled from her mouth, in time with the drip of blood. Half muttering, she wasn't entirely sure if their presence was even intentional.

"But if I untie you, you need to promise not to run away. I know that you won't, but you still need to promise. But I can't let you go. But you can't dance with me unless you're untied. Unless you stayed on your knees. Yes, your knees. I'm going to need you to stay on your knees, and we'll dance like that."

Finishing removing the belt fastening Scott's left foot, she slowly moved one hand over his skin.

Then she picked up her knife and sliced through his Achilles tendon.

Chapter 55

An ugly sound suddenly formed in Scott's throat, against his will. Pain lanced up his leg, searing through his nerve endings and his left ankle fell limp; unable to move. Tears formed in the corners of his eyes, stinging them and threatening to blind him.

No! he thought. *Eat it! Don't cry and don't scream! She's distracted! Quick- Before she does the other one!*

Adrenaline flooded his body, temporarily numbing him to the pain, and a desperate power took hold of him unlike anything he had experienced before. Wrenching his left hand against the restriction of the belt he pulled with every ounce of strength in his body, and more.

He felt the cold bite of metal against the back of his right ankle.

A sickening crack split the air, reverberating against the walls of the dimly lit room.

Scott had managed to wrench his hand free. Unfortunately, his freedom had come at the cost of his wrist and two of his fingers. Ripped from their sockets by the sheer force, they flailed uselessly in the air as he lost balance and the chair toppled. His foot caught Natalie in the face as he fell, sending her sprawling backwards, the knife flung from her grip.

Without a moment's hesitation, his two functioning fingers on his left hand frantically worked at the belt still binding his right wrist. The fingernail of his index finger was torn off as, in his desperation, he dug too hard at the buckle. He didn't care. He needed to free himself. To get out before she recovered.

The blood actually helped. The crimson liquid had lubricated the leather, allowing it to slide easier. Within seconds his right arm was free as well.

A mad strength possessed him, and soon he was on his knees, crawling towards the discarded knife. His speed surprised even him. With the tendons in his ankle severed, and his wrist still removed from its socket, almost his entire left side was dead. By all right and logic, he shouldn't have been able to move as fast as he did. And yet he did.

Fingers touching the handle of the blade, Scott was about to close them around it when he felt a grip tighten on the leg of his trousers. Yanking him back with a strength unbefitting her size, Natalie fell upon him with a scream of rage. Clawing her way up his body, teeth jutting and snapping from her barracuda mouth, she began to wrestle him, attempting to fight him into submission.

Ordinarily Scott would have had no problem fighting her off. But the situation was nothing but ordinary. His muscles cramping from the sudden usage, and overwrought with pain from his leg, he struggled to fend off the girl's thrashing attack. Ripping into him with her nails, Natalie tore at him with all the power of a vicious insanity.

Gripping her with his functioning right hand, in an attempt to push her back, Scott thrashed his legs in a futile attempt to kick her off of him.

Finally finding leverage by rolling onto his back, Scott kept his grip on her and reared his left arm back. Slamming his dislocated left hand into her already ruined face, the diminutive force was enough to temporarily stun her.

Momentarily free from Natalie's assault on him, he made a break for the door. Crawling along the floor, dragging his useless left foot behind him, he just about made it through the frame.

Not stopping for even a moment, he scrambled down the hallway, making for the beam of light at the end. Hot on his heels, Natalie charged after him, however was again stunned by a backwards kick from Scott's right leg. His heel slamming into the side of her knee, she fell to the floor and landed face-first on the carpeted floor.

Scott reached the stairs in less than a minute. Desperately tearing up them, on his hands and knees, his severed tendon screamed at him whenever even the slightest pressure was put on it. Tears burning in his eyes, he finally reached the top of the staircase, just has he saw Natalie beginning her chase after him, in earnest.

Gripping the wooden structure, he slammed the door at the top of the stairs closed, the wood crushing into the crazed girl's face as she reached the mouth of the doorway. Through the filter of the door, he heard a series of dull crashes as she tumbled back down the staircase.

Now bought some more time, Scott's vision darted around the room in which he found himself. Random details assaulted him through vision tunnelled by pain. Petunias in a vase on the windowsill; a countertop scattered with various letters and envelopes; the peel of an onion, missed during sweeping, sitting dejected in the corner of the room; an oven with the door left half open. He was in a kitchen.

A kitchen.

A kitchen meant knives; a means of defending himself.

Grabbing hold of a drawer handle with his still working right hand, Scott attempted to pull himself up. His hand slick with blood, however, he lost his grip and fell backwards, hitting his head against the floor. Pain shot under the skin of his scalp, prickling through what seemed like each individual hair in his head.

Gritting his teeth, Scott let out a guttural groan and abandoned his plan to find a knife. Pulling himself over the tiles, he began to crawl through the house in search of a phone.

What he found instead filled him with a horrific sense of fear and unease. Laying on his back in a growing puddle of rain and blood, his legs jutting out of the open doorway, was the body of a man. Lightning flashed through the door, illuminating the body in stark black and white, and thunder boomed in Scott's ears. Behind it, he could hear Natalie screaming his name as she tore up the stairs and came after him.

Fear pulsing in his throat, Scott wrestled with his conscience before deciding to abandon the man. Tears blurring his vision, he crawled over the man's bloody body and fled the house, into the storm.

Rain drowned his body, and his fingers dug through the soaking stones of the gravel pathway. The wound on his ankle continued to radiate pain up his leg and a shard of flint jammed into the soft flesh of his finger, exposed by his missing nail, sending a burning jolt through his hand.

Rolling out of the driveway, and into the road, he reared his head back and stared over his shoulder, back at the house. Illuminated by another burst of lightning, he saw Natalie appear in the doorway and start towards him. Before she had gone more than a few feet, however, the figure in the doorway moved. Grasping her by the leg, the dying man pulled her foot out from underneath her, in an attempt to seemingly restrain her.

A horrific rage-filled scream roared through the air as the girl fought against the man's limp arms. Again Scott saw her lift the knife, and the implement was driven down into the man's shoulder.

Fear still gripping him, Scott dragged his body across the road, reaching the bank of the bordering field. Fingers plunging into the mud, he pulled himself over the bank and into the mire left in the wake of the rain.

Ahead, through the descending curtain of rain, he could see the distant lights of Lindum, decorating the base of the valley. Lifting his body up, on trembling arms, he attempted to get a better view when he lost strength and tumbled forwards. Entering into a roll, he tumbled headfirst down the steep incline of the muddy field.

Sprinting over the road behind, Natalie leapt the bank and dived down the hill after him.

Chapter 56

The radio, fitted beneath his dashboard, pulsed with the thrum of heavy drum and bass. Windscreen wipers beat against the drowning glass with a heavy thrash, as if to the rhythm of the music.

Squinting his eyes, Masum Khalid peered past the downpour as he eased his foot off of the accelerator and turned down the volume.

Things were not at all going as he expected. His original plan was to take the country roads, to bypass the motorway traffic coming off of the industrial estate, and utilise the national speed limit to cut through the lanes at a fast pace. The rain, however, was putting a dampener on that plan. The roads were soaked, and the wind was beating against the frame of his sports car to such a degree that his driving was suffering. His steering was all over the place, and whenever he had to take a corner Masum had to slow right down for fear of sliding off of the blacktop.

Worse still was the persistent thunder and lightning. It cackled across the landscape in a deafening cacophony, distracting him from the roads and searing his nerves. Never in all of his years had he been so on edge.

Eyeing the clock hesitantly, he took a breath. There were still ten minutes until his meeting, and he wasn't sure if he was going to make it.

Turning a corner the lights of Lindum appeared on his right, through the veil of rain, as the road opened up into a straight stretch ahead of him. Increasing the pressure on his accelerator, Masum sped up and bore down on the road.

He hoped that, if he was late, the investor would wait for him. If he had any luck, his staff would think to delay any potential departure with the offer of free food and drink.

Masum considered calling ahead and explaining the traffic situation. His finger hovered over the touchscreen, built into his dashboard, and toyed with the idea of activating his hands free and dialling the investor's number. His eyes moved down and momentarily lingered on the device. Biting his lip, he mulled over the option, before he decided against it. Tearing his eyes away from the screen, he returned his attention to the road-

And hit the kid that had just staggered out of the field to his left.

Chapter 57

Water soaked the floor as David and Franko shook the rain from their jackets, striding into the entrance hall of Lindum Police Station. White panel lights illuminated them in a clinical glare of intelligent determination.

David's card beeped against the magnetic lock, releasing the door to the incident room, and the pair burst in in a flurry of purposeful activity. David reached the large table in the middle of the room within seconds, and began sifting through the various folders and piles of paper. Simultaneously, Franko moved to the front of the room and dashed his eyes over the evidence board. Fixed to the centre, partially obscuring the mostly erased phrase **"Pussy Hunting"**, was a large map of the wider Lindum area.

"Do you have that report?" Franko asked, his voice urgent in pace but level in tone.

David muttered under his breath as his fingers flicked through the bindings of a dense black folder. "Hang on, hang on, hang on..." Digits dancing over the sheathing glimmer of the plastic wallets protecting the reports, his pace was frantic. Twice he mistakenly thought he'd passed the report that he was looking for. "Got it!"

Eyes dashed over the sheet, flicking between it and the note that he held, still in the evidence bag, in his other hand. The handwriting definitely matched. The way the "D"s curled back onto themselves, and the "t"s looped were almost identical.

"Natalie Hunt!" he called out, as Franko focussed in on the map, ready to plot the address. "2 Burleigh Way, Lindum! Postcode: LM3 9XY!" Even as he read it out loud, a vaguely familiar feeling filled David's body. He recognised the postcode.

His train of thought was broken as Franko parroted it back to him. "It's one of the cottages out to the west. From what I can see, it seems to overlook the estate that the missing boy lives on."

"She also goes to the school where the first dump was made," David called back. "That's how she knew the schedule of the class, and about the security cameras." His eyes narrowed as he spotted something on the page. "Shit!"

Franko glanced over his shoulder. "What, what is it?"

"The fucking name of her cat. Smudge. Tabby cat, with a ginger striped pattern. Why didn't I notice it before? Shit. It's exactly the same as one of Odette Lewis' missings."

"That confirms your theory that she made the report to throw off our suspicions. She never had a cat; she just borrowed the name of one of the ones she killed." Leaning closer to the map, Franko inspected several marks that had been jotted onto the surface.

"But why Odette Lewis' cat? Why would she pick the cat of someone she ended up killing?"

"The report was probably filed before Mrs Lewis died," Franko said, anchoring his finger onto a single, labelled point. "Plus, given the situation, I think it's clear that she never intended to kill her. Look. Her house is right down the road from Mrs Lewis'. Killing someone so close to where she lives could only be accidental, given everything else we've seen." He narrowed his eyes. "The only thing we don't know is why she decided to kidnap the boy today."

"I think I've found that too, sir," David replied, standing as he held the report between his fingers. "Today's her birthday."

"And there's our trigger," Franko said, turning away from the evidence board and signalling to David. "Grab your coat. We're going to the house. Gather some uniforms too. But for god sake, make sure they don't turn their sirens on. We don't want to get him killed if she hears us and panics."

David nodded in confirmation and moved to head out of the incident room when his phone rang. Whipping it out, he blipped his thumb against the screen and pressed it to his ear, as Wilson's voice came through the device.

"Something weird is going on. I've called Rawlings four times, and he's still not picking up."

Noting his subordinate on the phone, Franko walked across the room. "What is it; what's going on?"

"It's Wilson," he replied. "He's saying Rawlings isn't there yet."

"This isn't like him," Wilson's voice again played through into his ear. "The idiot's always getting lost, but this is too long, even for him. He should be here by now; or at least should have called when he realised he was in the wrong place."

David relayed what the Detective was saying to Franko.

"Put him on speaker," the DCI said. "Quickly. We can't afford to be standing around too long."

"Like I was saying to Dave," Wilson's voice blared out of the phone, now held in front of David. "Rawlings hasn't called me, and he isn't picking up his phone either."

Franko lowered his brows and looked over at David. "And you gave him the correct address?"

"Yes." David nodded.

"You're sure?"

"Yes, yes." He fished his notepad out of his pocket and began to thumb through the pages. "I wrote down Scott's postcode, and read it out to Rawlings when I gave him the address. It's right-" He stopped short as he turned one page, and revealed a sheet of blank, lined sheets. "Hang on, it should be back here." David flicked the page back, and looked down at the postcode scribed on the paper. A dark realisation dawned on his face. A tremble of unease coursed through his body. "Oh no..."

Franko lifted an eyebrow and looked at him quizzically. "What?"

David lifted the sheet and peeled it apart. "These two pages are stuck together..." He looked over at the map. "The postcode I gave to him... It's the one for Odette Lewis' house." He shuddered, as an edge of anxiety touched his voice. "How many houses have that postcode? How many houses are on that road?!"

Franko hurried across the room and quickly studied the map. His voice took on a vacant hollowness. "Three."

"Guys, what's going on?" Wilson's voice, coming through the phone line, warbled with static as the storm interfered with the signal.

David and Franko both made for the door, hurrying to get out of the building.

"Wilson, get as many uniforms as possible," Franko commanded, his voice whirling into a mechanical authority. "Have them head to the location David is going to give you."

"Yeah, sure. As soon as you tell me what the hell is going on."

Even as he said the words, David didn't quite believe them. In spite of that, however, fear came through in his voice. "I think Rawlings is at our suspect's house."

Chapter 58

Scott staggered out of the field, ripping his dead ankle from the mud, using the force of his still functioning leg to push himself up. Stumbling out of the mire, his left leg came down with a jolt onto the Tarmac of the road, sending a bolt of pain up the joint. The limb unable to support his weight, he fell sideways.

As he did so, the high beams of a car fell upon him.

The car smashed into his right hand side, crushing his femur and rolling him over the bonnet. His head cracked the windscreen on impact, sending spiderweb of red and white over the glass, as the cracks filled with his blood.

Pitched ten feet into the air by the crash, Scott was surrounded by rain. Weightless, if only for a moment, he was turned end over end before finally falling and landing in the swamp of the field opposite.

Landing on his left elbow, the joint twisted sharply and a severe crack split the air as all three bones in his arm broke from the strain. The snapped limb dug into his side as he rolled, cracking three of his ribs with the pressure.

Coming to a stop several feet into the field, the pain tore through him like a freight train. It smacked him with the force, and left his very bones feeling the sear of fire.

There becomes a point where the discussion of pain becomes redundant. When describing how much something hurts can never quite do it justice. And Scott realised, in that moment, that if he lived through it, he would never be able to accurately describe what it felt like to anybody. Because in that instant, the burn felt like being possessed by the devil himself.

Sparks of scotoma danced in his vision in flashes of red and, combined with the disorienting rain, he felt like he was going blind. Everything was upside down. He had no idea where he was, knowing nothing but the bloodcurdling scream of pain.

Blood crawled out of his body and wormed deep into the earth, as if the ground were feeding on him. The dirt suckled on him hungrily, pulling life from his wounds.

Too riled by agony to pass out, Scott was filled with an overwhelming restlessness. He tried in vain to move his body but found his arms heavy and full of far too much sensation.

Choking out a breath, his broken ribs jabbed at his lungs, and he felt like he was being stabbed by a red hot poker. Even breathing became a struggle, the only thing keeping his ragged breaths regular being his brain's most basic fundamental instincts.

Roaring in his ears, all he could hear was the thrash of rain and the furious pounding of his heart. It was like he was drowning in static.

Nothing else even seemed to exist, outside of his own sphere of awareness.

Nothing, until he heard it.

Creeping over the horizon, it began to grow progressively louder, building until it pierced the haze of his lucid mind.

The sound of sirens.

Chapter 59

"Jesus Christ!"

St. Claire was on his way to the house when he saw the crash. Illuminated by a white burst of lightning, the whole scene was seared into his optic nerves like the negative of a photograph. His mouth opened, horrified, as he watched the car plough into the boy, tossing him through the air like a rag doll.

Pulling over into a muddy layby, he hurriedly got out of his car and climbed the bank of the field separating him from the collision. Passing him by, the other squad cars screamed up the hill and stopped outside of the cottage.

Concern knotting his stomach, he watched as the driver swung his car almost completely around and came to a screeching halt. A man in a suit hurriedly leapt out of the convertible to check on the kid. His hand was raised up beside his face as he began to phone for help.

Swearing under his breath in disbelief that the other cars had just passed by, he turned back to his patrol car and snatched up the radio.

"This is St. Claire. I've got a traffic collision down on Burleigh Way. Postcode LM3 9XY. Send an ambulance. Quickly. A kid's been hit by a car. Some kind of BMW; I can't see the plates from here, I'm going to move closer."

Glancing back over his shoulder, he looked down the slope of the field at the site of the crash. As he did so, his eyes opened wide.

Stepping out onto the road, covered in a mixture of mud and blood, a girl passed in front of the car's headlights. Catching the glare of the light, something metallic flashed in her hand. A knife.

She was heading straight for the driver.

St. Claire realised, in that moment, that the girl was their suspect. Panic grabbed at his heart with icy fingers, and he completely forgot procedure. His body reacted automatically, spurred by the urge to stop the girl. Dropping his radio, he leapt the bank and began to sprint down the muddy field.

Rain beat upon him, soaking his uniform, and mud sucked at his legs. Neither deterred him. Charging down the incline, he pumped his arms furiously, as if the motion would speed him up.

Please! his mind begged his body. *Please make it in time!*

*

Even as the thunder and lightning raged around her, an ever fiercer storm was exploding through Natalie Hunt.

Her thoughts were in complete disarray, to such an extent that it felt as if her body had been left to roam on its own. Her mind flickered with fragments of incomplete trains of thought, while a cordial of hormones and neural signals fired through her empty shell. Twitches shook her limbs and her eyes were unfocused; the overwhelming rush of chemical emotions riding her body in waves of destructive activity.

Scott had attacked her. He had tried to get away. He was getting away.

That wasn't right; there had to be some kind of mistake. Something that she just wasn't seeing.

Ever since she had first met him, Scott had been her only tether to even the concept of normality. Just by being visible to her, he had been her safety net. A means of escaping the torturous horror of her home life. Whenever her Mother hit her, or bathed her in boiling water, or stabbed her with the fork, Natalie had thought of Scott. Of the friendly smile he had offered her, the first day that they met. Whenever Daddy crawled into her bed, it was Scott that she thought of when he touched her. She would think of him, and imagine that it was *him* touching her.

He had been an obsession. A grounding force in her life that counteracted all of the sick, twisted and painful experiences. Like a human lightning rod.

His one act of kindness meant more than anything else she had ever experienced, in her miserable life. After all, nobody else had ever given a damn about her. Nobody else cared. He was the only one.

So he *had* to love her, the way that she loved him.

How could he not? No one else had ever treated her the way that he did; talking to her the way nobody else would; smiling at her.

So it had to be love.

Right?

But then he tried to get away. He had kicked her and hit her, the way her mother always used to, and the way the evil man had struck her.

Natalie knew that she didn't deserve it. There was no reason for his escape; no need for him to hit her.

When you do bad things, you are punished. However she hadn't done anything bad. She was only showing him how much she loved him.

A dark, vengeful feeling took her and shook Natalie to her core, thrashing through her and snapping at her nerves like a rabid animal.

It was the same as when her Mother had last beaten her. When, even though she was the one in the wrong, Natalie had been on the receiving end of the punishment.

Scott was deflecting onto her. The same way that her Mother did.

The thought of the betrayal was crushing. Natalie's chest constricted, like she was being held in a vice. Her breaths became short and her heart bruised the inside of her ribcage. She felt sick, like vomit and acid was going to heave out of her stomach and fly out of her mouth. The idea that the boy she loved so much could turn against her like that repulsed every fibre of her being.

And yet she knew what she had to do.

She needed to punish him.

Just like with her Mother and Father.

Hardly even aware of herself, Natalie stepped around the car and made for Scott's mangled form.

*

"Oh god. Oh fuck. Fuck! I need an ambulance here, right now! I- I've just hit a kid. He... He just ran out into the road! Please, you have to get someone!"

Masum Khalid, still in shock from the collision, trembled and stammered. Practically screaming down his phone at the emergency services, just stringing together a cohesive sentence seemed like the hardest thing in the world.

His heart was beating in his throat, and his tongue swelled, sticking to the inside of his mouth; dried out from the horror.

He slipped once on the mud as he stepped into the field where the kid had landed. Now that he was closer, the boy looked so much worse than before. He lay half on his back, mostly covered in a curdled mixture of mud and blood. Vacant eyes stared out of his face, through the veil of grime. His expression was blank, a dying light leeching from his expression.

"Oh shit, it's really bad," he said, not even listening to the operator's response. "What do I do? What do I do?"

He didn't want to touch the boy. It was like he was made of fragile glass; he felt like even the smallest movement would shatter him into a million pieces.

What if he has a spine injury? he thought, panic seething out of him. *What if I've fucking crippled him?!*

Nervous sweat seeped out of his body, beneath the expensive suit, and combined with the rain crashing down on him from above, ensuring that he was almost completely soaked through. His legs trembled unsteadily beneath him, quivering as they struggled to support him in the mire of mud.

The voice of the operator, more urgent and louder now, snapped him from his panic-induced daze. "Sir! Sir! Can you hear me? I need you to make sure that he's breathing. Please, can you check and see if he's breathing."

Masum's breath came through in short, sharp gasps as he began to hyperventilate. "Yes, yes... Yeah I'll check..."

Stooping and holding out one hand, Masum moved to hold his palm over the boy's mouth, when he suddenly felt a blow against his right hand side. It felt like he'd been shot. Pain radiated out from under his limbs and locked his muscles in a cramping tightness. He fell to his left and dropped the phone, writhing in agony as he grabbed at his side.

His spine arching from the horrific sensation, Masum's body turned over. Eyes squinted in pain, he just about made out the form of someone standing behind him.

The girl looked downright inhuman. Her body was mostly covered in an emulsion of dirt and blood. Her hair was matted and streaked with clumps of clay, hanging in tendrils around her ruined face. A nose, crooked and crushed, jutted from beneath her cold eyes, bubbling blood over the jagged teeth of her vampiric mouth. In her right hand she held a knife, the blade slick with blood.

She stepped past him, as if he wasn't even there.

And made for the boy that lay dying on the floor.

*

Scott looked up at Natalie through swollen eyes. Tears blinded him and a mist of red sprayed from his mouth when he tried to speak.

He gave in to his fear of death, a whimpering sound escaping from between his bloody lips. Scott crumbled, breaking down into sobs as tears flowed freely from his eyes. He wanted to go home. He wanted his Mum.

The urge to beg filled him, as Natalie reached down and grabbed the neck of his shirt, but no sound came out. His strangled breathing shot spears of pain, from his broken ribs, into his lungs.

Natalie moved her knife towards him.

This is it, he thought, as lightning whited out his vision. *I'm going to die.*

Thunder boomed in his ears and Natalie was blown off of her feet.

*

St. Claire crashed into Natalie with all of the force of the storm that beat down on the scene. Thunder rolled over the landscape, as if reacting to his action. Hooking one arm around her waist, his other grabbed onto her hand holding the knife. The girl's feet left the floor as she was tackled, and she came down hard in the mud, St. Claire's full weight on top of her.

Restraining her, he shook loose the blade from her grip and breathed heavily, his heartbeat roaring in his head.

St. Claire had heard about the strength of the insane before, but had never truly understood the concept until that moment. A madness gripped the girl, unlike anything he had ever seen before. So powerful and flooded with adrenaline was she, he had difficulty securing her wrists into the handcuffs. Even after snapping them into place, he kept a firm grip with one hand, for fear that she would break free.

Finally pulling his phone from the depths of his mud-caked uniform, St. Claire shouted down the receiver. "This is Constable St. Claire from Lyefield Police. I need an ambulance down on Burleigh Way. I've got a stabbing victim and a kid that's been hit by a car." Natalie started to scream and buck beneath him, but he kept his hold on her. His voice grew even louder, to dwarf the cacophony of her shrieking. "I'm also going to need a van! I've got the perp in custody!" As he said it, it dawned on him. "I've got her! I've got the Cat Hunter!"

Chapter 60

Natalie Hunt was carted away, just as Scott Willard's stretcher was being loaded into the ambulance. Not once did her voice die down, through the entire ordeal. She shrieked out her love for him, like a wailing banshee, continuing long after her vocal chords were torn.

Another ambulance peeled away from the house, carrying in it Detective Sergeant Timothy Rawlings. His left lung flooded with blood, he was lucky to be alive. Had help arrived even ten minutes later, he might not have made it.

Inside the house, the police had found the bodies of Alice Goodacre, Helen Raleigh, and Maria and Kevin Hunt. Alice's throat had been slashed, as had Kevin's. The only solace to be held was that their deaths were quick. Helen and Maria, however, were another story. Natalie had cut out Helen's tongue and stretched a strip of duct tape over her mouth, leaving her to the slow and torturous agony of drowning on her own blood. Maria was downright mutilated. She had been stabbed so many times, she was almost beyond recognition.

Upon searching her bedroom, David Stafford uncovered a diary of sorts. In it, Natalie detailed the horrific abuse she suffered, at the hands of her parents. As he thumbed through the pages, David was so unsettled he had to fight back the urge to cry.

Finding him reading in the bedroom, his hands trembling, Franko had placed one hand on David's shoulder and ushered him out of the house.

*

The office, in the middle of Lindum Police Station, was silent save for the dull hum of the computers. David peered down at one of the monitors, watching Natalie from the security cameras as she rocked back and forth, chained to the table in the interrogation room. Beside him, Wilson twisted his mouth into a shocked and sour expression.

"What the hell happened to her face?"

"She stabbed Rawlings in the throat, so he punched her in the face," David explained. "She swallowed six of her teeth."

"How on earth are they still alive?"

"Which one?"

"Both." Wilson turned away and grimaced. "It feels like I'm looking at some kind of creature down there."

David leaned back and stuffed his hands into his pockets. "Please don't."

"What, you're telling me you don't feel the same?" He jabbed a finger down at the screen and bared his teeth. "After what she's done... She's not human."

"I said don't."

Wilson persisted, his gaze hardening behind the lenses of his glasses. "She stabbed your partner. You're saying you don't feel anything when you see her?"

David felt something boil up inside him. He stared down the Detective and lowered his voice. "You want to know what I feel when I look at her? I feel pity. Pity because someone took a poor abused kid and manufactured a monster." Not once breaking eye-contact, he maintained a lead tone. "I read her diary. And when I did, I felt... Sad. Because if that little girl had been born to anyone else, she would have stood a chance. If things had been different... Nobody would have had to die."

"That doesn't change the fact that she killed five people," Wilson argued.

"I'm not saying that it changes anything. Those people are still dead; three people are still in hospital... She's done horrible things, and should be punished for that. That's not my argument. My argument is that this could have been prevented. This," he tapped the screen, "could be anyone. And that's terrifying."

As if there was nothing more to be said, David made for the door. Wilson might have called after him, but he was barely aware of the words. Slipping out of the half-open door, he paced down the corridor in an effort to calm himself. Heat seemed to radiate from the top of his head, and he leaned his forehead against the wall. Closing his eyes, he breathed deeply.

"It's not easy, is it?" came a voice from behind him. David turned and stared through blurry eyes at DCI James Franko. "She's not what you expected, I take it?"

David took a second to compose himself. "I... I expected someone more-"

"Evil?" He watched Franko study his expression, as he nodded. "Trust me, it seems difficult now — Christ, I know it does — but give it time and you'll be thankful. This one we can help. She's done some terrible things, but she's still young. She has time to get better. It's going to take a lot of therapy, but there's still a chance. Real evil, though... Real evil, you don't want to find."

"It's just..." He averted his eyes quickly, before returning his gaze to Franko's own mahogany orbs. "Everything that happened to her; everything in her diary... I feel so sorry for her."

"You do," Franko said, matter-of-factly. "You feel sorry for almost all of them. But that doesn't change what they've done. So the best you can do is put them away, and get them the help they'll need. With any luck, she'll end up in a hospital. Somewhere that can help her."

"You know, most people don't think like that."

"I know," Franko replied, shrugging. "And I'm not saying that what I think is right. I just thought that, if you're anything like me, you'll take solace in that."

Franko patted David on the arm and, for the first time, offered him a smile. The experience was so surreal that David was unsure whether or not it had actually happened, or if he was just imagining it. Either way, it had helped.

"And anyway..." the DCI said. "You should be proud of yourself. You solved this one. If you hadn't noticed the handwriting, we never would have made it in time. I'll be telling Braithwaite as much, too. No one can take that away from you."

Franko turned and nodded his head down the hallway. Fishing his hand out of his jacket pocket, he pulled out a debit card and wagged it in the air.

"Come on," he said. "St. Claire and I are going for a drink, so come and join us. I'm buying."

David hesitated. "What about the paperwork?"

"That'll keep. Something tells me you need this."

Chapter 61

Scott awoke from morphine dreams, his head swimming with lucid and vacant thoughts. Sensation returned to him. It started with his fingers. Ice caught the tip of his right pinkie before chaining through to the surrounding digits and harpooning up his arm. As the feeling reached his stomach, it jumped down to his legs. Like there was a piece of him missing. A hollow pit where something should have been.

The light from the ceiling panels stung his blackened eyes, forcing him to blink them closed again.

Behind his eyelids, he watched as fragments of memories replayed themselves in slow motion. He remembered being bound to the chair; he remembered what Natalie had done.

The urge to run overtook him, but his body didn't respond. Instead he watched as an astral version of himself began to run up the wall of the hospital room. His double's movements were delayed and sluggish, as if it were wading through tar. After what seemed like an eternity, it reached the ceiling and the scene faded to black.

When he woke again, it was already night. Horribly aware of the dark, his breathing sped up.

Scott used to like the night. It was quiet and peaceful, leaving him feeling at ease. But not anymore. The once comforting darkness seemed suddenly full of invisible threat. He half expected Natalie to come striding up to his bedside, a knife in her hand and needle shards of teeth jutting from her gums.

Tossing and turning in the bed, he attempted to roll onto his side, to try and find a light switch. The motion was not an easy one. His right leg was fixed into a dense cast and elevated by a kind of winch, while his left arm was fixed in plaster, up to his shoulder. His protective restraints did nothing to quell his unease; if anything they exacerbated them. He needed to banish the shadows, as quickly as possible.

Suddenly seeing a shape out of the corner of his eye, his heart lurched in his chest. Sat, hunched in the chair by the window, the figure moved slowly, drinking in deep lungfuls of air.

Allowing his eyes to adjust to the dim light, Scott lay shock still, frozen in place. Terrified that even the slightest movement would draw the attention of the figure, he held his breath.

The figure stirred, lifting her head.

Slowly inhaling, Scott's nose caught hold of a comforting and nostalgic scent in the air. Lavender.

His vision now used to the dark, Scott laid eyes on the face of his mother. Relief flooded through him, and he started to weep.

Chapter 62

"How you holding up?"

The hospital room was sparsely populated with few furnishings. A low chair was left abandoned in the corner, and a squat table sat beside the bed, upon which a cup of water and a framed picture of a cat had been placed. The curtains had been drawn over the window, leaving only artificial light to illuminate the room.

Rawlings sucked water through a straw and turned his mismatched eyes onto David, who stood lingering in the doorway. "I feel like shit, but I'm alive. Which is something..." He flinched in pain as he spoke, straining the stitches ringing his neck.

"I've gotta say... You're one tough son of a bitch," David said, folding his arms over his chest. "I talked to the boy. He says you grabbed her, when she tried to chase him out. And from what I gather, you'd already been stabbed at that point." He broke into a genuine smile. "Without you, she might have caught and killed him."

Rawlings scratched at the side of his head, again wincing as his IV line moved beneath the skin of his left arm. "Yeah, well... No good deed. She stabbed me three times."

"You got your own back, though," David retorted. "I saw what you did to her face."

"Thought she deserved something."

Pulling the chair out of the corner, David sat beside the bed and took a long moment to himself. "You know... I think I'm actually going to miss you."

"Shit, don't say it so loud. People might hear you."

David chuckled to himself and leaned backwards. "I'm actually trying to be nice to you. Don't make me regret it."

Rawlings smirked through his beard and pushed one hand back through his long, matted hair. "Actually... You grew on me as the week went on. Then again so did my verruca."

David burst into a genuine laugh, for the first time in a while. His eyes creased and crow's feet spread across his face. Reaching up, he wiped a tear out of his eye. "Like I said... I'm going to miss you."

Rawlings shrugged. "I guess I can say the same. I liked you better than the other Lyefield guys. Though that's not saying an awful lot."

David again sat in silence for a while, listening to the ticking of the wall-mounted clock. Again, Rawlings took a drink from his cup of water.

"You were right about the cats on the track, by the way," David said, breaking the silence. "She did dump them there, to get someone on their own. Helen Raleigh, nineteen years old."

Rawlings took a breath and stared off into the distance. "You'd think that would make me happy..."

"Not at all... I just wanted to say, you're good at your job."

Rawlings turned his odd eyes back to David, meeting his pupils in an unwavering stare. "Yeah. You too."

＊

Braithwaite and Franko stood staring over at the house, as if they could see the evil seeping out of it. The horrors that had occurred in the home had forever stained it, infecting it with the disease of pain. Lesions of the sickness spread out into the air around it and lingered, like the stench of death. Too long would it be until the horror was forgotten. The house would carry the stain until long after their bones turned to dust.

"Your lads did a good job," Braithwaite admitted.

"So did yours," Franko replied. "The media's going to be all over this," he added.

"Well, you can't expect anything else," the Superintendent stated. "A case like this... A serial killer in Lindum. The press is going to have a field day. It's a big talking point."

"If you want to go in front of those vultures, leave me out of it." Franko stuffed his hands into his pockets, his gaze still fixed on Natalie Hunt's house. Strands of police tape still hung between the beams of the garden gate. "I've had my fill. Twenty years on the Murder Squad is too long."

"What about all of those crime shows you were on," the older man said, with a smirk. "You were quite the celebrity back in your day."

"Not all they're cracked up to be," he replied. "I went on the shows to educate people, not because I had illusions of grandeur." He flicked his eyes over Braithwaite. "But if that is what you want, don't let me stop you."

Franko turned to leave when he spotted movement, coming down the slope of the field behind the house. Red-faced and ruddy, the young man wore a navy blue windbreaker and light blue jeans. Looped around his neck, a DSLR camera jumped and bounced with every step that he took.

He raised his voice and called out to the young reporter. "Hey! What the hell do you think you're doing?!"

Expecting the young man to run, he was surprised when the reporter continued past the house and jogged up to him. In his sweaty fist, he clasped a handheld recording device. "Hey, sorry about that!" he laughed. "Jessie Goodwin, Mayfair Star. You wouldn't happen to want to give me a bit of an interview? About what exactly's gone on here?"

Stunned by the brash nature of the man, Franko stepped back in disbelief. "Are you being serious?"

"Deathly," he joked. Crudely.

"Sorry, sir, but you're going to have to leave."

"Hang on a second," Braithwaite interjected, patting Franko on the shoulder as he strode past him. "You're from a local paper, right? Not one of those national ones?"

Jessie nodded, a shrewd smile curling his mouth.

Braithwaite smiled. "How about an exclusive?"

*

"I'm glad they've finally let you out," Pru said, beaming a smile over at Scott.

Both of his eyes were still black and swollen, and his limbs encased in cast, but he was otherwise on the mend. He sat in a wheelchair, his broken leg stretched out in front of him. As he smiled, he chewed the inside of his cheek.

"I guess they figured I was well enough to send home."

"How are you feeling?" she tilted her head in genuine sympathy, looking for anything in his expression.

"Honestly?" Sadness passed over his face. "Still guilty. If... If it hadn't been for me, Alice and Helen wouldn't have died."

"She was crazy," Pru said, her voice stern and forceful. "There was nothing you could do. As far as we know, she could have killed anyone. Listen to me." She moved as he looked away, so as to keep eye contact. "Listen to me. None of it was your fault."

Scott said nothing.

"Listen to me. None of this is your fault." Leaning towards him, she reached out and took his hand in her own. "Don't think like that, okay. Promise me."

Breaking into a sad smile, Scott nodded as the tears began to brim in his eyes. "Thank you."

"That's okay." Pru returned the smile and cocked her head to the side. "Just promise not to cry next time I come and visit, okay?"

Scott laughed, crying all the while. "Well I can't exactly help it, can I? Jesus, you're heartless."

Her usual attitude coaxing a laugh out of him, Pru joined Scott in chuckling.

The pair sat for a long time talking about nothing, but it meant everything to Scott. She could see it on his face. He had been through so much that he needed a sense of normality; something from his life before the horror to return to.

After two hours of conversation, and very little else, she promised to visit him every day. Scott replied with a laugh that she had better, or he would get the impression that she didn't care. She called him a bumhole and left with a smile on her face, thanking whatever God would listen for returning him safe.

Leaving Scott's house, she prepared to climb into her car when she noticed something out of the ordinary.

Pru saw the man, stood in the shade of a sycamore. He was leaning against the newly built wall that bordered the garden in which the tree had been planted. Tall and strong, his body was corded with tightly wound coils of dense muscle.

He seemed out of place in the suburban neighbourhood; an unfamiliar face that she had never seen before.

Clearly waiting for something the man moved listlessly, turning his attention up and down the street. The way that his eyes flitted about left her slightly uncomfortable and self-conscious. Almost like his vision was able to penetrate the very nature of whatever he looked at. When his gaze landed on her, he lingered for a second, like he was staring into her mind.

Lifting one hand, he waved pleasantly and broke into a grin.

Turing away, he walked several feet down the road and got into his car. As he drove away, Pru watched him leave. Through the white glare on his windows, she caught the man looking out; his eyes fixed on Scott's house.

Disappearing around the corner, down the road, the car's tail end reflected in Pru's eye.

*

Thinking to himself, as he drove away from the house, The Grinner readjusted the rear-view mirror and curled his mouth into a smile.

Afterword

When I started writing Pursuit, I never expected it to progress quite as far as it did. I have a really horrible habit of starting novels and then leaving them unfinished; something that I feared would become the fate of this book. However, the ultimate loss of interest never came. I watched as, over the course of this last year, the story took on a life of its own and became something much more than I had ever expected. I couldn't have gotten this far without the amazing support and help that I received from so many people and, as such, I would like to take the chance to thank everyone who helped me with bringing this story to fruition.

With matters of a forensic nature, I didn't have far to look. To my beautiful other half, you are the smartest, wittiest person that I know; never too busy to answer my questions and always supportive of my writing. I love you more than words can say.

Second, my friend Ellie. Even three years after we sat together in Chemistry, when I popped up as a message in your inbox, you were more than happy to help me. Without you, I would not have been able to convincingly write the scene in the Veterinary Surgery, or any of the procedure relating to missing or injured cats. You were a phenomenal help, and I wish you all the best for the future.

Next, the staff at my local train station. You probably don't remember me, but I was the strange man that would occasionally show up at the platform and ask questions about track obstructions. All of you could have very easily ignored me, however none of you did. You were always open to answer my questions, and seemed genuinely happy that someone was taking an interest.

For anyone interested in how I researched the investigative aspects of the story, "The Crime Writer's Guide to Police Practice and Procedure" by Michael O'Byrne played a big part in guiding me. It was extremely helpful and just an overall fantastic read, so please do pick yourself up a copy if you are interested.

Finally, I would like to thank everybody that in any way inspired me, during my writing of this novel. Life is built from experiences and relationships, and all of mine have contributed more than I can even relate.

20826882R00170

Printed in Great Britain
by Amazon